Praise for the incomparable romance
of *USA Today* bestselling author

SABRINA JEFFRIES

"Delightful."
Joan Johnston

"Humorous, sexy, and entertaining."
Romantic Times

"Her wit and passion will enthrall you."
Christina Dodd

"Luscious romance filled with sensuous moments
that will make your heart beat a little faster."
Oakland Press

"Intriguing . . . lively . . . occasionally bawdy."
Library Journal

"Wit, charm, and burning sensuality . . .
an absolute pleasure . . . anyone who loves
romance must read Sabrina Jeffries."
Lisa Kleypas

SABRINA JEFFRIES

A Dangerous Love

AVON BOOKS

An Imprint of HarperCollinsPublishers

AVON BOOKS
An Imprint of HarperCollins*Publishers*
10 East 53rd Street
New York, New York 10022-5299

Copyright © 2000 by Deborah Martin
ISBN-13: 978-0-380-80928-8
ISBN-10: 0-380-80928-1
www.avonromance.com

First Avon Books paperback printing: November 2000

Avon Trademark Reg. U.S. Pat. Off. and in Other Countries, Marca Registrada, Hecho en U.S.A.
HarperCollins® is a registered trademark of HarperCollins Publishers Inc.

Printed in the U.S.A.

10 9 8

To the Avon Ladies,
who've seen me through many tempestuous times.
To Micki, a truly superior editor.
And to lovers of Shakespeare everywhere.

Chapter 1

London
August 1815

> *Money speaks sense in a language all nations understand.*
>
> *Aphra Behn, English playwright*
> The Rover, *Pt. 2, Act 3*

"I'll be gone two weeks or more."

Marsden Griffith Knighton watched from the head of the large table as predictable excitement rippled through his staff. The last time Griff had left Knighton Trading helmless for so long, he'd established an office in Calcutta that tripled the firm's profits—and destroyed two of his competitors.

Even Daniel Brennan, his generally unimpressed man of affairs, straightened in his chair. Daniel rarely attended such meetings now that he managed Griff's substantial private interests, but Griff had a compelling reason to require his presence today.

"Are you leaving Mr. Brennan in charge as usual, sir?" a young trader asked.

"No. He's going with me." When Daniel gaped at him, Griff bit back a smile. Daniel was hard to shock, having been with Knighton Trading since the days when it gained its primary revenue from smuggled goods. "Mr. Harrison will be in charge."

The senior trader beamed at this evidence of preference. "So where are you off to now, Mr. Knighton? France? India?" Greed brightened his eyes. "China perhaps?"

Griff chuckled. "Warwickshire. This isn't a business trip. I have family there."

"F-Family?" Harrison stammered.

Griff could guess his thoughts. *But he's a bastard. Except for his poor mother, how could he have any family that would acknowledge him?*

"Yes. Family," Griff repeated with fierce satisfaction. "It's a personal matter of some importance." He paused, then continued in that firm tone his staff knew never to question. "One more thing—none of you is to mention this to anyone, not even my mother. As far as you're concerned, I *have* sailed to France or China, understand?"

A low chorus of reassurances followed.

"Good. You're dismissed. Daniel, I need a word with you."

His staff left without lingering, for they well knew he didn't waste time with frivolous chatter. Besides, Griff thought wryly, they probably couldn't wait to speculate upon the shocking news that he had "family." Years ago it would have angered him, but he'd worn the stigma of bastardy so long it hardly chafed his skin anymore. What it chafed was his purse, but he now intended to remedy that.

As soon as the office cleared, Daniel arched one blond eyebrow and lowered his massive frame onto the expensive chair before Griff's desk. "A personal matter?"

"It really is personal this time, believe it or not."

Gone were the days when he and Daniel engaged in whatever machinations, illegal or no, were necessary to make Knighton Trading succeed. The future of the company lay in respectability. And ironically enough, respectability lay buried in Griff's past.

Griff took his own seat behind the desk. "I've been invited to visit my distant cousin—the Earl of Swanlea. He's dying, and his estate, Swan Park, is entailed on me."

Daniel looked perplexed. "But how could it be entailed on you if you're—"

"A bastard? I'm not. Not in the legal sense, anyway."

Daniel scowled, his disappointment evident. Their bastardy was the one thing they had in common, since they were opposites in looks, manner, and education. The fair-haired Daniel had been brought up in the workhouse and then in a smuggler's gang. Griff, dark-haired and lean, had been raised and educated as a gentleman.

Griff forced a smile, and added, "Although my legitimacy isn't yet established."

"Either you're a bastard or you ain't," Daniel grumbled.

"*Aren't*," Griff corrected. "I'm not a bastard, though I can't prove it. That's why I accepted Swanlea's invitation."

Daniel's eyes narrowed. "Isn't Swanlea the chap you had me investigate? The widower whose three daughters are called the Swanlea Spinsters?"

"That's him." Griff handed Daniel a letter over the desk. "I received this last week, which is what

prompted the investigation. You may find it interesting."

As Daniel scanned the clumsy script, Griff surveyed his office. Summer sunlight crept in through
high windows that cost him a fortune in taxes. It
danced across marble sills and an Aubusson carpet
before disappearing beneath mahogany chairs. This
was his third office in ten years, each better situated
and more richly furnished. It lay in the heart of the
City near the Bank of England, loudly proclaiming
his success.

Yet it wasn't enough. He wanted Knighton Trading to rival even the East India Company. Thanks to
his distant cousin's timely offer, it might soon do
just that.

Daniel finished the letter and regarded Griff with
surprise. "So if you meet your cousin's terms, you'll
be the next Earl of Swanlea?"

"Yes. He'll give me the proof of my legitimacy
that I need to inherit his title and lands, which I
assume is my parents' missing marriage certificate.
In exchange, I'm to marry one of his daughters so
they may remain at Swan Park."

Daniel's eyes narrowed. "Don't you find it a mite
suspicious that the earl should 'stumble across the
proof in his family papers' after so many years?"

Griff snorted. "Of course I do." Indeed, he suspected the fifth earl of far worse crimes against his
family. But only a fool acted on past resentments.
And his purpose transcended any idle dreams of
revenge. "I don't care how he found the proof—I
want it. Once I establish my legitimacy, I can gain a
position on that trade delegation to China."

"So you actually intend to marry one of these
spinsters?"

"Give in to his blackmail? Never! That's why I
need you to come with me. I intend to get the

'proof' there. And while I'm searching Swan Park for it, I want *you* to distract the daughters. Entertain them, court them, do whatever you must. Just keep them out of my way."

"Have you lost your mind?" Daniel exploded. "Entertain three earl's daughters? They wouldn't even speak to the likes of me! How the devil can I distract them?"

Griff smiled. "By pretending to be me, of course."

"Me? As you? Not bloody likely. Your staff will be roaring at the thought of—"

Daniel broke off when Griff raised an eyebrow. "Christ, you're serious!"

"Perfectly serious. If I go there as myself courting, I'll have to be available. But as Mr. Knighton's man of affairs, I can roam the house at will. If I'm discovered, I merely have to reveal the deception to keep from being arrested. They won't accuse their cousin of thievery and risk a scandal. Whereas if they find *you* searching and learn of your background, the earl will have you hanged just to strike back at me."

Daniel's eyes narrowed. "You think him that much of a scoundrel?"

Griff considered telling him the entire truth, but decided against it. Daniel's moral code could be damned unpredictable. He might not cooperate if he realized how far Griff meant to go to establish his legitimacy.

"Yes. So I'll be the only one searching Swan Park. But don't worry—changing roles will be easy. I've never met the Earl of Swanlea or his daughters. Thanks to the rift between our families, they don't know how I look—"

"Ballocks! From the portrait I saw of your da, you're his very image. Black hair, blue eyes—"

"Which makes me look Irish—more Irish than you, anyway." Griff smiled smugly. Daniel's looks came from his English mother, and he'd been raised in England, so he bore no trace of an Irish brogue. "I'm told the earl never leaves his bed, so he need not see me. Why shouldn't he believe you're Mr. Knighton?"

The younger man's gaze flicked over him. "Because you carry yourself like a gentleman. And I carry myself like an Irish highwayman's bastard."

"Which is why they'd send you off to Newgate at the first sign of treachery." When Daniel rose to stalk the room, Griff softened his tone. "As Mr. Knighton, you'd be in your element. Unlike me, you're quite the charmer with females."

"Haymarket ware p'raps, but I don't know the first thing about charming ladies." Striding up to the desk, he planted his fists on it and stared down at Griff. "You're daft, y'know. It won't work."

"It *will*. Knighton is 'in trade,' so they'll expect a rough man. They'll overlook lapses in speech or manner because he's rich. For the most part, you can be yourself."

Daniel seemed to weigh Griff's words.

Griff pressed his advantage. "You want to run your own investment firm one day, don't you? This will give you essential training in social behavior—thrash any vestiges of the smuggler out of you." Griff smiled. "And I'll pay you hard currency for your efforts. A hundred pounds on top of your usual salary."

That got Daniel's attention. "A hundred pounds?"

"Yes. For that fund of yours." He paused. "I can't manage this without you. Besides, you might enjoy spending time with three young women."

"Three ugly shrews, most likely, or they wouldn't be called spinsters. Ten years of hard work and loyalty to you, and this is how I'm repaid."

"What if I make it a hundred and twenty pounds?"

Daniel regarded him shrewdly. "A hundred and fifty."

"Done," Griff said, offering his hand.

After a slight hesitation, Daniel shook it.

Griff grinned. "I'd have gone as high as two hundred."

"And I'd have taken fifty," Daniel retorted.

As it dawned on Griff that Daniel's resistance had been calculated, he erupted into laughter. "You rascal! I swear, you're Wild Danny Brennan's son through and through!"

Daniel drew himself up. "And legitimate parentage or no, you're a bastard."

"I'll never argue with you on that score, my friend." But before the month was out, Griff would prove he wasn't the unscrupulous upstart the world supposed he was. Then nothing would stand in the path of Knighton Trading.

Lady Rosalind Laverick, second oldest daughter of the Earl of Swanlea, was poring over Swan Park's expenses in a futile attempt to play pinchpenny when one of the footmen entered the drawing room.

"The outrider for Mr. Knighton has just arrived, milady," he announced. "The man is expected here within the hour."

"What? But surely Papa did not—" At his quizzical look, she stiffened. "Thank you, John."

She waited until he was well away before storming off to her father's bedchamber. When she entered, she was grimly pleased to find her sisters there, too. The youngest, Juliet, was tending Papa as usual, while Helena, the oldest, painted her in miniature. It was a cozy familial scene, one Rosalind cherished. But to preserve it, she'd have to change Papa's mind about his foolish plan.

He sat up in bed, the covers tucked around his wasting frame. Though never handsome, he'd once been very impressive, his height and booming voice cowing many a man.

He still possessed the piercing gaze and rigid chin that had made Rosalind tremble as a girl. But his body was now a heap of withered muscles and brittle bones, encased in skin that slipped around beneath her fingers whenever she grasped his arm or hand. Every time she saw him so beaten-down and ill, her chest ached.

Yet she dared not let sentiment interfere with her crusade. Not when the issue was so important. "Papa, I've been informed that Mr. Knighton's arrival is imminent." She marched up to the bed. "How could you? I thought we agreed—"

"*You* agreed, Rosalind. I told you that if any of you gels were amenable, I would arrange the match. And Juliet is amenable. So I wrote the man and invited him here."

Helena groaned, but Juliet merely blushed and ducked her head.

"Oh, Juliet, you foolish girl!" Rosalind cried.

"You don't understand—I don't mind marrying him!" Juliet protested from Papa's bedside. "Papa thinks it best, and I know my duty as a daughter."

"To marry without love?" Rosalind snapped at Juliet, ignoring her father's smug look. "You may think it your duty, as the bard says,

> to make curtsy, and say "Father, as it please you."
> But yet, for all that . . . let him be a handsome fel-
> low, or else make another curtsy, and say "Father,
> as it please me."

"Do not start quoting the wrong bits of Shakespeare again, gel," Papa put in. "Shakespeare is against you more often than not. Consider Desdemona. If she had done her duty by her father and refused Othello, she would not have died."

"As usual, you miss the entire point of the play," Rosalind retorted hotly.

"Oh, Lord." Helena stiffly rose. "Once you two drag Shakespeare into the argument, there's no resolving it." Gathering up her painting box in one hand and her cane in the other, she walked to the door haltingly.

"Where are you going?" Rosalind asked. She'd hoped for Helena's support.

Helena paused. "I want to put my paints away before our guest arrives."

"Don't you care that Papa is planning to—"

"Of course I care. Unlike you, however, I recognize that arguing with Papa is pointless. If you're not interested in marriage for yourself, hold your ground. I certainly have no intention of marrying Mr. Knighton, even if he would take a woman with my . . . shortcomings. However, Juliet seems more than willing to throw herself at him, and we can do little about that. Especially if she won't stand up for herself."

Rosalind watched in despair as her elegant older sister limped from the room. If only Juliet possessed Helena's strength of will or suspicion of men . . . Rosalind sighed as she faced her father and younger sister. But Juliet was as timid as the bland pink-and-white girlish gowns she insisted on wearing. And just as she refused to wear dramatic colors—like Rosalind's own vermilion chintz—she refused to disobey Papa.

"Papa," she persisted, "you act as if this man is

our only hope. But one of us might still marry, and
for love, too."

"You're twenty-three, gel, and Helena is twenty-
six. You will not find husbands now, not without a
decent dowry or sufficient portions. Helena may be
beautiful, but her lameness is a liability. And you
are not the sort of girl to attract a man—"

"You mean, I'm not beautiful." His cold recitation
wounded her. Just when she thought she'd inured
herself to Papa's heedless insults, they slipped past
her guard again. "My hair's as unruly as rusting
wire, and I'm plump."

"I was not speaking of your looks," Papa put in,
"but of your manner. Perhaps if you tried to be a bit
less—"

"Forthright? Well-read? Clever?" she snapped.

"Overbearing and tempestuous is what I was
thinking of," Papa retorted.

"I am *not* overbearing!" When he raised an eyebrow, Rosalind tossed back her head. "All right,
perhaps a little. But I could not run this estate for
you if I were otherwise." Oh, how had they gotten
onto this awful subject? "Besides, what about Juliet?
She might still marry for love, given time."

"Accept it, gel—there's no time left." Papa's rat-
tling cough only proved his point.

She skirted the painful subject of his illness. "We
don't have to marry, you know. We could earn our
way."

"Do not be silly. When Mr. Knighton evicts you—"

"I can go on the stage like Mama." At her father's
snort, Rosalind went on fiercely, "My looks may be
lacking, but I'm tall and have a fine speaking voice.
Helena could sell her miniatures. Juliet could do
something. Mama's actress friend, Mrs. Inchbald,
would help us find lodgings in London. If we
pooled our portions—"

"No!" Juliet put in. "We can't leave Swan Park! We can't abandon it!"

"Oh, blast, why not?" Rosalind snapped, glancing about the bedchamber with its crumbling moldings and shattered-silk drapes. "I see nothing worth sacrificing my darling sister for. What has this heap of stones ever done except make us the Swanlea Spinsters? If I must be a spinster, I'd rather be one in town."

"You wouldn't survive town," Papa growled. "You remember what happened to Helena. Besides, your mother was much happier as a wife than an actress. Such a life is not for you, nor for Juliet, either. She deserves better."

"Yes, but a forced marriage isn't 'better,' Papa. Especially when the man is, according to Mrs. Inchbald's letters, a scoundrel and a villain. You know that he had connections to smugglers and even sold smuggled goods himself."

"Out of necessity, and a long time ago. He is perfectly respectable these days."

"Mrs. Inchbald also said—"

"One moment, gel," her father broke in. He motioned Juliet to his side and whispered to her. She nodded. Then he looked at Rosalind. "Give Juliet the house keys. I need her to fetch my restorative from the pantry."

It was a flimsy excuse for getting rid of Juliet, but Rosalind didn't entirely mind. Handing her sister the ring of keys, Rosalind tapped her foot impatiently while the girl fled.

Then Rosalind squared off against her father, barely noticing the click of the door. "What's more," she continued, "Mrs. Inchbald says that Mr. Knighton is a . . . was born on the wrong side of the blanket. Doesn't that worry you?"

He broke into an alarming fit of coughing. Hurrying to his side, she thumped the middle of his back as Juliet always did. Apparently Juliet did it less vigorously, however, for he shoved her away, and growled, "Stop that, gel! I am not a bloody rug you beat the dust out of!"

Muttering to herself, she backed away. Ungrateful man! And they wondered where *she* learned to curse! Hah! How did Juliet put up with him?

As he dragged in several wheezing breaths, all her resentment vanished. Poor Papa. Not being able to leave his bed to order all of them about must drive him insane. It would certainly bedevil her. She returned to the bed, plumped up a fresh pillow, then eased it behind his back.

He settled into it. "Mrs. Inchbald is ill informed." He slid under the covers like a turtle withdrawing into its shell. "How could Knighton be heir to my title and estates if he is a bastard?"

"Oh." She frowned. "I hadn't thought of that."

"You see?" he mumbled, his face half-hidden by the sheets. "That is the trouble with you women— you never think things through. That is why women are so fickle. They let their feelings lead them about by the nose. One moment they love a man. and the next they—"

A flurry of activity in the hall startled them both. Servants called out, and feet pounded down the stairs. Rosalind rushed to the window, but couldn't see the front drive. Still, the sounds of hoofbeats and wheels crunching the gravel drive signaled the arrival of a coach.

Their cousin's.

"While I'd love to stay and listen to your wisdom concerning my gender," she said dryly, "I can't. Your precious Mr. Knighton is here."

She hurried to the door of the bedchamber, but

when she turned the knob, the door wouldn't open. She tried again with no success, then gawked at it, a horrid suspicion leaping into her mind. "Papa—" she began.

" 'Tis locked. I told Juliet to lock us in when she left."

She'd locked them in? Rosalind's temper soared. Curse the wretched girl's obedient nature! She kicked the door, wishing it was Juliet's backside, then whirled on her father. "What do you hope to accomplish by this, Papa?"

"I know you, gel. You'd run Knighton off before Juliet had a chance to meet him." Even the capricious firelight didn't disguise the Machiavellian gleam in his eyes. "So I told her not to let you out until our guest retires for the evening."

"If you think this will alter my behavior toward the man one whit—"

"It matters not." He rose, parting the covers like Neptune rising from the waves. "If you drive him off now, I will merely arrange the match by letter. After seeing Juliet's beauty and sweet temper tonight, he will agree to a match, never fear."

Blast! If Mr. Knighton left Swan Park believing that Juliet would make him a suitable wife, how could Rosalind prevent the marriage? She had no choice but to let him stay. But somehow she'd persuade Juliet that the man was wrong for her.

Papa's triumphant smirk vanished as he lapsed into another cough. She glared at him, refusing to go to his side. How was it possible to pity someone and also wish to throttle him? She loved Papa, truly she did, but his blindness drove her mad.

His coughing petered out. "One more matter, gel. I have a task for you to accomplish after Juliet lets you out."

"Oh?" she grumbled. "What task?"

"There is a locked strongbox in the desk in my study. I want you to fetch it."

"And bring it here?"

"No!" His gaze skittered away. "No, better put it where you can keep an eye on it. Your dressing room perhaps. Or in your writing table. Just until your cousin leaves."

Suspicions snaked through her mind. "Why? What's in it?"

"Only some papers I do not want him to see." He glanced away.

"What *sort* of papers?" she demanded.

"Just do as I say! And do not mention them to anyone, or try to open the box. Else I shall have your hide."

"But, Papa—"

"Promise you will keep it safe. Or I will have Juliet keep you locked up in here until you do."

She sniffed. As if he could manage that. Still . . . "Oh, all right, I promise." When he sank weakly back into the pillow, she added, "I do think, however, that if Mr. Knighton is so untrustworthy that you must hide your papers—"

"Merely a precaution. Nothing for you to worry about. Now let me sleep."

Rosalind gritted her teeth. Why must Papa be so bullheaded and secretive? He wouldn't tell her the truth, yet the more she learned about Mr. Knighton, the more alarmed she became. Something was rotten in Denmark, and it centered on her cousin.

Well, she'd learn what it was *without* Papa. Just see if she didn't.

Chapter 2

Such a set of tittle tattle, prittle prattle visitants!
Oh dear! I am so sick of the ceremony and fuss of
these fall lall people!

*Fanny Burney, English novelist, diarist,
and sometime playwright,* Journal

So this is *Swan Park*, Griff thought with unaccountable pride as his carriage raced up the majestic oak-bordered drive and past a shimmering pond alive with courtly swans. A refined air of ancient rank clung like ivy to the stone walls of the Jacobean manor, putting to shame his own impressive chateau. Perhaps once Swan Park was his, he'd establish himself here. Yes, it would sway even the most recalcitrant Parliament member.

"No wonder you want that certificate so badly," Daniel muttered across from him.

Griff chuckled. "It would be quite an addition to my properties, wouldn't it?"

As the house loomed up, servants streamed

through the entrance doors to form a long row on the terrace. In the center, two women presided over them.

"Tell me those two angels aren't your spinster cousins," Daniel growled.

Griff examined them through the dusty glass. "They must be, although there should be three of them. Perhaps the third is sick or tending their father."

Daniel scowled as the coach rattled to a halt. "Blast it, Griff, those beauties probably spend their days fighting off the gents. They'll see me for an impostor at once!"

"They're merely country cousins. You'll do fine." Griff watched as the taller woman limped toward them, relying heavily on a stout cane. "For the love of God, the dark-haired one is lame. She'll be glad of a man to pay her some attention."

"Are you blind as well as daft?" Daniel hissed. "Lame or no, she carries herself like a bloody duchess. She'll think me a clod ten times beneath her."

The women had nearly reached the carriage. Griff opened the door, then dropped his voice. "Just remember the hundred and fifty pounds."

Shooting a baleful glance over his shoulder, Daniel climbed down. Griff followed, wishing he'd instructed Daniel more thoroughly on how to act rich and powerful. The man usually had plenty of confidence, but these women seemed to drain his pride. Griff trod on his friend's heel deliberately, and Daniel straightened his spine and clenched his jaw. That was more like it.

Stepping forward, Daniel made a presentable bow to the taller woman. "Mr. Knighton at your service, madam."

"Welcome to Swan Park." Her voice was cool and

cultured. "I'm your cousin, Helena." Bracing herself on her cane with one hand, she offered Daniel the other.

Daniel held the woman's hand too long, provoking her to jerk it free with a flustered look. Griff groaned.

Gesturing to the girl at her side, Lady Helena added in a haughtier tone, "This is Juliet, my youngest sister."

The slip of woman gazed up at Daniel wide-eyed. "How do you do?"

"I'm fine, thank you," Daniel said, his accent credibly genteel if a bit coarse.

An awkward silence ensued. Then Lady Helena glanced back to where Griff stood. "And who is your friend?"

Daniel started. "Begging your pardon—this is Mr. . . . er . . . Daniel Brennan."

Griff bowed. "It's a very great pleasure to meet you."

When the women looked to the real Daniel for an explanation, Griff ground his teeth. Playing the subordinate was damned inconvenient, especially when Daniel stood there like a witless bull. Griff prodded him in the foot with his walking stick.

Daniel blurted out, "Mr. Brennan is my man of affairs. I hope my bringing him doesn't give you any trouble, but with so many business matters to discuss . . ."

"It's no trouble at all," Lady Helena put in evenly.

As she ushered them to the house, Daniel asked, "Don't you have another sister?"

Inexplicably, the younger woman turned scarlet. "Yes, our middle sister. I-I don't know where Rosalind's gone, but she'll be at dinner, I'm sure."

Lady Helena cast her sister a quizzical glance, and Lady Juliet ducked her head. *Very strange*, Griff thought. Why was the third sister hiding? Did she know of her father's plans to blackmail him into marriage? Did they all know?

At least they weren't shrews, which should appease Daniel. Lady Helena was formal and cold, and Lady Juliet was a milk-and-water miss, but neither seemed disposed to cause trouble, thank God.

At the doors, Lady Helena halted to point out the estate's boundaries for Daniel. Griff found it disconcerting to play Daniel's lackey. As a charity student at Eton, Griff had disliked being the target of condescension, and it was downright hateful to him now.

Then they entered the house, and the awful sight that greeted Griff knocked the wind from him. Father had described a vision of old nobility—veined marble arches and ancient tapestries hung on elegant walls. This was a nightmare of hell at its busiest hour.

Fiery red was the color of choice. The red-papered walls were punctuated by dark moldings and curtains in gold gauze with red-painted designs. Beside the staircase, a miniature pagoda sat atop a black-lacquer table. Indeed, Chinoiserie decorated the entire hall. Not to mention that a brilliant scarlet-and-blue Oriental carpet spanned the majestic room, covering up what his father had said was a floor of expensive Italian marble.

Apparently catching his stunned look, Lady Juliet ventured, "Rosalind recently had our hall redone. It's in the new Chinese style."

"I thought it was the old brothel style," Griff bit out unthinkingly. In the weighty silence that followed, it dawned on him what he'd said, to whom he'd said it, and most importantly, that he'd said it with a boldness unthinkable for an employee.

Daniel eyed him with something akin to glee.

"Please forgive my man of affairs. He has a bad habit of speaking his mind."

Griff suppressed a groan.

"R-Rosalind said the Chinese style was quite popular in L-London," the younger woman sputtered. "Is that not true?"

Daniel glanced furtively to Griff, who gave him a slight nod. "The style is still all the crack in many quarters," Daniel reassured the two ladies. "Mr. Brennan's tastes are duller than your sister's, that's all."

"You may inform your man of affairs," Lady Helena retorted in a frosty voice, "that my sister Rosalind manages the estate almost entirely alone under difficult circumstances, so I think she's entitled to a few eccentricities."

"I didn't mean to imply otherwise, my lady," Griff interjected, determined to placate the woman. And change the subject before her tongue stripped his skin. "Speaking of eccentricities, I noticed that you and your sisters bear the names of Shakespearean heroines. Rosalind. Helena. Juliet. Was that intentional?"

"Are you a lover of Shakespeare?"

He decided the truth wouldn't hurt. "Actually, I am. The comedies mostly."

"Thanks to our proximity to Stratford-upon-Avon, Papa is also an enthusiast. That, as you might guess, is why we're saddled with these names." She turned to Daniel. "What about you? Are you also fond of Shakespeare?"

"Not at all. Griff's the only one who's contracted the Shakespeare pox."

"Griff?" Lady Helena asked. "I beg your pardon, but who is Griff?"

Damnation, Daniel had already slipped up. Daniel

shot Griff a look of sheer exasperation, but Griff
suddenly realized that his cousins probably didn't
know his middle name. This might work to his
advantage. "Griff is my nickname," he quickly put
in. "That's what Knighton and the employees at
Knighton Trading call me."

"Y-Your Christian name is Daniel, isn't it?" Lady
Juliet stammered.

Griff thought fast. "Yes, but I'm called Griff after
the griffin." For Daniel's benefit, he added, "You
know—the mythical creature with the head of an
eagle and the body of a lion, who keeps guard over
gold and riches."

"That's right," Daniel chimed in, a mischievous
twinkle in his eyes. "It's because he's so tightfisted.
Why, only last week I wanted to pay a man two
hundred pounds for a service Griff thinks deserves
only one hundred and fifty. Isn't that right, Griff?"

Griff raised an eyebrow. "Yes. And I haven't
changed my mind. The man still has to prove he can
do a decent job."

"I expect he'll surprise you." At Griff's warning
glare, Daniel turned to the ladies. "When will I meet
your father—at dinner? I'm eager to talk with him."

Probably more eager to get it over with, Griff thought
wryly. If Daniel passed that test, they were in for the
duration.

"Oh, no, not tonight!" Lady Juliet cried. "I-I
mean, Papa is so ill you'd best wait until he's better.
In the morning, perhaps."

"But Juliet, surely—" her sister began.

"In the morning," Lady Juliet insisted. "W-Would
you gentlemen like some tea?"

Griff's eyes narrowed as Lady Juliet steered them
toward the parlor, chattering anxiously as they
went. All was not as it had seemed at first—these

two were hiding something, and their sister, who apparently ran the estate, probably had a part in it.

No matter. Their petty secrets would not deter him from his purpose.

Rosalind had been fretting for an age when she heard a key turn in the lock.

To her surprise, it was Helena. "You really *are* here," Helena said, her eyes reflecting shock at the sight of Rosalind waiting impatiently on the other side of the door.

Rosalind pushed past her out of the room. "Shh— Papa is asleep, and I don't want to wake him." As soon as she was in the hall, she asked, "Did Juliet send you to let me out?"

"Yes—she couldn't face your lecture. If I'd known you were here, I'd have come sooner. It's past eleven already." Helena closed the door. "I can't believe she did it. Papa doesn't surprise me, but Juliet—"

"I know. Wait until I get my hands on the foolish child. Where is she, anyway?"

Helena shot her a cautious look. "She's gone to bed, and you should wait until your temper cools."

Reluctantly, Rosalind acknowledged the wisdom of that. At the moment she was liable to throttle the girl. "I suppose Mr. Knighton is ensconced in a guest room?"

Her sister limped toward the grand staircase that led up to the first floor and their bedrooms. "He has retired for the night. Everyone has retired but us."

Rosalind scowled as she followed her sister. "I swear, if I'd been free, I might very well have barred him from the house."

"Which is why Papa had Juliet lock you in. You've lost now. Best to admit it."

"The man isn't the least respectable."

"So you say, but he isn't that bad. You might even like him."

"I doubt that." As they climbed the stairs, Rosalind slowed her steps to match her sister's awkward progress. "Tell me more. Does he speak like a gentleman or is he as coarse as I feared? Does he favor Papa in looks?"

"Not at all. He's rather massive and fair, nothing like the miniature Papa showed us of his father. His hair is blond with brown streaks, and he wears it long, like a lion's mane. His features are appealing, but they—" She broke off with a blush. "You'll see for yourself in the morning."

At the top, Rosalind regarded her sister thoughtfully. Helena never spared a glance for any man. "Well, if I don't show up at breakfast, come release me from the pantry or wherever Papa has told Juliet to stuff me."

Helena smiled tiredly. "Very well. And now I think I'll retire. I'm all done in." Patting Rosalind's hand, she added, "Do try not to worry."

"I'll try." As Helena entered her bedchamber, Rosalind went into her own across the hall, grateful to be once more amid its familiar, comfortable clutter. But long after the half-asleep maid helped her undress and departed, Rosalind lay awake in her bed.

How could she not worry? They'd welcomed a scoundrel into their home, one Papa didn't even trust, or he wouldn't have asked her to—

The strongbox! Curse it, Papa had said to move it to her room tonight!

Rosalind leapt from the bed and donned her wrapper. Since their guest had already retired, she could slip downstairs and fetch the box without anyone knowing. Snatching up the candle beside her bed, she hurried into the hall and toward the staircase.

She was halfway down the stairs and had rounded the landing when she noticed that a light shone beneath the closed door to Papa's study. She halted abruptly, her pulse quickening. No one should be about at this hour, not even the servants.

It had to be their guest. Was he lost? Or looking for something? Her lips thinned into a grim line. The strongbox. Papa had been right to worry. How dared Mr. Knighton sneak about looking for Papa's private papers! She'd set the villain straight, she would!

Racing down the stairs, she headed right for the study. She eased the door open, peeked in, and froze. The single candle lighting her father's desk also lit a man crouched behind it. He was clearly *not* their blond guest, for his hair was black as a gypsy's.

A gypsy! She jerked back, her heart thundering. Gypsies had recently plagued Warwickshire, but never Swan Park. Outrage swelled through her as she heard a drawer sliding open and its contents being searched. How dared he paw through Papa's desk!

She quelled her impulse to rush in. Even *she* wasn't so impetuous as all that. If only she had a weapon, something to hold him at bay while she sounded the alarm. Otherwise, he'd bolt with whatever he'd stolen—perhaps even Papa's precious strongbox.

She lifted her candle to scan the hallway. Some paintings, a spindly chair or two, and a bronze statuette too small to make an impact . . . Wait! What about the shield and sword mounted on the opposite wall? Quickly, she set the candlestick on the table and lifted the objects from their rack. The sword was heavier than she'd expected, but the stout oak shield with its leather bindings gave her a measure of security.

Without giving herself time to change her mind, she raced back across the hall and kicked the door open so hard it slammed against the wall. Brandishing the sword and hefting the shield, she plunged into the room, and cried boldly, "Stand to, thief!"

When the dark-haired stranger rose from behind the desk, she realized with a sinking heart that she'd grossly misread the situation. This was no gypsy. Gypsies didn't possess fair skin or eyes an unearthly shade of searing blue; they didn't wear expensive satin waistcoats or finely tailored silk breeches.

Then, to her mortification, a hint of a smile softened the man's angular features. "Good evening, madam," he said as he sketched a bow. "You must be Lady Rosalind."

Chapter 3

He that tries to recommend him [Shakespeare] by select quotations, will succeed like the pedant in Hierocles, who, when he offered his house to sale, carried a brick in his pocket as a specimen.

> Samuel Johnson, patron and critic of the theater,
> preface, Plays of William Shakespeare

Griff stared shamelessly at the Amazon flashing a sword in his face. By God, *this* was the third sister? This astonishing creature armed with weapons as ancient as the house itself? She couldn't be anyone else—her outrageous orange wrapper of Chinese silk could only belong to the same woman who'd defaced Swan Park's entrance hall.

And who seemed bent on defacing him.

He held up a hand as he edged around the desk. Swords were nothing to sneeze at, especially when wielded by a madwoman. "You *are* Lady Rosalind, aren't you?"

"You have the advantage of me, sir." Tossing back

a head of thick russet hair that fell nearly to her waist, she hefted the enormous slab of steel a notch higher. "You know my name, but I don't know yours."

Not mad perhaps, but certainly madcap. "I beg your pardon. I'm Knighton's man of affairs. Daniel Brennan at your service, madam. Most people call me Griff." He eyed her curiously. "Didn't your sisters tell you I'd joined your cousin for this visit?" When her sword wavered and confusion spread over her face, he suppressed a smile. "I take it they did not."

She recovered herself quickly. "They said nothing about a man of affairs."

"Ah." He nodded toward the weighty weapons she defied gravity to control. "That explains your . . . er . . . entrance. I wondered if you greeted all your guests with dramatic displays of the Swanlea arms."

If he'd thought to embarrass her, he'd failed. Her sword didn't waver. "Only when I find those guests rummaging through Papa's desk."

"Oh, that." Thank God he'd changed places with Daniel. He wouldn't have wanted to see how Daniel handled the Amazon. "I needed to jot down some notes, but I left my writing implements and paper behind. This seemed a likely place to find some."

She cocked her head, her hazel eyes alive with suspicion. "Do you often work so late?"

"I'm used to town hours—this is early for me." He glanced at the clock. "It's not yet midnight."

"I didn't know men of affairs kept town hours. I thought they had to be at work early every day."

Clever woman. And wary, too. She'd keep him on his toes. "My employer is casual about such things. I often attend late-night social affairs with him, and he allows me to keep what hours I wish. But you would know that if you'd joined us for dinner."

She grimaced. "I'd intended to be there. Papa had other plans, however."

The mention of her scoundrel father made him stiffen. "Does he often keep you at his side when guests arrive?"

A scowl marred the freckled brow fringed by short curls. "I'll ask the questions here, Mr. Brennan. You're the one in the wrong, after all." To emphasize the point, she thrust the sword out in front of her as easily as if it were a parasol.

By God, the woman was strong—most women wouldn't even be able to lift the thing. However gaudy its trappings, her lush body held surprising power.

Resting a hip on the desk, he said, "Ask what questions you like. Though now that we've introduced ourselves, you might dispense with the weapon. Unless you're afraid of a mere man of affairs."

"I'm afraid of no one." She spoke the words without a hint of boasting, as if stating a plain fact. A second later she lowered the sword to stand it on end like a cane. Leaning on the hilt, she surveyed him from head to foot. "I thought you were a gypsy thief."

"No, merely an Irishman," Griff quipped, remembering his role. "Though some would say that's nearly as bad."

"I have nothing against Irishmen, Mr. Brennan. Except when they're skulking about in the private areas of my home."

Casually, she bent to set down the shield. Without that obstruction, the candle on the hall table behind her sifted amber light through her flimsy garments to silhouette her body in astonishing detail. An image of large, rounded breasts, generous hips, and a nicely curved waist seared itself into Griff's suddenly distracted brain. Another not so distracted part of him responded instantly.

That annoying appendage knew what it wanted; tonight it apparently wanted the warrior queen. He shifted uncomfortably on the desk. Obviously it had been far too long since he'd had a woman. Why else would this one attract him? He liked quiet, elegant ladies with good taste and prudent tongues, not brash Amazons with penchants for flaming silk.

Yet when she straightened, it took a supreme effort to tear his gaze from her body and focus it on her face. Not that it helped. Her face interested him as much as the erotic shadow play of her body. Separately, each of her features seemed overdone, as if the Creator had gotten carried away with embellishments. Her chin was a bit protruding, her cheeks a little plump, her brows a shade darker and thicker than fashionable. Altogether, however, her face contained an arresting charm that reminded him of Titian's beauties. Indeed, he owned a Titian nude whose face resembled hers to an amazing degree.

Especially the lips. They were art come to life. He had a sudden insane urge to taste that erotic mouth, an urge he squelched ruthlessly by reminding himself of his purpose. A dalliance with the daughter of his enemy would certainly not serve it.

"If you don't mind my asking," Griff said in a futile attempt to draw his thoughts from baser considerations, "what would you have done if I *had* been a gypsy thief?"

She shrugged. "I would have held you here while I called for help."

He choked down a laugh. "Held me here?" At the sight of her raised eyebrow, however, he refrained from voicing his disparaging thoughts. This was his chance to elicit information, and he wouldn't get it by insulting her. "I see. Your father's desk must contain a great many treasures for you to show such concern over it."

Alarm flickered briefly in her face. "No! I mean, that's not the point. I don't want anyone stealing from Papa, even if it's only notes to the steward."

How intriguing. Did the desk indeed contain the certificate? He hadn't seen it there, but he hadn't had long to search before the warrior queen barged into the room. He shoved away from the desk. "Nonetheless, you took great pains to protect the desk's contents, so they must have value to someone."

"You seem inordinately interested in my father's desk. May I suggest that you wait until Papa actually dies before you inventory your employer's inheritance?"

Damnation, he'd been careless and given her the wrong impression. "This has nothing to do with my employer's future inheritance. I simply wondered if your father knows that his daughter risks her life for . . . whatever is in that desk."

A stubborn look settled over her face. "I wasn't risking my life. I was armed."

This time he didn't restrain his laughter. "Lady Rosalind, if you think you could have held off a gypsy thief with that relic of a sword for more than five seconds, you're a fool. You couldn't even have held *me* off with it if I hadn't let you."

"Hadn't *let* me?" She snatched up the sword again and brandished it in the air. "You think not, do you?"

How could he resist the challenge? Although prideful indignation swelled her chest, it was too lovely a chest to be exposed to the cruelties of any real thief she might encounter someday. The woman lacked common sense—she needed lessons in the world's dangers.

With the speed he'd honed during his days consorting with smugglers, he ducked under the sword and pivoted behind her, chaining her waist with his arm while his free hand wrenched the sword from her grip. Then he pressed the blade to the pulse in her neck and echoed her words, "I think not." He lowered his voice and bent his head so close his lips brushed her ear. "Never challenge a thief, my lady, unless you're well prepared to best him."

The rosewater scent in her hair clouded his thinking, not to mention the feel of her soft, trembling belly against his forearm and the curve of her waist beneath his hand. Insanely he wanted to inch his hand lower, to find the secrets between her thighs and fondle them until she trembled with pleasure instead of fear.

The thought further inflamed the part of him that shouldn't rear its lusty head. Not now, not with one of Swanlea's daughters.

Eager to make his point and escape her tempting body, he added, "You have more to worry about than the contents of your father's desk when you confront a man alone, especially as you are dressed. 'Beauty provoketh thieves sooner than gold,' you know."

She took a shaky breath, then whispered, "*As You Like It*."

"So you agree with me."

"No, you blasted idiot," she hissed. "*As You Like It*, the play by Shakespeare. That's what you quoted."

He was so astonished that he lowered the sword. That's when she struck, jabbing her elbow into his ribs with uncanny force.

Howling in pain, he released her. "Goddamn it to

hell!" He doubled over, the sword slipping from his hand to thud on the carpeted floor. A string of words leapt from his lips that he wouldn't normally speak in front of any woman, especially a lady. By God, the witch knew just where to place her blows! And she had an arm on her, too.

As Griff clutched his abdomen, she darted forward to snatch up the sword again, then backed away warily toward the desk. The Swanlea coat of arms on the wall behind her mocked him.

"Since you seem faintly familiar with Shakespeare," she remarked, "you will understand me when I say that no man, gypsy thief *or* man of affairs, will ever pick my lock and take the treasure of my honor by force."

He straightened stiffly. "*The Tempest*?" he croaked, sure he recognized her paraphrase from somewhere.

"*Cymbeline.*" One eyebrow arched upward. "But that was a good guess."

"So was yours about *As You Like It.*"

"Mine was not a guess. I know *As You Like It* as well as I know my own name."

"Do you?" Since he lacked Daniel's glib tongue around women, he generally relied on the bard for a few standard compliments. He'd used that particular quote with many women, but none had ever guessed its source.

And to think that she knew it. How unusual. Of course, any woman who'd use force to protect her "honor" was unusual.

Rubbing his tender ribs, he nodded toward the sword. "You realize I was only trying to make a point, not 'take the treasure of your honor.' "

"If you say so." The sword jutted out from her fisted hands.

"You don't believe me?"

To his surprise, she trailed her gaze down his body with the remote detachment generally used by men assessing a whore's physical attributes. It unnerved him, although his "sword" had no such compunctions and grew rampant beneath her look. What a bold vixen. Utterly unlike any peer's daughter he'd ever met.

Then she sighed wearily. "I believe you. A man like you needn't pick a woman's lock to take her treasure. I'll wager you can convince any woman to give you the key."

"What the hell does that mean, 'a man like me'?"

"A handsome ne'er-do-well." She tossed down the sword. "An Irishman who quotes Shakespeare to further his purposes. I suspect you know precisely how to gain entrance into any woman's bedchamber."

"But not yours," he couldn't resist saying. He wondered what she'd think if he told her that he generally gained entrance into bedchambers using gifts and cold currency rather than Shakespeare. It was more efficient, more dependable.

She glanced away, and for the first time since she'd entered the room, she looked vulnerable and young. "No. I'm not easily persuaded by flattery. All that flummery about beauty provoking thieves . . . you may seduce other women with your paltry knowledge of Shakespeare, but not me. I recognize a double-dealer when I see one: the sort of man who memorizes only those lines of great literature suitable for deceiving women."

That was harsh, even if partly true. Her other sisters hadn't been so wary either of him or Daniel. It intrigued him. He'd never met a female who hated him on sight, at least not since he'd become wealthy. "You have a poor opinion of me. That's hardly fair, given our short acquaintance."

"I think it more than fair when you consider that I found you rifling Papa's desk."

Damnation, couldn't he get her off that subject? "For pen and paper."

"Yes, of course. Did you find any?" She turned, and the edges of her silk wrapper swished open to reveal a flash of shapely calf before she circled to the back of the desk.

The one glimpse reignited his lust, burning up any memory of whether he'd seen pen or paper in the desk drawers. "No. But I'd only just started looking when you leapt into the room with sword and shield at the ready."

Ignoring his sarcastic tone, she bent forward to open a drawer, and two tempting swells of flesh threatened to spill from the wrapper. He gritted his teeth in a vain attempt to bite back his carnal thoughts. Did the woman have no modesty? He'd never survive a day in this house if she went around displaying her ample attractions with every motion.

When she straightened she held a sheaf of foolscap, which she offered to him over the desk. "Here is your paper. If you look in the drawer of the writing table in your room, you'll find a quill and ink. All the guest rooms are furnished with writing materials. I can only assume that our last visitor depleted the store of paper in yours."

Her challenging look roused his grudging admiration. Moving to the desk, he took the paper. Should he brazen his way through this any further? No. That was unlikely to work with this clever Amazon.

He tossed the paper down on the desk. "I see I've been well and truly caught."

A ghost of a smile touched her lips. "Only a fool would believe that a man of affairs would forget the tools of his trade at home. And I am no fool, Mr. Brennan."

"We've thoroughly established that."

When a second passed and he said no more, her half-grown smile vanished. She braced her hands wide apart on the desk, much as a man might, and unwittingly allowed him a glimpse down the front of her wrapper. "Will you explain yourself or not?"

"Not." His mind was far too diverted by the display of her assets to think of a plausible explanation. He'd have to stay clear of this woman, or he'd never achieve his purpose. She'd be a constant distraction.

A nearby clock struck midnight, its insistent chiming startling them both. When the clanging finally stopped she straightened, and he almost sighed with relief. Or regret—he wasn't sure which.

To add insult to injury, she crossed her arms over her twin temptations, hiding even the thinly draped shapes from view. " 'The iron tongue of midnight hath told twelve,' and I'm more than ready to retire. So would you stop being coy and tell me what you were doing in Papa's desk?"

Coy, for the love of God? She taunted him with flashes of her body, and *he* was coy? He'd built an empire on his reputation for being formidable. A woman, calling him *coy*! How his competitors would laugh to hear that tale over their brandy and cigars—

Cigars. Hmm. "I was looking for a cigar."

"A cigar?"

"Yes. I need a smoke before I retire, and I'm all out. Since Knighton doesn't smoke, I intended to see if your father kept some in his study." He paused, then continued more sarcastically, "I'm not by nature a cigar thief, but a man gets desperate when he's gone all day without. And I didn't realize you patrolled the halls at night fully armed. Tell me, do you always use the sword, or do you sometimes resort to pistols? I want to prepare myself in case you shoot at me one night."

"Very amusing. And if cigars are all you came down here for, why didn't you say so in the first place?"

"Surely you didn't expect me to reveal all my vices at our first meeting."

"You mean other than the ones you've already revealed?"

"Exactly." No point in arguing with the contentious woman. Besides, he wanted to be rid of her so he could resume his search.

But she seemed in no hurry to leave. She was opening drawers willy-nilly. Suddenly she pulled out a wooden box and thrust it at him. "Here, Mr. Brennan. My father's old cigars. We can't have you wandering about the house unable to sleep when the remedy to your insomnia is so close at hand. Papa hasn't smoked in years, so he won't mind if you enjoy them."

By God, she'd believed him! He took the box and opened it, feigning interest in its contents. The cigars appeared to be of fine quality. A pity he never smoked.

He closed the box and tucked it under his arm. "Thank you, that's most generous."

"Don't you want to smoke one now?"

"Here?"

"Certainly."

Was this a trick? Or did the woman truly have no idea what she'd proposed? "I may be a mere man of affairs, but I do know the rules of polite society. I'd never be so rude as to smoke in front of a lady."

"You have peculiar notions about propriety, sir. You find it acceptable to plunder your host's private possessions and hold a sword to his daughter's throat, yet you quibble over smoking a cigar in her presence?"

A smile tugged at his lips in spite of himself. "I'm not the only one with peculiar notions about propriety. You've shown no qualm about parading in your wrapper before a man alone at night. What would your father say to that?"

For the first time that evening, the Amazon blushed, the pretty color warring with the extreme orange of her wrapper. "Yes, well, I think it best that we not . . . discuss this incident with him. Or anyone else, for that matter."

Ha! Thank God for propriety's iron rules. Still, he couldn't resist teasing her. "Why should I remain silent? I've done nothing wrong. I was merely looking for cigars, remember?"

Alarm flickered in her lovely eyes. "You know the tale would do neither of us credit."

"I really don't see why *I* have anything to be ashamed of—"

"Blast it, Mr. Brennan, if you tell him—"

"Very well, I suppose I can indulge you." He shouldn't torment her so, especially when he, too, preferred that her father never hear of this little incident. "And since I seem to be playing the proper gentleman for once, I'll put an end to our improper meeting. Good night, my lady."

"Good night, Mr. Brennan. I'll see you in the morning at breakfast." With a stubborn set to her face, she stood there waiting. For him to leave, no doubt. Clearly she was taking no chances. Once he departed, she'd probably scurry about to check if anything were missing. And when she left, she'd lock the door behind her. He'd discover nothing tonight.

But he'd return another time, for it was clear she was hiding something, and he meant to find out what. "All right. Until breakfast." He started for the door, then paused and turned back as an overwhelming urge to have the last word seized him. "By the way, your line about the 'iron tongue of midnight'? It's from *A Midsummer Night's Dream*."

As her startled gaze fixed on him, he added, "So you see, I don't only memorize 'those lines of great literature suitable for deceiving women,' as you put it. In fact, I remember very well the rest of the passage." Very softly, he quoted, " 'The iron tongue of midnight hath told twelve Lovers, to bed; 'tis almost fairy time./I fear we shall outsleep the coming morn/As much as we this night have overwatch'd.' "

When his mention of lovers provoked yet another blush in those cheeks, a fierce satisfaction warmed his blood. Yes, the Amazon could be bested after all, and he'd found the way to do it. "While our 'fairy time' has been . . . er . . . enlightening, we've definitely 'overwatch'd' the night, Lady Rosalind. So you may wish to take care you don't 'outsleep the coming morn' and arrive late for breakfast tomorrow."

He flashed her a mocking smile. "Because if I arrive first, I'll be tempted to explain just why you are so late. And I have a suspicion that your family—particularly your father—would not approve."

Chapter 4

Zounds! I have been five minutes too late all my life-time.

Hannah Cowley, English playwright,
The Belle's Stratagem

After the maid finished helping her dress the next morning, Rosalind paced her room in the same state of agitation possessing her ever since Mr. Brennan had exited the study last night.

He'd as good as threatened her! Him—a man of affairs! Did he actually believe she'd quake in her boots for fear that he'd tell Papa what had happened? If he did, he was a fool.

She sniffed as she picked up her best lace shawl, tossed it about her shoulders, then headed toward the door. Let that scoundrel say what he wanted to Papa. She didn't care in the least. She'd simply go down to breakfast and continue about her business the rest of the day. No Irishman with devil-may-care looks and a running footman's well-formed body could frighten her. No, indeed.

And if he did speak to Papa? Then she'd reveal how the man had been snooping about in the desk, and Papa would laud her diligence.

Well, unless Mr. Brennan mentioned her . . . flimsy attire.

Scowling, she halted at the door, then turned back into the room. Papa wouldn't approve, to be sure. The curst Mr. Brennan had guessed aright on that particular.

Once more she felt the heat of a whisper against her ear—*Never challenge a thief, my lady, unless you are well prepared to best him.*

Blast! Mr. Brennan clearly realized that Papa wouldn't overlook this, especially after hearing the entire story—how the insolent man had dragged her hard against his body and steadied her with a broad hand too intimately placed on her belly, prompting the strangest whirligig sensation in that vicinity. How the heat of his hand had seared her through her wrapper and chemise . . .

Heat now seared her cheeks, too, launching her into a quicker pace about the room. That blackguard even had her blushing, for pity's sake! It was too much to be borne—this absurd reaction to him! It made no sense. Men of affairs weren't supposed to provoke such feelings in a woman.

But then, men of affairs were supposed to wear spectacles and cough a great deal. They were supposed to smell of dust and ink and moldy paper. They should be spidery men, all arms and legs and bulging eyes, like Papa's man of affairs.

They most certainly shouldn't be constructed of solid steel, sleek and hard as her ancestor's sword. They shouldn't smell of woodsmoke and leather or have eyes so blue that even with spectacles they'd be intoxicating.

She sank onto the bed and absently stroked the jade green damask, only a shade less bright than the stripes of the dress she wore today—her favorite. Mr. Brennan's rakish air and deft ability to disarm her made her wonder. Could he be one of Mr. Knighton's smuggling companions, brought here to tally up the estate's valuables before Papa was even in the grave? Yes, that must be it.

Yet how odd that he knew Shakespeare. It seemed unlikely that a smuggler would read *A Midsummer Night's Dream*. On the other hand, as Shakespeare wrote, "the Devil can cite scripture for his purpose," so why couldn't the Devil cite Shakespeare?

There was also his skulking about to consider—she didn't quite believe his tale about the cigars. What if he had indeed been searching for Papa's private papers?

Sliding to the foot of her bed, she opened her wooden trunk to check on the strongbox. Thank God Mr. Brennan hadn't had time to find it last night. As she studied its heavy padlock, her curiosity blossomed. Its contents certainly seemed important to both Papa and Mr. Brennan's employer, who no doubt had put the man up to searching the desk in the first place.

Well, if finding the box was Mr. Brennan's task, she would prevent him from succeeding. She wouldn't let him out of her sight, no matter what the consequences. Even if he wasn't looking for it, knowing her enemy couldn't hurt her. Mr. Brennan might unwittingly provide evidence of his employer's poor character that she could use in convincing Juliet to defy Papa. Surely Papa would never force Juliet into marriage if the girl truly didn't wish it.

She shoved the trunk lid shut. Yes, that would be her plan—to unravel the men's secrets and thus win this battle.

With renewed determination, she rose and swept toward the door. Let Mr. Brennan say what he would at breakfast. She'd counter every accusation with one of her own. He wouldn't best her—no indeed.

Hurrying from her room, she nearly collided with Juliet, who was coming up the hall. As Juliet's gaze swung to her, the girl blanched. "R-Rosalind?"

"Good morning, dear. Headed down for breakfast?"

"Yes." Juliet eyed her anxiously. "Y-You aren't furious at me?"

"For what?" She paused. "Oh, yes, for locking me in Papa's room." Her encounter with Mr. Brennan had blotted it right out of her mind.

"I'm so sorry I did it," Juliet whispered, pleating the skirt of her lemony satin gown with nervous fingers. "Are you very angry?"

How could she rail at the girl when the poor dear looked so remorseful? "Not anymore. You *thought* you were doing the right thing."

"I did! Truly, I did." Turning, Juliet lifted her skirts and walked toward the stairs. "I know Mr. Knighton's past concerns you, but it isn't as if he were a smuggler himself. And anyway, Papa says it was a long time ago. There are worse things he could have been—like a drunkard or a rakehell or a friend of that awful Lord Byron."

Rosalind rolled her eyes, but Juliet did have a point. Mrs. Inchbald's letters hadn't mentioned any character traits that would make the man a poor husband. Nonetheless. . . .

"You won't rail at Mr. Knighton about the smuggling, will you?" Juliet went on.

"Really, Juliet, I'd never be rude to a guest." Not rude enough to send him running to Papa, in any case. She didn't want to earn another evening locked away.

A sunny smile transformed her sister's features. "I'm so relieved to hear you say that. I don't like it when we're at odds. It's quite vexing."

"Yes, it is," she said, and meant it. After Mama had died bearing Juliet, Rosalind and Helena had tried as best they could to take their mother's place. At six and nine years old respectively, they'd coddled Juliet with great affection. They still did.

She was everyone's darling—and with good reason. At seventeen, the girl already possessed a stunning figure and rich hair of spun gold. The three of them all had the Laverick hazel eyes, but Juliet's shone as green as brilliant emeralds when she wore the right color. Rosalind's more often bore a strong resemblance to that dull moss growing on the trees in the deer park, no matter what color she wore. Juliet was far too pretty for an unsavory character like Mr. Knighton.

"So," Rosalind remarked, as they approached the stairs, "what do you think of our cousin? What can I expect?"

Ducking her head, Juliet hurried down. "He's nice. Very gentlemanly."

Eyes narrowing, Rosalind hastened after her sister. "You liked him, did you?"

Juliet shrugged and quickened her pace.

"Then you did not." Aha! Perhaps there'd be no need to expose Mr. Knighton's secrets after all.

"No. I-I mean, yes!" She glided down the stairs like a sleepwalking Lady Macbeth. "Oh, I don't know. He's all right, I suppose."

Rosalind caught up with her and stayed her with one hand. "But something about him troubles you."

When Juliet started to protest, Rosalind pressed a finger to her lips. "Don't pretend with me, dearest. Your face is as easy to read as a child's primer."

That was the wrong thing to say. "I'm not a child," Juliet retorted in a hurt tone, "and nothing is troubling me. I can do this. Truly, I can."

She sounded as if she were trying to convince herself. Rosalind sighed as the girl continued down. When had Juliet become so determined to save Swan Park? For a girl used to floating through life on a dream, she was suddenly very set on martyring herself to Papa's cause.

You weren't much older than her when you took on the task of caring for an invalid father, a desperately ill sister, and a failing estate.

Yes, well, that was different, she argued with herself. *I had no choice.*

Juliet probably felt the same. With a sigh, Rosalind caught up to her sister, resolving to say no more for now. Perhaps it would work itself out. Perhaps Juliet's fears would convince her to turn off this disastrous course.

When they reached the lower floor, they fell into a more sedate pace on the balding carpet and headed for the dining room. A man entered the other end of the hall, so tall and solidly built that he blotted out the light from the arched window behind him. After spotting them, he waited at the door to the dining room.

"Did the blessed creature grow in the night?" Juliet muttered under her breath.

Rosalind kept her voice low as well. "That's our cousin?"

"Yes, that's Mr. Knighton."

She scrutinized the man she'd already cast as the villain of the piece. He didn't look like a villain. He looked like a field laborer in gentlemen's clothing,

awkward and uncomfortable and wary of his surroundings. Papa's valet, assigned to Mr. Knighton
for the visit, must have tied his cravat too tightly, for
the man tugged at it so often he was in danger of
unraveling the knot entirely. His clear discomfort
had the strange effect of making her feel sympathy
for him.

It did not, however, seem to do the same for
Juliet. The young woman lagged behind Rosalind
fearfully. For pity's sake, the man was smiling,
which transformed his rawboned features into
something almost attractive. So why did he intimidate Juliet?

As they drew near and Rosalind realized how
large he was, a suspicion leapt into her mind. The
man *was* rather gigantic. And Juliet was so very
petite . . .

"You needn't bother with him, you know," Rosalind whispered. "If he frightens you, then—"

"Someone has to marry him," Juliet interrupted.
Rosalind couldn't help noticing that she didn't deny
her fright. "You and Helena refuse to do it, so the
task falls to me."

"Dearest—"

"Enough!" Juliet hissed, though tears shimmered
in her eyes. "I shan't live out my days as a Swanlea
Spinster, and if I don't marry Mr. Knighton and
we're thrown from Swan Park, that is exactly what
I'll become!"

Rosalind signed. The young could be such trage-
dians. "There's still time for you to find another
man to marry."

"You think so, do you? Helena missed her chance
because of her illness, and you missed it because of
your responsibilities and because Papa won't take
us to London. Well, I won't miss mine. I won't let go

of my only chance because of silly qualms about Mr. Knighton's size. I will adjust to it. I *will*."

Oh, what was the point of reasoning with the foolish girl when she was so blasted stubborn? But somehow Rosalind would make everything right. She owed it to Juliet to see her happily wed to a man of her choice, not an ox who terrified her.

Mr. Knighton bowed as they reached him, an action that only accentuated his size, since when he brought his head down to three-quarters mast, it was still a good foot above Juliet's. Quickly, her sister stammered through the introductions.

He politely overlooked the girl's nervousness. "It's a pleasure to meet you, cousin," he told Rosalind. "Your sisters have told me much of you."

"You mustn't believe a word." Extending her hand, she settled into the familiar role of mistress of the manor. "No one can exaggerate a person's faults quite so effectively as a sister."

He took her hand briefly before releasing it. "Then I hope you'll give me the privilege of learning your virtues so I can counter your sister's exaggerations. If indeed they were exaggerations."

When coupled with a winning smile, his charming words almost disarmed her. Almost. "Why, Mr. Knighton, I am impressed. You're far more talented at flattery than your man of affairs."

A thin blade of alarm sharpened his gray eyes to steel. "You met Griff?"

Griff? Oh, yes, the scoundrel *had* said people called him that. "I did. Last night." Without elaborating, Rosalind peered through the door into the empty dining room. "And where is Mr. Brennan this morning? Still abed, I take it?"

"Er. . . . yes. He tends to keep town hours."

Precisely what Mr. Brennan himself had said.

Had Mr. Knighton already spoken to him and heard of her attack last night?

If so, he hid it well, for his expression showed only polite disinterest. "I'm sure he'll be along soon. Shall we go in to breakfast?" His smile included Juliet, who watched him doggedly, as if that might help to dissolve her fear of his great bulk.

"Of course." Rosalind stepped between him and Juliet to take the arm he offered, and her sister sighed with relief.

Yet it wasn't Mr. Knighton occupying her thoughts as they entered the sun-drenched dining room. Mr. Brennan had outslept the coming morn—ha! And after all his veiled threats to reveal their embarrassing encounter, too. Who had the upper hand now?

Better yet, this would allow her to question Mr. Knighton without Mr. Brennan's interference. Or Papa's, for that matter. She waited until the three of them were seated, with Mr. Knighton beside her and Juliet opposite him. While the servants set platters of scones and sausages and shirred eggs on the table, she took up the teapot and began her inquisition. "I suppose your company is a rather large one, Mr. Knighton?"

"Yes, very large." He leaned back to allow her to pour him some tea. "The London office of Knighton Trading alone employs thirty people."

"Thirty!" She poured a cup for herself, adding a generous dollop of cream. "That's a great many indeed. You must tell us how you came to establish such an impressive concern."

She sipped her tea and awaited his reply, eager to see if the man could answer without alluding to his trading company's unsavory beginnings.

"It's too dull a tale for fine young ladies like you."

He glanced toward the door. "Speaking of young ladies, where's your other sister this morning?"

Rosalind wasn't about to let him change the subject. "Oh, Helena is with Papa. Now, about the founding of your trading concern—"

"Is she preparing him for visitors?" he broke in stubbornly. "Does that mean I'll meet your father after breakfast?"

That brought Rosalind up short. "You haven't met Papa yet?" She turned to her sister. "Juliet, why hasn't Mr. Knighton met Papa?"

Juliet's face turned a mottled shade of red. "Because Papa wasn't feeling well last night, remember?"

"He was no worse than usual when I was in—" Juliet's kick under the table came at the same time as her memory. "Owwhh, yes. Right. Papa wasn't feeling well." Twice now her encounter with that blasted man of affairs had made her forget her imprisonment. That the scoundrel had such an effect on her was vastly annoying.

Across from her, Juliet lifted the cover off a platter and sniffed. "Mr. Knighton, do you like shirred eggs? It's our cook's specialty, so you must try some. We have truly superior eggs here at Swan Park."

That launched them into a discussion of Cook and her talents, which led to a discussion of the kitchen's capacity, which led them far afield into a discussion of where they got their coal. Rosalind bided the changes in subject impatiently, eager to return to the topic of Knighton Trading. Meanwhile, she used the opportunity to observe Mr. Knighton.

He wasn't at all what she'd expected. He lacked Mr. Brennan's arrogance and annoying certitude about his own opinions. Mr. Knighton seemed as nervous as Juliet and as determined to be friendly. He was polite and charming. His table manners were a bit rough—he ate an enormous amount and had some trouble negotiating the cutlery—but otherwise he was quite amiable, not in the least the ogre she'd anticipated.

Still, she wouldn't let his apparent good nature lull her into complacency. She waited for an appropriate break in the conversation, then plunged in where she'd left off. Only this time she was more direct. "Mr. Knighton, is it true you once sold goods brought into England by smugglers?"

"Rosalind!" Juliet exclaimed. "You promised—"

"I'm merely making conversation." Rosalind fixed their cousin with a challenging look. "You don't mind talking about it, do you? It's widely rumored that you gained your success in trade by selling French brandy and silks brought in illegally during the war, so I don't think I'm speaking out of turn. It *is* true, isn't it?"

Mr. Knighton seemed at a loss for words, and Juliet was babbling a wild apology, when a rumbling voice sounded from the doorway.

"Attacking your guests as usual, Lady Rosalind?"

She swung her head around with a groan. She should have known bad timing would be one of that wretch's many vices. "Good morning, Mr. Brennan. We were just discussing Knighton Trading's origins."

"I heard." Casual and devious as any Iago, he sauntered into the room. "I'm relieved to see it's not only me you suspect of criminal activity, but my employer as well. Isn't there enough drama in your life without your having to create some?"

Juliet's relieved laughter bubbled into the air.

"You've taken her likeness exactly, Mr. Brennan! How did you know that Rosalind is so dramatic?"

"That's a secret, I'm afraid." A wicked smile spread over his lips as he took the seat directly across from Rosalind. He gestured to the servant to bring him food as if ordering servants about was commonplace for him, then went on. "Your sister begged me not to discuss our first encounter, and as a gentleman, I must abide by her wishes."

"A gentleman wouldn't even allude to it," Rosalind snapped. "And I didn't beg you. I don't care what you tell them, as long as it's the truth." But she rushed to tell her side first. "Did you enjoy the cigars after you went to so much trouble to find them? I assume it was your smoking rather than any further expeditions into our private rooms that caused you to 'outsleep the coming morn.'"

Mr. Knighton apparently found his voice. "Griff doesn't s—"

"Sleep late as a general rule," Mr. Brennan finished for him. "Yes, that's true. But you're right, Lady Rosalind. After you were so kind as to give me those cigars when you discovered me wandering the house—" He paused to shoot a pointed glance at his employer. "I ended up retiring very late."

Mr. Knighton opened his mouth again, then shut it. How very odd that Mr. Knighton would let Mr. Brennan intimidate him like that.

Mr. Brennan served himself some shirred eggs and sausages. "In any case, I hope my lateness didn't inconvenience anyone." He cast her a mocking smile. "Especially you, Lady Rosalind. I'm all too familiar with what you're capable of when your dander is up."

She had no qualm whatsoever about taking up the gauntlet he'd thrown down. "You gave me good enough reason to have my dander up, don't you think?"

He paused with his fork in midair. "Perhaps, but did you have to come after me with a sword?"

Mr. Knighton nearly choked on his juice. "A sword?"

"Oh, yes, our hostess is quite the swordswoman. Held me at the point of a blade and threatened to slit my gullet—"

"I did no such thing! *Now* who is being dramatic?" She attacked her eggs. "Besides, it was an honest mistake. I thought you were a thief. After all, I did find you rooting around in Papa's desk—"

"Looking for cigars. You wouldn't have assumed otherwise if you didn't have such a wild imagination, my lady."

"She does indeed!" Juliet interjected. "Rosalind wants to be an actress, you know."

"I would never have guessed," he said dryly. "Although that does explain her tendency to 'rush in where angels fear to tread.' "

When he continued to eat as if he hadn't just insulted her, Rosalind bristled. "Mr. Brennan, are you calling me a fool?"

"A fool?" He paused in the act of raising his steaming cup of tea to his lips. "No. Although even you must admit that your attack on me last night was foolhardy, especially in light of what happened afterward. If I'd truly been a thief instead of a—"

"Knave? Blackguard?"

"Rosalind, please don't be rude," Juliet pleaded with pink-tinged cheeks, but was ignored by everyone at the table.

Rosalind turned to Mr. Knighton. "Did you know your man of affairs has no sense of gentlemanly propriety whatsoever?"

"Do tell." Mr. Knighton leaned back in his chair,

his eyes twinkling. For some reason, her comment seemed to amuse him.

Not Mr. Brennan, however. "Propriety?" He tossed down his cup with such force that it fell over, and its contents sloshed onto the tablecloth. "You have the audacity to speak of propriety, madam? You can hardly blame me if I don't know how to react when a woman dressed like a soiled dove comes at me with a sword and shield! I doubt any man would behave with 'gentlemanly propriety' under such circumstances!"

A soiled dove! Now he'd done it! She leaned forward, determined to give him a piece of her mind.

"That's enough of your impudence, Griff," Mr. Knighton cut in before she could.

Rosalind sat back, a little mollified, though she wondered why it had taken the man so long to bring his insolent employee under control. And why that employee was now regarding his employer with a mixture of shock and annoyance.

"I don't know what happened between the two of you last night," Mr. Knighton continued, a little nervously, "but I won't tolerate rude behavior toward my fair cousins."

"What? *You* will not toler—" Mr. Brennan broke off abruptly as if realizing the full extent of his impertinence. With the precise motion of a man striving to govern his temper, he righted his cup. A long moment passed before he spoke again, eyes blazing. "Yes, sir, of course. I don't know what I was thinking."

"Now apologize to Lady Rosalind."

His gaze shot to Mr. Knighton, and a muscle jerked in his jaw. But he said through gritted teeth, "I beg your pardon, Lady Rosalind. I didn't intend any insult."

She might have believed him if not for his tone,

which was as insincere as a crocodile's tears. She glanced at Mr. Knighton, who seemed suddenly to be trying very hard not to laugh.

What on earth could he find amusing in the situation? His man of affairs was glaring at them both with murder in his eyes. Mr. Knighton should take care whom he allowed to conduct his business for him.

She strove to rein in her temper. "Your apology is accepted, Mr. Brennan. After last night I'm accustomed to your manner of speaking, and I'm sure you'll admit that I . . . tend to frankness myself."

When Mr. Brennan turned his hot blue gaze on her, he looked as if he exercised uncommon restraint to hold back a sarcastic reply. Then the beginnings of a smile stole over his lips, provoking her insides to tighten with an unfamiliar tension. She liked him better angry. When he was angry she didn't feel this strange connection to him, this intoxicating feeling that he understood her better than anyone ever had.

"Well, that's all right then," Juliet put in quickly, the peacemaker as always. She dabbed at her lips with her damask napkin, then laid it across her plate with typical feminine delicacy. "Perhaps if you're all finished with breakfast, we can go to Papa's room. He's expecting us."

"Since I was late to breakfast and am not quite finished," Mr. Brennan remarked in far too casual a tone, "why don't the rest of you go on without me?" His gaze swung to his employer. "You won't need me, will you?"

"No, of course not."

"I'll finish here and take a walk about the estate. If that meets with your approval."

Despite Mr. Brennan's perfectly subservient words, she couldn't shake the feeling that he was issuing an order—and he seemed very comfortable doing so. Their arrangement was peculiar indeed.

Of course, if she had a man as . . . unpredictable as Mr. Brennan working for her, she might be tempted to acquiesce herself for fear he'd murder her in her sleep if she didn't.

"That's a fine idea," Mr. Knighton responded. "We don't want to overwhelm his lordship by tramping in all together. The ladies and I will go on without you."

Not a chance, Rosalind thought. She wouldn't allow that smuggler to do more foraging for Papa's papers. "Actually, there's no reason for *me* to go, either. Papa really does prefer smaller groups of visitors." She flashed Mr. Brennan a brilliant smile. "I'll join you, sir. You'll need help finding your way about the estate."

His lips tightened into a disapproving line. "Begging your pardon, Lady Rosalind, but I didn't have a nursemaid when I was three, so I certainly don't need one now. I'm perfectly capable of navigating an estate alone."

"I'm sure you are—indeed, you demonstrated a remarkable proficiency for it last night, and in a strange house, too. But you'll miss much of interest on our grounds without one of us along to point things out. No, it's imperative that I accompany you."

With a worried glance at her, Mr. Knighton shifted his bulky frame in the chair that was ill equipped to hold such a Goliath. "I was hoping to have you help *me*, cousin. Won't your father like it better if all his daughters join us when he meets me for the first time?"

"Nonsense," she said gaily. "It'll be cozier without me. He won't even notice I'm gone. And Mr. Brennan should certainly have company."

Mr. Brennan drummed his fingers on the table, probably to keep from using them to throttle her. "Perhaps since you're so fond of the bard, Lady

Rosalind, I can put this in terms even you will understand. 'I thank you for your company; but, good faith, I had as lief have been myself alone.' "

As You Like It again. " 'And so had I,' " she quoted back. "However, since Swan Park is still Papa's estate, and I'm still the one who runs it, I must insist upon acting as your guide. After all, I'd hate it if something happened to you that I could have prevented."

"What of your reputation, my lady? You shouldn't walk out alone with a man."

She laughed. "At twenty-three, I hardly need a chaperone, sir. Besides, this is the country. We don't observe strict proprieties here, I assure you." She'd done pretty much as she liked for the last few years, so who would stop her? Certainly not Papa, under the circumstances.

For a moment Mr. Brennan looked as if he might argue more, then resignation seemed to dull his enthusiasm for further argument. "Very well, whatever you wish. Though I warn you I'm a fast walker and can go for hours without any rest."

"Excellent, so can I. It's settled then." She turned to her sister. "Juliet, why don't you and Mr. Knighton go on? I'll wait here for Mr. Brennan to finish his breakfast, and then we can embark on our tour of the estate."

"To be truthful," Mr. Knighton put in, "I need a word with Griff in private. If you ladies wouldn't mind waiting for us in the hall . . ."

"Of course we don't mind," Juliet said, rising hastily from her place. "Rosalind?"

Rosalind rose, too, and followed her without a word. Now that she'd won, she could be gracious enough to let the men plot alone for a moment. But their plotting would accomplish nothing. Mr. Brennan would not get at Papa's papers on *her* watch.

Once she and Juliet were in the hall, Juliet rounded on her, her face a mixture of admiration and worry. "You didn't *really* draw a sword on Mr. Brennan, did you?"

"I certainly did. And you would have, too, if you'd seen what he was doing."

Juliet peeked back into the dining room, her lashes fluttering like the wings of startled birds. "Not me. He frightens me even more than our cousin. I don't know how you find the courage to speak to him as you do."

"No one is born to courage, Juliet. Courage is a habit you develop after cowardice has gotten you nothing." She squeezed her sister's shoulder. "You'll learn it as you grow older, trust me."

Juliet shook her head. "I'll never be as brave as you. Or Helena, for that matter."

It suddenly occurred to Rosalind that her insistence on sticking close to Mr. Brennan would have another unwanted result. "You don't mind that I'm leaving you alone with Mr. Knighton, do you? You'll be all right?"

"I'll be fine. We're going straight to Papa's room anyway." Juliet glanced at her from beneath half-closed eyelids. "You . . . er . . . seem very eager to join Mr. Brennan."

"Not eager." She peered into the room, wondering what Mr. Brennan was saying to Mr. Knighton with such animation at the other end of the long dining room. "But I must keep an eye on him. I think he's up to no good." At Juliet's drawn-out sigh, she added, "Don't tell Papa, however—not until I'm sure what he's planning. I can handle this on my own."

Oh, yes, she would handle that devious man of affairs. Even if it meant sticking to him like flypaper for the rest of the men's visit.

Chapter 5

He is only honest who is not discovered.

Susannah Centlivre, English playwright, The Artifice

"**B**y God, why didn't you dissuade the damnable woman from going off with me?" Griff hissed at Daniel over the table.

Daniel shrugged. "I tried, but she insisted. You heard her."

"I don't care. You were supposed to prevent her. I can't; I'm no longer in charge, remember?" He scowled. "You obviously do, since you used your newfound station to chastise me publicly."

"Don't grumble at me! This was your idea, not mine. And if you can't control the bloody woman, how the hell do you expect me to?"

"How the hell do you expect *me* to search the house with her on my heels?"

"I have no idea." Daniel leaned forward, concern on his features. "I take it you didn't find the proof last night."

"No. She caught me before I could finish searching the desk. There's something in there that prompted her concern, but it might not be what I'm looking for. The damnable piece of paper could be anywhere." When Daniel shot him a look that said *I told you so*, he growled, "I'll find it eventually, don't worry."

"In the meantime, what do you intend to do about her?"

"Do? Damnation, I don't know." Glancing across the room and into the hall, Griff noted how Lady Rosalind and her sister eyed him and Daniel with ill-disguised curiosity. He feigned interest in the sausages growing cold on his plate, shoving them about with his fork. "Since I roused her suspicions last night, I'd best humor her whim this morning."

"Do you think she's guessed what you're up to?"

"I doubt it." He couldn't imagine that the earl would tell his daughters the true history of his dealings with the Knighton family. From the little Griff had gleaned of their characters, they would be appalled. "I think she's a suspicious woman in general. And she feels some sort of responsibility for the estate."

"Maybe you should try charming the girl. Flattery softens a woman."

"It may work for you, but you know I'm bad at it, especially with a woman as clever as this." He poured himself more tea, taking note of Swanlea's expensive china. At least the man had better taste than his daughter. "Besides, I tried it last night. She took offense, told me I was a ne'er-do-well, then peppered me with questions about why I was in her father's study."

"She's no soft, weak-willed light-o'-love, I'll give you that. Never met a woman like her before—so ready to speak her mind and all."

That was a fine understatement. "Maybe I should make myself so disagreeable that she'll eagerly abandon me."

"That's playing to your strengths, all right."

Griff glowered at him. "It's playing to her rank, you ass. She's a lady—squiring a man of affairs about can't be her favorite choice for entertainment."

"I'm not so sure. A woman who'll come after a man with a sword . . . Did she really do that?"

"Oh, yes. Thrust a shield in my face, too." Griff speared a sausage and bit off the end, then chewed it thoughtfully. "And all the while wearing only her chemise and wrapper. I swear the cheap silk was sheer enough to see through—I wouldn't have paid that trader Hung Choi a farthing for it."

"Hmmm, this grows more interesting each time you tell it. When you said she dressed like a soiled dove, I thought you meant her gown was gaudy."

"That goes without saying." He nodded in Lady Rosalind's direction. "Look at that assault-upon-the-eyes she's wearing today."

The dizzying striped print of bright yellow and green rivaled her handiwork in the entrance hall. Didn't the woman own a single piece of clothing that wasn't vividly colored? And how did she still manage to look so damnably alluring in the things?

Daniel cast her a furtive glance. "I don't notice anything wrong with it."

"You wouldn't."

Daniel bristled. "See here, you got no cause to insult me. I'm doing what you asked."

"Not entirely. I'm still saddled with Lady Amazon. You were supposed to play to *your* strengths and charm the woman out of my way."

"Can I help it if the woman can't be charmed?"

"Well, maybe she can be frightened off, if I can only think how to do it." Griff mused a moment.

"She wasn't entirely bold last night, after all. I did shut her up when I put a blade to her throat." He threw down his silver fork. "I've got it! Did you see how she backed down when I lost my temper this morning? She's confident when rebuffing a gentleman, but I'm not a gentleman, am I? I'm *you*—a highwayman's son and an erstwhile smuggler. Doing her father's bidding is one thing; keeping company with a dangerous fellow like me is quite another, even for an Amazon."

Daniel went still. "You're not going to tell her all that, do you hear? Unless by some chance the old bastard outlives you all, I'll have to deal with these women after you inherit, y'know. While you'll be in London running Knighton Trading, I'll be packing them off to some cottage. No sense in making it more difficult by teaching them to fear me. They'll hate me enough as it is without thinking I'm a bloody criminal."

Daniel's sudden reticence about his past took Griff by surprise. Although the man had never announced it to the world, he hadn't bothered to hide it either. Indeed, he sometimes dredged it up if it would help him gain the advantage in his business dealings. Playing a wealthy gentleman was obviously affecting his vanity. "They won't think you're a criminal. Besides, once it's over and they know of the masquerade, they won't believe anything I said while it was going on."

"All the same, I don't think you should tell."

"And I don't think you should reprimand me before God and everybody, but that's part of the masquerade, isn't it? Even if you did get carried away." Griff drained the rest of his tepid tea, wishing for something stronger. "After that performance, I ought to demand my money back—you're having too much fun to be paid."

A reluctant smile crossed Daniel's lips. "And it

might be worth losing the money. You should have seen your face when I told you not to be impudent—"

"Wait until this is done," Griff grumbled. "I'll show you impudence, you dog."

"Of course you will." Daniel laughed. "If there's anything left of you after the harridan is finished."

"I'll get the better of her, you'll see." *Now that I have a plan*. He shoved back from the table and stood. "I might as well go to it. She doesn't look as if she intends to leave my side anytime soon."

"For that I really am sorry." Daniel rose from his chair, sobering. "I have the best of this; the other two ladies are prettier and more quiet, more the sort of woman you prefer."

"Yes." Although a man could conceivably change his preference, couldn't he?

He dismissed that possibility with great violence. This ridiculous attraction came only from having seen the woman in her wrapper. A few hours with her would surely sour any fascination nurtured by last night's lust. Perhaps it was just as well she was foisting herself on him today. If he began thinking of her in those terms, he'd find himself regretting his plans for Swan Park and her father.

"Wish me luck meeting your cousin, the earl," Daniel murmured.

Griff thought grimly of the old sot scheming in his bedchamber down the hall. "I'm glad it's you meeting him and not I." Despite years of restraining his anger at the earl, he found it hard to do so now. Swan Park had roused old resentments. He wondered if he could manage even bare civility if forced to talk to the bastard.

Daniel shot him a sidelong glance as they neared the door. "What if the earl asks about the marriage arrangement?"

"Put him off. Say you're still making up your mind."

"I only hope I can convince him that I'm you."

"Don't worry—talk to him as you talked to me at breakfast and you'll be perfectly believable."

Daniel gave a low laugh. "I'll remember that. And don't go rousing Lady Rosalind against Daniel Brennan or I'll make you pay me even *more* for this scheme, see if I don't."

Griff didn't answer. He'd keep Daniel's secrets if he could, but if they happened to slip out . . . A former smuggler and a highwayman's son would surely send her running.

He reached the hall and nearly smiled when he saw Lady Rosalind turn away as if she hadn't been spying on them throughout their conversation. He'd never seen a woman so incapable of subtlety.

He held his arm out to her. "Shall we go?"

True to form, she ignored it to stalk off down the hall with all the dignity of a great lady. It was quite a performance, but he'd seen the woman flouncing about in her wrapper—she was about as dignified as an orange seller at the theater.

"This way, Mr. Brennan," she called back. "There's much to see and no time to waste."

Casting a wry glance at Daniel, he followed her. At least he could enjoy the view, he thought, as his gaze swung unerringly to her generous hips. That dramatic gown clung far too sweetly to her curves for a man's sanity. Didn't she know her walk wasn't the least demure, that it rivaled a courtesan's for sheer seductiveness?

Probably. It would be just like the damnable woman to try feminine wiles on him. Well, they wouldn't work. He could withstand the attractions of any woman—especially his enemy's daughter—

if he made a concerted effort to control his wayward
thoughts.

Now if only he could control his wayward cock . . .

Percival, the Earl of Swanlea, sometimes wondered how long he could endure this agony of living. He could not breathe deeply without setting off
the coughing. His muscles ached down to the bone,
and he could feel the disease creeping beyond his
lungs and into the rest of his body, destroying its
very fibers.

Most of all, he missed Solange. If not for the girls,
he would give up his struggle and join his beloved
wife in the great beyond. But he must see all his
daughters secure ere he died, no matter what physical pain it cost him, and that meant finding one of
them a wealthy husband. Which was why he'd
taken this risk with Knighton, of all people.

It was a great risk indeed, bringing him here.
Only the breath of Death on his face, coming closer
with each passing night, dared him to try it.

He glanced over to where Helena sat at his writing table, bent over her painting-box contraption as
she daubed lightly at some ivory squares. Where
she got the ivory he did not know, but then, no one
told him anything now that he was infirm.

He could still deduce some matters for himself.
For one thing, he knew Rosalind was wrong about
Juliet. His youngest was clearly eager to marry
Knighton—he could tell from the modest way she
hid her face whenever the marriage was mentioned.
And he knew, no matter what Rosalind protested,
that his middle daughter was peeved over Juliet's
marrying first.

But whatever her reasons for protest, he would
ignore them—for if he did not make peace with his

old enemy's son, all his daughters would lose their home and the chance of a secure future.

Helena sighed softly over her work, irritating him with her bloody eternal patience.

"Will he come soon?" Percival snapped.

"Yes, Papa. Juliet is bringing him upstairs after breakfast."

"Good. I am anxious to see him."

The door swung open only moments later and a man stood in the doorway behind Juliet, dwarfing her with his amazing height.

Leonard's son, stalwart as a castle. After all these years, the babe Percival had wronged stood before him. Old feelings swamped him—resentment, anger . . . and heavier than them all, guilt. At least Leonard had sired a son when Percival had fathered no son at all. But that did not assuage his guilt much.

"Good morning, Mr. Knighton," Helena said, drawing Percival from his unpleasant memories. The girl used one hand on the desk to push herself to a stand.

She was remarkable—graceful and polished, despite her infirmity. She owed those qualities to Solange's training. Percival owed much to Solange himself. At least he could take pleasure in knowing she would be proud to see him here now with Leonard's son, making things right as best he could without ruining the girls' lives.

The thought stiffened his resolve. "Come in, sir, and let me see you."

As Juliet flitted into the room in all her young, innocent splendor, Knighton followed behind. The man seemed to pay her charms little heed, which worried Percival.

He dragged himself up straighter in the bed.

"Close the door," he commanded. "We cannot have the servants sticking their noses in our business, eh?"

The big man nodded and did Percival's bidding, but once the door was closed, he approached the bed with a wary expression.

"Speaking of employees," Percival continued, "Helena tells me you brought your man of affairs with you to Swan Park."

"I did."

"Good, good." He hoped Knighton's reason for it was so they might draw up the marriage settlement with all due speed. "His name is Brinley or something?"

"Brennan." Knighton clipped the word off as if offended. "It's Brennan."

"An Irishman, eh? I suppose they have their uses." Percival gestured to the door. "Well, where is the man? Why is he not here?"

"We didn't want to crowd too many people into the room, Papa," Juliet broke in. "Mr. Brennan is with Rosalind. She's showing him around the estate."

That could be a promising development. If Rosalind stayed occupied with the man of affairs, she could not drive Knighton off with her bold manner and impudent tongue.

"Come closer, man," Percival demanded. "My eyesight is not so keen as it used to be. Let me get a better look at you."

The man advanced like a soldier preparing to meet the enemy. He was so tall the top of his head brushed the fringe hanging down from the canopy of the bed, and his broad shoulders blocked out some of the light.

Percival squinted up at him. "You do not resemble your father a bit."

"I look like my mother."

"You do not much resemble Georgina either."

Knighton seemed confused. "You knew her?"

"Of course. Did you not realize that? I mean, considering—" Percival broke off with a glance at Helena. The girls must not hear this. Besides, he should first determine how much Knighton knew. It was possible, he supposed, that Leonard and Georgina had told him very little. The case Percival had brought against Leonard had occurred when the boy was but a babe. "In any case, I knew her very well. Once."

"I . . . um . . . never heard her talk about you." Knighton stumbled over his words as if expecting any moment to have them contradicted.

That pained Percival, though he knew he deserved it. "No doubt she thinks badly of me." He dragged in a heavy breath that set off a fit of coughing. Juliet hurried to his side with a basin and his tincture of comfrey, while Helena stood by, looking helpless.

He spit into the basin, then swallowed some of the tincture and cleared his throat. "You see how my daughter coddles me, Knighton. I would not recommend a lung disease to anyone, but it has its compensations." He caught Juliet's hand and patted it. "My dear gel here is always hovering around me. She is my pride and joy, a good gel with a good heart."

For no reason that Percival could see, Knighton shot Helena a look. He, too, glanced over at his oldest, but aside from standing more stiffly than usual, she looked the same as always to him—reserved, serene, the perfect lady.

Dismissing the odd moment, he returned his attention to Knighton. "So what do you think of

Swan Park? I suppose your father told you all about it when you were a boy. Did his description do it justice?"

"Nothing could do it justice, m'lord."

Peculiar how Knighton's pronunciations were a bit vulgar, but he supposed that was to be expected from a man who worked so much in trade. Given all that Percival had learned in recent years about the man's childhood . . .

No, he would not think about that. It weighed too heavily on his conscience.

Better to get right to the important part of this conversation. "Well, we are pleased to have you here." He glanced over at Helena. "You and Juliet may go now. I should like to speak with Knighton in private."

Juliet fled the room with surprising speed as Helena gathered up her painting box and all its pieces.

That drew Knighton's attention. "Do you paint, Lady Helena?"

"Yes," she said quietly. "I paint miniatures."

"Are you painting a portrait of your father?"

"No, I'm merely touching up a copy of Mama's portrait."

"She does a bloody fine job with the little things," Percival remarked, proud as always of his eldest daughter's ability. "For a girl, that is. You must get Juliet to show you some of Helena's miniatures."

With a considering glance at Helena, Knighton nodded. "I'll do that."

"Papa is too kind," Helena remarked dryly as she walked past Knighton to the door. "I'm no artist. It's merely something to pass the time."

"Nonsense," Percival interjected, smiling at Knighton. "They are very pretty pictures. She puts all her energy into them, since she cannot ride or dance or any of that."

Something clattered to the floor, making Knighton turn around.

"I'm sorry, I didn't mean to startle you," Helena apologized in a choked voice, looking pale as she stared down at something that had dropped from her box. She started to leave—probably because picking it up would be too difficult with her weak leg—but Knighton quickly bent to pick up the object for her.

He handed it to her. "Nothing to be sorry about. Here you are."

Percival watched in rapt amazement as a blush spread over her cheeks. He had not seen his reserved daughter blush in years. Whyever was she doing it now?

She took what looked like a piece of her ivory from the man, never lifting her eyes to his face. "Thank you," she stammered in a manner very unlike her usual reserved one. Then, without a word of farewell to her father, she limped from the room.

When Knighton faced Percival again, his expression was stony cold. "You didn't need to remind her of it. I'm sure she has enough reminders as it is."

Percival was all at sea. "Remind her of what?"

"That she can't 'ride or dance or any of that.' "

"Pish, do not concern yourself over that. Helena is not a silly child to be bothered by such remarks."

"You don't know women very well, do you, m'lord?" Knighton remarked.

"I should think I know my own daughter." But this was not what he wanted to discuss with the man who held the future of Swan Park in his hands. "And speaking of daughters, how do you like Juliet?"

Something in Knighton's countenance struck him

uneasily, a flicker of distaste or even anger. Then it was gone. "I like her very well. So far."

"So far?" Percival echoed.

"I only just met her. I haven't had time to form much of an opinion."

Bloody hell, the man was delaying. He glared at Knighton. "But you do understand what is at stake, do you not? You understand what you must do to inherit."

Knighton stiffened. "I do. But you didn't say I had to make up my mind at once."

A chill shook Percival's old bones. "What is there to make up your mind about? The only way you will get the proof is if you marry Juliet." It was not entirely true—he did not want to die with his sins on his conscience. But he had to try this first, for he also did not want to leave his daughters destitute.

"You didn't say it had to be Juliet," Knighton said smoothly. "Your letter said I could choose any of your daughters."

Percival could not have been more astonished if Knighton had said he fancied the housekeeper for a wife. "That is true, but I did not think . . . You would rather marry Rosalind? Or Helena?"

The man's thoughts were impossible to guess from his wooden expression. "I don't know. How can I say until I know them better?"

The thought of remaining in this limbo any longer made Percival shudder, yet he was hardly in a position to protest. Still, he must not let the man drag his feet for long. There was not much time. "Very well. Stay here for a while to acquaint yourself with my daughters. In a week or so, we'll discuss this again."

Knighton's smooth smile unnerved Percival. "Thank you, m'lord. I promise you won't regret it."

Chapter 6

*Won't you come into the garden? I would like my
roses to see you.*

Richard Brinsley Sheridan, Anglo-Irish playwright
and owner of Drury Lane Theatre, to a young lady

The man was sly, she'd give him that, Rosalind
thought as she swept ahead of Mr. Brennan
into the deer park. It had taken her all morning, but
she'd finally figured out what he was up to.

"Don't tell me, let me guess," he said behind her
in his annoyingly snide tone. "We're entering the
Forest of Arden."

"You're thinking of a different part of the shire,"
she said dryly. "This is our deer park. It is widely
accounted to be the finest in all of Warwickshire."

She sucked in a deep breath of woodruff-scented
air and held it, eager for his answer. If her theory
were correct, he would now expound upon the deer
park's faults as he had with all the other portions of
the estate she'd shown him this morning.

Well, she would call him a liar to his face if he did. No one could possibly object to the deer park. Papa himself had overseen its progress through years of careful management.

With the air of a man examining a property for purchase, he scrutinized his surroundings. "It well warrants such praise."

She nearly collapsed in surprise. The man was actually admitting that some part of Swan Park met his high standards! "Do you mean to tell me that it does not 'require improvement'?" That had been his claim for every single room in the manor house.

He raised an eyebrow. "No, I don't think it does."

"You certainly can't call it a 'funeral pyre for foliage' as you did the greenhouse," she persisted.

"Very true."

"But wait, the deer park is dirty—I had forgotten how important cleanliness is to you. It must be, if you could call our dairy unclean. Your assertion came as quite a shock to my dairy manager, the woman we have all nicknamed Mrs. White Glove."

It was that absurd assertion that had led Rosalind to figure out his scheme. The foolish man apparently intended to provoke her into fleeing his disagreeable company, leaving him free to roam the estate alone.

His lips were twitching now. "Ah, but a deer park is supposed to have a certain amount of dirt, is it not?"

"It is indeed." She steered left to avoid tripping over a fallen tree that protruded into the path. Would he pounce on that as a potential danger to deer and hunter alike? Curious to see if he would, she halted in the path and faced him, sweeping her hand in an arc about her. "Do you mean to tell me that you see nothing whatsoever in our deer park to complain about? No flaws, no hazards, no disappointments?"

"Oh, it's a lovely deer park, I'll grant you that." His eyes twinkled. "But I don't think it wise to allow the woods to remain so thick this close to the house, do you?"

She couldn't help it—a laugh exploded out of her. Yes, the elms did crowd in upon the lawn, and the oaks seemed on the verge of squeezing the footpath out of existence, but that had always been one of the deer park's peculiar charms. And he knew it, too, the scoundrel, even if he was standing there looking at her with an expression of complete innocence.

"I'm sorry you find it lacking," she said, "though I believe the deer like it. They seem to prefer having a lot of trees about—probably something to do with staying hidden from hunters and hounds." An impish impulse seized her. "But I may be wrong. Perhaps we should find some and ask them?"

A smile played about his lips. "I was merely pointing out that woods this thick make it easy for poachers to hide. They could shoot a deer or bag a grouse and be away without anyone ever realizing it."

"Poachers. Hmm. I hadn't considered that. But you forget that this isn't London." Sobering, she added pointedly, "Nor is it one of your coastal towns with its enclaves of smugglers. We rarely have poachers around here, and if one should happen to show up, he'd be welcome to a deer or a grouse."

"Really?" His smile faded abruptly. "You weren't so friendly toward thieves last night, Lady Rosalind."

Blast, the man twisted the conversation against her as easily as he'd turned that sword against her last night. But she could do the same, couldn't she? Why not turn the conversation toward his master's secrets? Her previous three attempts had been rebuffed, but they'd also been more subtle. And subtlety had ever never been her strong suit.

She angled her head so her bonnet would hide her expression. "To my mind, a man who poaches a deer to feed his family differs vastly from a thief. The first is a poor soul struggling to survive; the second is motivated by greed, thus deserving the name of criminal."

"You're kinder than the law of the land. It makes no such fine distinctions. The law brands as a thief and criminal anyone who takes what doesn't belong to him, no matter what motivates his actions."

She shot him a keen glance. "You should know, shouldn't you?"

"What's that supposed to mean? Do you allude to your ridiculous assumptions last night? I thought we settled that."

"Actually, I refer to the man for whom you work."

His eyes shone a vivid blue. "Knighton, a thief? Why? Because he'll inherit Swan Park?"

"Of course not. Because of his connection to smugglers."

"Ah yes," he said tightly. "You must lead a very dull life, Lady Rosalind, since your favorite subject always seems to be the criminal population."

She studied him as he strolled to the nearby fallen tree and lowered his lean frame to sit on it. Was her supposition about him correct? Was that why mention of "the criminal population" disturbed him?

Yet when he gazed up at her from his seat, he didn't look disturbed. No, he looked amused . . . nonchalant . . .

Attractive, blast him. A man like that shouldn't be unleashed upon a woman alone. She'd found it difficult enough last night not to dwell on his male perfection in the poorly lit study. In the light of day, it was bloody well impossible.

The tree shifted beneath his weight, forcing him to widen his legs and lean back for balance. Her gaze shot straight to where his coat fell open to reveal sinewy legs well sculpted by kerseymere trousers that disappeared into polished leather boots.

Riding boots. Would he sit a horse well? They'd have to ride to reach the wheat fields and the tenant farms. She flashed on an image of him astride her father's best hunter, his muscular thighs gripping the sides of the powerful beast . . .

Her mouth fairly salivated before she caught herself. Dear God, she must rein in her woeful imagination. But who could fault her for it when there'd been no man at Swan Park in years with such nice . . . equipage? How she'd survive this one's arrival seemed uncertain.

But survive it she must. After all, she didn't even know if the man was married. That oddly depressing thought made her jerk her gaze back to his face. "Well? Mr. Knighton does have connections to smugglers, doesn't he?"

"Not that I know of. Even if he did, smugglers aren't thieves, my lady. They purchase their goods."

She eyed him askance. "Yes, but they steal the taxes owed to the government once they bring the goods into the country. And the men who sell the goods are guilty of it as well. Not to mention that they shouldn't have been buying French goods at all, since we were at war with France. Surely you can see how that makes them unsavory characters."

"I assure you my employer does not associate

with 'unsavory characters.' His business is completely legitimate."

"Now, perhaps. But I heard that it wasn't at one time." A thickening of clouds overhead obscured the sun and muted the already dim light of the forest. "You won't evade my questions as easily as you did this morning, so you might as well tell me the truth. Did Knighton Trading begin as an outlet for smugglers' goods? And don't change the subject."

There was no mistaking the humor glinting in his eyes now. "I wouldn't dream of it." Yet he merely tipped his head back to stare across the path. The hazy light showed lines of weariness cut into the high-boned cheeks and tanned brow. She followed his gaze to where a busy green woodpecker riddled a hapless chestnut tree with holes.

"Tell me," he continued, "do you think that bird will kill the tree?"

"You said you wouldn't change the subject."

"I'm not. Humor me and answer the question."

"All right." She stared at the woodpecker a moment. "I doubt he'll kill it. Woodpeckers are troublesome, but not lethal. And they need the grubs to survive."

"Exactly. One could say the same for smugglers. What they do is troublesome but not lethal to society, and in most cases they do it to survive."

"Did Mr. Knighton do it to survive?" she asked pointedly.

His gaze swung back to hold hers for a long, weighty moment. Then he cursed under his breath. "Yes. Knighton Trading was founded when your cousin bought French brandy from a smuggler and sold it at a profit to some of his Eton school acquaintances."

"I knew it!"

A muscle worked in his jaw. "He and his mother

had long been in danger of being sent to Fleet prison, since his father's death left them deeply in debt. Knighton did what work a lad can do to make money, but he earned more on that sale of smuggled brandy than he had in a year of odd jobs." Glancing away again, he added, "Or so he told me."

"Well, it sounds suspicious to me. If he and his mother had so little money, how did they pay for Eton?"

He stiffened. "His father had been the one to enroll him there. After the man's death, Knighton's mother managed to keep him at Eton for a few years as a charity pupil who worked off his expenses, but eventually that too became impossible, for the other debts were too high to manage."

"So he started buying goods from a smuggler and selling them for profit. He *did* do it more than once, didn't he? One could hardly build a trading concern on a single sale."

He rubbed the bridge of his nose wearily. "Lady Rosalind, has anyone ever told you that you have an annoying curiosity?"

"Nearly every day." She planted her hands on her hips. "Well? Am I right about Mr. Knighton?"

"Your cousin," he bit out, "hadn't the blunt to purchase a commission or the connections to find any other sort of advancement, so yes, he sold smuggler's goods."

Propping one booted foot against a dead branch of the tree, he leveled a penetrating look on her. "Tell me, when the opportunity came to sell brandy to wealthy schoolboys and thus provide for his mother and pay his father's debts, should he have refused? Told his mother to hie herself off to debtor's prison while he fled the country to seek his fortune? What would you have done in his place, my Lady Righteous?"

She knew only too well how difficult life could become when money was scarce, and her family hadn't even been in danger of debtors' prison. What's more, his words corresponded with what Papa had said—that Mr. Knighton had dealt with smugglers out of necessity.

Still, it was odd how strongly Mr. Brennan seemed to feel about his employer's situation. It certainly bespoke a close acquaintance.

She sniffed. "I suppose I might have succumbed to temptation temporarily. But once I found success, I would've broken off my association with criminals, I assure you."

"Aren't you the noble one," he said sarcastically. "Your cousin wasn't so noble. He succumbed to temptation for several years. He discovered that he liked paying off his debts and having the blunt to plow into his new trading concern. But then, he was more susceptible to temptation than you, my lady, since he wasn't born to privilege."

She bristled at his assumptions. "He might not have been born to privilege, Mr. Brennan, but he was born a man. Try being a woman for five minutes, and you'll rapidly discover that a man of the lowest station has more privilege than any woman. I have the privilege of being told I can't control my own money or govern my own life or seek the sort of future I desire. I have the privilege of running an estate alone, of looking after my two sisters and my father, with the knowledge that I can't even inherit the property I maintain. Such 'privilege' I could do without, I assure you."

He looked as if he might retort, but she cut him off. "Besides, it isn't a matter of privilege—it's a matter of right and wrong. You seem very sympathetic to free traders. I suppose you have firsthand experience with them?"

His eyes glittered. "Beyond working for my nefarious employer, you mean?"

"Precisely. You handle a sword very well for a man of affairs."

"And you handle a sword very well for an earl's daughter. Yet I haven't accused *you* of 'firsthand experience' with smugglers."

"Of course not. The very idea is absurd."

"Why? Because you're a woman? And I must be a smuggler because I'm Irish and handle a sword well? Women can be criminals, too, you know. And Irishmen who excel at swordplay can be respectable."

She colored. She hadn't meant her speculations to be so obvious as all that. "I didn't say you were a smuggler."

"You didn't have to. I've become adept at guessing what your overwrought imagination will conjure up." He rose from the log, a devious glint in his eyes. "But as it happens, you're right—I *was* a smuggler once."

She pounced on the admission with glee. "That's why my cousin hired you!"

"No. Your cousin hired me because I saved his life when my companions tried to murder him." He tipped back his beaver hat and a lock of sin-dark hair fell over his brow. "He was . . . impressed with my particular talents, and they've served him well through the years. No one has lived to complain of them, in any case."

A chill skittered along her spine before she caught the gleam in his eye. "Now you're teasing me."

"Am I?" Leaving the words hanging in the air, he strolled off down the path again with all the arrogance of a man sure of his own power.

She followed him, pondering this new strategy. Was he deliberately trying to frighten her? Or was this simply another tactic for ridding himself of her company? She would assume the latter, except for the unnerving memory of how easily he'd held that blade to her neck last night.

Increasing her pace until she walked beside him, she probed for more information. "What made you become a smuggler?"

Was that a smile she glimpsed on his lips before he averted his face? "What simple thief brags of his own attaint?"

"*Comedy of Errors.* Very good, you do know your Shakespeare. I don't mind if you brag, however. As you pointed out, I have a most annoying curiosity. If it isn't indulged, I'm liable to bedevil you with questions until it is."

"You're already bedeviling me," he grumbled. "But if you insist on knowing all the nasty details—"

"I do."

"—smuggling presented a welcome change from the workhouse where I lived from the age of six until I was given the chance at nine to join a gang of smugglers."

"The workhouse!"

"I can see how learning of my disreputable past would alarm you," he commented.

"No, indeed! I find it fascinating! You seem so . . . that is, I would never have guessed—"

"That I'm not a gentleman?"

"Oh, *that* I already knew," she quipped. "But I thought you might have been raised as one and were merely ignoring your education."

"Your flattery overwhelms me." He increased his speed until she was almost running to match his brisk gait through the drifts of leaves. "However, if my rudeness annoys you, you needn't continue in my company. I can find my way around now. I'm sure you have better things to do than accompany a disagreeable man about your estate."

He was really too sure of himself for words, believing she'd be so foolish as to fall for his ploys. Why, he'd probably never been a smuggler at all. Or lived in a workhouse.

"Oh, I don't mind," she said blithely. "I enjoy a good stroll around the estate, even with a dangerous criminal like you."

They continued in silence, the only sounds their hushed footfalls and the chatter of frolicking squirrels. Then it occurred to her that she could take advantage of his frankness—*if* she could believe a word he said.

"Tell me," she asked, "how did you come to be in a workhouse?"

He shrugged. "My parents died, leaving me to fend for myself. So I filched an orange from a fruit seller and ended up where all young ruffians end up." He brandished words like a weapon between them. "Needless to say, the magistrate recognized a potential menace to society when he saw one."

She didn't flinch; if anything, his tale intrigued her even more. "How did you lose both your parents at once? Was it the pox? Or a drowning accident?"

He snorted. "Do you ever mind your own business, Lady Rosalind?"

"Not where my family is concerned." When he shot her a black look, she added mischievously, "You're staying under our roof and roaming the place rather freely, so I think it only fair that you help me determine your potential for mischief. I can't have a genuine menace causing trouble on the estate."

"Then you'd best prepare yourself for trouble. I'm lower than even you could imagine. I'm the bastard son of Wild Danny Brennan and the English innkeeper's daughter who was his accomplice." He paused as if to gauge her reaction, then said in a blatant taunt, "They died on the gallows."

She gaped at him in sheer disbelief. The son of a highwayman? Why, the bloody liar! He couldn't possibly be related to Wild Danny Brennan—he wasn't crude or cruel enough to be the son of the Irish scourge who'd terrorized all travelers in Essex until he'd been caught in a tavern boasting of his successes. With his common law wife.

She shivered. Wild Danny Brennan *had* been hanged with a woman, a most unusual occurrence. And Mr. Brennan *had* introduced himself as *Daniel* Brennan. That must be rather more than coincidence.

"Is that why you use a nickname instead of your Christian name?" she probed. "Because you don't want people to make the connection between you and your father?"

A shuttered look veiled his features. "No. I'm called Griff because of the griffin."

"Ah, yes. How odd that Mr. Knighton would choose a smuggler and a highwayman's son to manage his vast treasure." As his hints of past dark deeds leapt instantly to mind, she added in a tone only half-teasing, "Though I suppose it's appropriate for him to keep a griffin at hand for tearing his enemies asunder."

"Tearing enemies asunder hasn't been one of my duties for some time," he said dryly. "Though I see I've affronted your delicate sensibilities. With my despicable background, I'm clearly unfit for your company."

He seemed suspiciously determined to lower himself in her esteem. Perhaps he'd merely adopted such a history for himself as an orphan because some family was better than none.

Or perhaps it was all true.

In either case, it merely increased her determination to keep an eye on him. And though it was horribly shameful to admit, his tales about his criminal past also captivated her. It *was* rather dramatic, wasn't it? The pauper and son of criminals made good. *If* it were true.

"My sensibilities aren't the least affronted," she said. "Certainly no one would call them delicate. After all, you can't help what your parents did, only what you do yourself. You chose a better path when you had the chance. You didn't become a thief."

"Except for that little dalliance with smuggling," he pointed out.

She hid a smile. "Yes, except for that. But you're respectable now."

"Respectable. But not a gentleman."

"Which is probably just as well. You're already more particular in your tastes than any gentleman I know. I shudder to think what your opinion of Swan Park would be if you came at it from a gentleman's viewpoint. As it is, you consider it inadequate in every respect."

"Not in every respect." His reluctant smile softened his rigid jaw and uncompromising mouth. "It has a very nice deer park."

"Except that the trees grow too closely together."

"Exactly." He paused, his steps slowing a little. "So I haven't offended you with my criticisms?"

He sounded so hopeful, she nearly laughed. "No, indeed. As far as I'm concerned, you and your employer are free to alter Swan Park however you wish after my sisters and I are gone."

Only when he looked sharply at her did she realize what she'd just revealed. Dear God, she shouldn't have spoken so hastily. Papa would take her over his knee if he learned that she'd practically told Mr. Brennan that she didn't expect a marriage to occur.

But then, Papa had refused to consider any of their feelings—so perhaps she should present them to someone who might be more interested. In the process, she could point out a few damaging facts that might dissuade Mr. Brennan's employer from taking on a debt-ridden estate and three spinsters with scant portions. Yes, perhaps Mr. Knighton ought to hear that his tidy arrangement with Papa wasn't so tidy after all.

And the best way to inform Mr. Knighton was to inform his man of affairs.

Chapter 7

Griff had no idea what to make of Rosalind's comment. After this morning, he had no idea what to make of the woman at all. She'd endured his criticisms with surprising equanimity. She'd even laughed at him, as if she'd guessed his tactics.

She probably had. He gained hourly proof that the woman was even more clever than he'd given her credit for. She'd run Swan Park adequately, despite her eccentric methods. Granted, he wouldn't have painted the outside of the dairy a periwinkle blue to compensate for the "dull" white on the inside. But the facility itself was scrupulously clean and seemed to have a superior output, judging from the cheese she'd made him sample.

He wouldn't have hired as grooms three itinerant actors from Stratford-upon-Avon, who at first seemed incapable of anything but reciting *As You Like It* for milady's pleasure. But they'd done a decent enough job with the stables when one considered that her horseflesh served only to carry her and her sisters about the estate and into Stratford.

With such knowledge of her capabilities, he couldn't let her strange comment about leaving Swan Park pass with no explanation. "What do you mean, 'after my sisters and I are gone'? Surely if one of you marries my employer as your father plans, you would all continue to live here."

She loped down the path ahead of him. "Just because Papa has offered us up like cattle to be auctioned doesn't mean we'll go meekly to the slaughter."

He followed her in a daze. "Do you mean to tell me that you and your sisters don't wish to marry my employer?"

"That's precisely what I'm telling you."

Damnation. Not only were they innocent of taking part in their father's blackmail plans, they weren't even eager to marry him. How in hell could that be? "You know you'll lose Swan Park if one of you doesn't marry Knighton."

"What do I care? It's a bloody inconvenience running an estate, I'll have you know. Especially one as deeply in debt as Swan Park."

"It's a great deal of work, I'm sure."

"It's not the work I mind." She glowered at him as if he'd just insulted her. "I'm not afraid of work, for pity's sake."

"Then why—" He broke off as an image of her brandishing a sword leapt into his mind. "Ah, yes. It's the *kind* of work that annoys you. Too dull, I would imagine."

Her exaggerated sigh gave him his answer. "Not all of it. I like overseeing any redecorating or construction. I like supervising the staff. I like planning dinners."

"Overseeing, supervising, planning." He smirked at her. "You like being in charge, don't you?"

She shrugged. "I suppose I do. But the other duties are so tedious. I hate going over the books with our steward and settling stupid tenant squabbles and attending to a thousand boring details. I do it because I have to—because no one else will—not because I like it."

He wondered if that were entirely true. She could let the "boring details" fall by the wayside; plenty of people did. But he wouldn't argue that point. Instead, he played devil's advocate. "All right, so you don't enjoy running the estate. But you needn't abandon it entirely. If Knighton marries one of your sisters, he'll run it, or pay someone else to run it. You can just live here, you and your sisters, and enjoy yourself."

"I don't want to live here, no matter what happens," she surprised him by saying. "What is there to enjoy in Stratford? I want to live in London."

He should have known. "Then you should marry Knighton yourself and have him take you there."

For the love of God, what was he saying? "Knighton" wouldn't marry any of them, even her, he reminded himself. Indeed, if matters went as planned, the entire family would be evicted from Swan Park within a matter of months.

The thought roused his conscience from the dead.

She scowled. "Marry Knighton? No, indeed! I wouldn't do so for all the wealth in England!"

The insult sent his conscience fleeing back to its grave. "That's a bit strong, isn't it?" The woman ought to be glad *anyone* would marry her, consider-

ing her years and her . . . peculiar ways. "Does the
thought of marriage to Knighton disgust you so
much?"

She blinked at his acid tone. "No . . . yes . . . I
mean, it's not *him* I object to, not exactly. It would be
the same with any man Papa picked without considering my feelings. This isn't the Dark Ages, after
all. Women ought to be free to choose their own
husbands, don't you think?"

His pride remained bruised, although he agreed
with her in principle. "And I suppose you want to
be free to choose a husband who hasn't built his
business on smuggled goods."

He expected her to deny it, but she met his gaze
steadily. "Now that you mention it . . . yes. How
could I respect a man who put fortune above every
other consideration—above morality, law, and
honor?"

He stalked resolutely ahead to prevent her from
seeing his anger. What did she know about putting
"fortune above every other consideration"? She had
her deer park and her servants and probably a portion as well. It might not be large, but then, *large*
was a relative term, wasn't it? Long ago, large
would have meant twenty pounds to him. She'd
never known a life like *that*, he'd wager.

Still, the more he considered it, the more her
response astonished him. He was used to women
who "put fortune above every other consideration,"
who'd been willing to overlook his questionable past
if it meant being the wife or even the mistress of the
very rich Mr. Knighton. Yet here was a woman who
actually considered his money a liability, a demon-
stration of his poor character. He didn't know
whether to admire her ideals or deplore her snobbery.

As if realizing she'd insulted him, she caught up,

and murmured, "It's not only the smuggling, you understand. I believe a woman—people—ought to marry for love."

He glanced at her. She stared off down the path as if she looked toward a future where some man might fall in love with her. It was hard to believe this Amazon had romantic notions about marriage. Mercenary, yes, or even condescending. But romantic? Extraordinary.

"Isn't that an unusual point of view for someone of your station?" he asked. "Doesn't your sort believe it's as easy to fall in love with a rich man as a poor one?"

"I don't know what 'my sort' believes, but I personally believe it isn't easy to fall in love with anyone, rich or poor." She cast him a sidelong glance. "And what do you believe? That a man should marry a rich wife when he can? Or perhaps you already have a rich wife back in London."

"No," he said firmly. "No planned or actual wife, rich or poor. I have . . . other matters that concern me more than marriage right now." Matters that might make it even more difficult for the Swanlea Spinsters to marry. He squelched the guilt that rose in his chest.

"So you don't plan to marry at all, for money *or* for love?"

"Not for money, and certainly not for love. I don't believe such a dubious emotion exists—I've never felt it myself. People merely mistake desire for love, a dangerous error that induces men to act like fools and women to choose bad husbands when their . . . er . . . urges to lead them into disaster." A caution he ought to remember when dealing with Lady Rosalind—for if anyone could lead a man into disaster, it was she.

"What a cynic you are. From what I understand, love differs vastly from desire."

"But you don't know for certain? You've never been in love yourself?"

Her gaze swung to his, startled, then wary. The gold flecks in her hazel eyes echoed the glint of sunlight on the glossy oak leaves overhead. He held her gaze, a strange tension building in his chest as he watched faint color tinge her cheeks.

Then she snapped her gaze back to the path ahead. "No, I don't think so."

He resisted the urge to ask her the next logical question—if she'd ever felt desire—since any answer was liable to fire his own "urges." "Don't you think you'd remember if you had been in love?"

That made her smile. "Yes, I suppose I would."

He suddenly wanted desperately to prevent her rare smile from vanishing. "Then your objection to marrying Knighton has nothing to do with some secret and vastly inappropriate suitor you've stashed away."

Laughter bubbled out of her, light and airy and immensely satisfying to hear. "No, indeed not."

"What about your sisters?" he asked, ruthlessly reminding himself of his greater purpose, which would be better served by delving for information than by flirting with Lady Rosalind. "Have they any suitors hidden away?"

"Not that I know of." She walked with a more relaxed gait now, her limbs looser, more fluid, as if telling him her thoughts on marriage had freed her to be more comfortable with him. "But I don't check the deer park regularly. And there's always the stables—you did find the grooms very incompetent, as I recall. They could be suitors in masquerade."

Fanciful woman. He knew very well she hadn't

been taken in by his criticisms. "Yes, who knows what devious elopement plans one of them might be hiding?" He crunched along through the leaves. "So your sisters don't wish to marry Knighton either?"

She hesitated before answering. "Juliet is difficult to read—unlike me, she desperately wants to remain at Swan Park. And Papa presses her on the matter constantly. Despite all that, however, I think she'd balk in the end."

By God, these sisters were particular about their husbands. He began to understand how they'd achieved their spinsterhood. "I take it she shares your aversion to free traders."

"No. To tell the truth, I don't think she cares about that. It's simply that . . . well . . . Mr. Knighton seems to frighten her."

"Frighten her? Why, Da—. . . Knighton would never hurt a woman."

"I'm afraid logic doesn't enter into it with Juliet. She's only seventeen, you know."

He mused a moment. "She does seem timid."

"Exactly! She's very shy and petite, and I think his size alarms her."

That he could certainly believe. Daniel's size alarmed half the women Griff knew—though they generally lost their alarm when Daniel turned his Irish charm on them. "What of Lady Helena? Wouldn't she marry my employer to ensure you could all continue at Swan Park in perpetuity?"

She shook her head sadly. "Helena's experiences with suitors have been unhappy, I'm afraid. One man in particular—a Lord Farnsworth—thought to marry her for her money despite her lameness. They were engaged, but he jilted her when he discovered Papa was telling the truth about her pitiful dowry."

"That's detestable!"

She favored him with an approving look. "It is, isn't it? I've tried to tell her that he was merely one scoundrel, but she remains unconvinced. Especially since a number of men have disdained her for her lameness. She's too disillusioned with men to consider marriage to Mr. Knighton. Though she may wish to live here, I don't think she'd marry to ensure it."

"And we've already established why you wouldn't marry to save the estate. Besides, you want to be an actress, don't you?"

"Indeed I do." She tossed her head back proudly.

"You'd throw all this away to go on the stage." He could still hardly believe it.

"Why not, if it's what I want?"

"Because you don't know the true nature of what you want," he snapped. "It's a degrading profession. Actresses work long into the night for little pay and less respect. They're regularly accosted by men who consider them barely better than whores, and they don't even have the luxury of a secure living, for they might be booed off the stage after their first performance, never to be allowed to return."

"So you've been an actress?" she said sarcastically. "You speak so familiarly about that life I can only assume you've lived it."

Saucy witch. "I don't have to live it to know what it's like. I go to the theater."

"As do I. Yet my impression of an actress's life differs markedly from yours. Fancy that."

"You go to the theater in a provincial town; it's not the same in London. I assume that you mean to go on the stage in London."

"Of course." She tipped her nose up. "As my mother did."

He'd forgotten that the late countess had been an actress. That explained where Lady Rosalind had gotten the fool notion to be one.

"By the way," she went on, "Mama never spoke of it as a degrading profession. I believe she regarded it rather fondly."

"It's easy to regard something fondly when you're well out of it," he growled.

"Oh? Do you regard your childhood in the work-house fondly?" She shot him a cat-in-the-cream smile.

He met it with a cold glance. "It's exactly because I've been treated like a pariah for my background and profession that I know you wouldn't like the theater. You were raised for something better, whether you accept it or not."

If anyone knew what it was like to be raised for something better and denied it, he did. Knighton Trading had come hard-won, and he'd cut his ties to the tricky world of smugglers as soon as he'd gained enough success to manage it.

"So you think I'd be better off marrying your employer?" she asked archly.

"Of course! An innocent like you throwing away Swan Park for the bawdy house of the theater? It's absurd, especially when you can continue in your pleasant situation merely by marrying—"

He broke off with a groan. The damnable vixen had his head so twisted around, he didn't know what he was saying. For the love of God, why was he trying to convince her? He didn't *want* her to marry him!

"You're entitled to your opinion," she bit out, "but it doesn't change how my sisters and I feel. None of us want to marry your employer. It was most generous of Mr. Knighton to consider Papa's proposal, but we shan't change our minds. Nor will we fault him if he decides to look for a wife where his attentions are better appreciated."

He gaped at her. The woman was actually refusing a marriage offer he hadn't even made! Of course, technically Lady Rosalind hadn't refused *him*—she'd refused Daniel. That fact only slightly assuaged his trampled pride, however.

They emerged suddenly from the woods onto a hillside that sloped down toward the fruit orchards below. The sun had broken through a phalanx of creamy clouds to make the air once more sticky, warm, and tangy with the scent of crushed grass.

They paused at the top of the hill to survey Swan Park, but he felt as if the ground fell away from him in every respect. All his expectations about his visit had proven wrong. The spinsters wished to remain spinsters. They weren't shrews, but amiable and attractive. And they were all too eager to hand his inheritance over to him unencumbered.

Yet one thing hadn't changed—he still didn't have his parents' marriage certificate. So although he'd happily oblige the ladies by leaving, he couldn't.

He considered striking a bargain with Lady Rosalind: She could wheedle the certificate out of her father, and he would leave as she wanted. But he feared she was too intelligent to accept a simple bargain. She'd ask why he wanted it, how her father had come by it, what the history of it was. And once she learned all his plans . . .

No, that wasn't a chance he could take. So until he found what he wanted, he—or rather, Daniel— must continue to pretend an interest in an alliance, despite what Rosalind thought and Griff himself desired.

"I perfectly understand what you're saying."

Griff stood viewing the land—*his* land—with his hands gripped together behind his back. "But I fear you won't convince my employer. He seems amenable to your father's plan." He slanted a look at her. "I doubt he'll refuse it merely because of your assertions."

"What!" she cried, rounding on him. "You mean he truly *wants* to marry one of us? But why? He'll inherit Swan Park one way or the other, so what possible advantage could marriage to one of us give him?"

He shrugged. "Prestige. He has money—now he wants something more. Possibly a better position in society. Or perhaps he's simply enamored of you all. In any case, he can hardly make a decision about your father's proposal on only one day's acquaintance. He'll probably want to remain here at least a week or so."

With a snort of disgust, she started off down the hill. "Well, that's just wonderful. Your blasted employer is looking for a wife, and my foolish father sanctions the entire idea, so what my sisters and I want doesn't even signify."

"I didn't say that," he said as he followed her down the hill, unable to take his eyes off her fetching derriere.

"Men!" she grumbled. "They never learn! 'What is wedlock forced but a hell?' Shakespeare wrote that while locked in his own unhappy marriage, yet his words go unheeded."

Did the woman quote nobody but Shakespeare? He was fond of the bard himself, but he didn't consider every pronouncement the greatest wisdom. Not to mention that her sweeping interpretation of an obscure passage to suit her needs irritated him. "No one knows if Shakespeare's marriage was unhappy or not."

"For pity's sake, he left his wife here in Stratford-upon-Avon for nearly thirty years while he pursued his own interests in London. I don't know about you, but I don't call that marital bliss." She faced him, her eyes shadowed with anger beneath the brim of her bonnet. "And what kind of man seeks to marry a woman against her will, anyway?"

"I take it we're no longer speaking of Shakespeare," he observed dryly.

With a sniff, she set off down the hill again. "Why the bloody hell does my cousin want *us*? Doesn't he know we're the Swanlea Spinsters? We don't marry for money or station—so why doesn't he seek elsewhere for a wife? He's rich enough and heir to an earldom beside."

"He is indeed." He couldn't suppress his grin, for she did make Knighton—him—seem like an idiot. And she clearly didn't know of his supposed bastardy.

She misunderstood the source of his humor and glowered at him. "If Mr. Knighton thinks that forcing one of us into marriage—"

"For the love of God, woman, calm down. I didn't say he'd force anyone to marry. I only said he wouldn't leave merely on the strength of your dislike of him."

A bare patch on the hillside impeded her progress, her bootheels sinking into the soft earth with every step, and that seemed to further infuriate her. "So we're stuck with you and my cousin for weeks, while he decides if he wants to marry one of us."

"If you keep showering us with this effusive hospitality, I doubt it'll be weeks. For my own part, I hope it's less."

"Now see here, Mr. Brennan, I didn't ask you to come here and complicate my life with your snooping about and your—"

"Snooping about?" His gut tightened. So she still suspected what he was up to. He couldn't have that, or she'd dog his every step. He said derisively, "What on earth do you mean? Why would I be snooping? What would I be looking for?"

She stiffened. "I-I have no idea. But you're clearly intent upon ridding yourself of me for *some* reason."

He thought quickly. "Mere expedience, I assure you. My employer pays me to determine what improvements the estate will require once he inherits. I can accomplish that aim quicker without a woman underfoot telling me where to go and what to see."

As he'd hoped, she took offense. "You men are always so blasted pompous." She glared at him. "I don't see why having me about wouldn't be a help."

She was so caught up in reprimanding him, she missed seeing the stone jutting from the hillside until her bootheel caught on it and she pitched forward. Instinctively, Griff grabbed her elbow, swinging her around into his arms to prevent her from tumbling down the hill. She clutched at his shoulders to steady herself.

Then they froze, locked in an embrace on the hillside. Her eyes lifted to him, the pupils narrowing to pinpoints to take him in so close. Too close. Although he'd stood easily this near her last night, she hadn't been facing him. He hadn't been gifted with an intimate view of her sun-dappled cheeks nor her feathery brown lashes nor the finely wrought lips that parted on a breath exactly as they'd part beneath his kiss.

Damnation, he mustn't think of kissing her. Because if he kissed her, he'd surely do something more stupid.

He wouldn't stop with kissing.

He ordered himself to release her, but his hands paid him no mind. His thumbs already stroked her ribs, moving higher, itching to be bolder, to touch the untouchable. And now his lips considered rebellion as well. They wanted to press against her fragile eyelids, her impudent chin, and certainly her lush mouth.

It was her fault, the way she looked at him now as if she desired him, too. And those parted lips. Damn them for daring him to kiss them. He'd never been a man to refuse a dare.

He started to lower his head, but the brim of his hat collided with the brim of her bonnet, and that brought her to her senses. With a little "Oh" of alarm, she released her death grip on his shoulders, then wriggled free of his embrace.

"Are you all right?" he heard himself say as she retreated. Was *he* all right? Would he ever be all right again? His stiffening cock said he wouldn't.

Half-stumbling, she turned away from him, then hastened down the hill, moving markedly faster than before.

"Slow down," he cautioned as he strode after her. "If you don't, you're liable to twist your ankle on this slope."

"That would certainly be convenient for you, wouldn't it?"

"What the devil does that mean?"

"Then you'd be rid of my company for good."

She increased her mad pace in long, rushing strides. Though he grew increasingly alarmed, she obviously had no concern, for she flung words over her shoulder at him like a whist player dealing cards. "I hate to disappoint you, Mr. Brennan, but I'm giving you no excuse to be rid of me. You might as well face it—I shan't leave your side no matter what you do."

"You're leaving my side now," he growled, and grabbed her arm to slow her down, but she snatched it from his grip immediately. Catching her skirts up to an indecent height, she raced down the hill. It was a miracle she didn't tumble to the bottom.

What had come over her? Why was she running from him like a woman possessed?

Then it dawned on him. She was running from the same thing that had consumed him seconds ago when he'd stared down into that intriguing face. Passion. There was no mistaking it. The blatant attraction between them was driving her away.

That was it! He'd been wrong about last night—it wasn't the blade at her throat that unnerved her, but his hands on her, his body against hers. She might pretend immunity to such things, but he'd recognized the flare of need in her gaze moments ago. She wasn't immune, and that damn well frightened her.

He smiled broadly as he slowed to a stroll. At last he'd figured out his Amazon's most secret fear. So she feared passion, did she, especially from a man whose character she held in contempt? Very well, then passion he'd give her. He'd send her fleeing for good.

An obnoxious voice in his head mocked his aims, saying they had nothing to do with driving her off and everything to do with his itch to get his hands on her. He ignored it. Besides, he deserved some enjoyment out of the woman after she'd tormented him all morning.

The thought of what he intended to do made him quicken his steps as he neared the bottom of the hill and the avenue of short trees. He entered it to find her waiting for him, a gleaming beacon of color against the line of dark trunks. Here her striped gown wasn't garish, but a slivered ray of sunlight amidst the brilliant green leaves and rich purple globes hanging over her head. Here she radiated an earthy allure that took his breath away and made his loins tighten painfully.

Yes, he deserved a taste of her—a little taste. Just enough to drive her off and quench his absurd need.

"This is our plum orchard," she announced as he neared her. "I thought you might like to see it as long as we're here. We have an apple orchard and a stand of cherry trees on the estate, but our plums are particularly fine, don't you think?"

At the moment he didn't care about plums or cherries or apples. But he'd play along to lower her defenses, since she looked as if she might bolt again if he took one step toward her.

The trouble was, she would never go far, or at least not far enough. So he'd have to frighten her so much she'd flee his presence for good. He stared up into the wizened branches heavily laden with newly ripened fruit. "I don't like plums," he said truthfully.

Frustrated laughter pealed from her. "Why does that not surprise me?"

He cut his gaze back to her as an idea took shape. "Plums are tart, and I don't like tart fruit. When I put something in my mouth, I want it to be plump and sweet and juicy."

He let his gaze drift to the parts of her that fit those qualities so well, then exulted when her breasts rose and fell rapidly. She understood his meaning, was alarmed by it. She even blushed a little before whirling away to approach one of the trees.

This is working. She's as skittish as those deer who seek the comfort of Swan Park's thick woods.

"These plums aren't tart." She kept her eyes care-

fully averted from him. "You're thinking of dam-
sons, which are used for pies." Removing one of her
gloves and tucking it in a pocket, she then reached
up to pluck a plum from a low-hanging branch. To
his surprise, she turned to hold it out to him. "Here,
taste it," she challenged him.

Even naked Eve in the Garden of Eden couldn't
have looked so tempting as Rosalind did with one
bare hand offering him ripe fruit. What was she up
to now?

A rampant eagerness to find out assailed him. He
stepped closer and removed his own gloves. Holding them in one hand, he reached for the fruit with
the other.

Instead of taking it, however, he imprisoned her
wrist and forced her hand with its prize up to
within easy reach of his mouth. Her lips parted in
surprise, and her eyes turned a delicate shade of
greenish gold as she watched him bite into the
plum, yet she didn't pull away or throw the plum at
him or flee.

No, she fixed her gaze on his mouth. As if she
tasted the plum herself, she moistened her bottom
lip with the pink tip of her tongue, sending a jolt of
need straight to his cock. When he swallowed, she
did, too, and the working of her smooth throat captivated him.

Damnation, he thought as he snapped his gaze
back to her face, it wasn't supposed to happen this
way. She should be slapping him, raging at him,
stalking off in a huff. Yet she stood there frozen, lips
parted and eyes huge in her face.

She needed more prodding, that's all. With delib-
erate boldness, he slid his mouth from the plum to
her sticky hand and sucked the tangy plum juice off.

"You're right," he murmured. "It's not tart at all."
He lapped plum juice from her wrist, triumph surg-

ing through him when he felt her pulse stammer beneath his tongue. "It's sweet . . . delicious."

He waited for her to bolt, yet she stood motionless while he licked her hand clean of juice. His grip on it tightened as he thought with longing of licking a path beneath her gown and all over the fulsome body she'd unwittingly displayed last night.

When she cleared her throat, he knew instinctively she would protest any further outrages. Before she could get the words out, he turned her hand up to her own mouth, and urged, "Here, eat some yourself. I know you're as hungry as I am."

Her dusky lashes dipped down with uncharacteristic modesty, making it clear she understood what kind of hunger he meant. Yet curiously she obeyed him, taking the plum between her fine, even teeth and tearing away a sliver, just enough to satisfy the letter of the law. A single drop of juice trailed fatefully down her chin, and he bent his head forward to catch it on his tongue.

It was an outrageous thing to do, but not nearly as outrageous as what he planned next. He lifted his mouth the half inch needed to meet her lips, then kissed her.

He kept the kiss light, soft, tender. Though he ached to make it deep and slow and hot, his aim was to frighten her, not make her accuse him of assaulting her.

Unfortunately, when he broke off the kiss and drew back, she didn't slap him or run or even protest. Instead she gazed at him with a wide-eyed look of wonder as the plum dropped from her fingers. "You do . . . have a talent for . . . kissing, don't you?"

Damnation. Obviously, this would require a bit more than he'd anticipated. He dropped his gloves, slid his arm about her waist, then dragged her flush against his body. "What did you expect? You said I was no gentleman."

This time he held nothing back, surrendering to the fiery need sparked by last night's encounter. Lost in the scents of plums and sunshine, he ravaged her lips as thoroughly as he ached to ravage her body.

To his shock, she kissed him back. By God, she kissed him back, with an enthusiasm unimaginable in a woman of her station and limited experience. So much softness, so much temptation . . . how could he resist it? His hat tumbled off as he pressed closer, running his tongue along her virgin lips until they gave way and allowed him entrance to the silken depths of her mouth. She stiffened a little at the intimate coupling of their tongues, then went fluid and limp in his arms, making him exult.

He delighted in how she leaned into him for more, how she twined her arms about his neck, sending her shawl floating to the ground. It made him stab his tongue deeper, harder, nearly losing his slender hold on his control.

This is mad, he thought. But it was less mad than not touching her, not kissing her. If he didn't have at least a taste of her he'd surely snap before the week was out, would throw her over his shoulder and carry her off to bed like Petruchio claiming his shrew.

He was in danger of doing so anyway. He needed to fill his hands with her bountiful breasts, to tear off her outrageous gown and explore all her secrets until her cries of pleasure echoed in the orchard. She was summer ripening to excess, and he was damned well ripening to excess himself. Only her virginity kept him from pressing her down to the plum-spattered earth, lifting her shirts, and planting himself between those smooth white thighs.

If she didn't stop uttering those enticing little sighs, however, his conscience would vanish in the wake of his lust. It already took all his will not to grip her hips and urge her against his erection.

"Oh, Mr. Brennan—" she purred against his lips.

"Griff," he said savagely. "Call me Griff, sweet Rosalind."

What was he doing? Had he lost his mind? He should be driving her off so he could be free to search for the certificate.

Yet he rebelled at the thought, especially now when she pressed tentative kisses along his jaw and down his neck. She was every bit as passionate as he'd expected. Nuzzling her hair scented with lilting notes of rosewater and soap, he made no move to end the delirium.

By God, how could he when all he wanted was another taste, another kiss? Yet he feared that after that kiss ended he'd want another . . . and another and always another, until she'd enmeshed him in desire.

He must stop this. Soon.

All he needed was a few more moments—then he'd put her away from him and return to his real purpose in coming here, his real purpose in kissing her.

Just a few more moments of heaven . . .

Chapter 8

Can spirit from the tomb, or fiend from hell,
More hateful, more malignant be than man—
Than villainous man?

Joanna Baille, Scottish playwright, Orra

Why must he be so good at this? Rosalind thought as she welcomed Griff's delicious kisses. His mouth was firm and secret, the mouth of a man who'd probably tasted every kind of darkness. It moved roughly on hers, too insistent to deny.

Not that she intended to deny him. Now that he'd carried her this far, she couldn't go back. That's what came of being cursed with a weakness for pleasures of the flesh—for apple tarts spiced with cinnamon that melted on the tongue, silken fabrics caressing the skin, hot baths soothing the body . . . and now for a handsome, virile man kissing her senseless. How could she deny herself this luscious and transient delight?

It seemed perfectly natural to let his hot tongue surge inside her mouth, to let it delve deep in velvety strokes that left her gasping. It seemed perfectly right to let him yank loose the ties of her bonnet and shove it off her head so he could kiss her more thoroughly.

She'd known he would eventually demand repayment for her plundering his past; she just hadn't known it would be so exciting and hot . . .

And dangerous. They shouldn't do this. Oh, no.

"Griff, I—"

"Shh, lovely Rosalind . . ." Another kiss, another all-consuming kiss wrung her dry—but this time he flattened her body against his, pressing his hips into hers.

Something hard in his pockets dug into her lower belly. A pistol? she thought wildly, then jerked back from him in fear that she'd make it go off. A thrilling little chill went through her. He'd certainly be the kind of man to carry a dangerous weapon.

"What's that?" She stared down between them at his trousers.

"What's what?"

He bent to kiss her again, but she angled her head back before he could. "In your pockets," she whispered. "You've got . . . something in your pockets."

"Something in my—" He broke off with a groan, staring down at her with eyes of molten cerulean blue. "Unless you're using a country euphemism for male arousal, there's nothing in my pockets."

Male arousal? She stared at him uncomprehending until it dawned on her what he meant. Then she blushed to the roots of her hair. "Oh. I did know what horses and cows . . . that is, I've seen them, but . . . I didn't think people . . . I-I mean men would . . ."

"Yes, men would. And do, when they're aroused.

And you've damned well got me aroused right now, my sweet."

She buried her flaming face in his cravat. "You must think me a great ninny."

"That wasn't the word that came first to mind, no." With a chuckle, he nibbled her earlobe, then ran his tongue inside the enclave of her ear. "Virgin maybe. Seductress, most definitely. But not ninny."

She shivered as his mouth toyed with her ear. She'd never known tongues could be used so delightfully to seduce. Or that ears could be so sensitive to it. The starchy smell of his cravat swirled with the tang of his sweat to produce a scent that was all male and surprisingly enticing.

He shifted her in his arms, reminding her of his strength. Last night it had surprised her, but now she knew how he'd developed it—first in the workhouse and then sailing boats across the choppy waters of the Channel.

That knowledge should make her shun him, make her accept he wasn't the man for her. Yet his fascinating background intrigued her and deepened the thrill, making it nearly impossible for her to push him away.

He apparently felt differently, however, for he drew back to murmur, "We shouldn't be doing this, Rosalind."

That was true, yet it piqued her that he could put her aside so easily when she couldn't bear to let go of him. On impulse, she raised up to kiss his lips. He froze, and then to her great satisfaction groaned and began feeding on her mouth as recklessly as before.

This time she was the one to draw back, leaving him gasping for breath. "You were saying?" she teased.

His gaze dipped to her lips. "I was saying . . .

I . . ." He shook his head as if to clear it. "I was saying we must stop this."

A pity he was right. "Must we? No, don't answer. I know we must." With regret, she loosed her hands from around his neck and let them drop to her sides. Suddenly the enormity of her actions hit her. "I don't know what came over me."

"The same thing that came over me." He bent to pick up her bonnet, then handed it to her. As she put it on, fumbling with the ties, he went on. "That's why we . . . shouldn't spend any more time alone together. You're far too much temptation for me."

A bleak foreboding settled in the pit of her stomach. "What do you mean?"

"Exactly what I said." His face grew shuttered. "We shouldn't have any more of these solitary meetings. It's best we stay apart from now on."

That's what she'd thought he meant. Except he didn't mean that at all, did he? A sickening wave of self-disgust rolled through her. She'd been a fool, an utter fool. She'd thought he was truly attracted to her, that he felt the same irrational desires as she did.

But he didn't, of course. This was merely one more attempt to frighten her off. Shame and betrayal mingled in her breast, making it hard for her to breathe. Dear God, he hadn't meant any of it! Curse him to hell!

She whirled away to go stand beside a plum tree. How could she so foolishly have fallen for the most ancient trick in the male arsenal—seduction? Not only fall for it, but embrace it, even revel in it! Why, she'd acted like a . . . a soiled dove!

For shame! By now she ought to know that overindulging her appetite for worldly pleasures never came to any good. But this time her enjoyment wouldn't result in only nausea from a surfeit of sweets. This time she'd suffer the pain of lost dignity and self-respect.

She stiffened her spine. No, her dignity was one thing she would salvage. Though she ached to berate him aloud for his perfidy, she mustn't or she'd risk revealing how easily he'd enticed her. The wretch would delight in his success at convincing the stupid earl's daughter that a man with his looks and talent in the sensual arts would actually enjoy kissing an overgrown spinster.

She heard him pick up his hat and knock dust off of it, and tears inexplicably welled in her eyes. She bent her head to hide them. Blast him! She wouldn't cry! Only silly lovesick girls cried, and she wouldn't let him see her behave like that. But she *would* make him admit to his ploy. Oh, yes. She'd have that satisfaction at least.

Smoothing her features into the mask of a coquette as best she could, she faced him again and smiled. This was no different from any other role a real actress might play. Now if only her insides would stop shaking . . .

"Dear God, I'm so silly," she said in a teasing tone that felt utterly unnatural. "I actually thought we were . . . um . . . having some genuine fun." Harsher words clamored to be spoken, but she squelched them ruthlessly. There were better ways to skewer a man. "I should have known you were only trying another of your ploys. Really, Mr. Brennan, you shouldn't be so obvious when springing your traps."

He went very still, gripping his hat tightly. "What the hell are you talking about?"

"Why, your kissing, of course. It was every bit as expert as I would've expected." Indeed, it had exceeded any expectation. "But I suppose you intended to frighten me off with your skill. You know, alarm the virgin and that sort of thing."

"Don't be absurd." But his suddenly shuttered gaze loudly proclaimed his guilt.

Blast him! "A pity I didn't act as you wished." She heard the hurt creeping into her tone and willfully forced it down. "I didn't behave like a proper lady and slap your face or banish you from my presence. That's what you wanted, wasn't it?"

She wished she *had* slapped him after the very first kiss. Now it was too late to take back her shameful, wanton reaction. It was too late to pretend she hadn't been swept up in the thrill. It wasn't too late, however, to pretend immunity to his betrayal.

He watched her in silence, a muscle flexing and unflexing in his jaw. She cursed him for looking more appealing than ever with that hooded gaze and the raven swirl of hair at his left temple that betrayed a cowlick.

"I suppose my enthusiastic reaction took you by surprise." She leaned casually against the tree trunk. "If you'd only told me what effect you wanted, I might have obliged you with a stellar performance. I can play the proper lady when I want, you know." She gave a huge sigh. "But alas, I did not, thus forcing you to alter your plan."

Clapping his hat on his head, he stalked up to her at the tree. "I have no idea what you're talking about."

For pity's sake, he sounded almost remorseful. But that was impossible. Mr. Brennan would never be remorseful—not the man who'd probably invented an entire life history merely to drive her off.

"You know precisely what I'm talking about," she snapped. "After my response, you decided to humor the country girl, correct? Let her have some fun, then tell her she was too much for a poor male like you? I suppose you thought a spinster who rarely received such attentions would do anything you asked after a kiss like that."

She choked off her words before they revealed too much. It took her a second to go on. "But I am not a muttonhead, and I recognize a shameless ploy when I see one."

His eyes chilled her, starkly ice-blue. "So you think you've found me out."

"I know I have." Her heart sank. What had she expected? That he would deny it? One thing about Griff she'd noticed—when he was caught, he admitted it. But a tiny part of her had hoped she was wrong.

"All right, perhaps it was a ploy at first, but once we kissed—" He glanced away, then continued harshly, "I'm not quite the talented deceiver you take me for. The part about your being a temptation was no lie."

"Of course it was—"

"No." He reached for her, and she swatted his hand away. "No, it was not. I swear it."

She searched his face, despairing of ever knowing the truth. He had this . . . horrid ability to make his claims sound plausible. "I don't believe you." She shoved the words through a throat clogged with unshed tears.

Anger flickered in his face. "Even I can't feign arousal, my sweet. Trust me, I'm not that accomplished an actor."

She pasted a blithe smile to her lips. "Oh, but you're wrong. You've played your role very well."

A wary look entered his eyes. "What role is that?"

"You know what role. Or roles, I should say. The ones you've been trying on in your determination to rid yourself of my company. All that making yourself disagreeable and pretending to be a smuggler and a highwayman's son and—"

"I really am a smuggler and a highwayman's—" He broke off. "Accuse me of playing any role you wish. Except the one of lover."

The word *lover* struck her with brutal force. There had indeed been a few moments during their kisses when she'd thought of him as a lover. Foolish, foolish girl. "I'll admit," she said shakily, "you played that particular role more convincingly than the others, but not convincingly enough to fool me."

She pushed away from the tree and tried to pass him, but he grabbed her shoulders to stay her. "You do us both a disservice if you think that was a role. I meant every word, and those kisses weren't counterfeit." His gaze dropped to her lips, and he lowered his voice. "You do tempt me . . . 'for still temptation follows where thou art.' "

"So desperate to drive me away that you'd resort to the sonnets?" she quipped to cover the turmoil he created in her breast.

"Desperate to make you believe me, yes."

Furious at his masterful ability for telling her what she wanted to hear—and for making her heart pound like a silly schoolgirl's—she wrenched herself free of him. She wouldn't fall for his tactics again. From now on, she was swearing off devious men and their kisses. Or at least this devious man's kisses.

It took all her will to keep her voice light and amused, when she just wanted to crawl into bed and cry. "Well, then, if I do tempt you, you'd best get used to it. Because no matter what ploys you try, I'm not leaving your side. For the duration of your visit here, I intend to be your bosom companion."

When he raised an eyebrow at her choice of

words, she couldn't prevent a faint blush. Hastily she added, "You'll simply have to learn to live with your urges, *if* you ever really had any."

"What about you and your urges? I wasn't the only one enjoying those kisses, Rosalind."

"*Lady* Rosalind," she said, glad to gird herself in the proprieties for once. "Of course I enjoyed them. You're very adept at kissing, Mr. Brennan—"

"Griff," he corrected angrily.

"*Mr. Brennan.* But I didn't enjoy them enough to wish them repeated."

"Liar. I tempt you, too. Admit it."

"Not in the least." Picking up her shawl, she swung it around her shoulders with a flourish that belied the increasing difficulty of maintaining her role. "So you might as well forget using temptation to drive me off. I'm immune to your kisses now."

She prayed he believed her. Because she very much feared that despite the way he'd deceived and manipulated her, she wasn't in the least immune. Not to him.

Chapter 9

*Your two friends, Prudence and Reflection, I am
informed, have lately ventured to pay you a visit;
for which I heartily congratulate you, as nothing
can possibly be more joyous to the heart than the
return of absent friends, after a long and painful
peregrination.*

Charlotte Charke, English actress,
A Narrative of the Life of Mrs. Charlotte Charke

Amidst Lady Juliet's chatter, Daniel's attempts
at charm, and Lady Helena's reserved silence,
Griff sat and watched Rosalind eat heartily of the
cold ham and half-moon slices of cheddar on her
plate. True to her words, she gave no sign of being
affected by their kisses, nor had she from the
moment they'd left the orchard. On their walk back
to the house, her conversation had been brisk and
engaging, and though she'd effectively skirted discussion of their activities, it hadn't seemed deliber-
ate.

As for him, he'd been too angry—and aroused—
to do more than grunt responses to her comments.
They'd arrived at the house to find everyone awaiting them on the terrace, where luncheon had been
served.

Now Rosalind sat and ate beneath the kindly sun,
wearing a countenance as serene as her older sister's. And he sat wearing a countenance that was
anything but. Perhaps she was immune to temptation, but he damned well wasn't. He still hadn't
subdued his willful cock, and just when he pacified
it a bit, one look at her made it rear its demanding
head again

How could she sit there so calmly, conversing
and joking as if nothing had happened between
them? He had no interest whatsoever in the innocu-
ous conversations of their companions, and certainly no appetite for food or drink.

Except for the vintage he'd accidentally uncorked
in the orchard. The one called Lady Rosalind.

That was a rare vintage indeed—champagne
where he'd expected vinegar—and he craved more.
But he couldn't have more. She was fruit of Swanlea's vines, for the love of God! Had he lost his mind
to be thinking of her this way?

Yes. Because the thought of swearing off her particular liquor was bedeviling him.

But not her, it seemed. Gone were her virginal
wonder and ardent gaze. She hadn't lied when
she'd said she could play the proper lady when she
wanted. Is that what her self-possessed air was—a
role? Or did she truly care no more about their
shared kisses than she would the notes of a sonata
vanishing on the breeze?

If this were a role, she played it well, sitting there
so demure and prim as if butter wouldn't melt in
her mouth. By God, he would *make* butter melt in

her mouth, if it took him the rest of the day. How dared she make light of their kisses when they'd utterly distracted *him* from his purpose?

"You're not eating, Mr. Brennan," Juliet chirped. "Does the food not please you?"

He glanced down at his full plate. "The food isn't the problem." He tried to catch Rosalind's eye, but she was suddenly intent upon drinking her wine. His eyes narrowed. "As it happens, your sister and I got so hungry on our walk that we ate a plum in the orchard."

"You mean plums," Juliet cut in with a giggle. "Surely you didn't share one."

He hesitated just long enough to make Rosalind's gaze jump to his, a hint of alarm in its depths. But she misunderstood his intention— he didn't wish to expose her, only make her expose herself to him.

"No, of course not," he lied. "But it was a foolish indulgence, since it killed our appetites for anything else."

He knew Rosalind took his meaning, though she made no sign of it. Instead, she leaned forward to cut a nice swath through the meat on her plate. "Speak for your own appetite." She lifted the portion nearly to her mouth, then paused with the fork midair. "Mine is perfectly intact, at least for healthful food like this."

"Do you claim that plums are unhealthful?" He felt everyone's eyes on him, but paid them no heed. Let them think what they would. He wanted to make her acknowledge he hadn't been the only one affected by their kisses.

"Oh, they're very good in their place, but they can be cloying. As you've already noted, all it takes is a single plum to make one ill."

"You misunderstand me. The plum didn't make

me ill." He lowered his voice deliberately. "If anything, it made me crave more . . . plums."

He'd hoped for a blush, but all he got was a stony stare. "Earlier this morning you said you didn't like plums. You're a most fickle creature, Mr. Brennan."

"Not at all. After you coaxed me to taste one I discovered that eating truly superior fruit changes one's opinions on the subject."

"Well, Mr. Brennan," Juliet put in before Rosalind could retort, "you and Rosalind had a dreadfully dull morning if all you talked about was fruit." The girl yawned prettily.

"The one thing I would *not* call it is boring." Griff kept his gaze fixed on Rosalind. He would unsettle her if it killed him. "And we discussed other subjects. Shakespeare, for example—one of the sonnets. We had an interesting discussion about temptation, didn't we, Lady Rosalind?"

She showed no reaction, though a quick glance around the terrace revealed that at least two of their companions were now very interested in the conversation. Daniel watched them with narrowed eyes, and Lady Helena had stopped painting the miniature she'd taken up after finishing her meal.

Yet Rosalind remained immune. "Are you sure it was one of the sonnets? I recall speaking of Shakespeare, but I thought it was *A Comedy of Errors*. All that talk about thieves, remember? When we discussed your childhood in the workhouse? And your fascinating family connections?"

Damnation. She certainly picked her weapons well. Daniel had straightened in his chair to glare at Griff.

As if knowing how much trouble she'd caused, she smiled. Then she leaned toward her younger sister without taking her gaze from Griff. "The man has a most intriguing background, Juliet. His father was a highwayman, for pity's sake—Wild Danny Brennan. Can you believe it?"

Griff groaned. Daniel was going to kill him.

"No!" Juliet exclaimed, regarding Griff as if he'd suddenly transformed into a snake in their midst. Then she spotted her sister's calculating look and gave a nervous giggle. "Oh, Rosalind, you're teasing me again, aren't you? You're really too awful sometimes."

"No, I'm perfectly serious. Mr. Brennan gave me all the details. Didn't you, Mr. Brennan?"

Griff snatched up his wineglass and swigged a healthy mouthful, then stared into its ruby depths to keep from looking at Daniel.

Rosalind continued to pound nails into his coffin. "Mr. Brennan says he was once a smuggler, too—a very disreputable man. You must take care with him, Juliet. He's been warning me about his dangerous character all morning."

Griff swirled the wine in his glass to prevent himself from leaping over the table and throttling the loose-tongued woman.

A noise erupted from Daniel that sounded like a cross between a growl and a curse. "The two of you certainly had an interesting tour of the estate."

"Oh, we did indeed. Mr. Brennan has been blackening his character for me by the hour." She glanced at Daniel. "Unless, of course, he was telling me tall tales. Was he?"

Griff stiffened as Daniel leapt from his chair and began lumbering back and forth along the terrace like the bear at a bear baiting. Goddamn it, he'd better support the story. If Daniel made him look like a liar to her, he'd thrash the man into the next county!

Daniel stopped to fix Griff with a blistering stare meant to fry him where he sat. "Well, you see, m'lady—"

"Knighton," Griff interrupted, setting down his wineglass, "remember that fellow you think should be paid two-hundred pounds? I'm beginning to agree that's probably a fairer sum. Or even two-hundred and fifty. What do you think?"

"Don't change the subject," Rosalind bit out, then stared imploringly at Daniel. "Mr. Knighton? *Was* Mr. Brennan lying about his parentage?"

Daniel looked from her to Griff in sheer frustration. Finally, to Griff's vast relief, he sighed and threw himself back into his chair. "Does it matter? If I say he's lying, you won't believe me. You'll think I'm only covering up the follies—and loose tongue—of my man of affairs, won't you? Especially when his words reflect badly on me."

Daniel's comments seemed to surprise her. "I don't see how any of that could reflect badly on *you*. You aren't responsible for the sins of Mr. Brennan's parents, if indeed there were any. You didn't know him when he was in the workhouse. And from what he told me about how you met, you can be excused for hiring a man who saved your life, even if he was—or claims he was—a smuggler."

Daniel's gaze swung back to Griff, slightly mollified. "You told her that? About how we met?"

Griff nodded.

Rosalind looked confused now. "Are you saying it's . . . all true? What he said?"

Wearily, Daniel leaned back in his chair. "Yes, it's all true. But believe me, it's far in the past, and Mr. Brennan wouldn't—"

"Don't mistake me, Mr. Knighton," she broke in, an odd remorse softening her face. "I-I wasn't accusing you of anything, or implying that you'd erred in hiring him or bringing him here or—"

"Then what *were* you doing, Rosalind?" Lady Helena spoke after remaining so silent all afternoon. A disapproving frown rippled her smooth brow. "It seems to me you meant to embarrass someone—if not Mr. Knighton, then Mr. Brennan. You'd do well to remember they're both our guests, no matter how you feel about it. You've exceeded the bounds of courtesy this time, and you know it."

Griff relished Rosalind's clear discomfort at the rebuke. He'd begun to think nothing shamed the brazen creature.

"You misunderstand me, Helena," Rosalind answered. "I assumed Mr. Brennan was lying, or I would never have brought it up. He's been telling falsehoods to . . . tease me, and I had thought this to be one of them. Indeed, I'm surprised to hear I was mistaken."

She spoke with such dignity he felt like a cur for exulting over her embarrassment. Ironically, he *had* been lying—at least about himself. She'd been astute enough to realize that.

Daniel, the other liar, took up her cause. "It's not Lady Rosalind's fault," he remarked to Lady Helena. "Knowing Griff, I'm sure he did something to rouse your sister's temper. Lately he's had an unhappy habit of alarming young women with stories of his days in the smuggling business. Apparently your sister doesn't alarm so easily."

He shot Griff a warning look. "You see all the trouble you've caused for nothing, man? How you've gotten my fair cousins into a miff? They'll want nothing to do with me now that my man of affairs has proved disreputable."

"That's not true!" Juliet protested feebly.

Griff stood abruptly and clapped his hat on his

head. He'd had enough of this. If he stayed here another moment, he was liable to expose the entire masquerade with his quick tongue. "I'm sure you can soothe all the ruffled feathers in the henhouse, Knighton. It's what you do best, isn't it? Meanwhile, I have work to do, so I'll take my leave of you all and spare you my annoying presence for a few hours."

Rosalind jumped to her feet, obviously intent on keeping to her threats to shadow him. "But I have more of the estate to show you."

He was in no mood for another of her tours. "Show your 'cousin' Swan Park's delights if you wish, Lady Rosalind, but leave me out of it."

When he stalked off toward the house, he heard the damnable woman's boots clicking on the granite as she hurried after him. "If you plan to work in the library," she said imperiously behind him, "I'll keep you company—"

"No!" He halted and turned on her. That was the last thing he needed—the suspicious Rosalind draped over some chair, watching over his shoulder, unwittingly tempting him to try her resolution not to "succumb" to his advances.

A sudden brilliant idea seized him. He lowered his voice so only she could hear his words. "As it happens, I won't be working in the library, but in my bedchamber—sitting on my bed."

He let his gaze rake her body with the utmost insolence, stopping deliberately at the point where her shawl half hid her full breasts. "If you wish to keep me company there, I'm more than happy to oblige." He brought his gaze back to her face very, very slowly. "There's plenty of room in my bed for both of us, I'll wager. Just say the word, and we'll go upstairs together."

To his fierce satisfaction, a blush began in the

vicinity of her breasts and crawled rapidly up her
neck to her face. "You know very well I'll do no
such thing!" she hissed under her breath.

"What a shame. At the moment, I can think of
nothing more satisfying than stopping your
mouth—and so far I've found only one effective
method for it. I think you'll agree it has its . . . pleasures. For both of us."

She trembled from head to toe, but her eyes were
alight with anger. "I'll *die* before I let you kiss me
again, you . . . you cad!"

Well, well—he'd finally raised a reaction out of
the woman. She was obviously *not* immune to his
kisses. " 'The lady doth protest too much
methinks,' " he quoted in gleeful delight. "And if
you keep following me around like a bloodhound, I
may decide to prove that you do enjoy my kisses.
Only next time I won't stop at kissing."

Ignoring her rage, he pivoted on his heel and
strolled into the house without a backward glance.
Let her stew for a while. He knew the truth now—
she was not unaffected, and kisses *could* drive her
off. So until she stopped accompanying him everywhere, he would insist on kissing her . . . everywhere.

He glanced back toward the earl's apartments in
the east wing. Rosalind might bedevil him, but she
no doubt bedeviled her father even more with her
nonchalant refusal to save Swan Park by marrying.
A bitter smile crossed his face. How ironic that his
enemy should have to rely on his daughters to hold
on to his estate. He hoped that stuck in the old
man's craw.

He strode down the hall to the west wing,
climbed the two flights of stairs, and had nearly
reached his bedchamber on the second floor when

he heard footsteps behind him again. Surely after
all his threats Rosalind wouldn't persist in following him. Grimly, he turned to look back. But it
wasn't Rosalind approaching.

It was Daniel. And the giant was not happy.

With a sigh, Griff waited for him. As the man
drew near and started to speak, Griff held his finger
to his lips, then gestured to the door of his bedchamber.

As soon as they'd entered, Griff closed the door.
"Daniel, I—"

"Don't try any excuses on me," Daniel snapped.
"I had good reasons for asking you to keep silent,
but you didn't care. You behaved as you always do,
without a thought for anybody but your bloody self
and your bloody Knighton Trading. Well, I put up
with it most of the time, but today . . ."

He trailed off with a shake of his head. "You
shouldn't have told them, and you know it. It ain't
wise."

"*Isn't* wise," Griff instinctively corrected.

Daniel's cold gaze held a warning. "And don't be
telling me how to bloody talk either. I do it right
most times, as you well know. You're in the wrong,
Griff, and for once have the decency to admit it."

"I don't think I am," Griff retorted.

"That's because *you* don't have to live with my
reputation—*I* do. Goddamn it, I'll be the one dealing with them, the one trying to convince them we
mean them no harm. Even pretending to be you,
I'm not liked. I frighten the youngest girl out of her
wits half the time, and the eldest may be beautiful
but . . ." he snorted. "She's a real lady, so she
despised me even before you told them all that rot.
Bloody haughty wench, makes me want to take her
over my knee. If you don't get me out of here, I'm

liable to do it one day, too." He held out his hands as if in the act of squeezing and added, "Her backside makes a man just want to—"

He broke off at Griff's laugh, then said stiffly, "She'll drive a man crazy is all. She's nearly as bad as Lady Rosalind. And what the devil am I supposed to do with *her*?"

"I can handle Lady Rosalind," Griff reassured him.

"I've seen how well you handle her. What do you want to wager that the she-devil is standing outside your door right now waiting for you?"

"She wouldn't dare," he ground out.

"You think not?" Daniel strode to the door and laid his hand on the knob. "Five quid says she's out there waiting for you."

"Five quid it is," Griff snapped as he stalked up to the door.

Daniel swung it open for him, and Griff stepped out into the hall. Then groaned. Standing in the hall were Rosalind and a footman.

She immediately hurried over. "I was just coming to tell you—I've asked John to be your companion: show you the estate, help you with Papa's ledgers and such." Her tone grew acid. "Since you made it clear that my company would prod you into ... misbehaving, I thought I'd offer you someone else to help."

Of all the— Damn the woman, did she never give up? "Lady Rosalind," he growled, "I do not need *anyone's* help."

Her expression was suspiciously innocent. "But you did say you were assessing the estate for your employer. I should think you'd wish all the help you could get, considering how little time you might have here."

He heard Daniel's barely smothered laughter

behind the door. Damnation! He'd thought himself so clever with his threats to kiss her, but that had merely challenged her to bedevil him another way. He almost suspected she knew what he searched for, except he couldn't imagine her father telling her the truth.

Now she had him trapped, and she knew it. If he insisted on dismissing the footman, she'd know he'd lied about his reasons for "skulking about," as she put it. Then she'd be following him again, which presented far more dangerous problems. But a footman might be less suspicious of his motives and might even help him unwittingly.

And a footman would not make him burn.

"Very well," he clipped out, "when I'm finished with my work in here, I'll come seek your footman's help."

"He'll wait for you," she responded with a lift of her impudent chin.

The witch thought of everything. "As long as it's him and not you. Because if you keep following me, I promise to make good on my threats."

Her blush told him she understood. With some satisfaction, he reentered his bedchamber.

"Easiest five quid I ever made," Daniel commented with a smirk.

"Shut up, unless you have other suggestions for how I might rid myself of that termagant." That fetching termagant, whose aptitude for war—and feminine attractions—rivaled those of the battle goddess Athena. And who already had him itching to taste her again.

Daniel snorted. "The wench should've worked for you in the early days. God knows what you could have done with her in your employ."

Not much, Griff thought sourly. He'd have been too busy trying to seduce her. Within a week she'd have had him offering her Knighton Trading for a chance at bedding her.

"If you're worried about that footman," Daniel went on, "why don't you use the servants' stairs?"

"What do you mean?"

"Over there." Daniel nodded toward a portion of the wall. "See that panel, the ornamented one behind the bureau? It's a door leading to the servants' stairs."

Griff was already heading across the room. "Are you sure?"

Daniel followed him. "I nearly jumped out of my skin this morning when I heard a knocking inside the wall in my room. It was the valet. He said all the servants come and go through those stairs. And the ones in the east wing."

Griff had heard of such staircases, but never seen one. Then again, he rarely visited estates like this. Once Griff moved the bureau aside, it was easy to find the door handle disguised as an ornament. But when he tried to open the door, it wouldn't budge. He felt along the seam. "It's painted shut."

"I don't think they receive many guests. Your room is the only one on this floor being used at present. The servants probably don't even come up here."

Griff drew out his penknife, then cut carefully around the door until he'd freed it. It opened into a damp, empty stairwell clogged with cobwebs. He broke them with his arm, then stepped into the stairwell and peered down. Pieces of furniture cluttered the last few feet. Apparently, the stairwell was used for storage now. That's why the servants who'd entered his room had used the main door.

But he could get around the furniture. If he were careful and avoided the servants, he could come and go as he pleased. All he need do was pretend to spend a few hours working in his room each day. If he spent the rest of the time with Rosalind's footman, she might not guess what he was doing for some time. And he could search at night, too.

He came back into the room grinning. "Excellent—Rosalind won't suspect a thing."

" 'Rosalind'? You're calling her by her Christian name now?" Daniel shook his head in disgust. "Why don't you just bed the bloody woman and be done with it?"

Griff stiffened. "Bed her?"

"You know you want to."

Had he been as obvious as all that? "That's absurd." Pivoting away from his too perceptive friend, he strolled across the room and removed his coat for his sojourn in the servants' staircase. "As you said before, she isn't the sort of woman I prefer."

"Then you probably shouldn't put your hands all over her in private."

Griff went still. "What the hell are you talking about?"

"I saw how she looked when the two of you returned from your 'tour.' She was all rattled and rosy-lipped, her bonnet askew. Looked to me like some man had been having himself a fine time sampling her attractions."

"All right, so maybe I kissed her," Griff muttered as he jerked at the knot of his cravat. "She was annoying me, and it shut her up. That's all it was."

"And is that why you scowled at her the whole meal? I could almost hear you thinking how you wanted to lay her down and spread her legs right there."

"Don't talk about her that way!" Griff whirled on Daniel. "She's not one of your dockside light-skirts, for the love of God!"

Too late he realized how easily he'd fallen into

Daniel's snare. Daniel was watching him with eyebrows raised. "No, she isn't," he said softly. "She's
the sort of woman a man marries—the sort *you*
ought to marry."

Griff smothered the bewitching idea before it
could take root in his brain. "Marrying Lady Rosalind is out of the question."

"I don't see why. You want the woman, don't
you?"

He thought about lying, but Daniel knew him too
well for that. "Yes. Insane as it seems, I want the
woman, but only in the physical sense. And I want
the document proving my legitimacy more."

"Why not have both? A wife you desire—an
earl's daughter, for Christ's sake—and those papers
that make you clear heir to an estate and a title."

"It's not as simple as that."

"Why not?" He lowered his voice. "Because your
pride balks at letting their father win? If I could
have a woman as fine as all that only by swallowing
my pride, I'd be choking it down so fast I wouldn't
taste it. But I can't. Women of Lady Rosalind's kind
are denied to me and always will be. You don't
know how bloody fortunate you are."

The vehemence in Daniel's voice surprised him.
He'd never thought of Daniel as having dreams or
hopes or disappointments. The Irishman had
always been ready with a joke or a humorous tale,
never letting on that he might want more than what
he had. Griff had always been so focused on his
own plans that he hadn't considered what Daniel
might be planning—besides the aim to gain enough
money to build his own concern, that is. But then,
Griff understood that goal. It had been his own.

He tried another tack. "You seem to be laboring
under the impression that Rosalind would marry
me if I asked. She's made it very clear she wouldn't,

not even to save Swan Park. Apparently, none of the daughters is amenable to their father's plan, least of all Rosalind. She seems to find my character faulty."

"You mean, *my* character, since she thinks I'm you."

"I mean both our characters. She despises Mr. Brennan because of his smuggling past, which she considers akin to thievery. And she despises Mr. Knighton because he used what she considers unscrupulous means to gain his fortune. I couldn't succeed with her in either incarnation."

"Ballocks. If you courted her, she'd marry you. I noticed how she looked at you, too. She wants you. It would take no effort at all for you to bed her, and then she'd marry you willingly. No woman wants to be left ruined."

He groaned at the erotic images Daniel's words brought instantly to mind. Bedding her would indeed take no effort. He wanted her so badly he could scarce think of anything else.

"Just marry her," Daniel went on, "get the papers, and be done with it so we can go home. I'm tired of this bloody farce. I don't want to do it anymore."

Damnation, the man would force him to explain everything. Unfortunately, the explanation would not sit well with Daniel—especially if he felt as kindly toward the Swanlea daughters as it appeared. But it was clear that if Griff didn't provide an explanation, he'd soon lose Daniel's help anyway.

With a curse, Griff turned and strode to the window. He surveyed the estate that would be his, and sooner than Daniel yet realized. "If I marry Lady Rosalind," he said quietly, "Swanlea's 'proof' will be of little use to me."

"Why?"

"Because it's not proof that I'm the *heir* to the Earl

of Swanlea." He faced Daniel grimly. "It's proof that I *am* the rightful Earl of Swanlea."

Daniel's jaw dropped. "What the devil are you talking about? You can't be the earl unless your father . . ." He trailed off with a look of shock.

"Was the earl. Or the heir presumptive." A bitter laugh boiled out of Griff. "Why do you think Father amassed so many debts when I was young? Because he was a fool with money? No. He was supposed to inherit the title and Swan Park from the fourth Earl of Swanlea, the current earl's predecessor. Father expected to pay off his debts with that inheritance. But Father died before the fourth earl, so when the fourth earl died, the title and the property went to the next in line after my father. And long before then, it had been determined that I was *not* the next in line."

"Because you were believed to be a bastard?"

"Not believed to be—proclaimed one legally. Shortly after I was born, Rosalind's father went to court to prove that my parents weren't married. He did it with the express purpose of ensuring that I couldn't inherit. With no record of their marriage, it was easy enough for him to persuade the fourth earl—and then the courts when Father disputed it—that my parents had borne me in sin."

Looking stunned, Daniel dropped his huge frame into the chair beside the writing table. "Bloody hell. Bloody, bloody hell." He glanced up at Griff. "So you think that's how the old man obtained the proof of their marriage? He stole it to achieve his aims?"

Scowling blackly, Griff leaned back against the windowsill. "I don't know for certain. Swanlea visited my parents shortly after the place where my parents had registered at Gretna Green burned down. A few months after his visit, my father went to get their marriage certificate out of his desk and discovered it gone. Quite possibly it had been gone since the day of Swanlea's visit. I suspect he saw the opportunity to cut me off and took it."

"The villain! How could he treat your parents so ill? Your father was his cousin, for Christ's sake! And from what he said, I gather they were all once friends."

"He might have been a friend to my father once," Griff said tightly, "but he was never friend to my mother. I doubt he would have associated with the lowly daughter of a theater manager in Stratford. The previous earl despised Father's unequal alliance with her—that was what first provoked their elopement and later led the earl to believe Swanlea's claims about my illegitimacy."

With a frown, Daniel leaned forward to brace his elbows on the writing table. " 'Tis very strange then. Swanlea told me this morning that he knew your mother. He even called her by her Christian name."

"What?" Griff had always assumed she hadn't known the man personally.

"Besides," Daniel went on, "Swanlea married an actress himself, so he couldn't have been so critical of theater folk as you think."

Griff shook off the unease roiling in his belly. It didn't matter if Swanlea had ever known Mother; the man was no less a scoundrel. Nor did it change Griff's plans.

"In any case," Griff said with an air of finality, "whatever he once was to my parents, he ended up their enemy. That's why he wants me to marry one of his daughters before he'll give me the proof: He thinks that if I get it in my hands without any strings attached, nothing will prevent me from having him stripped of his title and his family thrown off the estate he stole."

Daniel's eyes narrowed. "I see. And is that what you intend?"

Griff stared him down. "In one respect. When I find that certificate, I fully intend to use it to strip Swanlea of the title that belongs to me. As soon as possible."

Disapproval was stamped on Daniel's face. "Aren't you afraid of what society might think? What good is a bloody title to you if those whose influence you seek think ill of you for getting it?"

"Society won't think ill of me, I assure you. Given the choice between championing a usurper or the wronged heir to a title, society will side with the wronged heir every time. It does not like to see its rules flouted."

"What about Swanlea's daughters?"

Swanlea's daughters. Rosalind. Griff's throat felt suddenly tight and raw. "What about them?"

"If you strip Swanlea of his title and property, they'll share in his disgrace. And his poverty."

A stab of guilt made Griff wince. "I don't intend that, never did. I have no quarrel with the daughters." Especially now that he'd met them. He drummed his fingers on the windowsill. "I'll make sure they're well provided for, give them dowries so they can find husbands."

"But even if you provide for them, their lives will be ruined, tainted by scandal. Even money might not buy them husbands then."

"They don't want husbands anyway," Griff snapped. "According to Rosalind, they choose to be spinsters."

"You don't believe that."

I believe a woman—people—ought to marry for love. Griff shook off Rosalind's wistful words. "They've never had much hope for marriage in any case, and my money will only improve that hope."

"But why not just find the marriage certificate

and wait until the old man dies? It can't be long. Afterward you can have the legalities done quietly, inherit the estate and the title, and everyone will assume you weren't a bastard after all. Then you won't even have to worry about the girls. I'm sure their father has left them something."

"I can't wait until he dies—that might take years. I've seen plenty of men supposedly on their death-beds go on to outlive their children."

Daniel's voice rose in outrage. "So it's years—why do you care? Since when is a title or an estate so important to you? You have all the money you need, and Knighton Trading is doing well."

Griff recoiled. Though he'd expected Daniel's reaction, he hadn't expected it to bother him so much. "You don't understand," he ground out. "As soon as I become the Earl of Swanlea, I'll be allowed into the House of Lords. I'll be in the perfect position to put myself on that delegation to China. And that must be done before this year is out, or I lose my chance at it."

Daniel stared at Griff as if seeing him for the first time. "So that's what this is all about—your precious delegation and Knighton Trading."

Damn the man for his self-righteousness. "Yes, Knighton Trading—the company that put you where you are, or have you forgotten? Without my company, you wouldn't have a position. Nor would the other hundred or more people in my employ. You wouldn't have a small fortune in that fund of yours, nor any chance at owning your own business. Disparage my methods all you want, but without them, where would you be?"

Daniel tilted his head up proudly. "I've never criticized your methods before this. I've never had to. But then, you've never set out to ruin four people for the sake of Knighton Trading."

With an oath, Griff shoved away from the window. "That bastard ruined my entire family for the sake of this estate. At least I intend to look after his family; that's more than he ever did for me."

He paced angrily in front of the writing table. "Do you know what they used to call my mother at Eton when they thought I couldn't hear? Knighton's whore. I was 'Knighton's bastard' and she was 'Knighton's whore.' My parents had another wedding after the scandal, but it didn't change public opinion about her. Or me. After all, I'd been declared a bastard in the courts, before God and everyone."

Striding up to the writing table, he planted his fists on it and glowered down at Daniel. "After Father died, do you think Swanlea came offering his help? No, indeed." He talked past the pain tightening his throat, the pain he'd sworn would never infect him. "Now he wants me to marry his daughter for the proof that's rightfully mine. What would *you* do? Marry her? Make it easy for him? Is that what you think I should do?"

"I don't see how marrying his daughter would make it any easier for him. It wouldn't prevent you from stripping him of his title. I know you want vengeance, but—"

"This is not about vengeance!"

Daniel regarded him with quiet accusation. "Isn't it?"

"No!" He paced the floor again. "It's about getting on that delegation. If I marry Rosalind, do you think she'd stand idly by while I humiliate her father publicly? While I make it even more difficult for her sisters to marry? Not Rosalind. She'll fight me tooth and nail. As I said before, if I marry her, my parents' marriage certificate is virtually useless to me. I couldn't act on it without making an enemy of my wife."

He leveled a solemn gaze on Daniel. "No, I'll have that certificate without the daughter, just as I planned." He couldn't resist adding, with a hint of sarcasm, "And you'll have your two hundred and fifty pounds."

Like a bow strung taut, Daniel sprang to his feet. "I don't want your money anymore. It was different when I thought you only wanted to prove your legitimacy. I didn't blame you for that or for not wanting to marry for it. A man has a right to claim his property without having to marry. But this—" He broke off with a snort of disgust.

"Are you refusing to continue with the masquerade?" Griff snapped, his hands drawing into fists at his sides.

"I told you I'd do it and I will, but for a week and no more. That should give you ample time to find your bloody documents." He strode for the door, then paused to look back at Griff, a strange disquiet in his features. "But it'll be my last week in your employ, do you hear? Swanlea may be a villain, and having met him I can say for certain he's an arse, but he's old and he's dying and he seems to want only one thing—to secure his daughters' futures. Can't say I blame him for that."

Eyes darkening, Daniel laid his hand on the knob. "You, on the other hand, are willing to ruin them just to further your ambition. Well, there are some things even a highwayman's bastard can't stomach."

The words haunted Griff for long hours after Daniel left.

Chapter 10

The mind naturally accommodates itself, even to the most ridiculous improprieties, if they occur frequently.

Fanny Burney, *English novelist, diarist, and sometime playwright,* Evelina

Griff was up to something. Rosalind knew it. But she couldn't figure out what. Aside from a marked tension between him and his employer, she'd noticed nothing that might signal his intentions.

Her footman's reports had been unrevealing, and going near Griff herself had become increasingly difficult. Whenever she attempted it, even in the company of others, he whispered the most outrageous things to her when no one else could hear. Allusions to plums abounded—the man had no imagination at all. Nor did it help that Juliet, completely misunderstanding Griff's words on the terrace that day, now made a point of having plums at every meal. Plums that he ate only to torment her.

This morning she'd insisted on riding out with him and Mr. Knighton when John was required elsewhere. Griff had repaid her amply for it, especially once he'd discovered she didn't ride sidesaddle. Every comment about riding had seemed to mean something naughtier. And he'd shown her just how well he could control a horse, for as they'd ridden he'd brushed his leg against hers several times with such precision that the horses never touched or shied.

But the worst had been when he'd helped her dismount. He'd held her waist much longer than necessary and remarked in a low voice that the sight of her astride was guaranteed to "fill his pockets." It had taken her a second to recognize the allusion. To her shame, more than her cheeks had grown heated when she did so. As if sensing the warmth pooling low in her belly, he'd laughed heartily. The insolent scoundrel!

Now she sat near the billiard table at the east end of the long first-floor gallery that stretched between the two wings. Griff played against Juliet while Mr. Knighton lounged in a chair and cheered Juliet on. Rosalind had almost left them to it, reluctant to attract any more of Griff's sly maneuvers, until she'd realized that he would thus achieve his purpose to drive her away. Her pride wouldn't let him have even the smallest success in *that* aim.

The table was ancient, bought by Papa before she was even born. He and Mama used to play billiards—she remembered that, a sweet hazy image from when she was a little girl. Papa had laughed and teased Mama while Helena begged to be allowed to play, too, and protested that she was nearly nine, surely old enough to play billiards.

After Mama's death, Papa had stopped using it.

Rosalind could only suppose it brought back painful memories. But the three girls had all played billiards. What else was one to do in the long winter months when even books grew tedious, and there was no company to speak of? Unfortunately, after Helena's illness she'd claimed she could no longer play, but Juliet and Rosalind still played often. Juliet hadn't really mastered the game, but Rosalind was quite good, though she'd had no chance this afternoon to show her skill.

Unfortunately, watching Griff play was a torment—his smooth handling of the cue, the flex of his muscles as he bent over the table to shoot, his low laugh of triumph when he won. It spurred her imagination too dreadfully. Instead of gripping a cue stick, he was gripping her waist, and instead of bending over the table to shoot, he was bending over her body to kiss and fondle it. And his low laugh of triumph became a groan of need as he lowered himself . . .

Dear God, she thought, blushing violently. Why couldn't she prevent these scandalous fancies playing repeatedly in her head? But she knew why. All his contradictions of background and speech and behavior fascinated her. One moment he seemed a gentleman, the next a rogue. Being unable to figure him out vexed her exceedingly.

Well, at least he wasn't sneaking about the house anymore. Perhaps she'd imagined it all in the first place. The night they'd met, might he really have been searching for cigars? And the next day, might his pride have been pricked when she'd insisted on staying with him, thus prompting him to try all those tactics to be rid of her?

It was possible, but it seemed unlikely. Still, why hadn't he balked more at her restrictions? Although he did disappear into his bedchamber every afternoon to work, John stayed right outside his door. Another footman took the night watch. She would suspect the men of falling asleep at their post, except that she'd checked on them a few times, even late at night, and found them always vigilant.

Probably this was Griff's plan to lull her into complacency so she'd relax her guard and he could return to his snooping. Well, she didn't intend to relax her guard until the day he left Swan Park.

But as the afternoon dragged on, Rosalind felt herself dozing off. She'd had trouble sleeping last night, imagining sounds inside the walls when none of the servants would be about. She was just considering going to her bedchamber for a quick nap when a ball entered a pocket with a sudden thunk, and Juliet let out an uncharacteristic whoop.

"I win! I win!" Juliet crowed, brandishing her cue in the air with childish joy. "I've beaten you at last, Mr. Brennan, admit it! And after only three games, too!"

"You have indeed." Griff's tone was indulgent, kind. It suddenly occurred to Rosalind that he'd played rather worse this game for no apparent reason. When he turned away from Juliet and a look passed between him and Mr. Knighton, she realized that he'd allowed Juliet to win.

The realization wound around her heart with insidious warmth, like the lion's tail of the griffin he was named after. His action had cracked Juliet's painful shyness as Mr. Knighton had been unable to do, and Rosalind found herself grudgingly grateful to him for it. Over the past three days, Juliet had been anxious all the time—either silent entirely or answering only when spoken to. She was more comfortable with Griff than with Mr. Knighton, but the reason for that was obvious: Juliet did not worry about having to marry *him*.

Rosalind sighed. Unfortunately, from what she could see, Juliet's anxiety hadn't swayed the girl from her course. Indeed, she was already glancing uneasily at Mr. Knighton to see if her unladylike behavior had offended him.

Suddenly Griff loomed up in front of Rosalind, blocking her vision as he held out a cue stick to her. "Now that your sister has trounced me, Lady Rosalind, I thought you might like the chance to do the same."

The blatant challenge in his gaze dared her to accept the invitation. Very well—it was high time she reminded him of her ability to best him.

With a smile, she rose and took the stick from him. "I can hardly think of anything that would give me more pleasure than trouncing you, Mr. Brennan."

"That's my 'Lady Disdain.'" His eyes gleamed as he quoted from *Much Ado About Nothing*. "'She speaks poniards, and every word stabs.'"

"I do my best." She brushed past him and went to the end of the table, removing her gloves as she went. "But my poniards must need sharpening, since you keep coming back for more, and I've yet to see you bleeding."

He set the cue ball and the red in position on the table. "I'm glad you limit yourself to words and don't know how to fence. Judging from how well you wield a sword, I might find myself unmanned." He waved his hand to the table, indicating that she should go first.

She grinned. "A tempting prospect indeed. But I'll settle for trouncing you at billiards. How many points shall we set the game at?"

"Fifty seems a nice even number."

"Fifty it is." With a smile, she took a series of shots that potted the red, potted her cue ball off the red twice, and then potted the red again. She would have sunk it a fifth time if the table hadn't been so uneven, causing the ball to stop an inch short of the pocket.

Mr. Knighton gave a low whistle and rose from his seat to survey the table. "Christ, m'lady, where'd you learn to shoot billiards like that?"

She stepped back from the table. "One of our footmen taught me." She turned to Griff, who lounged against the near wall with his arms crossed and his gaze shuttered. "That's four points, I believe. Your turn, sir."

He ambled to the table, placed his cue ball, and then shot a spot-stroke. "Your footmen have a wide variety of duties." He took the red out and positioned it again, then shot an impressive cannon combined with a winning hazard. "They teach billiards and act as personal assistants to wandering guests. I wonder how they find the time to be footmen."

She winced when he potted the red neatly. "As you'll soon discover, all our servants are quite versatile. So if it weren't the footmen performing those services, it would be someone else—the butler, the coachman—"

"The lady of the manor?" he quipped as he paused in setting up a shot.

She raised an eyebrow. "If need be."

The red had dropped into the pocket nearest her, so she fished it out for him. When she leaned across the table to hand it to him, however, his eyes weren't on her hand, but lower. Only then did she realize her shawl had come unknotted and she was displaying far too much bosom. With an unspoken oath, she started to draw back, but his hand closed quickly over hers to stay her, and for a second she couldn't move.

She shot a pleading glance at her cousin, but he and Juliet had wandered down the gallery to look at the portraits of the Swanlea ancestors. They were deep in discussion with their backs to the table. Neither of them noticed Griff's hold on her.

His smooth, warm hand was so large it enveloped hers, but not so large as to imply a brutishness of character. His fingers stroked hers, reminding her of how those same deft fingers had walked their way up her ribs while she and he had stood on the sun-drenched hill.

Sweet need unfurled again in her belly. No, she thought angrily, she wouldn't let him do this to her! He only did it to provoke her.

Yet when she tried to withdraw her hand, he held it captive a moment longer. "As much as I might enjoy having the lady of the manor act as my assistant," he whispered, "I don't want to take her from her other, more pressing duties."

"Then you and your employer should return to London where you belong," she said archly.

"Why? Do we annoy you?" His corrupt gaze drifted to her half-exposed bosoms. "Or are you afraid that we'll uncover . . . your secrets?"

Despite her fervent wish to prevent it, her face flamed. He grinned, then took the ball and released her hand. Wishing she could stuff the ball in his shameless mouth to silence him once and for all, she sprang back and quickly knotted her shawl in place. Billiards clearly provided too many opportunities for unseemly contortions of the female body. The least she could do was cover up those parts Griff insisted on ogling.

She glanced at him when she was finished, only to find him smirking at her. Let him smirk. It was better than his ogling. Or making wicked remarks—the ones she found so disturbingly titillating.

He followed his previous stroke with three spot-strokes in rapid succession, recapturing her interest in the game. She had to admit Griff's skill impressed her. She'd guessed correctly before—he'd surely allowed Juliet to win. But when Rosalind got the chance to shoot again, she'd show him that not all of the Swanlea spinsters were fumble-fingers with a cue stick.

Her chance came a few shots later, just as she suppressed a sleepy yawn. He came around to her side of the table and assessed his next shot with great seriousness. From her vantage point, she could tell he was aiming for a white hazard, but their table wasn't the best, and he missed it, thanks to a tricky carom off two cushions. By that time, he was seven points ahead.

He stood back while she set up her own shot most carefully, for he'd left her cue ball in a devilish position. After a few moments of her bending over to sight down the stick, eye the pocket, then sight down the stick again, he murmured behind her, "If you're doing this purposely to tempt me, you're succeeding."

She glanced back at him quizzically only to find him eyeing her backside and the raised skirts that revealed a goodly length of her stockings. She glared at him. "If you don't like being tempted, Mr. Brennan, you should keep your eyes on the game where they belong." Without moving an inch, she returned her attention to the table, though it was difficult now not to imagine his interested gaze on her derriere.

He chuckled. "Who says I don't like being tempted?"

Gritting her teeth, she shot. And missed, of course. That's what she got for letting the bloody man drive her to distraction.

When she straightened angrily, she turned to find him so close his gray trousers brushed her skirts. "Excuse me, Mr. Brennan," she bit out, but he didn't move away.

He darted a quick look over to where Mr. Knighton and Juliet were still at the other end of the gallery. Juliet was explaining the history of each earl, and to his credit Mr. Knighton was patiently enduring the explanations. Unfortunately, he was also paying no attention to his man of affairs.

Who now leaned even closer, mischief dancing in his eyes. "We should place a little wager on this game."

"What sort of wager?" She tried to step back, but the table prevented it. He was too close for rational thought, too close for anything but remembering what had happened the last time he'd stood near her. Her pulse began to race.

"If I win," he murmured, "you call off your dog."

She suppressed a groan. She should have known he would eventually come back to that subject. Tilting up her chin, she asked, "And if I win?"

"You won't win." When she looked at him askance, he smiled and added, "Very well. If you do, I'll . . ." he thought a moment, "I'll arrange for you to audition for Richard Sheridan."

Her eyes went wide. "*The* Richard Sheridan? The owner of Drury Lane Theatre? The man who wrote *School for Scandal*?"

The blasted man grinned, knowing he'd baited his hook well. "The very one."

He looked far too sure of himself. She eyed him skeptically. "You know him well enough to arrange an audition?"

"Let's just say that Sheridan and I share an affection for fine French brandy, which we indulge occasionally."

"How would a man of affairs come to know a famous character like Sheridan?"

That seemed to catch him off guard. Then he shrugged. "My employer is a patron of the theater, and has a small investment in Drury Lane." He nodded toward Mr. Knighton. "If you don't believe me, ask him."

She glanced down the gallery at her cousin, who was still absorbed in her sister's prattling. Mr. Knighton invest in Drury Lane? Impossible! At dinner last night the ox had been entirely unaware of who John Dryden or Christopher Marlowe or even Homer was, despite his Eton education. Indeed, she'd begun to doubt he possessed such an education at all. It was highly unlikely that he loved the theater.

As if realizing the source of her disbelief, Griff added, "Actually, I instigated the investment, since it provided him—and me—with a very nice private box at Drury Lane."

That made more sense. Whatever his other faults, Griff did seem to possess a genuine interest in the theater.

"Well?" he prodded. "Do you accept the wager?"

She still hesitated. "Only if you answer one question."

"All right."

"Why are you so eager to be rid of my footman? He's merely there to help you."

"I don't need help. In any case, I'm accustomed to going where I please, when I please, without an audience. Have you ever tried reading documents with a servant two feet away trying to be unobtrusive? It's damned annoying."

When he put it that way, she saw how he might find it so. Besides, she intended to win the game. And the possibility of auditioning for Sheridan—

Richard Sheridan—was irresistible. "Very well. I accept your wager."

"Rosalind!" her sister cried from down the gallery. She and Mr. Knighton were headed back to the table. "Whatever are you and Mr. Brennan whispering about? I thought you were playing billiards."

Griff broke away from Rosalind with a rakish smile. "We are, my lady, we are." He caught up his cue stick. "Your sister and I are about to become very serious about it."

She'd thought they were already serious about billiards, but he soon proved her wrong. When he took the table this time, there was no flirting, no teasing innuendoes, no wavering from his purpose. He went to it with the single-mindedness of a sportsman. Indeed, he gained twenty points more before a slip of the stick ruined his shot.

She took her place with great trepidation, no longer as certain of winning. She should have made him start over for the wager. Now he was twenty-seven points ahead—a great gap indeed. If she lost, she'd have to spend more time in his presence, which would be terribly unwise—not to mention she'd lose the Sheridan audition.

By careful attention to her aim, she managed a string of red and white hazards. She wasn't as good at cannons and so didn't even risk them, even though they'd let her increase her score more quickly. Nonetheless, she'd already passed his score by four points when she potted his cue ball.

She and Juliet groaned at the same time.

"My turn." Griff gloated as he removed his cue ball from the pocket and spotted it.

Then he began to play with all the expertise of a true proficient. She should have known that a former smuggler would excel at billiards. No doubt that was how he and his criminal companions had entertained themselves.

As the score passed forty, she tensed. He aimed, and she leaned forward on the opposite end of the table to watch. In the split second between his drawing back and his sending the cue stick forward, his eyes veered from the table to her. He missed the shot and cursed.

Scowling, he rounded the table, then stopped beside her to murmur, "Getting desperate, are you?"

"What do you mean?" she whispered back.

"Much as I usually enjoy any glimpse of your . . . charms, I hardly think it's fair for you to thrust them into my line of sight when I'm shooting."

She glanced down and blushed to see that her shawl had come unknotted again. "I hadn't noticed," she said truthfully, reaching to retie it again.

"Of course not."

The blasted scoundrel didn't believe her! She hesitated a moment, then defiantly removed her shawl and tossed it over a chair. If the surly wretch insisted on attributing such tactics to her, she might as well be hanged for a sheep as a lamb.

From there on, she did her best to distract him whenever he shot. It wasn't that difficult. Apparently, given the choice between concentrating on his cue stick or ogling a woman's breasts, a man chose ogling every time. Its predictability was almost comical.

Unfortunately, it didn't take him long to find a suitable revenge. Whenever *she* shot, he passed just close enough to whisper comments so imaginatively scandalous that he never failed to draw a reaction from her—usually a missed shot.

It soon became obvious they had abandoned the game of serious billiards for "naughty billiards."

Juliet seemed oblivious to what was going on. When she did hear the comments, she apparently didn't understand them, and the ogling was something she was too innocent to be bothered by. Though Mr. Knighton was not so oblivious, he oddly chose to say nothing. She did, however, catch him watching them both with an inexplicably gleeful expression once or twice.

The game dragged, since neither progressed very far at a time—a point here, a point there, then a missed shot. Still, they were forty-nine to forty-nine when Helena approached along the gallery.

"What's going on?" she asked as she limped to a chair and took a seat.

"Mr. Brennan and Rosalind are playing billiards," Juliet said cheerfully, "and they both need only one point to win. But they're playing very badly, even worse than me. They've both missed their last three shots. We'll be here all day if this continues."

Helena eyed the table curiously, then glanced at Rosalind. As she took in Rosalind's décolletage, her disapproval was obvious. "It's no wonder Rosalind's having trouble. She must be freezing without her shawl, and that would surely deflect her aim."

Rosalind cursed inwardly. "I'm perfectly comfortable."

"No," Griff interrupted, "Lady Helena is right." He strode to where she'd left her shawl, picked it up, and brought it to her. "Here, my lady." With an utterly disgusting smile, he settled it around her shoulders. "This should help."

"Thank you," she retorted through gritted teeth. Just wait until she got Helena alone.

At least it was her turn to shoot and not his, and he wouldn't dare make any of his nasty comments with Helena nearby. Rosalind took careful aim at the easy red hazard before her. All she had to do was shoot. That's all.

Yet her hands were clammy, the cue stick slipping around in them like an eel. She couldn't fail now. She mustn't! For if she missed this shot, he was sure to make his. And there would go her chance at Sheridan.

She aimed, shot, and then watched with glee as her cue ball hit the red perfectly, sending it toward the pocket with a pure grace. But then it slowed as it neared the pocket. No, not again—it couldn't happen twice! She couldn't be so unlucky! Not now!

But she was. The ball danced on the edge of the pocket, then retreated half an inch to a position even a novice couldn't miss.

To his credit, Griff didn't even smile as he took the easy shot. But once the red disappeared into the pocket with a plop that echoed in her mind, he broke out in a grin. He glanced at her younger sister. "There, Lady Juliet. It appears we won't be here all day after all."

Rosalind watched numbly as he rounded the table, then came up beside her and offered his hand. She wanted to break her cue stick over it, but she had better manners than that. Glumly she held out her hand, expecting a brief press of fingers.

She should have known better. With the predatory gaze of an eagle carrying off a hare, he bent over her bare hand and kissed it. His lips were warm and soft against her skin, and they lingered for what seemed like forever, yet when he straightened she knew it had only been seconds.

"We are well matched, you must admit." He released her hand.

"I suppose," she said ungraciously.

His expression hinted at some other meaning for *well matched*, but she chose to ignore it and dwell instead on the disappointment of having lost her audition. It was safer than dwelling on the press of his lips against her hand.

He waited until her cousin had begun to ask Lady Juliet about playing another game, then stepped up close and lowered his voice. "I'm going to my room to work for a while. When I come out, I expect your footman to be gone."

She'd forgotten that in losing her part of the wager, he'd won his. Now she'd have to find another way to shadow him or else move the strongbox where he'd never find it. If indeed he was looking for it.

She swallowed, then nodded. With a final smile of triumph, he strode down the gallery to the west-wing stairs leading to the second floor where his room lay.

Bitterly disappointed by her loss, she turned to find Juliet telling Mr. Knighton that she didn't want to play billiards anymore.

He faced Helena. "What about you, my lady? Do you play?"

"No," was her cold answer.

When he looked offended by the short response, Rosalind explained. "Helena says her leg prevents her, that it's hard to balance on one leg and shoot." It was nonsense, of course, but she'd never determined if Helena believed it or was simply using the excuse to keep herself apart from people, as she did in other respects. She added, "But she used to beat me routinely before her illness."

Helena glared at her, but Rosalind had always thought it best to be honest. Besides, she rather liked her cousin, even if he were a bit coarse and had once consorted with smugglers. It pained Rosalind to see Helena treat him so coldly, even though Helena had been reserved toward all men of late.

Mr. Knighton hadn't taken his eyes from her older sister while Rosalind was speaking. Now he walked silently to the far wall. Lifting an armchair, he brought it back to the pool table and positioned it so that one arm was parallel to the rim, with about a foot of space between the table and the chair.

He glanced at Helena. "Couldn't you sit on the arm of the chair? Then you wouldn't need your legs at all to play."

A dark flush spread up Helena's neck. "That's highly impractical, Mr. Knighton. The chair would have to be moved and positioned to my order for every shot."

Bracing his hands on the chair back, he shrugged. "That's why you must play billiards with a great lummox like me, m'lady. I've lifted bigger loads a thousand times. If I can't move a wee thing like this, then I ain't much of a man."

Rosalind's heart melted.

But Helena appeared unswayed. "The arm of the chair won't hold my weight."

"Yes, it will." He pressed down on the arm to demonstrate. Then he strolled up to where she sat, still eyeing him warily. He held out his hand. "In any case, you won't know until you try it. And I promise to catch you if it breaks."

Helena stared at his hand for a long moment. Rosalind saw the flash of yearning in her face. It had been many years since Helena had played billiards, and many more years since a man had treated her so courteously.

"Go on, Helena," Rosalind prodded. "Mr. Brennan and I gave Mr. Knighton no chance at all to play, and if Juliet won't play and I'm too tired, you're the only one left."

Helena rolled her eyes, but clearly recognized she was trapped. With a scowl, she took his hand and let him help her rise. As she hobbled to the arm-chair, she muttered, "If it tips me over, Mr. Knight-on, I shall hold you responsible."

He only grinned in answer, then helped her settle herself onto the chair arm.

When the two of them began their game, Juliet pulled Rosalind down the gallery, well out of earshot. "Look at him," she whispered. "He's so kind to Helena."

Rosalind watched as Mr. Knighton hurried to set up the balls for the game. "Yes, he's a kind man, I think."

"It's such a pity that she dislikes him so," Juliet said mournfully. "This morning she called him a great oaf and said she'd never marry a man like that."

"You know how foolish Helena has become about men. She'll find any excuse to refuse them."

"Well, she has more than an excuse in his case, I'm afraid. She thinks he's only out for what he can get. She thinks he wants to marry an earl's daughter who can teach him how to behave in society. So there's no chance of her marrying him—Helena's pride wouldn't allow it." Juliet worried her lower lip. "And you've got your eye on that man of affairs—"

"I do not!"

Juliet shook her head. "Deny it all you wish, but I can see you like him."

"Not in the least." She was intrigued by him, fas-cinated by him, tempted by him. But *like* him? That was far too bland a word for what he made her feel.

"So if neither of you will marry Mr. Knighton, it's left to me." She said it with a tone of mournful acceptance.

"Now, dearest, you mustn't feel like that. None of us needs marry him. I told you, we can—"

"Leave Swan Park forever. I won't do it."

"I don't know why not," Rosalind snapped.

Juliet's lower lip trembled. "You don't understand. You never did."

A plaintive note in Juliet's voice gave Rosalind pause. "Why don't you explain it to me then?"

Afternoon sunlight streamed through the gallery's mullioned windows, spangling Juliet's golden hair and glinting off the sudden tears in the girl's eyes. Rosalind's heart broke at the sight. She took her sister's hand and squeezed it. "Oh, Juliet, please tell me what has made you so determined to marry against your heart."

"I have to marry Mr. Knighton. I have to!" Juliet bent her head, several gilt curls falling over her brow. "It's all my fault that we'll lose Swan Park, so I must prevent it."

"How could it possibly be your fault?"

"Because if . . . if Mama hadn't died giving birth to me, Papa would have been able to have a son." Tears rolled down her angelic cheeks. "And then the estate would never have been entailed away."

So that was the source of all Juliet's stubbornness. With wrenching sadness, Rosalind tugged her sister into her embrace. "Oh, my dearest, don't even think it. It's not your fault women die in childbirth. And Papa could have had more children if he'd chosen to remarry. But he didn't. How can you blame yourself for that?"

"B-Because Papa b-blames me," she whispered through her tears.

A surge of protectiveness made Rosalind clutch her sister tightly. "Do you mean Papa has told you it is your duty to marry Mr. Knighton because—"

"No, of course not!" Juliet rubbed the tears from her cheeks with her small fists. "Papa would never say it like that. But I know he blames me. It's in his face and voice whenever he speaks of Mama, whenever he speaks of my marrying to save Swan Park. He doesn't have to say it—I know what he feels."

Rosalind felt helpless in the face of such youthful misapprehension. Their father could be stern and misguided sometimes, but he did love his children in his own way. "I'm sure he doesn't blame you, dearest. None of us do, not even Papa."

Juliet jerked away, more tears coursing down her face. "I knew you wouldn't understand."

"But I do! I only think that—"

"That I'm a silly girl who imagines things. Well, I'm not imagining this, no matter what you say to spare my feelings. I'll prove to all of you I can do my part for the family, the way you have by taking care of Swan Park. That's why I *shall* marry Mr. Knighton even if I don't . . . love him!" And with that impassioned speech, she whirled and ran off down the west-wing stairs.

"Juliet!" Rosalind called out, running to the top of the stairs to look down, but her fleet-of-foot little sister was already halfway down. There was no point to remonstrating further with her when she was in her present mood, anyway.

Rosalind shook her head balefully as she returned to the gallery. Blast it all. Juliet's determination to "save" the family was rooted more deeply than she'd realized. She and Helena had probably coddled the girl too much, made her feel as if she could do nothing to help. Now they would pay for it dearly.

She collapsed into a nearby chair, her mind in turmoil. Oh, however were they to unravel this coil? Juliet wouldn't be satisfied until Swan Park was saved, and clearly she took that to mean she must marry Mr. Knighton. Unless Rosalind could think of how to stop it before it was too late. To her knowledge, Mr. Knighton hadn't yet offered for any of them—Papa would have crowed over it—but this limbo couldn't continue forever. Mr. Knighton had a business in London, after all.

A delay was what she needed, something to give her time to think of a plan that would suit all of them. Papa had sprung this on them so quickly, she'd hardly had time to consider their choices.

The trouble was, she had no control over the situation, no way to predict when the engagement would occur, how long it would last, or what would be done. The only way to gain control would be to agree to marry the bloody man herself.

Rosalind's heart began to pound. Yes, that would work! If she agreed to marry Mr. Knighton herself, she could play the skittish fiancée: insist on time to plan the wedding, do all manner of things to make him change his mind about marrying any of them . . .

She scowled. There was only one problem with that plan: He would never marry her. He wanted a woman like Juliet—the perfect, socially acceptable wife.

With a sigh, she stood. Perhaps she could find some way to tempt him in her direction. She'd have to think on it, for this was by far her best plan to date. She yawned. First, however, she'd take a nap. She always thought better after she'd slept. Or maybe some solution would come to her in a dream.

Only when she was halfway down the gallery did she remember she'd promised to send John away before Griff left his room again. Blast.

According to the clock, he'd only been in there half an hour, so she had plenty of time. He generally

spent over two hours working in his bedchamber in
the afternoon. Still, she wanted it done. Then she
could nap, and consider her plan further.

She strolled back to the west-wing stairs and
climbed to the second floor. John lounged in the hall
outside Griff's bedchamber as always, but rose
quickly from his chair when she approached.

"Mr. Brennan has been in his room for some time,
my lady," he reported.

She listened at the door, but could hear nothing.
She sighed. "You may go. And you may return to
your usual duties from now on."

He nodded, too well trained to question the
whims of the lady of the house. She started to leave,
too, then stopped, assailed by curiosity as always.
What did Griff do in there every day? She seldom
saw him and Mr. Knighton discussing business, so
how did he come to have so much work all the
time?

She plastered her ear to the door for a minute. An
ominous silence was all she heard. Of course, writing letters and such didn't make any noise. But one
would think there'd be the occasional scrape of a
chair or something. And he couldn't spend the
entire time writing letters, could he? His hand
would cramp.

Her eyes narrowed. Come to think of it, he didn't
post any great quantity of letters. Hmmm. How
very odd. What *did* he do in there?

With sudden resolve, she rapped on the door. No
answer. She rapped again, this time with more
impatience. Still silent.

Suspicion tightened her brow into a black frown.
Had he gotten past her footman? There was only
one way to find out. She tried the door, but it was
locked. Blast.

Now determined to ferret out his secret, she

withdrew her ring of keys, then tried several until she found the one that unlocked the door. She started to turn the knob, but hesitated. It would be awful if he were sleeping or something, and she burst in upon him.

Then again, she could always claim she'd only come to tell him the footman had been dismissed or some such nonsense, couldn't she? Feeling secure in that rationale, she opened the door and entered.

The room was empty—completely and utterly empty. She stood with her hands on her hips and cursed. No doubt John had popped down to the kitchen or something earlier, and Griff had left while he was gone.

As she scanned the room, she noticed that Griff's coat was thrown across a chair and his waistcoat and cravat hung from the handle of the clothes-press. Could he have changed clothes before he left? But why? And why only those pieces of clothing? No, it seemed more likely that wherever he was, he was in his shirtsleeves. Yet that was uncharacteristic of the well-dressed Mr. Brennan.

Then something else caught her eye. The bureau had been moved away from the wall. She moved nearer. There were cracks in the paneling behind it . . . And it hit her with sudden force how Griff had left his room.

Through the servants' door, the *sealed* servants' door. Curse him! Leave it to Griff to discover the door none of them ever used.

She opened the door, glanced down the stairwell, and saw the assorted furnishings blocking the stairs. She'd been told that the upper stairs were unsafe, which was why no one used them. Clearly that had been an exaggeration, for Griff obviously did.

Well, she thought grimly, he must be very proud of himself. All this time he'd been sneaking out

whenever he wanted, for as long as he wanted, and
she hadn't even realized it. And he'd made such a
big to-do about their wager, too!

The more she thought about it, the more infuriated she became. So he wanted to move about the
house at will, did he, sneaking into other people's
rooms, searching for God knows what? The man
was a rat. She wished she knew exactly what he was
up to, for knowing his plans might help her determine her own.

Frustrated, she turned to his writing table. Several papers were scattered on it. Did any of them
belong to her family? Approaching the table, she
stared down at the confusion, then realized most of
it dealt with the business of Knighton Trading.

A slow grin crossed her lips. If Griff insisted upon
nosing about her house where he didn't belong,
perhaps she should do the same. Who knows? She
might even be lucky enough to stumble across
something that would reveal his employer's true
intentions. Then she could go to Papa with her suspicions, and he'd have to listen.

She glanced over at the closed door to the servants' stairs and hesitated. She wouldn't want him
to find her here alone, not after what he'd threatened.

Still, it had only been a short while since she'd
seen him last, and he always stayed away at least
two or three hours. Surely she had time to do some
snooping of her own and be gone before he
returned. Feeling deliciously devious, she settled
herself into his chair and picked up a sheaf of
papers. She'd stay only a few minutes, that's all.
Just long enough to find out what he was up to.

Chapter 11

The bliss e'en of a moment still is bliss.

Joanna Baillie, Scottish playwright,
The Beacon

Griff trudged up the servants' stairs, weary to the bone and hungry besides. It must be near time for dinner. He usually didn't search for so long, but if Rosalind had held to her word her footman would be gone, so who'd notice? She could hardly sit outside his door waiting. And if she did, it would serve the vixen right to wait a long time.

As usual, he'd found nothing. There were plenty of documents—he'd even stumbled across the family Bible with its list of marriages, births, and deaths—but his parents' marriage had not been recorded at all. And he'd found no sign of his parents' marriage certificate.

Damnation. The earl must have a safe secreted away somewhere, probably in his room. That was where Griff really needed to look—but the old bas-

157

tard never left his bed. And Daniel had given Griff
only three more days.

Daniel, that self-righteous scoundrel. They'd never been at odds before, not like this. With his
sleeve, Griff wiped the sweat from his grimy brow,
streaking soot across the lawn fabric. He stared at it
in the staircase's dim candlelight. Long ago, he
wouldn't have soiled his shirt so heedlessly, for
every shirt cost him more than he could afford.
Now he could soil them at will, even throw them
away if he liked.

*Since when is a title or an estate so important to you?
You have all the money you need, and Knighton Trading
is doing well.*

His hand balled into a fist. Daniel would never
understand. It wasn't about money. It was about making Knighton Trading strong and powerful, worthy of
respect. In his small-minded way, Daniel failed to consider the larger good—the people Griff employed, the
trade that would be stimulated. How dare the man
imply that Griff had only vengeance in mind, that he
merely sought to further some petty ambition? Daniel
was wrong, and he'd surely see it in time.

Griff reached the piled-up footstools, broken
chairs, and bric-a-brac and climbed warily over
them. On his first trip down the stairs, when his leg
had fallen through a step, he'd discovered exactly
why the servants never used this route. Now he
was more careful where he trod.

At least he no longer needed to do this too often,
not with Rosalind calling off her footman. He only
hoped it didn't mean a renewal of her appearances
at his side—that was one war he was rapidly losing.

All his tactics to put her off succeeded only in
arousing him. When they were together, it was a ver-
itable feast of sensual innuendo. The first course—
her searing questions. The second—his spicy

answers. The third—her delicate blushes. Then it all repeated again in endless stimulating variations until it finished with him wanting her for dessert.

What had started as a method to drive her away had become a dangerous erotic game, one that could only end with her in his bed.

He shook off the thought. That was impossible, of course. Seducing a virgin was unacceptable. He had no intention of marrying her, and she certainly had no desire to marry him. So why did he persist in thinking of it?

Because the woman was an "original" in every sense of that overused appellation. Wealth didn't impress her; flattery didn't sway her. She ordered everybody in the household about, yet her servants spoke fondly of her, and her footmen sang her praises endlessly. She had an annoying tendency to call a spoon a spade, yet her wildest plans often succeeded despite her haphazard manner of executing them. He'd even grown to like her outrageous preference for brilliant-hued gowns. Intense colors suited her.

What most kept his desire simmering, however, was remembering how she'd kissed—throwing herself into it, excitement barely tempered by innocence, passion cloaked in wonder. How could such sheer enthusiasm fail to rouse a man's basest instincts?

Damnation, after this afternoon's dance of billiard seduction, he didn't know if he'd survive another day without throwing her over his shoulder like a slavering beast and carrying her off to his lair.

He reached his room and entered quickly, telling himself he was merely eager to exchange the dank musty stairwell for the brightly lit bedchamber. But the truth was he couldn't wait to prepare for his next skirmish with Rosalind.

He'd already shut the door behind him when he spotted her. The object of his ridiculous obsession sat in a chair with her head slumped on his writing table. He halted in shock, wondering if the intensity of his need might have conjured her up. But no, if he'd dreamed her into his bedchamber, she would already be naked. Instead, she wore the bold emerald gown he'd imagined ripping off with his teeth during their game of billiards.

Frustrated lust rapidly twisted into fury as he realized the woman had actually sneaked into his room. She'd unlocked the door and entered without his permission or knowledge. By God, was nothing sacred to the warrior queen?

He caught sight of the sheaf of papers spilling from her slack fingers, and his blood thundered in his ears. What had he left lying about? Was there anything to reveal his deception? Stalking to the table, he peered over her still form at the papers fanning out from her hand.

They were nothing of consequence, just bills of lading. No doubt their tediousness had put her to sleep. But had she done this before—come in here while he was gone, perhaps even during the day while he'd been with her footman?

It didn't matter—it would *not* happen again. It was one thing for her to tease and taunt him; quite another for her to intrude on his privacy. He refused to tolerate such behavior. He lifted his hand to her shoulder to shake her, then spotted the chunk of quartz he'd been using to weight down papers.

With grim purpose, he picked it up and hefted it. Yes, that would do nicely. Moving to one end of the table, he leaned over and dropped the rock as near her head as he could without hitting her. It struck the oak with a loud thunk.

She shot up, her eyes glazed with confusion, her cheek red and bearing finger-shaped creases.

The instant she spotted him, he bent forward to

plant his fists on the writing table, and growl, "What the hell do you think you're doing in here?"

The sheaf of papers slipped from her hand to drift like molting feathers to the floor. "Why I . . . there was . . ."

"You have no right to let yourself into my *locked* room without my permission, and you know it!"

For a moment, she just gaped at him, her agitation evident in her jerky breathing. Then she glanced over to the bureau pulled away from the wall, and her eyes narrowed to slits. "You have the audacity to accuse *me*? How many locked rooms have *you* entered without *my* permission? Tell me that!"

"As many as I pleased." He smothered any flare of conscience. Every room in this house belonged to him in principle, which meant he had the right to search them. "It's not as if I had a choice. You refused to allow me privacy, so I took some."

"You gave up the right to privacy when you began snooping about my home!"

Anger exploded in his brain. Catching her under the arms, he lifted her bodily from the chair. "And you gave up the right to courtesy when you let yourself into my room! Now get out!"

He released her, and she stumbled back a step, clearly shocked by his rough handling of her. But as usual, his Amazon remained undaunted. Steadying her shoulders, she scowled at him. "I'm not leaving until you tell me what you're up to. You went to a great deal of trouble to make sure you could move freely about the house. I want to know why. What are you looking for?"

"A place where I'm not bedeviled by nosy women!"

She sniffed. "I won't be put off by your surliness. I want to know the truth, and no amount of bullying will dissuade me from finding it out."

He glared down at the vixen, momentarily at a loss. Then her rosewater scent drifted through his senses, and an acute awareness of her body crashed through all his anger.

Rosalind was in his bedchamber. Alone. With him.

He ate her up with his eyes. Her shawl lay somewhere on the floor, leaving bare the two creamy half-moons of flesh above her green bodice. Like lily petals floating on a turbulent sea, they rose and fell madly with her angry breaths. He watched entranced, before dragging his gaze back to her trembling chin and her full, parted lips.

Those damnable lips that never failed to jolt his cock erect.

"If bullying won't teach you to mind your own business," he grated out, "I know what will."

Grasping her by the shoulders, he lowered his head, but before he could kiss her, she whispered, "Don't you dare!" in a tone almost pleading. It made him hesitate until she added, "Don't you dare kiss me, Griff Brennan!"

Hearing her marry his name to Daniel's was the last straw. "You can't say I didn't warn you," he rasped. Then he brought his mouth down hard on hers.

He'd expected a struggle from his battle goddess, but what he got was a perfect stunned stillness. Perhaps her nap had lowered her defenses. Or perhaps she was as randy as he'd been from the minute he'd seen her in her wrapper brandishing a sword.

He didn't know; he didn't care. The most tempting female ever to plague a hot-blooded male was in his arms in his bedchamber. And he desired her. Damnation, how he desired her!

He forced his tongue past the barrier of her lips, winning entrance after a moment of effort. With a deep groan of satisfaction, he laid siege to her mouth. And what a glory of a mouth—soft and warm and inviting, tasting of the cinnamon from those apple tarts she seemed to love. He could feed on it all day and never be satisfied.

But unwise though it might be, he needed more than kissing this time. A great deal more.

Rosalind could feel the difference in him, the urgency and determination. Curse him, he only wanted to distract her from learning the truth. So why was she letting him?

Because he did it so bloody well. His unyielding hands held her head still for a series of hungry kisses that made her pulse stammer and start and leap. His splayed fingers tugged restlessly on her coiffure, dragging it free of pins already loosened by her unplanned nap. Her hair tumbled down her back like a flag of truce unfurling.

That frightened the devil out of her. What in God's name was she doing? She had her sisters to think of and Papa's strongbox.

With a burst of will, she tore her lips from his. "I shan't let you do this. I shan't . . . let you distract me."

"Why not?" he growled, raining kisses over her cheeks. "God knows you've distracted me for days."

She jerked back from him. "Don't lie to me!" She couldn't bear to have him pretend again and hurt her as he had the last time he kissed her.

His gaze searched her face. "Lie to you? About what?"

Focusing on the grimy shirt that further attested to his devious activities, she gulped breath after breath. "You may think me . . . too stupid to realize what I lack, but I do know my deficiencies. I know I don't possess the beauty and form required to excite a man's . . . urges, and that you do this only to distract me from your secretive plans. You couldn't possibly find me—"

"Lovely? Seductive? Maddening?" Grabbing her

by the shoulders as if to shake her, he laughed harshly. "All this time I've gone insane trying to keep from kissing you, while you actually believed . . ." He held her at arm's length, his gaze raking her with thoroughly blatant desire. "Trust me, Rosalind, you don't lack a damned thing. Except the good sense to stay the hell away from a man who spends his nights lusting after you."

Her breath caught in her throat. The truth of his need was written in his face—in the starkly drawn jaw, the haunted eyes . . .

The lips lowering to hers again. She groaned as she surrendered to his kiss, with a thrill born of knowing that he desired it, he desired her.

Worse still, she desired him. Until now she'd resisted him only by reminding herself how he used seduction to drive her away. But if he truly wanted to seduce her, she was hopelessly lost—because God knows, she wanted it.

From the way he kissed her, he realized it, too. He tore down her barriers as if they were straw, scattering them like forgotten treasure beneath the griffin's talons.

It took all her effort just to angle her lips away to beg. "I know you're not always the rogue you pretend to be, Griff," she murmured desperately against his whisker-rough cheek. "Please . . . please don't play the rogue now. For once, play the gentleman."

She should have known better.

"It's not the gentleman you want." He kissed her ear, worshiping it with his mouth and then his tongue. Excitement spun through her body in widening waves. "And why shouldn't I play the rogue when you're playing the wanton?"

Blast the man for knowing her secret vices so well. Her hands already mocked her protests by sliding around his waist. His chest was nearly naked, with only a lawn shirt covering it. She could feel his ribs through the fabric, feel his muscles flex and purl beneath her questing, curious fingers. The intimacy of touching him so freely intoxicated her.

His hands swept down her arms to her waist to urge her against his bulging trousers. "You're tempting me again," he rasped against her ear.

"Then release me."

"You first." He pressed hot, openmouthed kisses along her jawline. "I'll let go if you will."

She couldn't. She wanted to, she earnestly did. Griff's caresses fogged her mind when she needed to think clearly. But she was incapable of letting him go.

Feverishly, she tried another tack. "If you don't stop this, I'll . . . I'll tell Papa." It sounded ridiculous, a child's threat, and she regretted the words as soon as she said them.

Especially when he chuckled in her ear. "I'd like to hear *that* conversation." He nipped at her earlobe, then mimicked her in a low voice, " 'Mr. Brennan kissed me when I let myself into his locked bedchamber and fell asleep by his bed.' " His breath warmed her ear. "You might as well tell him you came to me willingly."

"But I didn't!" she protested, arching her head away from him. "And I certainly didn't mean to fall asleep!"

He branded her neck with a searing kiss. "I suppose you didn't 'mean' to prance about in your wrapper the night we met, or let me kiss you in the orchard." Walking her backward to the bed, he growled, "Little girls who play with fire shouldn't go crying to Papa when they get burned."

Taking her by surprise, he tumbled her back onto the bed, then quickly covered her body with his, fitting himself between her legs, lying in the valley of her skirts between her thighs. His heavy weight and intimate position should alarm her; instead it felt indecently delicious.

"I'm not a little girl," she whispered fiercely.

The eagle gaze of the griffin traced a greedy path down her neck to where her breasts, rising and falling more quickly under his rapacious look, nearly spilled from her gown. "No," he said in a husky whisper, "you're definitely not a little girl." He shifted one hand to cup her breast through her gown, kneading it so scandalously she gasped. "But you've tempted and teased me for days, my sweet, and now it's time for a reckoning."

Delectable shivers danced down her spine. How would a griffin take a reckoning? she wondered with a frisson of excitement. But she knew. Oh, yes, she knew.

Because his lips now took a reckoning of hers, pillaging every inch without conscience. His tongue took a reckoning of her mouth, plunging rashly, possessively into its depths. And his hand slipped underneath her back to take a reckoning of her gown's fastenings, finding them shamefully easy to tear loose.

She wrenched free of his mouth as he worked her gown from her shoulders, then slowly down past her breasts. "Griff, you can't—"

"Clearly, I can," he said hoarsely. He abandoned her gown at her waist only to reach for her chemise ties.

Eyes widening, she caught his wrist. "Do you intend to ruin me?"

His gaze locked with hers, wild, needy . . . insistent. "No. Only to satisfy some of my cravings. And yours." To her utter shock, he bent forward to drag the tie of her chemise loose with his teeth. A rakish grin crossed his face as her chemise gaped open to reveal more flesh. "Let me look at you. Let me see what you 'lack,' my sweet." He shook his wrist free of her hand and dragged down her chemise to bare a plump breast for his dark, devouring gaze.

His breathing quickened, grew ragged. " 'From the east to western Inde,' " he quoted softly, " 'No jewel is like Rosalind.' "

"You're a devil indeed to use Shakespeare against me," she protested, though secretly delighting in his fulsome compliment.

And the heat of his admiring gaze that sparked a fiery blush to lick along her naked skin. Dear God, this was more than playing with fire—it was playing with gunpowder, with pistols, with cannons.

That was the trouble—danger made it even more thrilling.

Then he bent his head toward her shamelessly naked breast. "Griff, what do you think you're doing?" she whispered in alarm.

"Tasting my favorite variety of plum," he quipped, then closed his mouth around the rosy nipple.

She'd never been so shocked. But shock gave way to excitement at the first devilish flick of his tongue. Soft sighs spiraled out of her as he began sucking and teasing and caressing her breast. Enthralled, she slid her eyes shut to savor the wonderful heated pleasure. Oh, heaven . . . this was heaven . . . It was turning all her insides wild. His fingers slipped inside her chemise to pluck at the nipple of her other breast, and she nearly fainted from the surge of sheer delight.

When she made some low sound in her throat, he stopped sucking her breast to murmur roughly, "You've convinced me about the sweetness of plums, Rosalind. I'm a convert forever."

He tweaked her other nipple, and her eyes shot open at the tumult it unbridled deep in her belly. He was watching her face roguishly. "Shall I taste another?" His eyes gleamed at her as he kissed down the slope of her breast into the valley, then licked his way up the other side. "Would you like that?"

"Yes, oh yes." The words were out of her mouth before she could stop them.

With fervent hunger, he tasted and sucked, and she arched up for more, clutching his head to her breasts as he alternated between each with headier and headier caresses. His hair was rumpled satin in her hands, a delight to stroke. But she wanted to stroke other things, touch other parts of him, and soon she was curling her fingers restlessly into his lawn sleeves as if she could tear them off just by pulling.

With a laugh, Griff levered himself up from her. "Did you want something else, my lady?"

Wordlessly, her face burning, she unbuttoned his dirt-streaked shirt. His smile faded abruptly, replaced by a look of rampant need. Harsh breaths jerked out of him as he braced his upper torso off her with both arms to allow her better access.

When she'd dispensed with the last button, he rose up on his knees only long enough to pull off his shirt and toss it on the floor. His arms were thicker than she'd realized, his shoulders broader, but that was all she had time to notice before he fell on her again like the ravening half-eagle, half-lion creature he was. She dragged her hands eagerly over warm velvet skin and bold masculine muscle that leapt beneath her touch.

His mouth at her breasts, however, soon made her insensible of anything but a strange urge to thrust her pelvis against him. When she did, he groaned and ground himself into the juncture between her thighs, making her gasp with pleasure.

"If you keep that up, my teasing vixen," he

growled against her breast, "I won't be responsible for my actions."

Teasing vixen, was she? Some naughty instinct made her arch against him again, if only to see what he'd do. He tore his mouth from her breasts, then hovered above her, jaw taut and unyielding as he stared down into her face. Without moving his gaze, he shifted his body off to lie at her side. She couldn't prevent a murmur of disappointment, but it was short-lived, for his hand seized her skirts and dragged them up her legs.

"Gr-Griff?" she stammered.

"Little girls who play with fire . . ." he murmured thickly.

And his mouth crashed down on hers once more. This kiss was blatantly carnal, however, fraught with smoldering flames and dangerous promises. Dimly she felt her skirts clear her upper thighs. Then his hand cupped the sweet aching place between them, startling savage urges to life within her loins. For a moment, all he did was press the heel of his palm against her, kneading her, making her squirm restlessly against the hand that didn't quite satisfy.

Then something slid inside her.

She twisted her mouth free. "What are you . . ." She trailed off as what felt like his finger delved deep, in an intimate stroke that wrung a moan from her. "Ohhhh . . . Griff . . . that's . . . dear God, it's . . ."

"*Indescribable*, judging from your curious inability to speak."

He was gloating over her, blast him, and she couldn't even rouse any anger to retort. "Indescribable, yes. Oh, do it again."

"Witch," he whispered with a devilish chuckle, then did it again. And again. And again, until soon two fingers were caressing her, making her writhe against his hot, hard palm in a restless urge for more.

"You like that, do you?" His voice sounded tense and guttural now, as if it cost him great effort to speak. "You like that, my wanton Amazon?"

She loved it, reveled in its luxury of sensation. If that made her a wanton, then she was a wanton indeed. At last she understood about the dairymaid she'd caught laughing and blushing in the barn with the groom, her blouse all undone and her skirts rucked up around her thighs. Though Rosalind had fled in embarrassment, she'd thought of the woman as a wanton for days after.

Now she knew how easy it was to be a wanton. And how very, very delicious. The strokes of his fingers quickened, tugging her forward into a hidden forest where beasts roamed to ravage virgins as he ravaged her. Yet she wanted his ravaging . . . oh, yes . . . she felt as if she were running through the woods to meet it . . . faster and faster as he drove deep into her . . . over and over and over . . .

The explosion came like quicksilver lightning, tightening her loins, dragging a low, shameful cry from her lips as she arched into his hand.

She finally sank back onto the bed, half-sated, half-bereft, though his thigh still lay heavily across hers and his fingers lingered inside her. A second passed, during which the only sound in the room was his rapid breathing and her faint gasps, before he withdrew his hand from between her legs and wiped it on his trousers.

Sudden embarrassment seized her. Trying to hide her face from him, she turned her head into the coverlet, but couldn't escape him there, for it smelled of him, musky and male.

"Rosalind . . . damnation, Rosalind . . ." he growled as he bent over her to scatter ardent kisses along her neck, her jaw, her cheek. His whiskery skin scraped her, heightening the varied delights of his kisses. Then his breath warmed her ear. "Touch me, too," he whispered. "I want your hands on me. Please . . . Only a little . . ."

Her gaze flew to his. Touch him? All this time he hadn't asked her to do anything, hadn't even said *please*. But the unquenched ache of desire hardened all his features as he stared down at her.

He caught her hand and flattened it against the bulge in his trousers. "Touch me, my sweet, or I'll go mad."

She nodded fiercely, overwhelmed by a desire to please him as he'd pleased her. When she curled her hand around the clothed rigid flesh, it jerked beneath her fingers.

Groaning, he shoved it against her hand. "Yes, darling Rosalind . . . like that but . . . harder . . ."

She smiled with feminine satisfaction as she took firmer hold of it. With a growl, he thrust against her hand, then hungrily drove his tongue inside her mouth with deep, bold strokes

She rubbed against the stiff thickness in his trousers, increasing the pressure as he caressed her breasts and lavished fiery kisses over her cheeks and brow. Her curiosity about that part of him intensified until she cursed the layer of kerseymere that separated her hand from his flesh. Well, if he could pull up her skirts . . . She fumbled to release the buttons of his trousers.

He froze and caught her hand to halt it. "No, my sweet. I already want you beyond endurance." Raw need sculpted his face. "And if you take my cock out, I swear I'll bed you, virgin or no."

For a moment, she simply stared at him stunned, the word *cock* ringing in her ears, so crude and coarse. Then the rest of his sentence hit her, and she realized the enormity of what she was doing. What she'd just done.

"Dear God," she whispered as horror swept over her. She jerked her hand back from him. "Dear God, oh, dear God . . ." she kept chanting as she rolled off the bed.

Frantic to cover herself, she grabbed at the front of her gown and yanked it up, but it wouldn't stay because he'd unfastened it. Vainly she twisted her arms behind her back to reach the buttons while sheer mortification overtook her.

He leapt from the bed with a curse. "Calm down; you'll tear it!"

"Blast you!" she whispered, as he moved behind her and began deftly fastening the buttons. Her breath stuttered from her in quick gasps. How humiliating to have to rely on *him* to hook up her gown. And why must he be so very good at it? That could only mean one thing.

"You probably do this all the time," she said with irrational jealousy, "play the lady's maid for all your women—"

"*All* my women?" he bit out. "You make it sound as if I have a damned harem."

"For all I know, you do!" It dawned on her that she hardly knew him. He might actually keep a mistress. Or two or three . . . He'd probably had virgins before, too, prettier ones than she.

Her heart sank under the horrible thought. "How you must be congratulating yourself on seducing me into acting the wanton not once, but *twice*!" she lashed out. How could she have been so reckless?

"Seducing you?" He swung her around to face him, frustration tightening his features into a scowl. "Don't blame me for this! I warned you what could happen. I didn't ask you to come here, of all places! I tried to throw you out!"

It was true, curse him. She'd brought this on herself. Even now, with his hands gripping her shoulders and his bare male chest only inches away, all firm and muscled and sprinkled with hair, she wanted to have him kiss her again, take her back to the bed.

She covered her face with her hands. Dear God, she truly was a wanton. "You're right." She pulled away from him. "I'm entirely at fault."

"I didn't say entirely—"

"This can't happen again, do you hear? It mustn't! You have no interest in marriage and I—"

"Want to be an actress," he finished coldly. "Yes, I know. You made that perfectly clear before."

She lifted her head to stare at him. An actress? Dear God, that dream seemed so remote from this wretched muddle. And she couldn't help noticing that he hadn't denied his lack of interest in marriage.

Knowing his past, she'd be surprised if he had any pangs of conscience about what they'd done. He certainly wasn't the sort to marry a woman who practically threw herself at him every time he kissed her.

Not that she *wanted* the rutting beast to marry her. No, indeed! The last thing she needed was an impudent, devious man of affairs with a criminal past ordering her about.

Still, if he and his employer stayed here much longer, she didn't know how she'd resist him. She'd never excelled at self-denial. If he continued these . . . cursed sweet seductions of his, he would either take her virtue, leave her with child, or both. It was one thing to be a spinster and quite another to be a ruined pregnant spinster.

She must stop this madness. She must do something to put Griff—and his employer—out of harm's way, before she succumbed entirely to him and Juliet married Mr. Knighton. She could think of only one way, one plan that might work.

Bending to scoop up her fallen shawl, Rosalind headed toward the door.

"Where are you going?" he ground out from behind her. "We must discuss this."

"What's there to discuss? We agree it shouldn't happen again, and I intend to take steps to ensure it doesn't."

"Take steps? What the hell do you mean?"

She hesitated at the door. "I've been foolish and selfish. I thought I could stop it."

"Stop what?"

"All of it. Your being here. Juliet's marrying Mr. Knighton. But I've tried and I can't. And the longer I wait, the more chance . . ." *That I'll yield to you.* She sucked in a painful breath. "There's only one way to stop it. Helena won't marry him, and I refuse to let Juliet marry him, so that leaves only one of us to offer herself in marriage."

She forced herself to meet his gaze, to say the words that might buy her temporary protection. "Me."

Chapter 12

Nobody can boast of honesty till they are tried.

Susannah Centlivre, English playwright,
The Perplex'd Lovers

Griff stared at Rosalind, dumbfounded. His Athena stood there with her hair tumbled down about her shoulders and her lips still reddened from *his* kisses, and she talked of marrying another man? Daniel, whom she believed to be her cousin?

He must have misunderstood her. "You've obviously scattered my wits. I could have sworn you just said you wanted to offer yourself in marriage to Knighton."

She swallowed, her gaze fixed to the floor. "That's precisely what I said."

The thought of her planning to marry *any* other man after the intimacies they'd just shared sent rage boiling up through him, unreasonable, unpredictable, and ungovernable.

"Over . . . my . . . dead . . . body," he enunciated in a low growl.

Her head shot up and for a long moment, she stared at him speechlessly. Then stubbornness glinted in her eyes, and she headed for the door again. He grabbed her by the arm, forcing her around to face him.

"Let go!" she cried. "You have no say in this whatsoever!"

"Why the hell not? You nearly let me bed you! That gives me all the say I need!" She opened her mouth to retort, but he cut her off. "Don't try to convince me you were unaffected by our activities. This time I know better. I forbid you to marry him when you obviously want *me!*"

"You *forbid* me? Why, you arrogant bastard—you have nothing to do with it!"

The word *bastard* reverberated in the room, striking an ancient chill along his spine that evoked Eton's cold garrett and the cruel taunts in the halls. Icy fury froze his blood as he backed her against the closed door and planted his hands beside her shoulders to trap her. "You didn't seem to mind my arrogance or my bastardy a few minutes ago when I had my fingers inside you."

For a moment she only gaped at him, two spots of color blooming high on her cheeks. Then she slapped him, the impact of her hand against his cheek echoing in the room. "How d-dare you!" she sputtered. "Y-You are the crudest man I've ever met!"

"Not half as crude as Knighton, trust me," he snapped, thinking of Daniel's frequent visits to the London trollops. "Nor even as crude as you, my sweet, who are leaving one man's bed to throw yourself into another's."

He might as well have struck her back, for hurt

drained her eyes of their sparkle and leached her face of color. With a strangled whimper that would have melted stone, she slumped against the door, turning her head to lay her cheek against the oak panel. "That should not surprise you. You've already noted that I'm a wanton."

Tears trembled on her lashes, flooding his conscience with guilt and dissolving his anger. Damnation, he'd made her cry. Self-loathing filled him as he shoved away from the door. What kind of monster had he become?

That was easy to answer: the green-eyed kind.

He was jealous. Of himself, for the love of God! He'd never been jealous in his life, and this was beyond ridiculous. If she wanted to marry "Knighton," that was *him*. If by some chance she actually wanted Daniel—which he doubted—Daniel wouldn't marry her anyway. So why torment her?

"Damn it, Rosalind, I didn't mean . . ." He rubbed the cheek she'd slapped, which still stung. He should have known his Amazon would give as well as she got. Not that he didn't deserve it. "I shouldn't have said that. Any of it. I know you're no wanton."

At her long silence, he swung his gaze back to her. She was staring past him now, tears streaming down her face and her shoulders shaking with the fruitless effort to contain them.

Something tore inside him. "You're *not* a wanton. It's not your fault I took advantage of the attraction between us."

"But it's . . . my fault that I . . . let you." She was sobbing now, struggling to speak between great gulps of air. "That's why I . . . must end this."

He didn't know which was worse—her pitiful sobs or her determination to get away from him. Forcing himself to stay calm this time, he approached her. "End it how? By marrying Knighton?"

"Would you have me . . . marry you instead?" She groaned, then added quickly, "No, forget that I said it."

He went very still. He *could* marry her, couldn't he? Until now, he'd been convinced she wouldn't consider him—or rather, Brennan—as a prospective husband. But if she would take him as Brennan, thinking there was no advantage to such a marriage, then she'd surely take him as Knighton—

Damnation, what was he thinking? That couldn't be what she'd meant. "I thought you wanted to marry for love," he said softly, searching her face for a sign of her true feelings.

Rubbing her tears away with her fist, she bent her head to focus on the shawl she twisted in her hands. "Yes, of course. I couldn't possibly marry you."

The sharp words scraped at his pride, a reaction he tried doggedly to ignore.

She lifted her tear-streaked face to him. "Besides, you don't want to marry, do you? You said so in the deer park. You said other matters concerned you more than marriage."

Other matters. Memory slammed into him. He couldn't believe he'd been so caught up in this that he'd forgotten his situation. If he married Rosalind, he'd have to reveal his identity, what he wanted . . . everything.

He stared down into her face, so hesitant, so expectant . . . so enticing. The possibility of marrying her tantalized him. She would belong to *him*, every fascinating, delightful, lush inch of her. And all he had to do to have her, aside from convincing her to marry the "wicked" Mr. Knighton, was—

Give up his plans for China.

He groaned. She wouldn't understand his purpose or accept it, not Rosalind with her lofty morality. Delegation or no, she'd certainly never marry him if she knew he planned to strip her father of his title. So marrying her would mean giving up the other.

It would mean letting Swanlea win. *Your pride balks at letting their father win . . . I know you want vengeance . . .* Ruthlessly, Griff shoved Daniel's words from his brain. This was not about pride or vengeance. It was about business, that's all. A very large, very significant business with hundreds of employees who depended on him.

With a low curse, he whirled away from her to pace the room. It was madness even to think of marrying her with so much at stake. For the love of God, the woman even said she didn't want to marry him. What sane man would consider choosing such a woman over the possibility of expanding his business threefold?

Daniel would, he thought. *Women of Lady Rosalind's kind are denied to me and always will be. You don't know how fortunate you are.*

He stiffened. Daniel was wrong. Griff knew precisely how fortunate he was—to have a growing company on the verge of becoming a major power in the world of trade. Unlike his sentimental man of affairs, he could appreciate that advantage.

So marrying her—telling her the truth—was out of the question. Unfortunately, however, she wouldn't be making her foolish offer to *him*, but to Daniel, and Griff couldn't let it go that far. If she offered herself as wife to "Knighton," Daniel would have to refuse. Swanlea would demand that Daniel offer for one of the others, and when he didn't, would throw them both out. That would end Griff's search for the proof.

He must change her mind on this. He faced her,

again noting with a stab of guilt her fruitless struggle to contain her tears. Damn the woman—could she never do anything delicately? The sight of her so vulnerable cut him right to the heart.

He steeled himself against it. "You said you wouldn't marry me, so why would you marry Knighton? You don't love him either, do you?" When she shook her head no, he couldn't stop himself from adding, "So you've decided to be mercenary. His wealth has convinced you."

"No! How could you think it?"

He didn't think it, not really. Although he'd grown accustomed to grasping women in recent years, she'd never struck him as one. But he wished she were. It would be easier to hold fast to his purpose if she were a greedy harpy.

"Why then?" he asked quietly. "As I recall, you swore *not* to marry merely to save Swan Park."

She took a shuddering breath. "Unfortunately, Juliet has no such compunction. I didn't realize until today how strongly she feels on the subject."

"Then let *her* marry him, if that's what she wants!" Because Lady Juliet was the sort to wait until Daniel proposed, which Griff would never allow to happen.

"But she doesn't want it—that's the trouble. She simply has this . . . insane determination to make sure we don't lose our home."

"He has to ask her first, and to my knowledge, he has not." *Nor will he.*

She tilted up her chin. "Then my proposal will help him make up his mind. That's all I want—to have this blasted business decided."

"Even if it means you marry Knighton?" he asked hoarsely.

Her gaze skittered away from his. "Yes."

He strove mightily to control his temper. "What if he refuses?"

"He won't, unless he decides not to marry *any* of us. I intend to make him a very good proposal. He'll get no better from my sisters, so if he won't take mine, he might as well leave."

Damn her. She placed him and Daniel in a devil of a position. And what the hell did she mean by "make him a very good proposal"?

"If you do this," he warned in a last-ditch effort to prevent her from forcing Daniel into a choice, "I'll tell Knighton about our intimacies. He won't want a wife who's been carrying on with his man of affairs."

Her gaze shot to his, eyes glittering like a ruin of crushed gold and green glass. "Tell him if you wish. Though I don't think he'd want a man of affairs who's been toying with his respectable female cousin."

Griff groaned. She would then expect Daniel to dismiss him or something absurd like that. He couldn't win.

She squared her shoulders. "Besides, such . . . intimacies won't happen again no matter what his decision, so it hardly matters."

Absurdly, that pronouncement infuriated him. "You can't offer to marry him," Griff growled.

"Why not? So far you've given me no compelling reason against it."

She tossed back her head. By God, she'd never looked more tempting. With her hair wild and free, her cheeks and lips flushed with color, and her hands planted on her abundant hips, she was the very essence of warrior queen preparing for battle. A sensual, desirable warrior queen.

Damn her to hell. Giving her no warning, he

stepped forward and caught her head to hold it still, then kissed her hard, driven by a mix of desire and yes, jealousy. Though she tried to wrench free, he refused to relent until she opened her mouth and took him inside. Then he thrust into it over and over, hungry, desperate. He sandwiched her between his freshly aroused body and the door. With a whimper of need, she strained against him and locked her arms about his waist. That only enflamed him more.

In seconds, he had his hand in her bodice kneading her soft flesh, thumbing her sweet nipple, inciting himself to madness again. Barely conscious of anything but pure raging lust, he ground his erection restlessly into her loins.

She stiffened. Then she shoved him hard, sending him stumbling back away from her. With the look of a wounded animal, she fumbled to straighten her clothes.

"You wanted a compelling reason?" he snapped. His breath came in desperate gasps as he strove to regain control. "That ought to be compelling reason enough for you."

She dragged her shawl around her shoulders and clutched it tightly to her chest. "It is. It's a compelling reason why I *should* marry him," she whispered. "Because if this goes on any longer, you'll use my desires to make a h-harlot of me."

"Rosalind—" he began, but before he could say more, she tore the door open and fled into the hall. He ran out after her. "Damn it, woman, come back here—"

He skittered to a halt as he realized he wore no shirt, no coat, no waistcoat. Although the hall was empty, he couldn't run after her like this. Not unless he wanted the entire household to know what they'd been doing.

A string of oaths poured out of him as he watched her bolt for the stairs, then hurry down them. Surely she didn't mean to find Daniel *now*. For the love of God—

Racing back into his room, he dragged on his clothes, cursing at the endless buttons defying all his attempts at speed. He had to stop her. He had to talk to Daniel and make some decision about how to handle this before she reached the man.

He had to keep her from ruining everything.

Rosalind rushed down the stairs, wiping away tears with every step. The blasted double-dealing wretch! Griff was outraged that she would marry his employer, yet he wouldn't think of marrying her himself. No, he wanted only to dally with her, to take her virtue and her self-respect. And he knew he could do it, too, with the merest brush of his hands over her wayward body.

She burst onto the first floor, not even stopping to glance behind her. Griff might be following her. He seemed determined to prevent her in this, though she didn't understand why. He acted like a jealous husband, only he wasn't her husband nor ever planned to be. All the same, he could cause trouble if he found Mr. Knighton before she could make her proposal. She must reach Mr. Knighton first.

She strode quickly along the gallery toward the billiard table. To her vast relief, Mr. Knighton was still playing billiards with Helena, though it must have been two hours now at least. Rosalind noted wryly that they'd dispensed with the farce of the chair. Helena braced her body against the table and balanced on her good leg as she aimed.

Rosalind heard the knock of ivory against wood all the way down the gallery, then saw Helena glance up at Mr. Knighton with a taunting smile.

Juliet was right—it *was* a pity that Helena wouldn't marry him. He was such a charming man. But somehow she couldn't imagine elegant Helena with raffish Mr. Knighton.

They looked up as Rosalind approached. When Helena's eyebrows lifted half an inch at least, Rosalind realized she probably resembled one of Macbeth's witches with her hair tangled around her shoulders and her gown utterly disordered. But she gave her sister no chance to remark upon it.

"Mr. Knighton, I hate to disturb you, but I must speak to you in private. It's a matter of some importance."

Alarm rose in his rawboned features as his gaze scoured her from head to toe. "Why . . . of course, Lady Rosalind, if you want." He cast Helena a quizzical glance, and she shrugged in response.

The sound of a door slamming upstairs quickened Rosalind's pulse. Griff, blast him. "We can talk downstairs in Papa's study," she said urgently, and gestured to the stairs. "This way."

"Can't it wait until I finish my game with your sister?" Mr. Knighton protested. "It shouldn't take us more than a few minutes—"

"No!" She caught their exchange of glances and deliberately softened her tone. "No, it must be now."

"Very well, if you insist." He offered her his oak of an arm, and she took it, trying to ignore the unmistakable tramp of booted feet nearing the stairs on the floor above them.

Thankfully, they made it into the east-wing staircase without Griff having emerged from the west-wing staircase. Nonetheless, she hurried Mr. Knighton down and into her father's study with all due haste.

"What's this about?" Mr. Knighton asked.

She shut the door and fumbled for her keys, but

they'd apparently fallen out of her skirts when she was in Griff's room on his bed . . .

Blast, she thought, a blush heating her cheeks. Well, perhaps Helena wouldn't tell Griff where they'd gone or he wouldn't think to ask. Perhaps he wouldn't even follow her. She could always hope.

Swallowing hard, she left the door to face her massive cousin. He'd planted himself in front of Papa's desk like a pugilist awaiting a fight, his expression wary. Now that the moment had come, she felt panicky. Curse Griff for forcing her into doing this before she'd had all her plans settled.

And curse Papa for making it necessary in the first place. How fitting that it should happen in Papa's study, where his presence lingered in every emblem of power—the leather-bound books, his massive chair, the Swanlea coat of arms on the wall. Well, she'd satisfy Papa for the moment, but only to gain time to undermine his plans.

Yet how did a woman convince a wealthy man to marry her when all she possessed was a tiny dowry and no fine qualities to speak of? What could she possibly offer to tempt him?

Something must. She had to make this proposal appealing enough so he'd accept it. Otherwise, Juliet and Papa would continue with their plans, and she'd still have to deal with Griff.

"Lady Rosalind?" he prodded. "If you'd rather do this later—"

"I have a proposal for you," she blurted out.

Eyes the color of wet slate examined her. "What sort of proposal?"

Think, blast it! "I know Papa is interested in having you marry one of us. And I gather you're considering the possibility."

He looked startled. "Um . . . well . . . Yes, I s'pose I am."

"Have you—" She broke off as footsteps sounded in the hallway, heading for the study. She edged toward Mr. Knighton and lowered her voice. "Have you made up your mind on the subject?"

Mr. Knighton tugged nervously on his cravat. "Lady Rosalind, this is . . . a bit irregular, isn't it? I can't exactly—"

"Because if you haven't, I'd like to suggest that you choose me."

The color drained from his face. "Choose you?"

"For a wife, blast it!" She struggled to contain her temper, then added more evenly, "I wish to marry you." That was about as forthright as a woman could possibly be, short of dragging the man bodily to a church. "What's more, I think I can suggest terms that will make you want to marry *me*." As soon as she thought of them, which had better happen this very moment or she was sunk.

The door behind her swung open so hard it slammed back against the wall, making both her and Mr. Knighton jump. Curse it all, couldn't Griff have waited a few minutes more before blustering in here? And what the devil did he plan—to lay out everything that had happened between her and him?

She gritted her teeth. Not if she could help it.

"I must speak to you, Knighton," Griff ground out behind her. "Now!"

Mr. Knighton's mouth opened, but nothing came out. His bewildered gaze swung from Griff to her and then back to Griff. He surveyed his man of affairs questioningly. Then he turned to regard her just as consideringly. At last a strange little smile, like that of a jester amused by his own jokes, spread over his face.

He settled his hip on her father's desk and braced one hand on the oak surface. "I have to speak to you, too, Griff. Do come join us. We're in the midst of a fascinating discussion—one I believe you'd find interesting."

Rosalind colored to the roots of her hair. She didn't have to look behind her to feel Griff throwing off sparks like a bonfire.

"I must speak to you now," Griff repeated, enunciating every word. "Alone."

Mr. Knighton crooked one eyebrow upward. "It can wait." He gestured to a chair close to Rosalind. "Come sit down. I may need your advice in this matter of Lady Rosalind's."

There was a long pause, then a low curse before Griff entered and closed the door. He pointedly passed the chair to walk instead to the window near the bookshelves.

"I-I see no need for Mr. Brennan to be here," she protested. "This doesn't concern him."

"*Everything* concerns my man of affairs," Mr. Knighton retorted. "I make no decisions without his advice. So if you want my attention, you'll have to speak with him here."

Groaning, she risked a glance at Griff and instantly regretted it. He leaned against the windowsill, arms crossed over his crookedly buttoned waistcoat and his tailcoat, which sorely needed ironing. Wild strands of inky hair hung down over his creased brow, and he wore no cravat.

But worst of all was the way he stared at her. If eyes could strip a person, his had already shredded her garments where she stood, as if to remind her that he knew her true self and wouldn't allow her to present a false one to his employer.

Well, she had no intention of presenting a false one. She intended to be perfectly honest with her cousin . . . in what she chose to tell him, that is.

With Griff's daunting presence renewing her resolution, she returned her gaze to Mr. Knighton to find him regarding her with an expression of pure mischief. Though his apparent amusement briefly unsettled her, she refused to let it deter her.

"Go on, Lady Rosalind," he remarked. "I believe you were saying something about wishing to marry me?"

"Yes." She closed one clammy hand around the ends of her shawl. "Exactly."

Griff's audible oath sounded above the anxious beating of her heart.

Mr. Knighton appeared to ignore it. "You mentioned something about terms."

She took firm hold of herself. "Yes. As I said, I think you'll approve of the terms I'm prepared to offer if you marry me."

"What terms would those be?" Griff snapped from his stance at the window. When she glared at him, he added coolly, "Mr. Knighton pays me to assess any contract he considers."

She glanced to Mr. Knighton for help, but he merely shrugged. "He's right. I'd never sign one Griff didn't examine first." The man's cheeks quivered as if it cost him an effort to keep a straight face. "However, I do make the final decisions. So tell me your terms."

"Very well." She twisted the corners of her shawl together and tried not to think of Griff brooding in the corner like his namesake standing guard over the master's treasure. "First of all, I know you have a business to run in London. If you marry me, I won't expect you to bother with Swan Park. I'll continue to run it for you if you wish."

"Quite a noble sacrifice," Griff said acidly, "since you detest running this place."

"Shut up, man," Mr. Knighton commanded. "Let

the woman speak her piece." Then he flashed her a dazzling smile. "Go on."

She swallowed. This was more difficult than she'd expected, rather like putting one's goods on display at the fair. One's worst goods, unfortunately. "Unlike other women you could marry, I wouldn't expect a large sum for pin money nor make exorbitant demands on you for gowns and the like. Such things matter little to me anyway, and if I reside in the country, I should hardly need them."

Mr. Knighton's upper lip twitched. "What if I want you to live in town with me?"

"That would be your choice, of course." She tilted up her chin. "But in such a case, I'd ask that you fit me out in a manner becoming my station and position."

"That could become expensive," he remarked dryly.

"You'd make the decisions in that matter. I'd accept your choices for such expenses without complaint." A loud snort from Griff made her stiffen. "Indeed, I wouldn't cost you nearly as much as most women. I wouldn't even cost you as much as my sisters, for they're both the sort to require costly gowns and jewels." Well, that was an exaggeration, but close enough.

Mr. Knighton rubbed his chin thoughtfully. "That might appeal to most men, but I'm so flush in the pockets these days, I can meet the needs of even a spendthrift."

Her eyes widened. If he didn't care about money, then what? What else did a man want that he might not get from the average wife? Most men wanted beautiful wives, she knew, but she could do nothing about that. If she'd thought she could tempt him

with her person ... but that would never work,
even if she could lower herself to do so. Besides,
men of his sort kept mistresses and—

Yes, of course. *That* was what men wanted—free-
dom to behave as they pleased, wife or no. "I'd be a
most convenient wife in more than cost, sir. No matter where you choose to have me reside, you'd be
free to live your life as you please. I won't expect
you to give up your ... bachelor activities after
we're married."

His eyes fairly twinkled at that. Men were so
bloody predictable. "Bachelor activities? What
exactly do you mean, m'lady?"

Surely he didn't expect her to spell it out. "Um ...
you ... you may spend all night ... out in town, if
that's what you wish."

"You mean, at a club or gambling? I don't much
cotton to gentlemen's clubs, and a man doesn't get
as rich as me by risking his money on cards."

The cursed wretch would indeed make her spell
it out. "Yes, but ... well, I also wouldn't mind if ...
that is ..." She blushed. "If you and some woman ..." Dear God, how could she put this delicately?

"I believe, sir," Griff interjected in a tone of pure
ice, "that Lady Rosalind is giving you permission to
fornicate whenever, wherever, and with whomever
you wish."

So much color flooded her cheeks she probably lit
up the room like a chandelier. But Griff's obvious
contempt stiffened her resolve. What right had he to
judge her? At least *she* wouldn't do any "fornicat-
ing," the way he'd probably done many times. And
had tried to do with her this afternoon, blast him.

She met Mr. Knighton's astonished expression
determinedly. "Though your man of affairs puts it
crudely, he's correct. That's precisely what I'm of-

fering. If we marry, I won't complain about your keeping a mistress or visiting . . . certain ladies." Her tone grew cynical. "I believe I can safely say that few women—my sisters included—would be so accommodating."

"How very true, Lady Rosalind." Griff left his corner to approach the desk where Mr. Knighton quietly watched the two of them. "I would even venture to say that *no* woman would be so accommodating. Unless, of course, she has her own plans for 'entertainment.' A lover kept in abeyance, perhaps?"

She couldn't mistake whom he meant, for he raked her with a heated gaze clearly intended to remind her of how easily she'd succumbed to his advances earlier.

"Griff!" Mr. Knighton growled. "You will not insult—"

"It's all right, cousin," she broke in, her pulse pounding. "I should like to address Mr. Brennan's insinuation." *Before the wretch ruins everything.*

She pinned Griff with a cold look, though her knees threatened to buckle. "I'm being so accommodating to your employer because I recognize our unequal circumstances. He has little to gain by marrying me, whereas I'll gain a great deal. Since my accommodating nature is all I have to offer, I'd be stupid indeed to jeopardize my position with reckless liaisons, don't you think?" When he merely continued to glower at her, she added, "I'm not stupid, however. Nor am I a harlot."

Mr. Knighton's sharp intake of breath made her wonder if she'd gone too far. But she couldn't regret speaking frankly when Griff was being so utterly unreasonable.

Griff stepped closer, and said nastily, "Apparently, Lady Rosalind, I misunderstand your definition of *harlot*. It *is* someone who sells herself for money, isn't it?"

The words hung in the room, so nakedly cruel they knocked the wind from her. She'd thought he understood her reasons, but obviously he hadn't. She couldn't stop her tears. They welled up freely and spilled down her cheeks while Griff looked on, his expression rapidly changing from anger to horror.

Only Mr. Knighton's hand under her elbow kept her from collapsing. Only his words saved her pride. "But we all understand the definition of *bastard*, don't we?" He leveled an accusing glare on Griff. "To my mind, it fits you bloody well."

Griff looked visibly shaken, as if he could hardly believe what he'd said himself. "Rosalind, I . . . By God, I didn't mean . . . Please forgive me. Damnation, I don't know what has come over me."

"Don't you?" Mr. Knighton snapped. "It seems fairly clear to me. Your concern for my assets and reputation has made you forget you're s'posed to be a gentleman." His fingers tightened on Rosalind's elbow. "But you needn't worry overmuch about it. You see, I think Lady Rosalind's offer is sound, even appealing. I'm going to accept it."

Rosalind's shocked gaze flew to her cousin at the same time Griff groaned. Did Mr. Knighton truly mean it? She'd won her position?

The burly man now regarded her with the same kindly concern he'd always shown Juliet, and for an instant, guilt overwhelmed her. He was acting upon the assumption that she'd honor a promise she never intended to honor.

Then he astonished her by winking. Absurdly, that reassured her. He clearly had a trick up his sleeve, though she couldn't imagine what. Or why it would prompt him to accept her offer when his man of affairs had practically called her a harlot.

She darted a furtive glance at Griff, wondering if he'd seen that wink. Judging from his look of pure shock, she supposed he hadn't. He opened his mouth, then shut it, then opened it again. But the only sound that came out was a strangled, "Why?"

"Lady Rosalind has made me an offer I can't refuse," Mr. Knighton explained. "An accommodating wife who'll run my estate for me? What man wouldn't want to have his cake and eat it, too?"

"But you can't— You wouldn't—" Griff began.

"Why not? Her father invited me here for that reason. I'll admit I thought her younger sister was more interested, but as Lady Rosalind says, Lady Juliet would probably not be near so accommodating."

"This is absurd, and you know it," Griff said hollowly.

"I don't find it absurd." Mr. Knighton eyed Griff with a gleam of satisfaction. "Can you think of any reason I should *not* marry Lady Rosalind? Aside from your complaints about her accommodating nature?"

Mr. Knighton seemed to be throwing that word *accommodating* around very freely. And every time he spoke it, Griff stiffened a fraction more.

When Griff made no answer, Mr. Knighton persisted. "Don't you have something else to say on the subject, or has the cat got your tongue all of a sudden? I swear you look as if a whole *delegation* of cats has got your tongue."

At the word *delegation*, Griff's eyes blazed. "I am merely thinking that Lady Rosalind has no idea what she's getting herself into."

"Then p'raps you should tell her," Mr. Knighton said evenly.

Perhaps one *of them should,* Rosalind thought. The interchange between the two men bewildered her. They spoke words she understood, but hinted at other meanings. Griff might be right—she truly had no idea what she was getting into.

Or what she *would* be getting into if she actually intended to go through with it. She pressed the back of her hand to her hot temple. This had become far too confusing.

"Well, Griff?" Mr. Knighton prodded. "Have you got anything to tell Lady Rosalind to dissuade her from marrying me?"

She glanced at Griff, but he refused to look at her. Instead, his gaze was fixed on his employer, full of an impotent rage so fierce it made her catch her breath. At last he said, "No. Nothing. If she wants to marry you and you want to marry her, then go ahead. I intend to continue as if nothing has happened."

What a strange statement. But what struck her most was the contempt with which he spoke it. Was it contempt for her? Or his employer?

Her new "fiancé" faced her with a smile. "Then it's agreed. I'll go to your father after dinner and offer for your hand. Tomorrow he and I will discuss the settlement."

A sudden inspiration seized her. "After that, I know you'll want to return to London to attend to your business, you and Mr. Brennan. I'm sure we've kept you from your work far too long already. I'll stay here and prepare for the wedding, of course."

Mr. Knighton stared at her. The oddest flicker in his gray eyes made her wonder if she'd been too obvious, and he'd guessed what she was about. Behind him, she heard Griff mutter something unintelligible beneath his breath.

Then her "fiancé" smiled. "Don't be ridiculous,

m'lady. My business affairs can wait. I want to take part in all the plans for the wedding. I wouldn't dream of leaving you here to do it alone, and so soon after our engagement."

Blast him. Well, it had been worth a try, and she didn't plan to give up. One way or the other, she intended to delay the wedding long enough to make arrangements for her and Juliet and Helena.

"So don't concern yourself about Knighton Trading," Mr. Knighton went on genially. "Griff and I planned from the beginning to be here at least a week, and it's already half-gone." He shot Griff a glance. "Isn't that right?"

Griff looked as if he were strangling on his own blood, but he managed to choke out a curt, "Yes, sir."

Mr. Knighton turned back to her with an even broader smile. "Now, why don't you go on and start those wedding plans? And don't worry over the expense neither. I don't mind paying for it if need be." His eyes twinkled merrily. "I have plenty of money, y'know. Just ask Griff."

She didn't dare look at Griff, much less ask him such a question. But she was rabidly eager to escape his condemning stares. "Very well," she told Mr. Knighton. "I'll see you at dinner."

"Certainly, m'lady." To her surprise, he placed a proprietary hand in the small of her back and led her to the door. "Until then."

Only after she'd left the study and made her way to her bedchamber did she allow herself to crumple. She hoped she could indeed delay this wedding indefinitely . . . or at least until she figured out a way to escape this nightmare. Because if she couldn't, she might find herself in quite a pickle.

Chapter 13

Jealousy, the old Worm that bites.

Aphra Behn, English playwright, The Lucky Chance

"That was the finest display of jealousy I've ever seen," Daniel remarked as soon as he'd closed the door and was sure Lady Rosalind was out of earshot. "Damned inspiring, as a matter of fact."

He grinned. Griff looked a sight—half-dressed, rumpled, and as angry as a charger with a wasp under its saddle. Daniel could hardly keep from laughing in his face. Served the selfish bastard right to have his plans torn asunder. He hoped that fire-eating spinster dragged Griff into an early grave, her and her *accommodating* nature.

"I am *not* jealous!" Griff hissed. "I'm only appalled that— Damn it, how dare you accept that proposal of hers when you know you're lying about your identity!"

"Me? I'm just carrying on *your* lies. I gave you the chance to tell her everything, but you didn't take it."

196

"I couldn't do that!"

"No, I s'pose not. If you told the truth, the Swan-lea Spinsters would discover they've been clutch-ing an asp to their bosoms all this time." Daniel raised an eyebrow. "Though from the way you and Lady Rosalind look, my guess is that m'lady clutched *your* asp to *her* bosom all afternoon. Or p'raps you even got your asp inside her. Mustn't have been too satisfying for the wench, if it sent her running to me."

Stripping off his coat, Griff stalked grimly toward him. "You goddamned son of a bitch whoreson, I'll break your damned jaw for talking about her like that—"

"You can try." Daniel removed his own coat and waistcoat and stood his ground with fists drawn. There'd be no talking sense to the bloody fool until Griff vented his spleen. Besides, Daniel was spoil-ing for a fight himself. He'd had enough of Griff's sly tactics. "Go on, hit me. It'll be worth it to see which one of us Lady Rosalind fusses over when we show up at dinner with our faces bashed in. Not to mention what her da will think when I ask for her hand this evening."

Griff halted but adopted a fighting stance, clearly so furious the idiot needed all his control to keep from tearing out Daniel's heart with his bare hands.

"But I'm sure you'll think of some clanker to tell them," Daniel taunted, "since you're so bloody good at lying. You wouldn't want to reveal the real reason you fought me—that you're so jealous you can't stand to think of Lady Rosalind touching me, much less offering to marry me." He lowered his voice. "And that you're such a cork-brained arse you won't marry her yourself."

Griff's fist shot out so quick that, even watching for it, Daniel narrowly missed ducking. With a bellow, Griff launched himself at Daniel, knocking them both to the floor. Then they were rolling across the expensive rug, pummeling each other with fists. Griff landed a cracking facer to Daniel's unguarded jaw that Daniel answered with a hard punch to Griff's belly.

Griff's grunt of pain was music to his ears. Christ, but he hadn't enjoyed anything so much since the old days, when they used to siphon off the hot blood of youth with a good tavern brawl. Nothing like a fistfight to knock sense into a man, and if anybody needed sense knocked into him, it was Griff.

They were well matched: Daniel had size while Griff had speed and got in more blows. But Daniel's scrapping had been bred deep and honed early, so he took punishment well, like the great lumbering lout that he was.

Several punches later, however, Daniel realized Griff had something in his favor that overtook Daniel's talents by a furlong: his jealousy. The older man's rage kept him pounding away at Daniel like a bloody blacksmith at his anvil long after Daniel's enthusiasm for the fight had waned and he'd fallen back on defensive moves only.

By the time Griff wore out his fury enough so Daniel could shove free, Daniel was cursing himself for ten kinds of a fool. He was getting too old for this, he thought as he staggered away from the reeling Griff. Next time he needed to knock sense into the blackguard, he'd hit him in the head with a brick, for Christ's sake, and finish it quickly.

They stumbled to opposite ends of the room, clawing breath into their lungs as they faced each other. With satisfaction, Daniel noted the blood trickling from Griff's split lip and the great bruise rising up on his thick noggin. Daniel straightened, then groaned as his own bruised muscles protested the motion.

Rubbing his aching shoulder, he glanced about the room. It wasn't a pretty sight. Books scattered hither and yon, the rug streaked with blood and sweat, chairs shoved aside and the plaque with the Swanlea crest tilted sideways. He scowled at Griff, then winced when even that hurt. "Looks like you got more expenses to lay to your account with the old earl. Between this and the wedding expenses, the affair may cost you an entire day's profits at Knighton Trading."

"Very funny," Griff grumbled as he wiped blood off his face with the cuff of his grimy shirt. "There won't be any damned wedding expenses, and you know it, you fool Irishman."

Daniel chuckled. He always knew Griff's hot temper had spent itself when the swears grew milder.

Stumbling to a chair, Griff dropped heavily into it. "Why the hell did you tell her you'd marry her? What were you thinking, for the love of God?"

Daniel stood swaying, preferring not to stretch his aching muscles by sitting down just yet. "I was thinking I didn't have much choice. What was I s'posed to do? Refuse her? That would get back to her da, and he'd demand I choose one of the others. You haven't found your bloody document yet, have you?"

Griff grunted in answer.

"Besides, I only did what you told me to do. 'Court them,' you said. 'Entertain them and distract them,' you said. I remember it clear as day. 'Do whatever you must to keep them out of my way.' Well, offering to marry her damned well covers all of those."

"Yes, but she'll think you meant it." Casting Daniel a foul look, Griff threw his head back against the chair. Then he groaned and leaned forward again, rubbing at the back of his skull where Daniel had knocked him hard earlier. "Haven't you ever heard of breach of promise, Daniel? Mr. Knighton offered to marry her, but you're not Mr. Knighton. We'll be skinned alive in court."

"You're such an arse, y'know that? The last thing Swanlea will worry about after we leave is some bloody breach of promise. He'll be too busy fighting your assault on his title and his property, not to mention trying to stay alive long enough to get his daughters settled in a cheap cottage in Stratford."

The quick flash of guilt over Griff's features gave Daniel great satisfaction. Maybe the idiot had a conscience after all, buried somewhere beneath all his ambition. Gingerly, Daniel made his way to an overturned chair and righted it, then lowered himself onto the hard seat.

"Besides," he went on, "I can't see Lady Rosalind going after a man for breach of promise, can you? And certainly not one she dislikes so much she's happy to send him off nightly to his mistress and his whores. No, she only wants the marriage to keep Swan Park in the family, and since she can't even do that once you find those papers, she'll most likely be relieved not to have to marry me *or* you." He settled back against the chair. "Especially since the real Mr. Knighton called her a harlot to her face."

Wincing, Griff sank low into his chair. "That was a stupid thing to do."

"I'll say so. You're lucky she didn't have a knife in her hand, or you might be missing your 'asp' now."

Griff shook his head. "I could have handled a physical attack; what she did was worse. I hate seeing a woman cry as it is, but with *that* damnable female . . ." He wearily scrubbed his hands over his face. "She never does it softly—oh, no. None of those discreet tears and delicate sniffs for the Amazon. When she decides to cry, she damned well puts everything into it."

"Then you've seen her cry before," Daniel commented slyly.

Griff stiffened. "What makes you say that? You think I go around making women cry?"

"You said, 'she never does it softly.' Which means you must have seen her do it more than the one time."

Staring past him, Griff shrugged. "So what if I did? Apparently I have a certain . . . talent for making Rosalind cry."

"That's not likely to help you win the girl."

"Win the girl?" Griff snorted. "Surely you don't think that I—"

"I do indeed. It's plain as day you want her, and not just in your bed, either."

"That's absurd," Griff muttered.

Daniel raised an eyebrow. "Is it? A man doesn't insult a woman so bitterly unless something powerful is driving him. You don't hate her, that's for sure. And the way you were letting jealousy ride you—"

"Stop saying it was jealousy, for the love of God! I merely wanted to prevent her from putting you in a difficult position."

"Yes, your concern for me was evident at every moment," Daniel quipped.

Griff scowled at him. "How could I be jealous of myself? It was me she set out to marry, you know. You just happened to be wearing my name at the moment."

"P'raps. Or p'raps she disliked you making advances to her and decided to protect herself by throwing in her lot with a bigger, handsomer chap." When Griff shot up in the chair looking wild-eyed again, Daniel broke into loud laughter. "Look at yourself, you fool. That wench has you twisted into knots."

Griff slumped back into the chair. "If she does, it's with unrelieved lust. I haven't had a woman in a while, she's available, and she's . . . interesting. That's all it is."

"You're a bloody liar, you are."

"That's the trouble with you Irishmen. You're too sentimental about women. You confuse simple lust with a deeper emotion."

Daniel bit back a smile. If Griff couldn't see what he felt for the woman, Daniel sure as hell wouldn't convince him of it. Though he'd enjoy watching the man squirm over it. "So you haven't bedded her yet."

There was a slight hesitation. Then Griff said, "No." He added gruffly, "Though not for lack of wanting to. But I draw the line at seducing virgins."

"Good to know you draw the line somewhere," Daniel said dryly.

With a black scowl, Griff levered himself out of his chair. "At least I'm not deceiving the woman, leading her to think I intend to marry her. I'm not making any false promises. That was your idea."

Daniel wondered if he should tell Griff his suspicion—that Lady Rosalind didn't plan to marry anybody. The woman's eagerness to send him back to London had been too bloody obvious.

"It's curious how Lady Rosalind changed her mind about all this," Daniel remarked. "I thought she told you she didn't want to marry to save Swan Park."

"Yes, but that was before."

"Before what?"

He raked his hand through his already disheveled hair. "Damn it, I don't know. Today she said something about . . . realizing how serious Juliet was. She's marrying you to save Juliet from doing so. Apparently, she's convinced that Mr. Knighton will marry one of them for certain, so she'd rather it was her than her sister."

"Why?"

"I have no idea. That woman doesn't think like anyone else on God's green earth. She says she won't let Juliet marry you . . . me . . . Knighton. Perhaps she really does want to save the estate, and all her other claims were just a lie. I certainly would never have expected her to offer you what she did today."

"Me, neither." No, Lady Rosalind didn't intend to save the estate or even save her sister, despite what Griff thought. She was the fighting sort, not the sacrificing sort, and he suspected this was her new weapon.

Griff didn't seem to realize it, however. As Daniel watched, Griff limped to where his coat lay half-trampled, then picked it up and shook it out. No, the fool didn't know the first thing about women. His experiences were limited to ordering his quiet mother about and bedding the occasional whore or merchant's wife. These days his ambitions gave him little enough time even for that.

Daniel, on the other hand, had come to his ambitions late, having started his fund only a few years ago after a lifetime of reckless living. Daniel had been only seventeen when he'd met the twenty-one-year-old Griff. Even then, Griff had possessed the good breeding, sharp mind, and will necessary to reach his grand dreams. Daniel, however, had simply thanked his good fortune he'd found a generous employer who appreciated his peculiar talents. As fast as he'd gotten his pay, he'd spent it, mostly on whoring in the East End.

After many a night with the light-skirts, however, he'd learned a bit about how the fair sex thought. That was the secret behind his appeal to women. Oh, Griff could give them compliments and quote Shakespeare, but Daniel knew what they wanted. Well, what *most* women wanted, at any rate. A woman like cool Lady Helena—whose beauty excited him even while her manner annoyed him—was still a holy mystery.

But a straightforward woman like Lady Rosalind was easy to read. She was plotting mutiny—he could tell. Just like he could tell she wanted Griff. The air fairly crackled between the two.

Should he tell Griff his suspicions? He folded his hands over his belly and considered the fool, who was righting chairs and restoring books to shelves while cursing under his breath.

No, Daniel didn't think he would. Things had come too easy to Griff in the past few years—success, money, even respect. He wasn't accepted in the highest levels of society, but who cared? Griff had come further in ten years than some men came in a lifetime, but did he realize his good fortune? No. All he could think about was gaining everything he saw as his due, no matter who it hurt or what he had to do to get it.

But Lady Rosalind's proposal had thrown a large rock in the man's mill works, and Daniel would make the arse take it seriously. Daniel had a few rocks of his own to throw, besides.

"In any case," Daniel remarked, "we can turn this situation with Lady Rosalind to your advantage."

"How do you figure that?" Before Daniel could answer, Griff added, "If you're thinking of using this engagement to get the certificate from her father, you can forget it. His letter was clear on that point. I receive my proof on the wedding day and not before."

"I wasn't thinking about your bloody proof," he snapped, then caught himself when Griff glanced curiously at him. "Not about getting it from Swanlea anyway. But now that Lady Rosalind is my fiancée, I've got every reason to keep her busy while you're searching."

Griff hesitated with a vase in one hand, a book in the other. "What do you mean, keep her busy?"

"Courtship, man. Strolls in the garden at night, picnics on the grounds, that sort of thing. She can scarce refuse it when she's planning to marry me. And if anything will keep her out of your way, that ought to."

Griff didn't seem nearly as pleased by that as he should be, Daniel thought smugly.

"I don't know how wise that is," Griff retorted, setting the vase down on a side table none too gently. "You shouldn't lead her to hope for this marriage too much. I don't want her . . . hurt when the truth comes out."

"You can't avoid that," Daniel said dryly. "You're planning to destroy her father, remember? Besides, while you mightn't be interested in marrying, I am." At Griff's dire look, he added, "Not Lady Rosalind, of course. She's too lofty an aim for the likes of me. But courting her will give me practice for wooing some other sweet lass. Isn't that why you said I should do this in the first place? So I could learn to be more civilized? What's more civilized than courting a lady?"

Griff looked as if two demons fought for control of his soul—the jealous monster who had laid into Daniel, and the proud man of trade who couldn't yet admit the selfish nature of his plans for the Swanlea girls.

Pride won out. "Do as you please," he muttered, though the muscles in his jaw fairly creaked with stiffness as he said it. "Just be careful you don't . . . do anything to get us thrown from the place."

Daniel rose to help Griff straighten the room. "Of course not." He would only do what he needed to make Griff see sense. And it mightn't take much more, after all.

Chapter 14

All policy's allowed in war and love.

Susannah Centlivre, English playwright,
Love at a Venture

Griff stayed away from everyone all evening
while the deed was being done. He didn't go
to dinner, and he certainly had no part in Daniel's
talk with the earl, though he wondered what excuse
Daniel could offer for the mangled state of his face.

A more important matter required Griff's attention. He didn't know why it plagued him so, nor
why it carried him to Rosalind's bedchamber after
he was sure she'd retired. He only knew he couldn't
ignore the compulsion.

He rapped softly on her door.

"Just a minute," a muted voice said from inside.

Seconds later, the door opened a crack, and Rosalind's face appeared. The minute she saw him, she
tried to shut the door, but he shoved his foot in to
prevent it.

"Go away!" She glanced worriedly past him to her sisters' doors across the hall.

"I must speak with you."

"We have nothing to talk about."

"It'll only take a moment, and then I'll leave, I promise. Please let me in."

"You're not coming into my bedchamber," she said stoutly.

"Why not? You came into mine." When she glowered at him, he added, "I'll be a gentleman, I promise. I only want to talk, that's all. If you'd rather come out here—"

"No," she said quickly. "No, I-I don't want anyone to see you here."

"Then let me in."

"If you're so eager to speak to me, you can do so at breakfast."

"Considering how I look, I don't intend to be at breakfast." He held his candle nearer his face. "As you can see, I'd frighten your sisters."

Concern flickered in her eyes, and the door widened a fraction, giving him a glimpse of her unbound hair and flame-colored wrapper. He suddenly wondered if this was wise after all.

"What happened to you?" she whispered.

"The same thing that happened to Knighton."

One pretty eyebrow arched up. "You fell down a flight of stairs?"

He chuckled. "Is that what he told all of you?"

"Yes. He gave a very convincing account. Though I did wonder if you might have pushed him down it—you seemed rather angry at him this afternoon."

"I was." He paused. "And how did he explain the disorder in the study?"

"Disorder?" she asked, bristling.

"Don't worry, I'll—he'll pay for any damages."

"You're bloody right he will! Are the two of you so uncivilized you brawled right there in Papa's study?"

Griff shrugged. "He took umbrage with what I said, and I did the same. We settled the matter in the old-fashioned way." He leaned his shoulder against the door. "If you'll let me in, my bloodthirsty Amazon, I'll tell you all about it. If you don't, I'll stand here with my foot in the door until you do. What would your sisters say to that in the morning?"

She sniffed. "Has anyone ever told you you're a bully?"

"Nearly every day," he quipped, remembering her similar comment in the deer park.

Apparently she remembered, too, for a small smile graced her lips. But she still didn't open the door.

His patience was at an end. "Damnation, woman, you can see I'm in no condition to ravish you. After the battering my body took this afternoon, it would resist any attempt at such vigorous activity. So let me in!"

"Hold your voice down, for pity's sake!" The sound of a cough coming from one of her sisters' rooms apparently decided her. "Very well, you may come in for a moment, but I'll hold you to your promise to be a gentleman." She stood aside to let him in, and added, "Though I greatly fear you don't know what one is."

Biting back a smile, he entered the sanctuary and held his candle high to survey it as she closed the door. His lone candle illuminated very little, but it did flash off a great bed hung in green and tall windows draped with velvet curtains of what looked like the same green. Though he couldn't make out the shade, he laid odds it was vivid.

It pleased him to think of her wrapped in orange Chinese silk and lying in the verdant green, like jasper set in jade—full of Oriental mystery and sensuality. He clamped down on a sudden surge in his unruly cock.

He'd sorely lied about his inability to ravish her. He could ravish her quite cheerfully right now, no doubt about it. Then again, it would take a pummeling from *fifty* men before he'd hold back from bedding Rosalind. Even then, he'd want to kiss her and taste her breasts again and . . .

No! he told himself sternly. He'd promised her, though he regretted his promise when he looked at her in her wrapper, all soft and alluring, her lush "assets" only too well outlined by the silk.

She tugged nervously at the ties. "Why are you here, Griff? What do you want?"

What he wanted, he couldn't have tonight. "I want . . . to make sure you're all right."

"I'm fine. Now if that's all—"

"How did your sisters take your news about the engagement? I needn't ask about your father. I assume *he* was overjoyed."

With a little frown, she averted her gaze from him. "Yes, of course he was. He's pleased to finally rid himself of a spinster daughter." She paused. "And my sisters took it as well as can be expected."

Whatever *that* meant.

She looked at him again. "But surely you didn't come to ask after my family."

"No. I'm here to apologize."

Even in the dimness of the candlelight, he could see a welter of emotion in her face. Relief, confusion, and finally, anger. "You'll have to be more specific," she snapped. "What do you wish to apologize for? Trying to seduce me? Calling me a harlot in front of your employer? Acting like a beast—"

"Enough," he growled. "I see you have a number of sins to lay to my account. I won't apologize for trying to seduce you, since the only part of that I regret is not finishing it."

"Griff—" she warned.

"But I do apologize for the rest of it. That's why I came, and to make sure that you're well. We didn't part on the best of terms this afternoon." He had other motives, too, though they were wholly unwise.

She said nothing, but glided out of the small circle of candlelight to stand at a safer distance. Sheltered by darkness, she looked otherworldly, mystical . . . a golden Oriental idol come alive to protect her sisters from encroaching villains.

Villains like Knighton. Him. He rubbed the back of his neck, wondering how else to placate her. "I know you're not marrying Knighton for money, and I certainly know you're no harlot. It's just that when you started talking about being so damned accommodating—"

He broke off as a familiar red haze swam in his head. It had taken him all evening to figure out why her proposal had so angered him. Finally, he'd realized it was because she'd offered "Mr. Knighton" insane liberties to entice him into marriage after blithely dismissing any thought of marrying "Mr. Brennan." And for what? Swan Park, which she claimed to detest? Her sister, who seemed quite happy to marry whoever would save the estate? It made no sense.

"If I . . ." He paused and gritted his teeth, knowing he'd later regret asking this question. But he couldn't stop himself. He'd tortured himself all evening with thoughts of his behavior earlier. "If I'd asked you to marry me this afternoon in my bedchamber, what would you have said?"

The room was so still, he could hear her breathing quicken, a distressing counterpoint to the crackling of the fire. "You didn't ask me to marry you." Her voice thrummed through the darkness, adding low cello notes to that counterpoint.

"I know," he ground out. "But what would you have said if I had?"

"It doesn't matter anymore, does it? I'm planning to marry your employer."

He suppressed the exasperated retort that sprang instantly to his lips. Her ability to make him lose control over his tongue was truly astonishing. Never in his life had he spoken as heedlessly as he had around her today. "Just answer the question, Rosalind," he said, as calmly as he could manage.

"Why?" Bitterness threaded her words. "To reassure you that you could have me if you wanted? To save your blasted pride? Is that it?"

"No, of course not." But that was indeed part of it. Even knowing all her practical reasons for wanting to marry the man she thought of as Knighton, it chafed his pride to watch her pursue that course.

His other reasons were more noble, however. He'd come to realize that he needn't give up the idea of having her as his wife—he needn't change his plans for her father too much to have her. He still wanted the title, of course, but perhaps the matter could be settled less publicly.

Because he wanted both. He wanted the title that would gain him the China delegation and thus propel Knighton Trading into a position of great strength and power. And he wanted Rosalind. In his bed, in his life, forever.

Why shouldn't he have her, damn it? He didn't know for certain that she'd oppose his plans. His cause was just, after all, and Rosalind was the most fair-minded female he'd ever met. Surely she would concede that her father had wronged him and he deserved the title. From what he could gather, she didn't even get along with her father.

She did love her sisters, however. No matter how much money he offered for their financial care, she wouldn't want their names linked with scandal.

But she might brave it if she cared about him. This was the woman, after all, who planned to tread the boards. Surely that would tarnish her sisters' reputations more than what he intended.

He'd come here hoping to determine how she really felt about him before he took such a drastic step . . . Yet she clearly wouldn't tell him as long as he prevaricated. Very well. "Don't answer my other question, then. Answer this one: Will you marry me? Just forget about Knighton and marry me?"

He held his breath for her answer. If she said yes, he'd tell her the truth—all of it. But first, he had to know how she truly felt about him. Beyond desiring him, of course—after this afternoon he knew she desired him. Even now, her glance kept darting nervously to her bed. He was certainly all too aware of the bed himself.

"No," she finally clipped out.

He couldn't believe his ears. She was *refusing* him? How could she, after he'd spent all evening trying to decide whether to offer in the first place! "Why the hell not?" Then it dawned on him. "You think I can't provide for you, is that it? A man of affairs wouldn't have the income to support a wife." That was an answer he could understand, one that would disappear once he told her everything.

"It has nothing to do with your income, I assure you."

A bleak wind blew through him. "Then it's my . . . past you object to."

"No! It's because you don't *want* to marry me. You merely wish to beat Mr. Knighton, to salvage your pride. You can't bear that I'd offer my hand—

even out of practicality—to someone you hold in such contempt."

That stymied him. "What? I don't hold Knighton in contempt!"

"Don't you? I've heard how you speak to him, as if you were his better. Being naturally devious, you've taught yourself the ways of a gentleman, but he doesn't have your talent. He's not as polished as you, despite his supposed Eton education. So you despise him for his crude manners. And your marriage proposal is only an extension of your contempt, one more effort to show him up."

"That's arrant drivel!" Thanks to the masquerade, she'd misunderstood everything! What she viewed as contempt was only authority—years of taking charge had made it difficult for him to alter his behavior easily.

"Tell me something, Griff," she said softly. "If I hadn't gone to him today with my offer, would you even be here now?"

Her pain rang clearly in her words, sobering him. He wasn't the only person whose pride had been wounded. Much as he hated to admit it, her offer had indeed made him consider marriage further, and she was too intelligent not to realize it. But that didn't mean he wanted her because of some feeling of competitiveness toward Daniel, for the love of God. He wanted her for herself.

"It's not what you think," he said, determined to lay her fears to rest. "Knighton and I have an unusual friendship. We've known each other for ten years, and we speak more frankly to each other than most in our situation. I assure you, however, I have no desire to 'beat him' at anything." He swallowed his pride, and admitted, "I want you as my wife— it's as simple as that."

"Is it?" Her voice caught on the words. "All right.

Answer a question that's been plaguing me, and I'll consider your . . . proposal."

"What?"

"What have you been searching for so secretly at Swan Park?"

Damnation, that would be her question. And the simplest answer was the truth. It would certainly correct her misconceptions about his "contempt" for "Knighton," and she'd understand why he'd delayed in proposing.

He sighed. Yes, she'd understand all right. She'd understand that he meant to ruin her father. She might not care, but if she did, then he risked her refusing him. And then she'd also make sure he never got his proof. Why should he gamble when the woman wouldn't even admit she *wanted* to marry him?

"I haven't been searching for anything, I told you," he said evasively. "I'm only taking stock of the property—"

"Balderdash, sheer balderdash." She approached, the candle suddenly bathing her with light that glinted red in her hair and reflected hellfire in her eyes. "Don't treat me like a sapskull. You haven't even spoken to our steward yet or asked to meet Papa's own man of affairs. You would have done both right away if your concern had truly been for the future of the estate. Not to mention that I haven't smelled tobacco on you once. For a man desperate for cigars, you've been dreadfully remiss in smoking them."

By God, the woman had certainly paid close attention to his activities and come to some very astute conclusions. But he would expect no less of his Athena.

He tried another evasion. "If you're so certain I'm

searching for something, then why don't you tell me what you think it is?"

Rosalind heard Griff's question with a hint of alarm. It took all her will not to glance at the foot of her bed where the trunk with Papa's box lay. She'd already glanced at it too many times since he'd been in the room. "I have no idea. That's what I want you to tell me."

"You have no idea what I'm looking for, but you're sure I'm looking for something. If your suspicions are so sound, why haven't you said anything to your father? Had him throw me out?"

His snide tone rankled. She tilted up her chin and glared at him. "I'd planned to do that very thing this afternoon when I discovered the unsealed door to the stairs in your room. But then you . . . distracted me and afterward—"

"Afterward, you went to my employer," he bit out. "Come to think of it, why didn't you mention these suspicions to Knighton when you were offering yourself to him? Or have you forgotten he's the one I work for? You only seem to consider *my* motives suspect, yet I do what he commands."

He had a point, Rosalind thought. If Griff were playing some deep game, Mr. Knighton must indeed have something to do with it. But if they were both in it together, why had Mr. Knighton accepted her proposal when Griff had been so decidedly against it? Something wasn't right here.

"Very well," she said, "perhaps I *will* ask him about it later. But first I want to know what you have to say about it, since you're the one doing the searching."

He glanced away, and his profile gave her a new view of his battered condition, which easily matched that of his employer's. His upper cheek bore an ugly bruise, and the corner of his lip was crusted over where it had been split open.

She tamped down a sudden wave of tender concern. So what if he had fought over her? It meant nothing. Why, she wasn't even sure how much the fight had to do with her at all. Mr. Knighton clearly didn't care enough about her to fight anyone on her behalf. As for Griff . . . well, he was driven by pride, that's all. He seemed to have an inordinate supply of it for a mere man of affairs.

"Believe what you wish about my activities," he finally answered, "but I had no aim other than the one I've professed all along." He fixed her with an earnest look. "Besides, it has nothing to do with us, with why we should marry. I want to marry you. Isn't that enough for you?"

Pain seared her throat, not only at his refusal to tell her anything, but at the flat, unemotional tone of his proposal. He acted as if the very fact of his offering for a spinster like her ought to make her fall down at his feet in gratitude.

Well, he could wait until doomsday for that.

"While I'm terribly flattered that you'd deign to marry me—" she began frostily.

"What the hell do you mean, 'deign' to marry you?" he interrupted.

Tears stung her eyes; she struggled to hold them back. She wouldn't let him see her cry again! "You clearly lack enthusiasm for the prospect, Griff."

"Goddamn it, Rosalind," he roared, "what do you want from me?"

She blanched. "The truth. And some sign that you care about me." When his gaze darkened in a familiar manner, she added hastily, "Not merely about my physical attributes. You've made it perfectly clear you have that sort of 'caring.'"

"I didn't hear you making any such demands on

Knighton," he snapped. "You didn't ask *him* for the truth, or want *him* to care about you."

A shaft of sorrow pierced her heart. *That's because I don't want him to marry me. I want you.*

Dear God, it was true. She *did* want the wretch to marry her. To her shame, she realized she'd relinquish almost anything—her hopes for Juliet's future, her family, even her dream of being an actress—to marry Griff. But only if he truly wanted her.

The trouble was, he didn't. Another man had taken his discarded toy, and that had made him want it back. But not enough to tell her the truth or show that he cared for her. She wasn't even worth that to him.

With a sinking heart, she walked to the door and opened it. "I didn't ask for that from Mr. Knighton, because he'd already offered me something I didn't have—his willingness and ability to help my family."

She swallowed her tears. "You haven't offered me anything that I can see, not even a good reason for marrying me. Given the choice between two men who don't care for me—a gentleman whose offer may only suit my practical needs but who treats me with courtesy and consideration, or a selfish schemer who calls me names and only offers marriage in a fit of pique—I'd be a fool to choose the schemer."

His eyes narrowed to slits. "A fit of pique? The only one having a fit of pique, Rosalind, is you. I didn't offer for you this afternoon when I should have, so now you want to punish me by refusing me. Is that it?"

Her heart twisted in her chest. What was the point of arguing with him? He simply refused to consider anything beyond his own feelings. "Mr.

Knighton was right: you *are* a bastard, and I don't mean in the literal sense. Well, I already have Papa to deal with—I don't need another secretive, selfish bastard in my life."

His eyes blazed in the darkness. "Fine. And I don't need a meddling, suspicious harpy in mine. Enjoy your 'engagement' to your 'gentleman.' I suspect you'll find it vastly unsatisfying in the end."

He strode to the door, started to walk out, then returned to her side. Grabbing her about the waist, he pulled her to him for a hard, thorough kiss. At first she struggled, keeping her mouth firmly closed as he tried to deepen the kiss.

Then he urged her hips against his, forcing her to feel his arousal through her silk wrapper, and to her utter shame she yielded, a complete weakling as always when it came to his seductions. Her mouth opened of its own accord, and with a dark groan of triumph, he conquered it, stabbing his devilish tongue inside.

There in the open doorway to her bedchamber where anyone could see them, he kissed her like a lover, hot and deep, his hands sliding down to cup her buttocks and plaster her against his bulging trousers. He didn't relent until he'd reduced her to a boneless, quivering mass of jelly.

That's when he broke off the kiss to stare down at her, eyes gleaming. "It seems you're right—I *don't* know what a gentleman is. But next time you're with your 'fiancé,' my lady, remember that it isn't the gentleman whose kisses you crave, whose hands you want on you. It's the bastard's. And whether you admit it or not, it's the bastard you want in your bed."

Then the insolent devil left.

Long after he'd gone, she stood there shaking

with unfulfilled need. God help her, he'd spoken the truth. She did want the bastard in her bed.

But if it meant marrying him when he didn't care a farthing for her beyond desire, that was another matter entirely. She still had some say about whom she married, thank God. And though it probably wouldn't be Mr. Knighton, it would definitely not be Griff.

Chapter 15

Good humor, like the jaundice, makes every one of its own complexion.

Elizabeth Inchbald, English playwright,
A Simple Story

Over the next two days, Rosalind discovered that being engaged to a man she didn't wish to marry had decided disadvantages. To her annoyance, despite Papa's joy at the engagement, her sisters lacked enthusiasm. Rosalind had told Helena privately what she really intended, and to her surprise Helena had disapproved. She'd said it was awful of Rosalind to mislead Mr. Knighton like that.

But Rosalind could endure Helena's icy demeanor. It was Juliet whose behavior puzzled her. When Papa had given Juliet the news about the engagement, the girl had burst into tears and fled. Rosalind had scarcely seen her since.

Only today had Rosalind figured out the source of Juliet's discontent. The girl's heart had been set on saving the family and in her eyes, redeeming the grievous blow she'd dealt it with her birth. Rosalind had denied her that chance at redemption.

But Rosalind couldn't regret that. Juliet was too young to act as a virgin sacrifice.

Not that Rosalind was very good at it herself. She'd hoped her offer would rid her of Mr. Knighton; instead, it had drawn him in. Though she regularly protested that she didn't need him around to plan the wedding, the blasted man wouldn't listen. He insisted on spending time in her company, squiring her to town to order a fictitious gown, consulting with her and Cook about a fictitious wedding feast. She began to fear she'd soon find herself standing before a minister who wasn't the least fictitious.

Today he'd proposed a picnic on the grounds for the two of them. She dreaded so intimate an outing, yet she couldn't refuse without rousing suspicion. So she now awaited him in Swan Park's drawing room, trying not to fret and failing miserably.

She was woefully unaccustomed to courtship and certainly to a pretended courtship. Her previous encounters with men had all ended when her admittedly irascible behavior sent them running for the next shire. No man had ever come close enough to pierce her defenses, and she'd been happy with that state, since none of them had appealed to her.

Until Griff. A shiver swept her. Dear God, the last time he'd kissed her . . .

Hot need poured through her veins, despite her memory of his arrogant remarks. His absence the past two days—for he'd avoided her entirely—had illustrated painfully just how much she desired the scoundrel. He might be insolent and uncaring and a complete bastard, but he reduced her to a blithering idiot whenever he kissed her.

Thankfully, he hadn't done so again. He hadn't even been around. Her relief at being spared his unsettling presence had prompted her to ignore her suspicions about where he'd been spending his time. No doubt he was still occupied with searching for . . . whatever was in Papa's strongbox.

Well, that was fine, just fine. Let him search the place, the wretch. She'd tried asking Mr. Knighton about Griff's secret searches, but he'd claimed that his man of affairs merely did his job thoroughly. What a lot of fustian. She'd even told Papa of her suspicions, but he hadn't cared, except to make sure she'd hidden the box well. He refused to tell her what was in it, however, especially now that Mr. Knighton had agreed to marry her. The man would have to be looting the house before Papa would kick him out now, him *or* his man of affairs.

So she'd taken the precaution of moving the strongbox to her wardrobe, beneath her unmentionables. Not that Griff would balk at searching her unmentionables, she thought testily. Clearly, the man was wholly unacquainted with the concept of shame.

Very well—let him have whatever was in the blasted strongbox if he found it. Protecting it had brought her far too much trouble already. Let Griff rifle the house with impunity. As long as he didn't rifle her body with impunity, she was safe.

Now if only he'd stop rifling her thoughts at night in bed—

"Are you ready to go, m'dear?" came a cordial voice from the door.

Startled, she glanced up to find her curst cousin standing in the doorway. She walked toward him with a wan smile. "Of course."

Though his battered face was healing remarkably well, it added to his often incongruous appearance.

Sometimes he put her in mind of a bear bedecked in finery for a fair or the circus, stoically enduring the indignities of his inappropriate attire even though he'd prefer to return to his natural state. Today, however, he was a bear with a picnic basket, and that actually suited him.

"Where should we go, Lady Rosalind? You'll have to find us a spot, since I don't know the place too well yet."

She smiled and laid her hand on the arm he offered. "I fear we have few truly pretty vistas. We've not had a regular gardener for some time now, so our grounds have grown quite wild."

"I don't mind wild."

"Yes, but no doubt you miss London with its well-kept parks and gardens."

His eyes gleamed with mischief. "How could I miss London when I have such lovely company here?"

Having grown accustomed to his compliments over the past two days, she surprised herself by blushing like a green miss. Mr. Knighton might be unpolished, but he possessed a facility for gallantry that Griff lacked. It was a refreshing change from the whirlwind Griff invariably roused in her. But not so refreshing that she'd want the man around all the time. Whereas Griff . . .

She squelched that thought at once.

"Besides," Mr. Knighton went on blithely, "I've got no time for picnics in London, so this is a treat, no matter how wild the view." He cast her a teasing glance as they entered the foyer. "Though after we marry, I'll make time for picnics with my wife."

"That's an inducement to marry indeed," she choked out through the sudden guilt that swamped her. He really was a charming man. A pity she didn't want to marry him.

He led her outside with rough courtliness, and at her suggestion, they struck a path through the gardens and headed toward the woods that lay a quarter mile from the house. Soon they were following a dirt path through ancient oaks, willows, and elms.

"There it is," she said as a sunlit clearing came into view through the trees. "That's where the three of us used to play when we were girls. Papa hung that swing for us. There's even a tree house, though I suspect it's unsafe after all these years. The clearing is my favorite place in Swan Park."

"Looks near to perfect."

It took them a few minutes to reach it along the path, and in that time she grew increasingly uncomfortable. She'd forgotten how secluded it was. The trees formed an impenetrable shield that lent the area a disturbing privacy. Perhaps she should have brought her maid, but she hadn't thought it necessary. Until now, he'd shown no inclination to deepen their relationship.

When they reached the clearing, however, his solicitous behavior made her wonder if he intended to do so today. First, when he spread out a blanket, he apologized for his lack of foresight in not bringing a cushion for her tender hind parts. Then when they sat down to eat, he insisted on serving her himself, offering her the best pieces of chicken, the choicest apple. It felt alarmingly like a real courtship. What would she do if he tried anything more . . . intimate? Though she concentrated on eating, she watched him furtively all the while, alert to any sign of impending advances.

"You're looking fine as a fivepence today, m'lady," he said after devouring his third piece of chicken. When he began licking his fingers, she held out a napkin, and he took it with a grin. "That bonnet's quite fetching on you."

Oh, dear, she'd best squelch this line of conversation. "Thank you, but I'm sure it doesn't compare with what you see in London."

The corner of his mouth twitched. "Y'know, you must think everything in London is better, since you've mentioned its wonders about fifty times in the past two days."

Curse it—she really must learn to be more subtle. "I'm merely curious, that's all." *Curious to know when you'll be returning there.* "But surely most things *are* better—the fashions, the diversions, the people. You must find Swan Park terribly dull after the delights of town."

His face wore the most peculiarly strained expression, as if he tried very hard to keep from laughing. "Not dull in the least."

She took a lusty bite of apple and chewed thoughtfully. "But in London you can go to the opera or the theater every night."

"I don't like the opera or the theater."

"What about the British Museum? Or the Tower of London? I'd so love to see the menagerie at the Tower of London."

"I wouldn't even know what to do in a museum. And with my reputation I'm not venturing near the Tower of London." He was grinning now.

She slanted a glance at him. "What do you find so amusing, Mr. Knighton?"

"You, m'lady."

"Oh?" She wiped her mouth with a napkin, wondering if she had apple juice on her upper lip or something.

"Why don't you just come out and say it, for Christ's sake, and get it over with?"

"Say what?"

"That you want me gone to London so you can stop pretending to be engaged."

Her napkin fluttered to her lap. "P-Pretending?"

"Come now, Lady Rosalind, we both know you don't plan to marry me."

The woods seemed to close in around her. Dear God, how had she given herself away? Could Helena have told him her plans? "Don't be r-ridiculous," she stammered. "Why on earth would you think such a thing?"

"Because you've been trying to pack me off to London since the day we arranged to marry. Not to mention those 'terms' of yours even a dog wouldn't offer. You're not the sort to make an arranged marriage, especially with such poor conditions."

Rising to her knees, she began packing the remains of their picnic while wondering frantically how to salvage the situation. Why must she always give herself away?

"It's all right," he went on. "I don't plan to marry you, either."

Her gaze shot to him. "What?"

"I knew you didn't intend to marry me the day you made that fool proposal."

He was serious! She sank back onto her heels. "Then why did you accept it?"

"For one thing, you presented it so charmingly, I would've felt like a cad disappointing you." He grinned. "But mostly, I liked watching it make Griff jealous."

Heat rose to her cheeks despite her attempt to suppress any reaction. Surely Griff hadn't told him about the kisses and . . . all the other things. Oh, but what if he had?

She tried summoning up righteous indignation. "You don't mean to imply that Mr. Brennan and I—"

"I'm not implying it. I'm coming right out and saying it. I'd have to be chuckleheaded indeed not to notice what's going on between you and my man of affairs."

"There is *nothing* going on between me and Griff . . . I-I mean, Mr. Brennan . . ." She trailed off, face flaming. Dear God, how easily she betrayed herself!

"See here," he said, "I don't mind you being interested in my man of affairs."

"I'm *not* interested in him!"

"That's a clanker."

She glowered at him. "It is not! You have no reason to think I'm lying!"

"No reason? Let's see. Two days ago, you come running from the top floor where Griff's bedchamber is, with your hair down and your clothes rumpled. We go off in the study, then Griff comes in with *his* hair mussed and *his* clothes rumpled, raging about you wanting to marry me. After you're gone, he near beats me senseless over my agreeing to your offer. If you were in my shoes, what would *you* make of all that?"

Cringing at the graphic description, she sat back on the blanket again.

"So let's have some honesty between us. Admit it—you're interested in the man."

"Oh, all right," she grumbled. "Yes. I suppose I am."

With a triumphant smile, he stretched out on the blanket and braced himself up on two elbows. "You don't seem too happy about it."

A bitter laugh tumbled from her lips. "What's there to be happy about? The last time I saw him, he called me a 'meddling, suspicious harpy.' "

"When was that?"

She groaned. This was so mortifying. Thank God she had no intention of marrying Mr. Knighton.

Otherwise, this would squash that hope. Still, it was a relief to have someone to discuss Griff with, especially someone who knew him so well.

"M'lady?" he prodded.

"It was after your fight with him." She ducked her head to hide her blush.

Mr. Knighton chuckled. "Couldn't stay away from you, could he?"

"Don't assume that means anything. He only came to apologize, but as usual he ended up insulting me." And proposing to her and kissing her senseless, but she wouldn't think of that, let alone mention it.

"Oh, it means something, all right. I've known Griff a long time, and I've never seen him act like this around a woman."

"Like what?" she snapped. "Obnoxious? Arrogant? Rude?"

"Jealous." Mr. Knighton crossed his outstretched legs at the ankles. "He usually doesn't care enough about any woman to be jealous or obnoxious or anything else. Since he doesn't have time for wooing, he usually gets what he needs from the light-skirts and goes on about his business."

She didn't like the sound of "gets what he needs." The thought of Griff going to light-skirts for anything bothered her to an astonishing degree.

"You see, Griff is the sort who thinks only of his work," Mr. Knighton went on. "Knighton Trading is everything to him, y'know."

"I did wonder . . . He does seem to know so much about it while you . . . well—"

"Don't know a thing?"

"No, I didn't mean that," she protested, cursing her quick tongue.

He waved his hand dismissively. "It's all right. Griff's the one with the knowledge of trading." He added hastily, "Because of having been a smuggler, you see. He's got the connections, and he manages all of that."

The brains of the concern, she thought. And what advantage did Mr. Knighton bring to it? Not that she could ask; that would be rude.

She glanced at him with avid curiosity from beneath the brim of her bonnet. "So then he's not really your *personal* man of business."

"Er . . . yes. That he is. But most of what he does in that capacity is . . . related to the company." Mr. Knighton cleared his throat nervously. "Anyway, that ain't . . . isn't the point. Here's what I wanted to say, why I arranged for us to have this tête-à-tête."

Mr. Knighton sat up and leaned toward her, his voice turning earnest. "Griff has his eye on you, but he's never considered marriage till now, and he doesn't know how to go about doing it. A fine woman like you— Well, he knows you're far above his station, and he don't feel right asking you to lower yourself. That's the only reason he hasn't offered for you yet. You have to encourage him a bit, show him you like him, and—"

"It's too late for that," she cut in dryly. "Apparently I demonstrated my liking well enough. He's already offered for me."

"What?" He gaped at her. "When?"

"That time I told you about. When he called me a 'meddling, suspicious harpy.' "

Mr. Knighton sat back abruptly. "For Christ's sake, I knew the man wasn't a charmer, but you'd think he'd at least know enough to flatter a girl before he proposed."

"No, he called me that after I turned him down."

"You turned him down?" Shaking his head, he muttered a curse under his breath. "Why'd you go and do that for? You told me you were interested in him." He eyed her suspiciously. "It wasn't because he's beneath you, is it?"

"Don't be absurd. Mama was an actress, and I'd planned to become an actress myself. Why would I care about Griff being beneath me?"

"Lady Helena would care," he pointed out.

Rosalind sighed. "My sister might surprise you. Don't let her coldness fool you. She plays the ice maiden to keep from getting hurt." She cast him a sly glance. "Why? Is she your first choice for a wife?"

He looked as if she'd struck him with a poker. "No, indeed. Lady Helena's a mite too haughty for my tastes." His eyes narrowed. "Anyway, we weren't talking about me. We were talking about why you refused Griff. We both know it wasn't because of this imaginary engagement."

"True. But since he'd never have offered for me if not for this 'imaginary engagement,' I didn't see much point in accepting. He doesn't want me. He's merely angry because you have something he doesn't. That's all it is."

"Is that what you think, lass?" he said in a tone so gentle it made her throat ache.

"It's what I know."

He was silent a long time. The wind soughed through the trees, a mournful echo of her desolate heart. She tried to shake off the blue devils, but despite the sunny day and their lovely surroundings, she failed as miserably as she'd failed for the past two days.

"Tell me something, Lady Rosalind," he finally said. "Did Griff say anything to you about . . . that is . . . did he mention Knighton Trading? Or his work? Did he even say why he wanted to marry you?"

She shook her head. "He didn't say anything

except, 'Marry me. Forget about Knighton and marry me.' Oh, and he said, 'I want you as my wife. Isn't that enough?' "

"Bloody arse," Mr. Knighton mumbled. Then he glanced at her and frowned. "Forgive my bear-garden jaw, m'lady, but that's what he is."

"No need to apologize. I wholeheartedly agree with you." She stared past him at the old swing that mocked her turmoil with its wind-driven dance. "I didn't . . . expect a lot of flattery, you understand. But I should have liked a reason, something other than 'I want you as my wife.' " Her chest felt crushed under a weight of granite. "I should have liked to know . . . he cares for me a little." *And not just my body.*

"P'raps he does. Like most English, Griff's not good at knowing his own heart."

"But he's half-Irish. I thought the Irish were famous for knowing their hearts."

Mr. Knighton suddenly became very interested in picking up where she'd left off in stowing away the remains of their picnic. "Yes . . . um . . . but he didn't grow up among the Irish, you see. His mother was English; he was raised in England." He set the basket aside, then cast her a sad glance. "And we English are a nation of merchants. We know how to make money. We don't know as well how to make love."

He drew up one knee and rested his elbow on it. "That's the trouble with Griff, you see. He's spent his whole life making money—for me, that is—so he's never learned anything else. Now he sees a woman he wants, and he doesn't know why or how. He can't even put it into words for himself, so how can he put it into words for you?"

She thought back to how Griff had behaved—how he'd said over and over that he wanted her, but

wouldn't say why. What Mr. Knighton said made
sense. On the other hand, Griff simply might not
feel anything for her at all.

"Besides, did you tell him how *you* felt?" Mr.
Knighton asked. "Did you tell him you were in love
with him?"

In love with him? She started to protest the very
idea, but no words came out. Because he was right.
She was in love with Griff.

She closed her eyes and groaned. Blast it, she
couldn't be in love with that man! It would be too
cruel of Fate to play such a trick on her! She
couldn't, she mustn't!

But she was. She knew it as surely as she knew it
wasn't returned. Miserably, she shook her head. "I
couldn't tell him something like that. He didn't
even offer to marry me until after my proposal to
you. I couldn't be sure he felt anything for me
except—" She broke off with a blush. "Except . . ."

"Lust?"

The man certainly never minced words. She nodded, her blush deepening.

"There's something you got to understand about
men. A man's got three parts: his brain, his . . . er . . .
St. Peter, and his heart. Each part has got its own
needs, you see?" Glancing into the thick woods, he
sighed. "Griff's always answered the needs of his
brain and his St. Peter. But he's ignored the needs of
his heart, most likely because he didn't hear it calling, didn't even know it was there."

He stared earnestly into her face. "Then he meets
you, and all hell breaks loose. His brain's trying to
figure you out, his St. Peter is crying out for attention, and worst of all, his heart is clamoring to be
heard for the first time in the poor sod's life. All that
clamoring is confusing the man like mad. He

doesn't know it's his heart wanting something, since it never troubled him before. So he's only listening to his St. Peter. He figures if he satisfies it, the rest of the parts will settle down and let him go back to how things were. But that's not gonna work. He just don't know it yet."

She remembered Griff saying during their discussion in the deer park that he wouldn't marry for love, that he didn't believe it existed. *People merely mistake desire for love,* he'd said.

According to Mr. Knighton, Griff was doing the opposite—mistaking love for desire. "What if you're wrong? What if it really is only his . . . um . . . St. Peter?"

"A man laboring under those needs doesn't sniff around a virgin like you, m'lady. Making free with a virgin is a chancy thing, especially a wellborn one. But it's hard for a man in love to stay away from what he loves."

A thrill shot through her. *No,* she cautioned herself, *don't raise your hopes. Griff will only dash them as usual.* "I fear you assume too much about his affections."

"Do I? He damned near beat me to death for accepting your proposal. That isn't the behavior of an indifferent man."

She shook her head, unconvinced. "He merely hated that you'd gotten what he wanted, that's all. The night he proposed, he said nothing about his feelings for me. He kept complaining about you and why I'd marry you over him."

"Why didn't you tell him you didn't plan to marry me?"

"Because I thought he'd run to you and ruin everything, of course."

Mr. Knighton laughed wholeheartedly. "You two

are a pair. If you'd only be honest with yourselves and take a chance on each other instead of all this scheming, you might find you feel the same things."

"Scheming?" She sniffed. "We're not the only ones scheming. What about you? Why didn't you tell him *your* suspicions about *me*?"

"More fun not to." His eyes twinkled in the afternoon sun.

"At least my scheming had a purpose," she grumbled. "Yours was merely for entertainment."

"What purpose? You offered to marry me, knowing you weren't going to."

"I was trying to prevent a marriage, any marriage, with you as long as possible."

All semblance of his good humor vanished. "Didn't approve of me as a husband for your sisters, I s'pose." His jaw tightened as he stared off behind her into the woods.

"No, I didn't. Because you don't love either of them."

His rigid features softened. "You put great store by marrying for love, don't you?"

"Yes. Though Juliet would indeed marry you for your practical advantages. But she's far too young to marry, especially where she doesn't love."

"And Lady Helena would find even Prinny beneath her condescension," he said dryly, "not to mention a great rascal like me."

How strange. Mr. Knighton had brought up Helena *twice* now as a prospective wife. Could he have a serious interest in her?

"Anyway, it's a ticklish business," he went on. "Your father seems set on the marriage."

"Yes." She brightened. "But if you're not, just tell him so and go home. I was afraid you'd marry Juliet if I didn't step forward, but now I needn't worry. So you needn't stay here anymore. You and Mr. Brennan can return to London."

"Trying to get rid of him, are you?"

She stared down at the half-eaten apple in her lap. Turning it over in her hand, she murmured, "Perhaps."

"But he hasn't come near you in a couple of days, has he? So don't be packing us off yet. I'm not ready to run back to London. I like it here."

She eyed him askance. "If you're thinking of staying in order to further a possible marriage between Griff and me, you might as well give that up. It *won't* happen."

"That's not why I'm staying," he protested. "I've a right to look over the estate I'll inherit, don't you think? There's plans to make, improvements to consider."

"Is that your only reason?" She thought of Griff's search, which he'd as much as said was sanctioned by Mr. Knighton. "You have no other purpose?"

"What purpose could I possible have?"

She considered mentioning the strongbox burning a hole in her wardrobe, but decided against it. He wouldn't tell her, and her continued questions might rouse their suspicions enough to make Griff search her room.

"How long will you stay?" she asked. "How long will it take you to 'consider improvements'?"

"A few days, no more. As you said before, I've got a business to run in London."

She smiled. She could endure them a few days longer, especially if Griff continued ignoring her.

"In the meantime," he went on, eyes gleaming, "you and I should still pretend to be engaged, don't you think? It'll keep your father happy and your sister Juliet from running after me. And it'll drive Griff mad."

She confessed she liked that particular idea. "That sounds like fun."

He picked up the half-empty bottle of claret. Pouring them each a glass, he handed her one, then lifted his own in toast. "To short engagements, m'lady."

"To short engagements," she agreed. "But you shouldn't call me 'my lady,' you know; it sounds terribly formal. I give you leave to call me by my Christian name. Besides, every time you say 'my lady' it makes me feel like a dowager duchess with graying temples and a lorgnette." Not to mention that only the servants spouted "my lady" every other sentence, but she didn't want to embarrass him by pointing it out.

"Whatever you wish, m— Rosalind." He sipped his wine, eyeing her over the glass with a teasing look. "But I've seen a dowager duchess or two, and you don't look like them in the least, trust me. You're much too pretty."

Now that she had no more reason to fear his compliments, she could enjoy them, no matter how insincere. "Are you flirting with me, Mr. Knighton?"

"P'raps I am. Do you mind?"

Laughter bubbled up through her throat. "No. I don't think I do."

The rest of the afternoon passed pleasantly enough. They talked of the estate, of the upcoming harvest and Swan Park's dairy. He seemed interested in financial specifics—how much cheese and milk fetched at market, what portion of the profits went back into the dairy, how much they paid the dairymaids. That shouldn't surprise her—he was in trade, after all. Yet she'd assumed that the owner of a large trading firm would no longer bother with such details. They certainly weren't her strong suit, and more than once she stumbled over the actual prices.

After a while, he asked if the swing worked, and she assured him it did. Soon he was pushing her on it, sending her soaring high. It had been years since she'd swung. It made her feel weightless, free, happy. She could almost forget about Griff. Almost.

The sun had already dipped behind the trees when she slowed the swing. "We should probably go in," she told him with a tinge of regret. "They'll be wondering what happened to us."

"That they will," he said genially, circling to the front of the swing to help her out.

Then he froze in front of her and lifted his head to scan the trees. A slow grin spread over his face. Without warning, he bent and kissed her square on the lips.

She was so shocked she didn't even react. The kiss wasn't overly intimate, but it was soft and tender and certainly demonstrated the man's facility for kissing. While it didn't make her heart leap as Griff's kisses did, she suspected it would make just about any other woman's heart leap.

When he drew back, she gaped at him. "What in God's name was that for?"

"A certain gentleman is watching us," he murmured, eyes dancing. "The bloody jealous arse."

She angled her head just enough to see Griff approaching through the woods, face grim. Outrage made her heart pound. He had the audacity to spy on her "courtship," did he? Well, if he insisted upon such insulting behavior, she'd certainly give him something to see.

Rising from the swing, she threw her arms about Mr. Knighton's neck, then stood on tiptoe to press her lips against his.

She quickly discovered, however, that it was difficult to kiss a man with conviction when he was chuckling. Especially when she was chuckling, too. Indeed, the two of them were so overcome with laughter, they were hard-pressed to do more than keep their lips aligned long enough to produce a convincing kiss.

When she drew back she was fairly certain they'd hidden their humor from their observer. So she wasn't quite sure what possessed her to do what she did next.

Chapter 16

A willing heart adds feather to the heel.

Joanna Baillie, Scottish playwright, De Montfort

Griff halted to gawk at Rosalind. She'd stuck her tongue out at him? The witch had kissed Daniel, then turned, stared straight at Griff, and stuck her tongue out at him!

Of all the—

Perhaps he'd imagined it: the kiss, the taunt, the whole thing. She and Daniel stood apart now, looking perfectly civilized and cordial.

No, he *hadn't* imagined it, damn it. He'd watched them from a distance for some time, watching Daniel use his flatteries to make her laugh and flirt. When Daniel had kissed her, Griff's blood had flashed hot, then cold. Her return kiss had stopped it entirely.

Then she'd stuck her tongue out at him. Now he didn't know whether to be relieved or insulted.

He'd come out here swearing to rein in his temper, control his jealousy, woo her properly. When

239

she'd refused him because he'd made such a hash of
it, he'd sworn he would manage it better this time.
She'd been right that night—he hadn't given her a
single reason for marrying him other than desire.
And desire never swayed women as it did men.

No, this time he'd tell her everything, no matter
what her response. Half of her refusal was based on
her mistaken perception of his behavior toward
Daniel, and there was only one way to set that
straight.

Not that he'd changed his mind about the certificate—he wasn't that besotted. But he would marry
her in spite of it. If she would marry the pretend
Knighton to protect her sisters, then she'd marry the
real one for the same reason, wouldn't she?

One way or the other, he had to have the Amazon.
He needed her, every eccentric inch of her. It made
no sense—she wasn't the sort of wife he'd thought
to acquire. Earl's daughter or no, she and her forthright tongue would certainly never further his aims
for Knighton Trading. Besides, she wouldn't be an
earl's daughter once he acted on the certificate.

And yet . . . And yet two days of attempting to
ignore her had maddened him. He'd accomplished
almost nothing. He hadn't found the damnable documents, because he'd spent all his time pacing his
room and wondering what she and Daniel were up to.

Well, now he knew, didn't he? Griff swore under
his breath, then continued toward them like a can-
nonball headed unerringly for its target. A week
ago, Griff would have sworn Daniel would never
attempt to steal a woman from him. But that was
only because Daniel never had. It didn't mean the
scoundrel wouldn't try it now.

What if Daniel had told her everything, showing
Griff in the worst light? That night in her bedchamber she'd said that Griff's lack of income wouldn't

bother her. So it wouldn't bother her for Daniel either, would it?

If I could have a woman as fine as all that only by swallowing my pride, Daniel had said, *I'd be choking it down so fast I wouldn't taste it.*

By God, he'd be choking down Griff's fist if he even attempted it! How dare the man kiss her! How dare she kiss him back!

But she'd stuck her tongue out at him afterward, hadn't she? He clung to that thought determinedly. He would never make it through the next hour if he went thundering in like the damnable idiot Daniel took him to be.

Holding to his resolution proved difficult, however, when he approached to find Daniel wearing a self-satisfied grin. Griff dearly wanted to wipe it off the Irishman's face, especially after Daniel rested a proprietary hand on Rosalind's waist. She seemed far too comfortable with the man for Griff's satisfaction. Griff had never hated his man of affairs' easy manners with women as much as he did at that moment.

Although a cursory glance reassured Griff that her bonnet was intact, her gown unmussed, and her face devoid of any unusual glow, he still wanted to strangle Daniel for that kiss. Even if Daniel's motives were innocent, it was intolerable. And Griff wasn't at all sure they were innocent.

"Hello there, Griff," the devil himself said. "What brings you out here? Joining us for our picnic?" He exchanged a smile with Rosalind. "I'm afraid you've missed the best part, hasn't he, m'dear?"

The endearment so enraged Griff he nearly forgot the excuse he'd dreamed up for following them. It took him another second to get his temper under control enough to speak it reasonably. "You've been out here so long Lady Helena grew worried. She sent me after you."

"Did she now?" Daniel smirked at him. "Well, then, we'd best go in, hadn't we?"

He offered Rosalind his arm, but as she took it, Griff stepped forward to grip her other arm. "No. She and I have matters to discuss. She stays here with me."

"What am I supposed to tell Lady Helena?" Daniel asked.

"Whatever you must to keep her from coming out here."

"Wait a minute!" Rosalind wrenched her arm from Griff's hold and moved closer to Daniel. "I believe I have some say in this matter, and I'm not staying anywhere with you alone, Griff Brennan."

Brennan? Well, that was one consolation—Daniel hadn't told her about the masquerade. It would have sorely ruined Griff's own plans for breaking the truth to her. "I only want to talk to you, Rosalind."

Daniel fixed his penetrating gaze on Griff. "To talk, is it? Are you going to tell her then?"

Griff knew what he was asking. He gave a terse nod.

"You don't want me—"

"No," he said sharply.

"Very well." Daniel stared down into Rosalind's face with a tender look that tore through Griff's gut. "Stay here, m'lady, and hear the man out. It's important."

"I don't want to."

"Yes, you do." He patted Rosalind's hand, then added, "It'll be all right, I promise. A woman's got three parts, too, you know, though hers are made up differently. Just make sure you use all of yours when you listen to what the man has to say."

She raised an eyebrow. "All of them? I believe there's one I'd best keep firmly in check."

"Weeell . . ." He bent down, whispered something in her ear that made her blush violently, then tipped his hat and strolled off, laughing.

That blush sorely rankled. "What did he say?" Griff bit out as soon as Daniel was out of earshot.

With a coy toss of her pretty head, she glided to the swing and resumed her seat on it. "It's private. Surely you don't expect to know everything that goes on between me and my fiancé merely because you work for the man."

Me and my fiancé. Must the woman try so hard to drive him mad? Much more of this, and he'd be acting exactly as she'd criticized him for two nights ago.

How could he not when she looked so damnably fetching in that gown? Her color of choice today was a vibrant citrine orange that made him think of brightly wrapped candies only found in sweets stores. He wanted to unwrap it and suck it until it melted . . . in his mouth, his hands, his . . .

He bit back another curse. He had to stop thinking with his cock, or he'd never get through this discussion without ravishing her.

As if she knew the dangerous direction of his thoughts, she blithely walked her swing back in preparation for launching it. But before she could do so, he stepped in front and grabbed the ropes on either side to prevent her.

"Get out of my way, Griff," she ordered with that imperious lift of her chin that always enchanted him.

"First, tell me what Dan— . . . what Knighton whispered to you. And while you're at it, what was all that nonsense about parts?" She blushed again. Under any other circumstances, he would have found it intoxicating. Now it merely fueled his reckless temper. "Well?"

"I thought *you* were supposed to be telling *me* things."

"I am. I will." He released the ropes of the swing,

but only to grab her around the waist and lift her fully onto it. The motion parted her legs just enough to allow him to press forward between them, pushing her and the swing back and up. Now she was trapped on it with her legs straddling his waist and her face at his eye level. "First I want to know what Knighton said to you. Tell me what he whispered to make you blush."

She let go of the ropes to push him, but quickly grabbed them again when she began losing her balance. "Blast it, Griff, let me down!"

"Not until you tell me what he said."

"Why should I?"

She glared at him, and instantly the line from *Much Ado about Nothing*, "Disdain and scorn ride sparkling in her eyes," came to mind. By God, Shakespeare would have written ten more plays if he'd ever met *this* Rosalind.

He shook the swing a little. "Haven't you ever heard that it's impolite to talk about someone behind his back?"

"It's also impolite to spy on a person, but that didn't stop you." A gloating smile turned up her vixen's mouth. "Though I do think you saw more than you wanted."

"Tease me, will you?" He pushed her higher. "Do you think that's wise, considering where I've got you? You forget that your gentleman fiancé has left you out here alone with me. And your teasing has roused more than my temper."

He was looking up at her, but with her breasts at eye level, he couldn't stop himself from bringing his gaze down to where the two halves of her robinfront gown met at a point low enough to reveal a generous amount of bosom beneath the lace fichu.

"I know what you're thinking, you scoundrel, and I shall not let you—"

He buried his face in that sweet hollow, pressing an openmouthed kiss to her skin through the lace.

"Stop that . . ." she protested, then groaned when he reached for the fancy ribbon used to hold the gown closed in front.

He'd meant only to demonstrate that he had the upper hand, so to speak. He hadn't come here to seduce her; he'd come to present the truth logically and then convince her to marry him.

But faced with temptations too potent to ignore—their solitary location, the encroaching of dusk, and most of all, her luscious body trapped in his arms—he abandoned all reason and prudence. Only desire remained.

Feeling it pound in his head, his blood, his cock, he untied the ribbon, then unpinned her fichu and tossed it to the ground.

"Griff, don't . . . blast you . . ." she sputtered as he peeled open her bodice. He made short work of her chemise ribbons and had her chemise open and her breasts bared to his hungry gaze in the space of seconds. Her hands left the ropes to stop him, but he grabbed them and closed them back in place, holding them still.

Her breath came fast and hard, almost as fast and hard as his. He nuzzled one breast, drinking in her rosewater scent, relishing the soft, smooth skin fairly begging him to lavish caresses all over it. Then he kissed her delicious female flesh.

"You bloody—" She broke off with a gasp as he took the plump nipple in his mouth. "Oh . . . don't . . . dear God . . . ohhhhh, Griff . . ."

He sucked it fervently, laving the hard nub, teasing it with his teeth until she uttered a low, intoxicating sigh. He released one of her hands to caress her other breast, but she didn't let go of the swing. If anything, she pressed the weight of her breasts into his avid mouth and fingers.

"Yes, my sweet, yes," he murmured against her nipple. He wanted her willing, hot, and eager, the way he knew she could be, and by God he'd stay here all evening pleasuring her if that's what it took.

Though he doubted he'd last that long. Pleasuring her was already driving him insane. He needed to be inside her, to make her his. That way she could never refuse him, could she?

Yes, he thought as he sucked at each of her pebbled nipples in turn, that was his new plan. Make her his, forever.

Her skirts were already hitched up because of her straddling him, but he shoved them up further, then slid his hands beneath them and up along her hose, past her garters to the strips of smooth thigh at the top. No drawers. By God, the woman never wore drawers, and as always that made him frantic with need. He prayed she never adopted the new fashion, though it would mean him walking around in a perpetual state of arousal at the thought of her always bare and open beneath her skirts.

"Griff . . . I'll . . . I'll tell you . . ." she choked out. "I'll tell you what . . . Mr. Knighton . . . said . . ."

"I don't care what he said anymore." He found her darling cleft and fondled it with his thumb. She made some aching sound of pleasure low in her throat that sent lust thundering through his veins.

Slowly he rubbed the slick skin, then slid a finger inside her. By God, she was wet for him already, wet and hot and so damned tight. All he had to do was lower her a little to have her right there open and waiting for his cock.

Through the thick jumble of thoughts crying, *need to be . . . inside her . . . now,* he reminded himself she was a virgin. She required coaxing.

"Hold on, darling," he muttered. He pushed forward, lifting the swing higher until he could hook her legs over his shoulders. Shoving her skirts up past her thighs, he caught his breath at the sight of her so sweetly displayed. He had to taste her. Oh, God, he had to taste her.

Rosalind didn't know whether to be shocked or thrilled when he put his head between her thighs. Though her bottom was still braced against the upheld swing and her legs on his shoulders further secured her to him, she felt decidedly off-balance floating five feet off the ground.

Then his mouth kissed her *there*, and her insides went off-balance, too.

She'd never imagined such a debauchery. Its very outrageousness roused her, titillated her . . . delighted her. Especially once he used his tongue. Sweet Lord in heaven, this was too good not to be the worst sin in the world.

"Griff, you . . . should not—"

His answer was to drive his tongue deep inside her as he'd done with his finger. Dear God, what was this . . . how could he . . . oh, yes . . . yes . . .

She grew insensible of anything but the thrust of his tongue inside her. It lit up her insides, ignited them into flame. Throwing her head back, she closed her eyes and let the wild fury build in her as it had before in his bedchamber, her senses acutely aware of his every motion, her thighs gripping his head, her body feeling as if it floated around him while his tongue teased and taunted and made her insane.

Oh, dear God—this was why people warned virgins that these naughty things were wrong and sinful and bad. If they didn't, there'd scarce be a virgin over sixteen left in England.

She wanted to release the swing and clutch him tighter, but feared it would overbalance them both.

And the last thing she wanted right now was to make him stop. No, he mustn't stop . . . Sin or no, she wanted to have . . . this . . .

Abruptly he *did* stop, and only after she'd opened her eyes did she realize she'd released the swing to clutch his head and the board was sliding out from under her bottom. He caught her as her legs slid off his shoulders. Locking his heated gaze with hers, he let her body slip down him with aching slowness.

A smile gilded his face. "I think we'd best move to the blanket. I doubt either of us is limber enough to make love on the swing. Besides, I want to touch and kiss every inch of you. I want you naked."

Sanity began to penetrate her dazed senses. "Oh, but we can't—"

"Please, Rosalind." His smile vanished, replaced by a look of such haunting longing it made her shiver. "Let me make love to you, my darling. I need to make love to you. I need you. Goddamn it, I . . ."

He trailed off, and she remembered what Mr. Knighton had said about Griff not being able to speak the needs of his heart. But if Griff said he needed her, said he wanted to make *love*, surely that implied some deep feeling. After all, the first time he'd threatened to seduce her, he'd spoken of bedding her.

She glanced around the clearing, still well lit, though the sun had fallen behind the trees. "But here? Where anyone could—"

"If I could get you to my bedchamber without getting caught, I would, but I'm taking no chances. They're less likely to discover us here than there. And if someone does stumble upon us, it'll merely ensure that you marry me sooner rather than later. Because you are going to marry me, you know."

His confident smile made her want to clout him. "You, sir, are entirely too sure of your—"

He stopped up her mouth with the first kiss he'd

given her on the lips in two days, and dear God, what a kiss. Sweet, aching, possessive ... the way any decent kiss should be. It rapidly became more, however. His hands roamed her body with the proprietary confidence of a lover, tearing off her bonnet, shaking pins from her hair, sliding down her neck to shove her gown off her shoulders.

Then he had his hands inside her open chemise and was kneading her breasts and thumbing her nipples into hard, aching knots. She couldn't muster an ounce of protest. All thoughts of defying him scattered into the dusky evening sky with his every caress.

For two days, she'd wanted this, and yes, needed it, needed him. She didn't know why this curst man, of all men, made her feel whole, but he did. He spoke to the wildness in her that chafed under so many restraints. He understood her as no one ever had. And he cared for her. He might not say it, but he did. She was sure of it.

If he hadn't already asked her to marry him, she might resist his seductions out of fear for the future, but he *had* asked her and he *did* want her. At the moment, that was all the reassurance she needed.

Still kissing her with lavish excess, he scooped her up and carried her the few feet to where the blanket was spread on the earth. He set her down on it without breaking the kiss, as if fearing she might change her mind.

But she was beyond changing her mind. And when he began stripping off her gown, she started at once on his waistcoat buttons. He froze and stopped kissing her, but only in order to undress her more quickly. When she jerked at his coat lapels, he shrugged the coat off and then the waistcoat she'd unbuttoned. The rest of his clothes and his boots swiftly followed, leaving him wearing nothing but drawers full to bursting with his hardened flesh.

She scarcely had time to notice, however, before he ran his hands down her corset and said thickly, "Turn around, my sweet."

She obeyed with some trepidation—not at the thought of his taking off all her clothes, though. *That* gave her a treacherous thrill. But he'd never seen her without her corset, and she wasn't exactly . . . well . . . trim. He mightn't want her quite so much if he saw her abundant figure totally bared.

Her heart pounded as he worked at loosening her corset laces. Out here in the open, she felt painfully exposed, though the trees formed a welcoming shield and the time of the day—dinnertime—virtually ensured that no one would be outside on the estate. She wished the sun had already set, however. Then he couldn't see her quite so well.

By the time he'd peeled the hated corset off her and tossed it aside, she'd braced herself for his disappointment. He dragged her chemise over her head and let it float to the ground. Her stockings and boots were last to go, leaving her totally naked, still with her back to him.

His long silence pierced her confidence. Until she heard him groan tellingly. He stroked her ample hips and waist, sending delicate tendrils of delight stealing around her heart. Reaching from behind her, he filled his hands with her breasts. He nuzzled her hair, then her ear. "Oh, Rosalind," he said hoarsely. "You shouldn't wear corsets, darling. You shouldn't hide all this goddamned beauty in such a nasty contraption."

She swung around to face him, hardly believing what he said, but she couldn't mistake the blaze of need in his eyes or the worshipful way he stroked her body. Then he was kissing it . . . her shoulders, the upper swells of her breasts, the nipples.

He knelt on one knee and pressed a kiss beneath her breast at the top of a long indentation one of her stays had scored on her skin. It was the first of several following the line down her belly. "To mar this . . ." He kissed her again. "Too sweet flesh . . ." Another hot, delicious kiss. "Is a grievous . . ." A series of sizzling kisses. "Sin . . ."

By the time he'd reached the bottom and pressed a kiss into her thatch of hair, she could hardly contain the tears choking her throat. She'd never thought a man might actually *like* her body this way. To have it be the man she loved so desperately . . .

With a moan half of pleasure, half of love, she clutched his head to her. *I love you. No matter what you feel for me, I love you.*

For a moment they were locked that way, her stroking his thick raven hair, him nuzzling her thigh. Then he gazed up at her, his face marked with a griffin's predatory desire. "I want you, darling." He drew her down on the blanket. "I want you now."

Before she could even think, she was on her back with him kneeling between her spread thighs and fumbling with the buttons of his drawers.

"Wait!" she cried.

He froze, his eyes glowing with fervent need. "No, Rosalind, don't stop me . . . I can't bear it—"

"I won't stop you." Despite the blush rising in her cheeks, she sat up and reached for his buttons. "I just want to . . . Last time you wouldn't let me . . . take it out and touch it. Let me do it this time."

He sucked in a sharp breath as her fingers brushed his drawers. "Curious, are you?" he rasped.

"How could I not be?" Unable to meet his gaze, she shifted to kneeling before him, then began unbuttoning. "You teased me about the blasted thing often enough."

But now she understood why he'd spoken of it like a creature apart from himself. The second the buttons were undone, it sprang free of the stockingette, a wild beast escaping a cage.

Griff wrangled the drawers off, then knelt once more in front of her. "There," he whispered hoarsely. "Now you know what's been filling my pockets."

She stared at the instrument between them in undisguised fascination. How strange to see it so proud and impudent, springing up between his legs like a cocky lad.

Cocky. Dear God. Another blush heated her cheeks at the memory of that day in his bedchamber and what he'd called it. "So that's where it came from."

"What?"

"The word *cocky*. I never realized . . ."

He chuckled, then caught her hand and closed it around the thick, rigid flesh. "Yes, my inquisitive virgin. That's where *cocky* comes from. Men have nearly a hundred terms for their privates. Even your precious Shakespeare uses several."

"Does he?" She smoothed her fingers over Griff's privates, delighting in how it pulsed in her hand.

His eyes slid shut and a dark flush rose in his face. "You'll find . . . the plays have a whole new . . . meaning once you know of such things."

She stroked his intriguing shaft until he groaned. "Oh? For example?"

He frowned, obviously having difficulty thinking. "Remember Petruchio and Katherina? He talks about having . . . his tongue in her tail? And being a . . . 'combless cock' if she . . . will be his 'hen'?"

She released him abruptly. "What! That's what that means? I never dreamed—"

With a growl, he grabbed her hand and guided it back to him. When she wrapped her fingers tightly about him, he shuddered. "Shakespeare isn't . . . the least . . . respectable, my sweet. You chose your . . . favorite author well."

She sniffed. "Are you saying I'm not respectable, sir?"

He glanced down at her fingers and raised an eyebrow. "I wouldn't dare. Not when you've . . . got my cock in your hand."

Regarding the warm length of him thoughtfully, she tugged at it.

"By God, Rosalind, you'll kill me yet," he protested as he thrust into her fist.

"I don't like that word, 'cock.' I like 'St. Peter' better."

His eyes flamed at her. "Damnation, where did you hear that term?"

"From Mr. Knighton," she said unthinkingly.

"What?" He shoved her hand away and forced her back onto the blanket, hovering over her as he pinned her hands on either side of her head. "Why in God's name did he speak of a St. Peter to *you*?"

This was a strange position indeed, strange and titillating. Her every sense tingled with the awareness of him kneeling between her legs, the tip of his "St. Peter" bobbing against her triangle of hair. His body was poised above her so close she could see the vivid blue irises of his eyes, glowing down at her with a mix of jealousy and desire.

She swallowed. "He and I were talking about you—the parts of you. And how your . . . um . . . St. Peter part wants me."

He relaxed only a fraction. "That's not the only part of me wanting you, but I'll admit it's the most demanding one right now. Is that what all that nonsense about the three parts was?"

Licking her suddenly dry lips, she nodded.

He frowned, as if trying to remember what they'd said. A smile suddenly lit his face. "Which of your parts did you say you should 'keep firmly in check around me'?"

"Do you have to ask?" she retorted tartly.

His gaze seared heat down her body. "No, I don't suppose I do. Though it seems you've failed in that respect."

"It does seem that way, doesn't it?" She was surprisingly cheerful about it. She'd known it would be hopeless if he ever got her alone again. She hadn't a whit of self-control around Griff.

Besides, now that she knew she loved him, it seemed pointless not to share this with him. Especially since he was going to tell her his secrets and marry her anyway.

Shifting his weight so he could brace himself off her with one elbow, he reached down and fondled her in a very naughty manner, plunging his finger so deliciously deep that it wrung a gasp from her. "When Knighton left, what did he whisper in your ear?"

"It's a secret," she taunted him. Griff hadn't told her all of his yet, so she ought to be able to keep a few of her own until he did.

"Is it?" He thumbed her little nub enough to tantalize her, no more. Half-consciously, she tilted her hips up against his hand, then groaned when his fingers danced away. "Tell me, Rosalind," he whispered devilishly, stroking oh-too-lightly over her damp skin. "Or I'll tease you until you do."

"You're an awful man," she said, pouting.

"So I've been told many times." He dipped his finger inside her again, leaving her aching for more, so much more. "Rosalind?"

"Oh, all right! He said I should make *you* keep your St. Peter firmly in check until you told me the truth."

For a moment, he froze, a black look crossing his face. Then it was gone, replaced by sheer raw desire. "Too late for that," he whispered raggedly. "Because I'm about to put my St. Peter inside you, my sweet. And you're going to let me, aren't you?"

She barely had a chance to register the words or nod in response before he was kissing her again, rich, ardent kisses meant to distract her from what he was doing between her legs. As if that would work, she thought. She could hardly ignore the rigid staff sliding up inside her, filling her with exquisite pressure.

After all his teasing, it was almost too much. She felt anchored to him, joined to him so intimately they were one entity. She liked the feeling . . . until he kept moving farther in. She began to wonder how he could put so much of his St. Peter inside her.

She tore her lips from his. "Griff, surely you . . . it won't fit."

Obviously he'd reached the same conclusion, for he looked strained and by no means comfortable. Then he shocked her by saying, "Yes, it will, my sweet. Give it a chance." With a growl, he pressed farther into her. "God, you're so tight and . . . and warm. It feels so good to be . . . inside you at last."

"It doesn't feel quite so good to me," she muttered, for he was stretching her beyond endurance.

"I know, darling, I know." He thrust a little, then groaned as if he'd reached his limit. "And now I'm going to hurt you, I'm afraid."

"H-Hurt me?" she squeaked. "How badly?"

His jaw tightened. "Not too badly, I hope. I must pierce your maidenhead."

That sounded ominous.

"But it'll be better once it's done, I promise," he added. Bending his head, he sucked at her breast, making pleasure shoot through her veins. When her eyes slid shut and she tossed her head back, he murmured, "Forgive me," and thrust hard.

Something tore inside her, and she moaned at the sharp spasm of pain. But it was over quickly without hurting nearly as much as the words "pierce your maidenhead" had led her to expect. Still, it planted him so deeply, she couldn't even move without being utterly aware of his flesh filling her up.

She opened her eyes to gaze up into his taut features. "Can't we go back . . . to kissing? This is not . . . quite as pleasant." She wriggled her hips a bit, and he cursed.

"It will be even less pleasant if you keep that up," he warned. When she cast him a hurt look, he softened his tone. "You need to adjust to having me inside you. And I need to adjust to being inside you. Otherwise, I'll never do this right." He caressed one breast with his mouth, then kissed a path to the other. "Relax, darling. Try to relax."

Was he mad? How could she "relax" with him plunged so deeply inside her?

Then he started pressing tender kisses to her chin and her cheeks, teasing her lips with his tongue, nibbling on them with his teeth. With a melting sigh, she opened her mouth and let him slide his tongue inside.

As he fed on her mouth with growing ardor, he released one of her hands to fondle her where they were joined. A delicious thrill darted along her limbs. The more he fondled and kissed her, the more she felt herself opening up, softening . . . relaxing.

Then he moved inside her again, withdrawing his St. Peter a little, pressing it back, mimicking the velvet caresses of his tongue in her mouth. Her breath dried up in her throat. Dear God . . . this felt . . . carnal. Oh, yes, assuredly carnal.

She wiggled her hips. How interesting. She could make it even better just by undulating a little beneath him.

"Damnation, Rosalind," he tore his mouth from her to growl. "Yes . . . yes like that . . . yes . . . oh, sweet Christ, you're . . . priceless . . ."

So was he. With the sun setting behind his head, she could hardly bear to stare into his beautiful face with its stark, devouring look, a golden griffin swooping down to plunder her. *Her* griffin. There was something so . . . intense about being plundered. He was inescapable, thundering into her. His musky scent mingled with the smell of grass and spilled wine, his feverish breaths kissed her face, and his sweat-slick body surrounded her and was inside her, too, igniting wildfire in her loins, making her ache for the unknown, for him, for the two of them together.

His hands had freed hers and were firmly planted on either side of her as he thrust into her, building the excitement, driving her mad again. She gripped his shoulders and arched her body into him, mad with the need he provoked so rampantly inside her.

At last she understood—why lovers trysted. Why women risked all for their men. Why people spoke of the two becoming one. It was for this enthralling dance, this fiery union.

The union meant to be between a man and woman who loved each other. Tears leaked from her eyes. She couldn't stop them.

Then she felt his lips brushing her tears away. "Don't weep, my sweet," he said in a voice of aching tenderness. "I don't want . . . to hurt you. I . . . can withdraw—"

"No!" She dragged his head down to hers. "No. Just kiss me, Griff." Though his body thundered inside her, he kissed her with a gentleness that melted her heart.

I love you, she thought as he drove into her. *I love you, Griff.*

"You're mine now, Rosalind," he growled with

the fierceness of a griffin hoarding his treasure. He pounded into her as if to impress his claim upon her. "Mine forever."

With those words, the flood inundated her, waves of hot pleasure that made her cry out and writhe beneath him, digging her fingernails into his shoulders, straining up against his lean body. She was still drowning in the ecstasy when he plunged to the very heart of her and found his own release, crying out her name.

Then he collapsed on top of her. She hugged him fiercely to her as tears poured down her cheeks. *Mine*, she thought, as greedy as he to lay claim to her dark lover. He wanted her for his own. He hadn't spoken of love, but he wanted her for his own, and surely that meant something?

They lay there in perfect stillness as their breathing slowed, and their blood resumed a more natural rhythm. The sky above them was a miracle of shot silk in plum and rose and gold, the sun's own final ecstasy before it found its bed in the horizon. All lay still in the woods around them, as if even the birds hushed themselves before both miracles . . . the one in the sky and the one on the ground.

With a sigh, Griff nuzzled her neck, then pushed himself off her to fall limp on the blanket at her side. Then he tugged her into his embrace, so she lay half-sprawled across him, her head resting against his chest. Feeling shy with him now and terribly exposed lying naked in the woods, she couldn't bring herself to look into his face.

Yet she so wanted to know if he'd had the same heart-wrenching reaction to their lovemaking. She drew circles on his belly with her finger. "Griff?"

"Mmm?"

Oh, how did one ask such a thing? "Nothing."

He tipped her chin up so he could see her face,

then frowned. Brushing his thumb along the corners
of each eye, he wiped away the remnants of her
tears. "Why did you cry, darling? Did I hurt you?"

The endearment resonated deeply within her.
"No," she whispered.

"I tried not to. But I wanted you so desperately . . ."

"So did I," she reassured him. "I've thought of
nothing else for two days."

He lifted an eyebrow. "You seemed to have
another man on your mind earlier."

She laughed. "You're such a jealous fool. All we
did was talk about you. Your employer was deter
mined to convince me you cared about me. I
remained unconvinced."

"You talked to him about me?" he said incredulously. "But . . . you planned to marry him. Didn't
you think he might take that amiss?"

"I hate to tell you this, for it'll swell your head,
but I never planned to marry him."

"What? My God, you practically offered yourself
on a platter to the man!"

His jealous tone made her smile. She pushed up
on his chest to stare down into his face. A giddy joy
seized her at the thought of marrying him. "I'll have
you know that Mr. Knighton is far more perceptive
than *you*. He guessed at once I had no intention of
marrying him. I only wanted to delay him somehow, and I thought if I agreed to marry him, I could
lengthen the engagement indefinitely."

"You're saying it was a pretend engagement."

"Precisely."

"Then why did you let him kiss you?" he
growled, temper flaring.

"Because we *knew* you were spying on us, you
ninny, and he wanted to goad you. Besides, it took
me quite by surprise."

He clasped her neck, drew her down for a long, drugging kiss, then whispered, "There will be no more surprises like that, do you hear? Because you're mine now, my sweet. And if I ever catch Daniel kissing you again—"

"Daniel?" she asked, perplexed.

Griff froze, his face draining of color. "Damnation."

"Daniel? Who is Daniel? Wait, isn't your real name supposed to be—"

"Yes. I suppose it's time I told you what I'd come out here to say in the first place." He sighed. Moving her gently aside, he sat up. "If we're to be married, you probably ought to know my real name."

Fear startled to life in her breast. Why did she sense she wouldn't like this?

He ran his fingers through his hair in distraction, then gazed at her. "The man you know as Mr. Knighton is actually Daniel Brennan. And I'm not called 'Griff' because of the griffin. I'm called Griff because of my middle name, Griffith."

His long shuddering breath struck dread in her soul. "My entire name is Marsden Griffith Knighton. *I* am your cousin, Mr. Knighton."

Chapter 17

He that knew all that ever learning writ
Knew only this—that he knew nothing yet.

Aphra Behn, English playwright,
The Emperor of the Moon

Griff braced himself for her anger. At least now everything was out in the open. He'd always believed in plunging right in, and this was a matter he could no longer avoid, especially if they were to marry.

He *would* marry her, no matter what her reaction. Making love to her had sealed his determination. He'd never experienced such a joining with any woman—never. It still struck him with awe, with untrammeled wonder.

And with a fierce desire to make sure he didn't lose this precious connection with her.

He rose and jerked on his drawers, watching her warily. She'd already sat up, twisting herself into a tangle of limbs that hid the private areas of her body. Looking dazed, she drew the blanket up around her. With a twinge of guilt, he saw that it was stained with her virgin blood.

"Rosalind, say something," he growled as she stared sightlessly past him. "Call me a bastard, rage at me, anything."

"How can I call you a bastard?" she said in a small voice. "If . . . you're . . . telling me the truth, then you aren't one, are you?"

If ever he'd needed proof that she knew nothing of her father's plans, this was it. And she'd given him the perfect opening to spill out the rest of the tale.

He couldn't, though, not yet. How could he when she sat there so still and quiet, her silence putting the death knell to all his plans?

"Oh, but I am a bastard," he said hoarsely. "I should never have lied to you about who I was."

She shook her head as if to clear it. "You really are Marsden Knighton? My cousin?"

"Distant cousin," he reminded her.

A groan rolled from her. "I've been such an idiot. I should have seen it all along. The way you acted, the way you talked. I always wondered how Mr. Kni— How your man of affairs could put up with your insolence. It wasn't insolence, was it? You've always given him orders. You were merely acting as his employer."

Gratified that she finally understood that at least, he nodded.

She rose as if in a trance, tucking the blanket about her. "And his coarse manner—" Her gaze shot to Griff. "*He* is the son of the highwayman, not you. He's the one who lived in the workhouse for a time." A look of horror spread over her face. "Or was that a lie, too?"

"The only thing I lied about was my identity."

Though I haven't yet told you a hundred other things. "I gave myself Daniel's past and he took mine, but the details of our backgrounds are all true and they all match the names. It's only that what I said about myself belongs to Daniel and what I said about him belongs to me."

He could see her working it out in her mind, which alarmed him. Rosalind operated on emotion. She attacked with swords, she impetuously offered herself in marriage to save her sister . . . she threw herself passionately into lovemaking. To see her thinking the matter through instead of hurling the picnic basket at him worried him.

"So you're the one who went to Eton?" she asked. He nodded curtly.

"You're our cousin." She scrutinized his features. "Yes, of course you are. I only saw the miniature of your father once, but from what I recall you look much like him. I don't know why I didn't see it before."

"Because people see what they've been told to see. You didn't know us—you had no reason to suspect I wasn't Mr. Brennan."

At the sound of the name, her eyes went wide. "That means you're not even half-Irish. That's why he said . . . Ohhh . . ." She groaned and closed her eyes, obviously remembering something.

"What did *he* say?"

She shook her head. "Nothing. We just talked about the Irish and . . . It was nothing." She mused a moment. "So of course you're the one who made Knighton Trading such a success. How could I have been so stupid? I kept thinking you were the brains behind the company, but I couldn't understand how you'd hidden that from his investors so long or why you'd let him take credit for your efforts."

He laughed bitterly. "You know me too well to

believe I'd let anyone take credit for my efforts. As for Daniel—don't let his rough exterior deceive you. He's good at what he does, so good that his shrewdness about investments has enabled me to double my personal income in the past few years. He advises other men besides me. Indeed, he's soon planning to open his own concern."

He knew he was rambling, that she had no reason for wanting to know about Daniel, but he blindly sought to wipe away her look of betrayal.

She turned her face from him. It was dark enough now that he could barely see her, but he still hated having her turn from him.

"You asked me to marry you," she whispered, "knowing that I thought you were someone else. Didn't you think it significant enough to tell me?"

"Damnation, Rosalind, I'm telling you now!"

"Oh? Explain to me why you would even begin such a masquerade. And why, after you supposedly decided you wanted to marry me, you would continue it."

"*Supposedly?* Goddamn it, woman, there was no *supposedly* about it. The minute I saw you in your father's study, I wanted you. And after that day in my bedchamber, I knew I had to have you."

"You mean . . . in your bed."

"No! As my wife. I never lied about that."

"Yes, but that day in your bedchamber, you didn't offer for me. Why not? You could have just told me the truth then, told me I had nothing to fear, that you'd marry me yourself. Why did you wait until after I went to Mr. . . . to . . ."

"Daniel. His Christian name is Daniel. This will be easier if you call him that."

"Nothing about this is easy!" she cried.

Her shoulders shook violently, and he prayed she wouldn't weep. He couldn't stand it if she wept.

"I thought I was in . . . I thought I cared for you," she whispered, her features etched with hurt, "but whom did I care for? Not Griff Knighton, obviously. Certainly not Daniel Brennan. It was some . . . creation, a blend of you and your man of affairs."

"That's not true!" Why did she speak of caring for him as if it were in the past? He couldn't lose her now, not over this. He must make her understand. "It wasn't Daniel you accompanied about the estate. It wasn't Daniel you played billiards with or discussed Shakespeare with." Walking to where she stood enveloped in her blanket, looking lost, he reached up to caress the darling curve of her cheek. "It wasn't Daniel who made love to you."

At least she didn't recoil from his touch. "You still haven't told me why you would even begin such a deception. Or why you let it go on for so long."

His hand froze, and a sudden terror seized him. Damnation, he couldn't tell her the rest of it. How could he? She already felt betrayed and hurt. How much more would she suffer if he told her he'd come here on a search for something that would ruin her father and drag her sisters through scandal? How could he tell her he still planned to regain what was rightfully his?

He couldn't, not now. Once they were married, he'd tell her. By then, he'd know exactly what he intended to do. As matters stood, he didn't even know if she *would* marry him. So first he must secure her, then sort out the rest after they married.

It took him only a moment to think of a plausible reason. "When your father invited me here, he mentioned the possibility of my marrying one of you. To be truthful, I wasn't interested. I had no reason to marry, or so I thought."

"And you didn't need to marry to gain the estate," she put in tartly.

He merely nodded, incapable of lying to her so blatantly. "Nonetheless, I wanted to see Swan Park. My father spoke often of it, I knew I'd inherit it, and I was curious. So I devised a way of looking at it without being plagued by a group of women throwing themselves at me." He managed a faint smile. "Believe me, if I'd ever guessed you were all so violently opposed to marrying me, I would never have considered the masquerade. But I'd been told that you were . . . well . . ."

"The Swanlea Spinsters," she said, tipping her chin up with an amazing dignity for a woman in a blanket standing barefoot in the middle of a glade.

"Exactly. I thought Daniel could keep all of you occupied while I . . . surveyed the estate at my leisure. Of course, the longer the masquerade continued, the harder it became to admit to it."

He brushed her hair away from her face. By God, she'd never looked so fetching as she did in that blanket. It completed his image of her as Athena the battle goddess, except that she needed to drape it lower, to reveal her lovely breasts in all their glory.

He forced down his randy cock and continued. "By the time I realized I wanted you, I didn't know how to stop it. I wasn't even sure you were interested in me as Griff Brennan, much less as Griff Knighton. You were spouting all that bloody nonsense about marrying 'Mr. Knighton' to save your sister, and I didn't want you marrying *me* for that."

"So you kept lying, to make sure I'd marry you for yourself and not for your property? Is that it? You manipulated me and—"

"Now see here," he interrupted, his temper pricked by her outrage, "I wasn't the only one manipulating people. You weren't even really planning to marry Daniel . . . I mean, me. Knighton. You were no more honest with me than I was with you, damn it."

Her chin quivered. "I was fighting for my family. What were you fighting for?"

My company, my future, he nearly said, but didn't dare. "Rosalind," he said, mustering a reasonable tone, "I know I should never have engaged in such a reckless scheme, but it's done now, and I've told you about it. Can't you forgive me? Can't we put it behind us?"

Rosalind stared at him, not sure how to take his revelations. She wanted to hate him for masquerading and then continuing it so long, for making love to her while pretending to be someone else.

Yet how could she? His being the real Mr. Knighton made everything so much easier. She hadn't looked forward to telling her family she was running off to marry the wrong man, the one who could *not* save Swan Park. She'd dreaded dealing with Juliet's renewal of attentions to the man she believed to be their cousin.

Still, Griff had *lied* to her. Repeatedly. Egregiously. In her heart she knew she could forgive him that . . . if she were certain it was all she had to forgive. But though his explanation seemed plausible enough, she couldn't quite believe it. This had all been merely to keep the Swanlea Spinsters from bothering him while he looked over the estate? How could it be that simple?

She thought of Papa's strongbox and stiffened. "And what of all your sneaking about the estate? What of that?"

He glanced away, a muscle tensing in his jaw. "I told you. I wanted to assess the place. I don't work well with somebody hovering around, that's all." His gaze swung back to her, raking her boldly, making her blush. "Especially when the somebody is a fetching female who makes me burn. Who's making me burn right now, truth be told."

An irresistible need drew her gaze inexorably to his drawers. She swallowed to see that he didn't lie about *that* at least, for the stockingette clearly outlined his arousal. He seemed to grow even more as she stared.

"I find myself in this state nearly all the time when I'm around you, my darling," he said hoarsely. "Until now, I didn't think I'd ever find a woman I wanted so badly. It makes no sense, I know, but the minute I met you . . . well . . . something altered inside me. It's as if I was missing a part of me that I found when you entered my life."

His heart, she thought, remembering what Daniel had told her. *He doesn't know it's his heart.*

Other things Daniel said sprang into her mind: *His brain's trying to figure you out, his St. Peter is crying out for attention, and worst of all, his heart is clamoring to be heard for the first time in the poor sod's life. All that clamoring is confusing the man.*

The thought warmed her. Surely he loved her a little if he could speak so haltingly, so sweetly of his need for her. He might not know it was his heart speaking, but that didn't mean it wasn't.

"I want to marry you, now more than ever," he said in a low, urgent voice. "The question is—can you forgive me, will you forgive me enough to marry me?"

Blast him, he had a talent for reducing situations to their most basic. She even knew the answer she wanted to make. How could she not forgive him when she loved him so much?

After all, it was entirely possible the situation was exactly as he'd claimed. She could easily imagine Griff wanting to avoid being plagued by three spinsters. And she could see how his pride would have prevented him from offering for her sooner.

So why did she feel this uncertainty, this sense he wasn't being entirely truthful with her? Certain things remained odd. Why had Griff gone to such extraordinary lengths to secure his privacy in the past few days? His story didn't seem to warrant it. And what about Papa's bloody strongbox? Papa insisted it contained only papers, but why hide them? That made no sense.

She thought about actually mentioning the strongbox to Griff, but some instinct made her hold back. If he were lying about it, her mentioning it would make matters worse, for then he'd know of it. If he were telling the truth, then it was of no importance.

"Rosalind, darling," he bit out, "if you're trying to punish me with this silence, you're doing a good job of it."

His worry touched her. "I'm not trying to punish you. It's just that . . . this is so wholly unexpected. I'm still trying to take it all in." *I'm still trying to determine who you really are. And if I can trust you.*

"What is there to take in? I'm the same man you cared for, only with a different name and a less disreputable past. That shouldn't affect whether you care for me enough to marry me." When she remained silent, torn, he added in a rigid tone, "And if my blunders have destroyed your feelings for me, you could still marry me for practical reasons. I would accept even that from you."

"Practical reasons? I suppose you mean the advantages to my family."

He stiffened the merest fraction. "Yes. But more particularly the advantages to *you*. I'm rich, remember?"

"I ought to," she said coldly. "You reminded me

of it repeatedly that day in the deer park. As I recall, it influenced me as little then as it does now."

"You're a stubborn woman, Lady Rosalind."

"In fact, I believe I told you that I had so little interest in money I was willing to throw it all aside to go on the stage."

He sighed. "Then I'll have to find other enticements to tempt you from the lure of the theater, won't I?" Taking her by surprise, he caught her to him with an arm about her waist. The blanket slipped a little, but she didn't resist his embrace. She couldn't.

Brushing her cheek with his lips, he lowered his voice seductively. "For one thing, you and I are very well matched. You must admit it."

"Well matched in bed, you mean," she choked out. Curse him for his ability to fog her mind with passion.

"Everywhere." Clasping her chin, he forced it up so she'd look into his eyes, his beautiful, devious eyes. "What do you think are your chances of finding a husband who can match your knowledge of Shakespeare quote for quote?"

Another piece of the puzzle fell into place. Of course he knew Shakespeare. He'd been educated at Eton. Still, of all the things he might have said to convince her, that wasn't one she'd expected. It was rather crafty of him to use it, and Griff was nothing if not crafty.

She lifted an eyebrow. "We haven't yet established that you can match me quote for quote, sir."

He smiled at her taunt. "Then perhaps we should. Think of all the enjoyment we'll have doing so." He pressed a heated kiss to her cheekbone. "Think of the hours we can spend—" he kissed a path to her ear and nipped the lobe—"discussing all of Shakespeare's euphemisms for *cock*."

An unwanted thrill coursed through her. The man certainly knew how to use naughty words to his advantage.

Laving her too-sensitive ear with his tongue, he flattened her against his body. His decidedly aroused body. "There will be other advantages, too. You can redecorate my town house from top to bottom. You'll have two estates full of servants to order about."

"Why should I want that?" She was finding it hard to breathe, hard to think. She angled her head away, fighting down the surge of excitement that always deluged her when he started his blasted seductions. "I don't like running this estate, remember?"

"You said you only disliked the tedious details. Well, my darling, I have plenty of employees to take care of the tedious details, leaving you free to order everyone about." He kissed her neck. "And warm my bed."

She swallowed. Hard. "I suppose you consider warming your bed one of those 'advantages' in favor of my marrying you."

"Contentious woman," he muttered. "Shall I demonstrate again that we both consider it an advantage?"

He kissed her on the mouth then and stole the very soul from her body. Every sense stood to attention, her very skin came alive with heat. For a moment, she reveled in it, responding to his kiss with all the love in her heart.

But when he tugged at her blanket, she came to her senses. With a feverish burst of will, she wriggled from his arms to go stand a few feet away, clutching the blanket close like a shield.

"Rosalind?" he queried in concern.

"All right."

" 'All right' what?"

"I'll marry you."

His ragged sigh of relief echoed unmistakably in the clearing. "Good. Now come here so we can celebrate."

Only Griff could imbue the word *celebrate* with sheer carnality. She shivered at his delicious temptation, but resisted it. She couldn't lie with him again until she determined if all her fears were nothing. She'd nearly admitted she loved him before; if he took her again, she'd never keep from saying it. And her pride wouldn't let her lay her heart before him until she was more sure of him.

"No," she protested, "we'll be missed if we don't go in soon."

He stepped toward her. "Daniel will see to it that no one disturbs us."

"No," she said firmly. "I'm . . . a bit . . ." What? Tired? Sleepy? At shortly after sunset? What reason could she give?

To her surprise, he supplied the reason for her. "Sore. Of course." He flashed her an apologetic look. "I wasn't thinking. You were a virgin, and we were rather . . . vigorous in our lovemaking. You need time to recover."

She pounced on his reason at once, though she wasn't nearly as sore as he seemed to think. "Yes, precisely. I-I'm sorry—"

"You've no reason to apologize. *I'm* the one who should apologize. I should have realized you wouldn't be ready again so soon." He stepped up close to caress her cheek. "I'm sailing in uncharted waters, my sweet, since you're my first virgin."

"I'd better be the last, as well," she warned. "No matter what I promised Daniel, I won't play the accommodating wife for *you*. If you take a mistress after we're married, I swear I'll cut off your St. Peter, or whatever you call it."

He laughed. "Spoken like a true Amazon. But don't worry, darling, I don't want that sort of accommodating wife. Nor do I want a mistress. I want you and no one else, for the rest of our lives."

It sounded so good, so perfect. Too perfect, she thought as he bent to kiss her.

There was only way to be sure of his intentions and lay all her fears to rest. Tonight she must go to Papa with that blasted strongbox and make him open it, make him tell her what it contained. It had to be nothing—she was nearly sure it was nothing.

She prayed it was nothing.

Because if Griff proved to be lying about his reasons for marrying her, it just might kill her.

Chapter 18

There is not a passion so strongly rooted in the
human heart as envy.

Richard Sheridan, English theater manager
and playwright, The Critic

Half an hour later, after they were dressed and
walking back to the house, Griff couldn't
shake the unease plaguing him. He didn't understand it. He ought to be ecstatic now that he had
what he wanted. *Everything* he wanted.

He'd gained Rosalind despite the revelation of
his masquerade. She'd agreed to marry him. She'd
spoken of caring for him. She'd even threatened
him with emasculation if he ever took a mistress,
which he found decidedly promising. Her jealousy
surely meant she felt more than desire for him.

And he'd gained the certificate, or would on his
wedding day if the earl kept his promise. He'd done
it without alienating her from his affections, too,

thanks to his prudent decision not to tell her about the damned thing.

Yet he still felt unsure of her. He shot her a quick glance as they skirted the manor and passed under a window spilling soft light onto her face. She seemed . . . pensive, distant. Could she possibly know . . .

No, how could she? She was merely responding to the loss of her virginity and the many changes it had wrought. Because if she'd known the truth, she wouldn't have agreed to marry him. He was nearly certain of that.

Yet he'd have to tell her eventually. What a dilemma he'd created. To gain his place in the House of Lords and thus on that delegation, he must publicly establish his claim to the title. But if he claimed it publicly, whether before or after he married Rosalind, she would kill him.

He groaned. Was there no way around this without infuriating her?

Of course, she needn't know how he'd gotten the certificate. He could keep that between the earl and himself. And using it would mean little change to the family situation, because once he married Rosalind, he'd take up residence at Swan Park and all would be as it was before. He could even allow her father to remain in the master bedchamber. He was not a vindictive man, after all.

There would merely be the small matter of a public transfer of the title from her father to Griff. Possibly no more than a month. In the House of Lords. Before all her father's peers and a number of newspapermen, no doubt. Her father branded a criminal, her sisters pitied, his deception in wooing her aired before her.

He groaned again. Damnation, it wasn't fair! He deserved that title; it was his! She ought to be grateful he wanted to marry her after everything her father had done to him, damn it!

"If you groan one more time with such feeling, Griff," she said quietly at his side, "I'll know you're regretting your proposal of marriage."

His gaze swung to her. "I have no regrets on that score, believe me." It was true, God help him. No matter what difficulties marriage might present, he wanted to marry her more than anything he'd wanted in his life. Except that place on the delegation.

But he'd find a way to gain both. Perhaps her father would oblige him by succumbing to his illness in a timely fashion.

Guilt assailed him for even wishing something that would give her such pain. He groaned yet again. Catching her anxious look, he quickly said, "I'm merely trying to decide how to handle our entrance. I don't wish to embarrass you before your family. Is there a way to enter the house without being noticed?"

"Don't tell me you failed to uncover all the secret passages of Swan Park during your wanderings."

"I see that making love hasn't dulled your sharp tongue, my lady. Very well." He halted, swept her up in his arms, and strode toward the main entrance. "We can always go in like this. Get all the questions out of the way at once."

"Put me down, you rascal!" she hissed, darting a furtive glance at the windows they were passing. "For pity's sake, put me down!"

"As you wish." He released her legs so they slid slowly down his body, though he continued embracing her until he'd stolen a kiss. One very hot, very sweet kiss that left him panting for more.

She broke away, breath racing, eyes wide, lips reddened. "There's a side door behind there." She pointed to a row of hedges. "It leads to one of the servants' stairs."

When they reached the small door, she opened it, but he caught her arm to stay her. "I'll let you go up alone. I'll enter in front and distract everyone," he said.

"How do you intend to do that?"

He shrugged. "I suppose it's time I tell them about the masquerade, if Daniel hasn't already done so. That ought to distract them." He prayed that Daniel hadn't mentioned *everything*, however. "Are you coming down to dinner after you get inside?"

She dropped her gaze, probably embarrassed. "I . . . um . . . think I'll eat in my room tonight. I need a bath."

"Shall I join you for that bath later?"

"Certainly not!" she protested with a fiery blush.

He chuckled. "I suppose that will have to wait until after we're married."

She eyed him warily. "Surely you wouldn't be so incorrigible as to bathe with me."

"I'm afraid, darling, that I intend to be a most incorrigible husband." He grinned shamelessly. "You know very well that's why you agreed to marry me."

She sniffed, but didn't bother to deny it.

"I suppose sneaking into your bedchamber at midnight is out of the question, too?"

"It certainly is!"

He sighed loudly. But it was just as well. He should probably meet with her father in private to explain about the masquerade. With any luck, the fact that Griff was willing to marry Rosalind would mollify the man's anger over the deception.

Not that the man had any reason to be angry, considering his own treacheries. But if angered, the earl might mention the certificate to Rosalind, and it would be better if Griff headed that off. Indeed, it might be better if Griff kept her as far away from her father as possible until the wedding.

"Rosalind," he said, clasping her hand in both of his, "I'll need to go to London soon, if only to determine that matters are running smoothly at Knighton Trading. And I want you to go with me."

"But Griff, that would be highly improper—you know that! It's one thing for us to secretly . . . well, you know . . . but we can't let the whole world think—"

"You can take one of your sisters as chaperone on the short journey—surely Helena will do."

"What about Papa? And the estate?"

"Juliet can stay and care for your father as she already does. The estate will be fine for a few days." He caressed her fingers. "Once we're in London, you'll have my mother for a chaperone, and that should satisfy anyone's notions of propriety."

Briefly she looked stunned, then her face cleared. "Oh, yes, I forgot you have a mother. I'm so accustomed to thinking of you as the orphaned Mr. Brennan . . ." She trailed off with the slightest hint of accusation. "I'm afraid it'll take me a while to sort out your character."

Her words stabbed his conscience. Determinedly, he tugged her into his arms, kissed her with a thoroughness bordering on indecency, then drew back just enough to stare down at her. "That's all you need to know of my character, darling."

A shaky breath wafted from her, and she looked dazed. Thank God for his sweet Athena's natural passion, his best weapon for keeping her on his side. He must use it often to secure her.

A smile touched his lips. That would certainly be no trial.

His satisfaction deepened when she didn't resist

his embrace. "When do you want us to leave?" she whispered as he began stroking her beautiful, wild hair.

"Day after tomorrow, if possible. I'll need to settle matters with your father concerning the marriage, of course, and you and Helena will need to pack. But I see no reason to delay. There's much to do in London, and I want you to see Knighton Trading." He added mischievously, "The place from which all wickedness stems."

She snorted. "I suspect it's not the place, but the owner who is producing all that wickedness."

"Yes, and shall continue producing wickedness once he's married." He cupped her breast and bent to whisper, "All manner of wickedness."

She shoved his hand away. "No more of that now, Griff. If we're caught out here like this, I'll never recover from the embarrassment. I must go in before someone comes looking for me."

"Very well." Catching her hand up in his, he kissed it. "Good night, my darling. I'll see you at breakfast. Go on to your bath now, and dream of me while you wash your sweet little—"

"That's enough, Griff!" But though she shot him a chastening look as she scurried off through the door, he could hear her low laugh after it closed behind her.

He sighed. How in hell would he last until the wedding? No doubt he'd become an aficionado of cold baths before he got the chance to bed her again, for tomorrow they had much to attend to. With Helena as chaperone on the way to London and his mother as chaperone once they arrived, there'd be little opportunity after they left here.

Well, abstinence would only make the wedding night that much sweeter. A grin crept across his face. He intended to press for the shortest engagement in history. And knowing Rosalind, she wouldn't argue.

When he entered the house, the butler informed him that everyone was at dinner. Time to face the wrath of the other Swanlea spinsters. Not that he really cared what they thought; the only one he cared about was Rosalind, and she'd already agreed to marry him.

He entered the dining room and took a seat. "Good evening, all. Has Daniel been telling you about our little subterfuge?"

"Daniel?" Lady Helena asked.

"Subterfuge?" Lady Juliet echoed.

He sighed, then began explaining. Daniel said nothing, but merely ate his dinner, and Griff soon realized why. The damned Irishman wanted to watch Griff squirm.

Squirming was all Griff did for the next hour. He gave Lady Helena and Lady Juliet the same reason for the masquerade he'd given Rosalind, ignoring Daniel's questioning glance. By the end of dinner, after answering a hundred questions with considerable evasion, he found himself being roundly condemned by the two sisters.

"So you lied to us?" Lady Juliet said for what must have been the fifteenth time. "You've been pretending all along?"

"Yes, yes," Griff said impatiently. Rosalind had been more understanding, damn it. If she could forgive him, why the hell couldn't the rest of them? "Nothing has really changed, except that I'll be the one marrying your sister and not Daniel—"

"Who *also* lied to us," Lady Helena broke in, shooting Griff's man of affairs an angry glance. "No doubt you've been enjoying yourself at our expense, laughing at us for our stupidity and—"

"Now see here," Daniel retorted, "it wasn't like

that. This was all Griff's idea. I disapproved from the beginning, but I work for him, so I did what I was told. Trust me, I didn't like deceiving all of you."

Juliet patted his hand sympathetically. "Of course you didn't." Apparently, now that she didn't have to marry the big lummox or see her sister sacrifice to marry him, she could be easy around the man. "We all know your kind heart, Mr. Knight— I mean, Mr. Brennan." She leveled a blistering look on Griff. "It's your employer who has behaved badly, very badly indeed."

Griff glared at Juliet. "Before you start exonerating Daniel of all blame, you should know that he chose to do this. I didn't force him. He went along with it because he's being amply compensated. Two hundred and fifty pounds, to be exact."

"Two hundred and fifty pounds!" Lady Helena looked stunned by the amount. She turned a contemptuous gaze on Daniel. "I suppose I should expect no better from a man who was a smuggler and God knows what else. How could you resist such a large sum, after all?" Her tone grew wounded. "Then again, it must have taken a large sum for you to agree to endure a visit with us tedious spinsters."

She threw down her napkin and started to rise, but Daniel caught her arm. "Listen, Lady Helena—"

"Let go of me," she whispered, her eyes glittering with what looked like tears. "I should have realized you were being paid for all your kindnesses—for the billiards and the courtship of Rosalind and . . . You were being paid to entertain the spinsters. Well, you certainly earned your money. You fooled us all."

When Daniel began to remonstrate with her and Lady Juliet jumped in to defend him, Griff shook his head and left. Let the three of them sort it out. He was in no mood to deal with two fractious women tonight. After all, he still had a fractious earl to deal with, and he feared that would take all his patience.

Though Griff hadn't yet been in Swanlea's private quarters, he knew where they were. The study where he'd first encountered Rosalind and battled Daniel was situated in that wing on the same floor. So it took him only a few minutes to locate the earl's bedchamber.

He'd half expected to find a servant awaiting his lord's leisure outside it, but there was no one. Perhaps the man was sleeping. Should he come back? No, the sooner he could speak with the earl, the better. Easing the door open, he looked inside. It took a moment for him to adjust to the dim lighting provided by the lone candle on the earl's bedside table.

But a quick glance showed the man sitting up, though his eyes seemed closed. As Griff walked in and approached the bed, he considered what to do. Was the man merely dozing? Or did he always sleep sitting up with a candle lit?

One thing was certain—he was obviously more ill than Griff had realized. The earl was only fifty-odd years old, yet he looked a score older. An alarming rattle marked his breathing, and the skin of his face hung loose as a shroud. The entire room stank of possets and urine and death, chilling Griff to the bone, for it reminded him painfully of his own father's sickroom all those years ago.

He'd nearly decided to return early the next morning when the earl opened his eyes and spotted him. Before Griff could say a word, the earl's sleep-dazed expression stiffened into horror. Clutching his sheet to his chest, he shrank against the pillow. "So you have come for me, have you?" he gasped. "Is that how the judgment begins? I am taken to my grave by the man I most wronged?"

Griff stood frozen in the shadows. What the

devil? None of the daughters had said a word about dementia in their father. Was the wretch dreaming with his eyes open?

"I should have known they would send you." The earl coughed, never taking his eyes from Griff. "Who else should usher me into hell but you, Leonard?"

Then it hit him. Mother had always said that Griff was the very image of his father, but until now he'd thought she exaggerated. Clearly, she hadn't.

He started to step into the candlelight by the bed to let the man see him better, then hesitated. Some dark impulse made him say sharply, "And what have you done that I should usher you into hell?"

The earl's eyes blazed. "Do not torment me, ghost. You know what I have done. But I am trying to make it right. Please . . . If you will only give me a few more weeks to make it right, I will go willingly to my fate."

"Make it right?" Griff's blood pounded in his veins. "How do you intend to make it right?"

"Your son will marry my Rosalind. *That* will make it right."

It took a second for Griff to remember that the earl thought Rosalind was marrying Daniel. And that Daniel was Mr. Knighton.

"When they marry," the earl continued in a wheezing voice, "I will give him the marriage certificate, the proof of his legitimacy."

"Why not give it to him now? Why wait until after a wedding?" Though Griff intended to marry Rosalind either way, he wanted to hear the man attempt to explain himself, attempt to vindicate his despicable actions to a higher power.

"I cannot tell if your son is bitter about what happened. He seems amiable, but I know he has every right to hate me. If I give him the certificate, he might ruin us."

Griff clenched his fists at his sides. "But you agree that he has every right to hate you, to wish to ruin you."

"*Me*, yes. But not my family."

"So you'd deny him his birthright if he doesn't marry your daughter."

"No! Truly, I would not!" He struggled for breath, holding his hand against his sunken chest. "I would give him the papers regardless. I will not go to my death with his undeserved bastardy on my conscience."

Amazement coursed through Griff. Did he mean it? Would a dying man lie to a ghost? Griff gritted his teeth. Perhaps. A man who wanted to cheat death would say almost anything.

The earl's voice turned pleading. "Don't you see, Leonard? I love my daughters as much as you love your son. I had to try the other first, make sure my gels were provided for." He coughed. "Or what would become of them when I die?"

There was no mistaking the earl's sincerity. Guilt swamped Griff, staggering him. How could the earl's motives, which had seemed so reprehensible, now seem almost understandable?

"I think you will like my Rosalind for your son," the earl went on in a lowered voice. He took a deep breath, coughed a bit, then managed to control it. "She has the devil of a temper, and she is not so pretty as my youngest, but—"

"Rosalind is an angel!" Griff snapped. "She's a better daughter than you deserve!"

The man blinked at him. "So you know her? Yes, I suppose ghosts know everyone. You should approve—she is much like Georgina was at her age."

"Georgina?" Griff whispered, reminded of what Daniel had said about the earl knowing his mother.

Sitting up a little straighter, the earl struggled for

breath. When he could speak again, he said, "I no longer hate you for winning her. After I found my Solange, I was content without Georgina. Solange gave me my three gels, after all."

The words swam in Griff's brain. What did the scoundrel mean—without Georgina?

A cloud dimmed the old man's face. "But when you first stole her from me, I could not bear it. Otherwise, I would never have acted so rashly. Surely you can understand my feelings that day—" He dragged in a harsh breath. "When I went to see your babe, the one who ended my future. You would soon have the title and Swan Park. Then your heir would have it. And you had the woman I loved, too."

The earl had loved Mother? And Griff had never known? Mother had never spoken of it. But perhaps she hadn't known either. Griff held his breath, afraid to stop the man from talking. And just as afraid to let him go on.

The earl stared beyond Griff as if gazing into the past. "And I? I had nothing. You had Georgina, and I had nothing."

The words made Griff flinch. He knew what it was like to be left with nothing.

Then he cursed his momentary sympathy. The man who'd left Griff with nothing was the damned earl himself, for the love of God!

"You should never have invited me to visit," the earl choked out. Griff forcibly reminded himself that the man thought he was speaking to Griff's father. "It was too tempting, too easy to steal your marriage certificate when you went to fetch the baby."

"And you must have known about the registry burning down in Gretna Green," Griff prodded, fascinated to hear his own suspicions confirmed.

Swanlea nodded. "The old earl himself told me.

And I knew no one would ever find any witnesses to the wedding."

No, Griff thought grimly, not in Gretna Green, where the only witnesses were strangers more often than not.

The earl's voice was a thready murmur. "What I did was wicked, I know. How many times in the past thirty years have I told myself that?" He wheezed a moment. "But I thought you would *live*, damn you. You were not supposed to die so young. I thought, *Once the old earl dies, Leonard will be earl for his lifetime, but after Leonard dies, any son of mine will be earl. That is fair.*"

Swanlea began nodding as if agreeing with himself and his twisted thoughts. "I told myself, *he stole Georgina from me, so our families should share the title. By the time Leonard dies, his son will be well situated. What will he need with a title?*"

"But he was *not* well situated!" Griff hissed. "He was left with no money, a mound of debts, and a mother to support!"

"I know!" The earl gasped for breath a moment, then went on. "I tried to send Georgina money, but she would not take it."

"Liar!"

" 'Tis true! You know it is true! And there was little enough to send. What more could I have done, Leonard? By then, I had my own wife and daughters. To admit I had stolen the title would have meant ruin for my family. And you had a son, for God's sake!" He wheezed, his body shaking. "He could make his own fortune, and he *did*! He made you proud. I only had daughters, and I could not be sure of their future."

"You didn't need a son, damn you! You were a healthy man. You could have made your fortune yourself. But you were too cowardly for that. You preferred to let a poor twelve-year-old boy suffer instead."

The bitterness of remembered pain laced all his words. "You stood by and watched while the other boys called him 'bastard' unjustly. You did nothing when he was forced to consort with smugglers and thieves to stay out of debt. And you sat in your comfortable estate ignoring him while he withstood the contempt of men who by rights were his equals, because that was what it took for him to gain his success!"

"But he did succeed! That boy is richer than I have ever been!" The fervent protest sent the earl into a fit of coughing, which Griff watched with a strange mixture of anger and concern. He wanted to blot out the earl's words, ignore them, belittle them. Yet he couldn't.

Because despite all Griff had endured, he'd indeed achieved success, so much that the earl had been forced to come to *him* for help. It was hard to hate a man whose fortunes had fallen so far that he had to ask aid from the very person he'd wronged. A man who was dying a slow, painful death.

Yet it was no more than the man deserved. After all, Griff wasn't the only person the earl had wronged. "What about Georgina?" Griff asked cuttingly when the earl's coughing subsided. "If you cared for her, how could you have let *her* suffer? How could you have had me . . . my son proclaimed a bastard when it brought her such heartache?"

A pain too deep to be merely physical spasmed over the earl's face. "I was young and foolish. I believe I *did* want her to suffer some of my torment. She chose you over me because you would be earl. I had few prospects, but until you came, she planned to marry me. You know she did. She still loved me on the day you married. She told me."

Rage exploded through Griff. "You lie, old man!" He strode into the light with fists clenched. "You lie! My mother never loved you! Never!"

The earl gaped at him, then paled to a sickening white. Slowly, he surveyed the room as if to catch his bearings, his breath coming in sharp, hoarse gasps. Then he lifted a shaky finger to point at Griff. "Y-You're not Leonard! You're flesh and blood! Who are you? Tell me who you are, blast it!"

A weary female voice answered from behind Griff. "He's Leonard's son, Papa—and he's very much flesh and blood."

No! Griff thought, the blood draining from his face. *No, she can't have heard!*

Slowly he turned to find Rosalind standing in the doorway, but she wouldn't look at him. She stared past him to her father, her soft features trembling with pain.

Oh, God, how much had she heard? How *much*? His stomach roiled.

As she entered, she clutched an iron box to her chest. She'd obviously come from her bath, for she wore a less formal gown, and her pinned-up hair glistened. It was like looking at heaven from the ferry to hell.

Then she swung her gaze to his, and the clear betrayal in her eyes told him she'd heard far too much. It pierced him to the center of his heart.

"This, Papa, is your cousin," she went on. "Marsden Griffith Knighton. I'm afraid this is the real Mr. Knighton."

Chapter 19

Though those that are betrayed
Do feel the treason sharply, yet the traitor
Stands in worse case of woe.

William Shakespeare, *English playwright,* Cymbeline

Why did I have to be right? Rosalind thought. Why couldn't it all have been just as Griff said—a simple, foolish masquerade that he regretted now that he wanted to marry her?

Of course, he didn't really want to marry her, did he? He wanted something else. And having heard most of his conversation with Papa, she knew he had every right to it.

She dearly wished she hadn't come to Papa's bedchamber, or stayed when she'd heard Griff's voice. Ignorance would have been such bliss. Yet once she'd caught the drift of the conversation, she couldn't have left if her life depended on it.

On legs that threatened to give way beneath her, she walked to her father's bed.

"How long have you . . . been standing there?" Griff asked hoarsely.

She cut her gaze to him only long enough to see the bloodless cast to his features that nearly mirrored her father's. "Since Papa started talking about 'making it right.' "

Then she faced Papa, who was scrutinizing Griff's features in bewilderment. Hard to believe her ill father could once have been so heartless. He'd always been a gruff, cantankerous old fool, but she'd never thought him cruel. Yet she knew his tale was true, for it made sense out of all the other odd pieces of this bad play.

Now she knew why Griff had responded so angrily whenever she'd called him bastard. Now she knew why he'd even bothered to indulge her father's request, why he'd masqueraded, and what he'd been looking for.

Icy fingers gripped her heart. And yes, now she knew why he wanted to marry a great, ungainly spinster like her.

She approached the bed before her tears could spill out and betray her. "Papa, give me the key to the strongbox."

His gaze swung to her. "Knighton said he would marry you." He coughed fitfully, then shook his head. "But . . . but it was that other Knighton—the blond one."

"Rosalind is marrying *me*," Griff bit out. "Not 'the blond one.' And I am Knighton, as your daughter says."

"You needn't keep speaking of marriage, Griff," she whispered, not daring to look at him. "You'll have what you want. I'm sure it's in this box." She glared at her father. "It's in here, isn't it? Give me the key. Now!"

"Rosalind, darling—" Griff began.

"Please don't," she begged, his endearment torturing her. "This is difficult enough as it is. Don't make it worse by pretending." As she tried not to cry, she tightened her arms about the strongbox, not caring how the sharp corners snagged her gown. Turning her face away, she dashed a few wayward tears from her face. She wouldn't fall apart in front of him. Blast it, she wouldn't!

"Pretending?" Griff echoed. "Pretending what? That I want to marry you? Damnation, that's no pretense!"

She shook her head wildly. "Don't you understand? You can *have* the certificate! You needn't marry me for it. I'll give it to you. It belongs to you. If I'd known Papa was offering it to induce you to marry one of us . . . if he'd told me what was in here when he asked me to keep the strongbox safe . . ."

Tears choked her, pooling in her throat. She cleared it as best she could, then stalked up to the bed and glowered down at her father. "Give me the bloody key, Papa!"

Her father blinked, but meekly reached beneath his nightshirt and withdrew a thin chain from which hung a key. She didn't even attempt disentangling the chain. She snapped it with a jerk, then took the key and shoved it into the lock of the strongbox. Her fingers shook so badly it took her a second to get it open.

In that second Griff came to her side and laid his hand on her arm. "Please, darling, leave it be. I don't care about it right now."

"Don't care about it?" She twisted away from him, clutching the unlocked box to her chest as if it alone could keep her afloat in this sea of deceit. She met his stricken gaze with her own. "Don't say you don't care about it, Griff Knighton, because you lie! You cared enough to come here and switch places with your man of affairs. To spend every waking hour searching the house. And when I was suspicious of your activities, you cared enough to use every possible trick to rid yourself of me." *Even seduction*, she thought, though she didn't dare say it in front of Papa.

Her voice dropped to an anguished whisper. "And when you finally realized you'd never find it on your own, you cared enough about it to accept Papa's terms and ask one of the pathetic Swanlea Spinsters to marry you. So don't tell me you don't care about it, because you lie!"

"For the love of God, surely you don't believe—"

"Here it is!" she cried, yanking open the box. She pulled out a sheaf of papers and flipped through them until she found the odd-looking one from Gretna Green. Tossing the rest of it aside—box, papers, and all—she strode up to Griff with the only one that mattered. "Here it is," she repeated, waving it madly at him. "It's yours. Take it! Then leave, blast you!"

"I'm not leaving!" He ignored the paper. "Not without you!"

"He don't have to leave, gel," her father put in, " 'specially if he takes that paper. Once he's got that, it isn't our estate anymore. Don't you understand? He's the rightful earl. He'll take that before the College of Heralds and the House of Lords, and the title and this place will be his."

"I understand that perfectly, Papa." She shoved the certificate against Griff's chest. "But unlike you, I don't care. Because it was his from the beginning. You just stole it from him for a time."

Though shame flushed her father's features, he didn't give up. "All the same, I must consider you gels. If he marries one of you, he'll have reason to wait until I die. If he don't marry one of you and he's got that in his hands, he'll drag me into court. We'll all be shamed publicly, and that'll be the end of any future for you three."

An ugly realization made her belly churn. She stared at Griff incredulously. "Is that what you'd planned to do with it if you'd found it during your search? Is it?"

Griff hesitated just long enough for her to read the truth in his stark features.

"You bloody, heartless ass," she hissed. Dropping the certificate on the floor at his feet, she whirled toward the door.

He caught her by the arm and jerked her back. "Damn it, I would never leave any of you destitute. I'd already decided to provide for you. I have no quarrel with the rest of you, only him. Ask Daniel, if you don't believe me. But I need that proof of my legitimacy, and yes, I intended to find it on my own. It's exactly as I said this afternoon—when I came here, I didn't plan to take a wife."

"Until you were forced into it because you couldn't find the blasted thing!"

"No! I may have come here with other intentions, but that changed. I proposed to you because I want you as my wife!" He swung her around to face him, gripping her arms painfully tight. "You can't let this keep you from marrying me, damn you!"

"Listen to Knighton," her father put in shakily from his bed. "You know your duty to your family, gel."

When she stiffened, Griff shot her father a black look. "Shut up, old man! Can't you see you're making it worse? Don't you know *anything* about your daughter?"

With a low oath, he faced her again. The candle-light left most of his features in shadow, but that seemed appropriate since the scoundrel had left his entire character in shadow until now. "Listen to me, darling. If you heard our entire discussion, then you heard me describe you as an angel to your father. You did, didn't you?"

Bits and pieces of the conversation trickled into her head. Yes, she'd heard it, but reeling from all the other revelations, she hadn't paid it much heed.

When she said nothing, he went on. "Does a man say that about a woman he's being forced to marry? Don't you think if I'd wanted to marry you only because of the certificate, I'd have chosen the daughter who was most willing to marry, the one easiest to convince? Don't you think I'd have chosen Juliet if that's all that mattered to me?"

"You knew I'd never let Juliet marry you," she retorted hotly. "And Helena wouldn't marry you or anybody else, so that left only me."

"By God, woman, must you always be so damned stubborn?"

"Yes! That's what I am! I thought you knew it when you proposed. I even thought . . . maybe you liked it a little."

"I did! I do! I like that and a score of other things about you." Shooting her father a furtive glance, he drew her close and dropped his voice. "I thought I made it very clear this afternoon what I felt for you." His heated gaze fixed on her lips. "Do you think my lovemaking was all a role? That I could pretend to desire a woman, pretend to be jealous over her when I felt nothing at all?"

"Why not? You pretended to be a highwayman's son, a man of affairs, a former smuggler. You pretended to be half-Irish. If you hadn't quoted so much bloody Shakespeare, I would have thought you'd pretended to know your Shakespeare. Just now you even pretended to be a ghost." As all his lies hit her anew, she struggled to draw the breath to continue. "And . . . and the first time we kissed, it was only a pretense. You admitted as much."

"I admitted that it began as a pretense. It certainly didn't end as one." He added in a whisper, "And making love to you this afternoon was the most wonderful experience of my entire life."

She felt herself weakening. No, she wouldn't let him do this to her! "Griff, I don't know why you persist in this farce! You have the document—I give it to you freely. I understand why you did it, truly I do. I heard what Papa did to you." Tears flooded her eyes. Dear God, how much Griff had suffered because of Papa.

"It was a terrible, awful thing to do to a child," she went on. "As you told him, you have every right to hate him, to wish to ruin him. I don't blame you for it. So there's no need for you to marry me out of guilt or anything else. Just take the paper and let me be!"

"I'll never let you be, do you hear? As for guilt, let me disabuse you of the notion that anything so self-less as guilt drives me to marry you. I'm being entirely selfish. I want you. I intend to have you. You won't talk me out of marrying you."

She read the determination in his face with shock. Dear God, could he truly wish to marry her? But why? He'd still given her no plausible reason other than desire. Yet he did seem in earnest.

Unfortunately, he wasn't the same man she'd thought she was marrying. "What if I don't want to marry you anymore?"

He looked as stunned as if someone had just struck his thick head with a hammer.

She tilted up her chin proudly. "I see you find it surprising that a spinster with no future would refuse an offer of marriage from a wealthy and handsome young heir to a title. Most people would think I'm daft." Wrenching her arms from his grasp, she glared at him. "But then I *am* a bit daft, as you know, and I don't really care what they think." She ignored her father's groan. "I've no desire to marry a man I understand so little, whose aims in life are so opposed to my own."

Rage twisted his features into an ugly mask. "How am I any different now than I was this afternoon? You seemed perfectly happy to marry me then."

"That was before I knew that your elaborate masquerade was designed to wreak vengeance on Papa by publicly shaming him as well as me and my sisters."

"Vengeance!" He whirled away from her. "You and Daniel with your narrow minds! This is not about vengeance!"

"Oh? Then what is it about? Why else would you have set out to steal that certificate and use it to strip Papa of his title? You have a fortune, a thriving company. What do you need with a title?"

For a moment, she thought he wouldn't answer, for he stared away, his neck strained so taut she fancied she saw the pulse throb in it. "I have a thriving company, yes." He fixed her with a defiant look. "But how long would it thrive if I didn't seek to improve it and find it new markets? Next year a delegation is going to China to establish trade outside the confines of the East India Company. Every trading company in England wants a seat on that delegation, including me. As a bastard with a scandalous past, I have little chance of being considered. But as an earl in the House of Lords—"

Her heart sank. "Of course. You'd be in the perfect position politically to be included. That's why you must establish your legitimacy as soon as possible, isn't it? You must act before the decisions are made. I understand."

She blinked back fresh tears. Yes, she understood only too well. Daniel had said Knighton Trading was everything to Griff, and now she realized just how true that was.

"It's simply a practical matter, a business matter," he explained in that terribly precise tone he always used when speaking of his unscrupulous methods on behalf of his company. "If I could have found another way to achieve it, I would have, but I couldn't. I will, however, regain the title as discreetly as possible in deference to your family."

"So when you proposed to me this afternoon, you still intended to use that certificate as soon as you got your hands on it?" When he didn't answer, she took that for a yes. "What did you plan to do marry me and then go drag my ill father to the House of Lords so you could publicly proclaim him the worst sort of schemer? I'll admit he deserves it, but he's my father, after all. Did you think I would champion you?"

Averting his gaze from her, he yanked restlessly on his cravat. She hoped the blasted thing was choking him.

"I was hoping . . . that is, I planned . . . Damn it, I hadn't thought that far." His gaze shifted back to her. "But I did assume that when you knew the circumstances, you would see I had a right to the title."

The sad thing was, she did see he had a right to it. She'd merely hoped he might be noble enough not to exercise his right. But clearly she didn't know him at all. Griff had no noble instincts. Daniel was wrong in that respect—Griff wasn't ignoring his heart; he simply *had* no heart.

"Here now, man," her father protested from his bed. "You aren't saying you meant to use that certificate before I died. And shame my daughters?"

A terrible sadness came over her. "Yes, Papa, I'm afraid that's precisely what Mr. Knighton planned to do. Still plans to do, I suspect."

"Why not?" Griff said defensively. "It's mine by right, damn it!"

Rosalind sighed. All this time, Papa had thought his brilliant plan would save him from Griff's wrath and gain her and her sisters a future. Instead, he'd opened the door to the griffin, and now that the griffin had come he wouldn't depart without his treasure.

Well, there was one treasure he wouldn't get. "Yes, that title is yours by right. But *I* am not."

A look of panic came over Griff's face. "Why does the certificate make any difference? It changes nothing! We'll live here after we're married, and your family will live here, too. Yes, there might be a short period of scandal, but people will forget. None of you ever sought their good opinion before. I don't see why it matters now."

She thought of Juliet's desperate urge not to become a spinster and Helena's defensiveness about her limp. "No, why should it?" she said sarcastically. "My sisters are already odd ducks, after all. They can't find husbands even with their rank, so who cares if they lose it? Who cares if they're gossiped about behind their backs? My sisters are beneath your concern, aren't they? They're the daughters of a man who treated you badly, so you see no reason to protect their reputations."

A dark flush spread up his neck to his face.

"Of course, society will gossip about me, too, but not to my face if we marry. No one would dare

laugh publicly at the wife of the new Earl of Swanlea, with all his wealth and influence. But they'll
scorn me privately. I'll be the sister clever enough to
marry the real earl to protect my family from ruin."
She choked back more tears. "I'll be the whoring
sister."

"Don't ever call yourself that again!" Griff
exploded. "And since when do you care what they
think of you, goddamn it? Didn't you just say that
you don't?"

"The point is that you don't care what happens to
me or my family as long as it serves your purpose.
You'll do anything for Knighton Trading—whether
consorting with smugglers or defaming innocents—so what place could a mere woman like me
have in your life? Well, I can't marry a man who
cares so little for me."

She turned on her heel and walked out, afraid to
stay any longer. She'd fall apart in her room, away
from him.

When she heard him call her name, she increased
her pace. She wouldn't let him work on her with his
tempting words, for right now she'd be all too susceptible to them.

If she could hate him, it would be easy. If she
could consider him the villain of the piece, she
could set her world to rights again and thrust him
clear out of it.

But she couldn't hate him, knowing how dreadfully he'd been treated. Griff had Papa to thank for
his character, so she could hardly reprove him for it.
While he and Papa had been talking, she'd stood
there in horror, realizing the appalling ramifica-
tions, imagining Griff's life as a bastard. His sudden
and unwarranted poverty had driven him to awful
lengths. With shame, she remembered her ridicu-

lous moral posturing in the deer park. He'd done
what he could after a wretched betrayal, and she'd
chastised him for it.

Tears streamed down her cheeks. He'd spent his
life regaining something that had always belonged
to him, all because her foolish, cruel father had in
one petty act rent Griff's and his mother's life in
two.

She dashed the tears from her eyes. She understood, truly she did, yet she couldn't be part of it.
Papa might have ripped out Griff's heart, but that
didn't mean she had to marry the empty shell.

Hearing footsteps behind her, she glanced back,
then panicked when she saw Griff striding after her.
If he caught her alone, she would never stand firm.
He had that curst ability to make her lose all her
good intentions . . .

He was running after her, and she swung about
in alarm, wondering how to escape him. She'd
never make it to her bedchamber. She was nearly to
Papa's study, but didn't have her keys to lock herself in.

Then she spotted the ancient sword, back in its
spot on the wall. Grabbing it down, she brandished
it in front of her just as Griff reached her.

"Keep back, do you hear? I'm done with you! I
won't marry you, so leave me alone!"

The candlelight heightened his determined expression. "You're daft indeed if you think I'll let you
walk away from me now. I won't let this change
things between us, Rosalind."

He advanced on her undaunted, and she backed
up a pace, nearing the open doorway of the study
behind her. The reason for his nickname might have
been a fabrication, but it suited him well. He had a
griffin's predatory instincts and obsession with

rightful ownership. Like a griffin, he was fixed upon keeping his treasure.

The sword wavered in her hand. "I'll . . . I'll use this!" she cried, as much to convince herself as him. "I'll unman you with it, I swear I will!"

He paused, raising one jet eyebrow. "As I recall, you threatened to do that only if I took a mistress. And I haven't."

Utter despair possessed her heart. How could he be so blind? "Oh, but you have. You took a mistress long before you met me, one you'll never relinquish."

"What the hell are you talking about?"

"Knighton Trading—as demanding a mistress as any woman could ever be to you. She's one mistress I can't compete with."

Like the lion half of the griffin, he stalked her. "What do you want from me? That I abandon Knighton Trading's best interests? Is that what you want?"

She backed up into the study, for there was nowhere else to go. How could she use a sword on him? "I want nothing from you." Nothing she had any right to ask of him, anyway. She wanted him to give up the part of his plans that meant shaming her family. She wanted him to care that much for her. She wanted him to love her. "There's nothing you could give me that would entice me to marry you now. You've killed my feelings for you."

Fear flickered over his face, then was gone. "I don't believe you." He snatched a candle from the sconce and continued to advance, backing her all the way into the dark room. "I refuse to believe that the woman who shared every intimacy with me this afternoon could suddenly turn off her feelings merely because I'm pursuing what's rightfully mine." He closed the door behind him, then set the candle in the sconce near the door. "You still care—I know you do."

The longing in his voice pricked her raw. How dared he appeal to her feelings after trampling all over them earlier? "You know nothing about me and what I feel, you bloody ass," she whispered achingly.

He looked stricken. "Can't call me a *bastard* now that you know I'm not one?"

"Oh, but you are! Inside, you're still every bit a bastard! Is that what turned you into one? Being called one all the time?"

He shook his head wearily. "Your father is what turned me into one, my sweet. But he's happy to remove the stain, so I don't understand why you object."

"I don't object to his offering to remove it. Only to your accepting his offer when you know what it will do to my family—"

"Your family doesn't matter, don't you see?" he cried. "All that matters is us!"

"Not to me!"

"Damnation, Rosalind, I . . ." He glanced away, looking hollow-eyed and bleak in the shadowed room. "I understand why you are angry. I should not have deceived you about my purpose." His gaze shot back to her. "But I didn't tell you because I didn't want *this* to happen! I didn't want you to make the mistake of thinking that this matter between me and your father affects what you and I feel for each other!"

He stepped forward as if to touch her, and she leveled the sword at his chest.

"D-Don't come a-any nearer," she stammered.

"Or what? You'll stab me?" His jaw tautened. "You may be outrageous, but you're not given to murdering your lovers. And we both know you'd never unman me."

"Don't tempt me!" she cried hoarsely, and pressed the tip of the sword to his breeches.

With an expression of grim purpose, he closed his hand around the blade, gripping it so tightly that if she moved it even a fraction, it would slice open his hand. She froze, her gaze fixed on that terrible union of flesh and steel.

"Let go of the sword, darling," he urged. "You know you don't want to hurt me."

Curse him for being right! "What if I do? What if I want to hurt you as much as you hurt me?"

Guilt slashed across his features. "I didn't intend to hurt you, I swear it. And if I for one moment believed that you truly no longer cared for me, that you actually wish to hurt me, I'd leave tonight and never return. But I don't believe it, and neither do you."

"Because it doesn't suit your plans," she whispered.

"Because it's not true." He released the blade, but only to move his hand up to cover hers where it clasped the hilt. "Please, my darling . . . Do not send me away."

Such blatant need laced his voice that she didn't resist when he angled the sword away from between them, nor when he removed it from her numb fingers. But when he gathered her in his arms, tears began streaming down her cheeks.

"Oh, God, don't cry, my sweet," he murmured, wiping away her tears. "It tortures me when you cry."

"Then release me from this curst engagement," she pleaded.

"I can't." His lips brushed her hair, her brow, her temple. "I need you too much."

"To warm your bed, you mean—"

"No, for more than that," he whispered, dropping sweet kisses along her hairline. "And you need me. You know you do."

She did need him—that was the trouble. Because she needed him more desperately than he needed her. He might be missing a heart, but he certainly had all his other "parts," and he seemed to think two out of three were perfectly acceptable. She did not.

And yet . . . *Do not send me away*, his words echoed in her head as he covered her face with kisses, his tempting kisses that never failed to dissolve her into molten heat. With him, her body had a will of its own. When he kissed her ear, then tugged at the soft flesh of her earlobe with his teeth, she shivered in desire, and yes, *need*.

Oh, why must he always affect her in this way? He'd wrapped his greedy griffin's wings about her, and she didn't know how to fight free. How could she resist when the man she loved held her fast against the body she desired?

"I want you as my wife, darling." He dragged his fingers through her damp hair, dislodging pins until it fell down about her shoulders. "I want you to be my companion by day and my bedmate by night. I want you to bear my children—"

She drew back to stare at him wide-eyed. Children?

"You didn't even think of that, did you? Well, I did." Laying his hand on her stomach, he rotated it in a slow circle. "Our child might even now be growing in your belly—it only takes once. Can you tell me you don't want any child of mine?"

The candle above them lit his face with an unholy glow. He slipped his hand inside her wrapped gown to cup her breast, and since she wore no che-

mise, it was her naked flesh he held in his hand.
"Can you tell me that the thought of suckling our
son or daughter at this breast doesn't please you as
it does me?" The raw ache in his voice echoed in her
heart. "You can't, can you?"

She wanted to protest, to say he was wrong, but
she couldn't even lie about it. She hated herself for
it, but she couldn't.

When the silence stretched out meaningfully, his
eyes flashed wild and fierce. "I thought not."

"Oh, but Griff—"

He muffled her protest with a hot, needy kiss.
With slow, deep strokes, he explored her mouth, his
tongue mating with hers so deliciously that he
elicited a groan from her. His hand inside her gown
tenderly caressed her breast, and she leaned into
him, twining her arms about his neck.

Curse him for knowing so well how to tempt her.
Her body was already softening, readying itself for
him. As he fondled her breasts, they came alive, the
nipples tightening into little knots beneath his
ardent touches. It was only when he started fumbling for the ties of her gown that she found the
strength to tear her mouth away.

"It will be all right, Rosalind, I swear," he whispered. His breath wafted over her cheek, scented
with wine and spiked with his heat. "Only give me
a chance to prove it to you. Let me remind you how
good it is between us, how right."

She stared up into his face, and felt despair seize
her. She needed no reminding of how good their
lovemaking was. Every moment of the sweet desire
and bliss was fixed in her memory.

But lovemaking was no longer enough. No matter how drunk he made her with passion, she
would always have the sober morning and the real-

ization that he could never love her, that his only true love was his business. She couldn't marry him in the face of that cold truth.

As if sensing her thoughts, he cupped her face in his hands with a look of hungry desperation. "Stay with me now," he whispered. "Let me make love to you, my sweet Rosalind. I need you. I want you."

She hesitated. She needed and wanted him, too, but she could not marry him. And the longer she stayed with him, the harder it would be to refuse.

Her throat tightened as she realized what she must do. Later tonight, she would have to escape Swan Park, before he could wear her down with all his temptations. She would take her meager savings and go to London.

But before she left him forever, she would have one more time with him, one more hour of wondrous bliss. One more chance to show him what love really was, so that he would remember once she'd left him.

"Yes," she whispered.

Then she gave herself into his embrace.

Chapter 20

O, we all acknowledge our faults, now; 'tis the
mode of the day: but the acknowledgment passes
for current payment; and therefore we never
amend them.

Fanny Burney, English novelist, diarist,
and sometime playwright, Camilla

Griff could not believe it—he'd won her at last.
Even though this time had come harder, he'd
won her for good.

Yet even as they both worked feverishly at the
fastenings of their clothing, untying and unbuttoning and loosening, a nagging fear hovered at the
back of his brain. Was she truly his if only passion
kept her?

Why not? Passion was a powerful force indeed,
as his body already attested, crying out its need to
take her, to be inside her, to bury all his apprehension in the welcoming warmth of her loins. What
did it matter how he got her? In time she would for-

give him the rest of it. He would keep her in bed
until she did.

He ignored his screaming conscience, unwilling
even to think of losing her. He wouldn't lose her,
damn it, not over this. He would make everything
up to her in time, and tonight he'd start by making
every inch of her burn. Thankfully, this afternoon
had tapped enough of his need to allow a less fren-
zied lovemaking. He intended to use every minute
in heightening and satisfying her desire. She
wouldn't regret her decision. He'd make sure of it.

He shrugged off his coat and waistcoat, then his
shirt, but as he was reaching for his trouser buttons,
he froze at the sight of her pushing her gown off her
shoulders. With a smile as seductive as Eve's, she let
it slide down her luscious body to fall on the floor in
a heap of periwinkle silk.

His heart stopped. Beneath it lay blond lace
garters and white hose and naught else—no chemise, no petticoats, no drawers. Rosalind in all her
dazzling glory, kissed by candlelight, scented with
rosewater, and all his, every gorgeous inch. It nearly
brought him to his knees. By God, how would he
keep from ravishing her instantly?

As he stood mute, with his cock doing a mindless
dance at the sight of her, her skin pinkened and she
nodded to where his fingers had halted at his
trouser buttons. "Well?"

"Not yet." If he peeled them off now, he'd surely
fall on her like a starving madman, which was not
what he'd planned. "Come with me, darling."

Warily, she let him guide her over to the settee.

"Sit down," he urged, and she did as he bade.

"What are you—" She broke off when he knelt on
the floor and parted her legs. "Oh."

With an almost painful hunger gripping his loins,
he widened her thighs and spread the fleecy folds in

their juncture to gaze on the dewy female flesh he wished to kiss. Then he glanced up into her face. "You liked it when I did this before, didn't you? On the swing?"

Her cheeks were rosy, her eyelids lowered modestly, but she nodded.

Leaning forward, he murmured, "This time will be even better, I promise." Then he covered her soft petals with his mouth.

By God, he loved to taste her heated honeypot. Her woman's scent drove him insane. He entered her with his tongue, ignoring the demands of his erection to focus on building her own demand. He wanted her begging for him, turning to him and only him for satisfaction. He sensed that he held her only by the thinnest tether, and that wasn't enough for him.

Still, he didn't know how long he'd last. He could devour her whole right now, and it wouldn't satisfy his hunger. Nothing could ever satisfy his hunger for Rosalind except more of Rosalind.

More, he thought, using his fingers and lips and tongue to excite her. More, more, his need chanted. Soon his brazen temptress was clasping his head, pressing him against her, swiveling her hips forward to allow him better access. He caressed her velvet skin and drove into her with his tongue until he felt the tension rising in her, felt her shake beneath his mouth. When at last she cried out and surged against him, he thought he'd explode in his trousers.

He'd never known that pleasing a woman could affect a man so deeply. But then he'd never made love to a woman like Rosalind, who put her whole heart into it, who enjoyed the pleasure unabashed. It left him in awe. And rampantly aroused.

When she'd come to her senses enough to look at him through eyes still dazed with satisfaction, he said urgently, "My turn."

While she watched heavy-lidded, he stood and tore off his trousers, then his drawers, popping off buttons in his haste. Dragging her to a stand, he embraced her a moment, kissing her, fondling her breasts as she swayed into him, still dizzy with her own pleasure.

Then he sat down on the settee and drew her toward him. He'd intended to have her straddle his lap, but before he could maneuver her there, she dropped to her knees at his feet. "What are you doing?" he growled.

"You said it was your turn," she whispered, gazing up at him bewildered. "Isn't this what you meant? Can't a woman do to a man what you did to me with your mouth?"

While he gaped at her, she leaned forward and kissed his cock on the very tip. The damned thing nearly shot its seed right then, and it took all his control to haul her up onto his lap instead of shoving his flesh into her darling mouth.

"But Griff," she said, staring at him in perfect innocence as he positioned her astride his lap, "do women not—"

"Sometimes, yes," he said hoarsely. "But tonight that would bring our lovemaking to a quick end, so we'd best save that variation for another time."

"Another time," she echoed with a hint of regret.

He groaned. Would she ever stop amazing him? Nobody but the most experienced whore had ever offered her mouth to him like that, so *her* offering it was an astounding gift. He shouldn't be surprised, however, that his inquisitive darling would show interest in all the delights of love, even ones most women found disgusting. Indeed, she was already staring down at his rigid member with obvious curiosity.

"What I meant by 'my turn,' " he rasped, "is that

I want to sheathe my 'sword' inside you now."
Under her avid look, his cock behaved . . . well . . .
damned cocky. He filled his hands with her ample
breasts, tugging eagerly at the satiny nipples.

Her face flushed as she lifted her eyes to his.
"While we're . . . like this?"

"Oh, yes. You might find it interesting." God
knows he was finding it fascinating to have her
honeypot so deliciously exposed on his bare thighs.
"Can you guess what to do or shall I show you?"

A purely feline smile curved up her lush lips. "I
think I can guess." With an uncanny instinct, she
raised herself up and slid down on him so slowly,
he thought he'd died and gone to heaven.

"God, Rosalind . . . yes . . . oh, my darling . . ." He
grabbed her hips and shifted her until she fit against
him as tightly as the position would allow.

She clutched at his shoulders and stared down
into his face. "Now what?"

"Now you make love to me . . . as I made love to
you this afternoon," he managed to explain, though
the intense pleasure of being inside her honeyed
body muddled all his thoughts.

"You mean like this?" she asked, rising up and
coming back down on him, glove-tight and hot and
glorious.

He was too far gone to do more than nod and
thrust his hips up to urge her into continuing the
motion.

But she was a quick study, his Athena, riding him
into battle with her copper-tinged hair for a banner
and her generous bosom for a breastplate. Now that
he'd given her the chance to take control, she seized it
like the battle goddess she was, flaunting her sensual
power, her body clamping around his cock with an
urgency that matched his own. By God, she would
kill him for sure. And he hoped she did it often.

She gazed down at him, eyes alight, her hair a glorious tangle of damp curls about her face and shoulders. "Is this considered . . . very naughty?"

"Very," he bit out. "But we bastards . . . are a naughty lot . . . and we like our women naughty." He dragged her head down to kiss her, twining her hair about his hand.

With his other hand he caressed her breast. He loved her magnificent breasts. Merely touching them made him ache to taste them, so he broke off the kiss to fasten his mouth around one large, plum-hued nipple. When she gasped, he tugged hard at the sweet tip with his teeth and was rewarded this time with her long groan of pleasure.

He thrust up into her faster, and she quickened her pace in instant response to his rhythm. She rode him hard, his Amazon, sheathing him in hot silk, sucking him into her as if to steal his strength. He'd relinquish it willingly as long as she used it always for this, ever for this.

Soon the drive to fulfillment became too much to withstand. He was near to exploding, so he felt for the tiny nub nestled between her legs, stroking it to make sure she found her release, too. Then they finished the battle together, the drumbeat rhythm of their joining erupting into a climax so shattering they both uttered a cry as they succumbed to the victory, and he spent himself inside her.

As she collapsed against him, he clutched her tightly, possessed by a fierce joy unlike any he'd ever known. She was his, *his*, damn it. He'd never let her go.

He stroked her tousled hair from her face and pressed a kiss to her temple. He'd never thought to find such a wonder in Warwickshire. He only wished Swanlea had invited him sooner, for he begrudged every day he'd lived without her.

Sated and pleasantly tired, he lay down on the settee and pulled her on top of him. With a sigh, she settled her body on his. Though she wasn't exactly light, he liked having her weight on him, liked having her heavy breasts crushed to his chest, and her head tucked against his shoulder.

Rosalind, however, could hardly bear to have him holding her so intimately, knowing that she'd soon be leaving him. But when she tried to move off, he murmured, "Stay here a while, darling. I want to hold you." A hint of humor tinged his voice. "Besides, if you move, you'll stir up my St. Peter again."

She propped her chin on his chest and stared into his roguish face. "You have a very willful St. Peter, Mr. Knighton. Can't you control the thing?"

He grinned and suggestively thrust his barely subdued St. Peter up between her legs. "Apparently not. Besides, I see no reason to control it when your honeypot is so handy."

"H-Honeypot?" she choked out, fighting back a blush. "Don't tell me there are terms for a woman's privates, too."

"Probably as many as for a man's."

"Are any of *those* terms by Shakespeare?" she asked dryly. Really, men could be such children sometimes.

He chuckled. "Actually, yes. There's one you'd probably like—Venus's glove. You can generally tell what's meant from the context of the passage. Especially now that you know exactly how all your private parts work."

This was what she'd miss most about Griff. He never found her outrageous or shocking. Well, hardly ever. Even when he did, it seemed to excite rather than appall him. Dropping her gaze, she traced a figure on his chest with one finger, melancholy at the thought that she'd soon leave him.

He caught her hand and pressed a kiss to the palm. "I can guess what you and I will be doing with our nights—other than making love, that is. You're going to work your way through Shakespeare deciphering all the naughty parts, aren't you, my love?"

"I am not!" she protested, then stilled. *My love.* He'd never called her that before. She clung to him in a terrible confusion. Perhaps she was being too hasty in her decision to leave for London. Perhaps . . .

Curse him, she'd known this would happen if she let him seduce her. She'd known he would turn her heart upside down. Feeling lost, she slid off him and crossed to where her gown lay.

"Where are you going?" he asked in a rumbling voice.

"I thought I'd dress. It's late, you know." Too late.

"I'd hoped to stay here a while longer."

If only they could . . . But no, that wouldn't do. "We can't, Griff. Someone might find us." She needed time to make her decision. Because if she did leave, it should be as soon as possible or he'd catch up to her easily on the road.

She also needed to talk to Helena. Helena would help her either way.

He propped himself up on one elbow. "Very well. We'll move to your room."

She stifled a groan. "No, we won't. If we go there, we're liable to fall asleep, and the maid will find us together in the morning."

"Who cares? We're marrying anyway."

She thought quickly. "I know . . . but . . . It would be embarrassing." She drew on her gown, trying to ignore the disappointment in his face.

"All right. I suppose I can wait until we're married." He sat up and stretched his legs out, obviously quite self-satisfied and completely unabashed about his nudity.

"Aren't you going to dress?" she asked when he just sat there. She fastened her gown.

"What's your hurry? I'll dress in a minute." He shot her a rakish grin. "I'd rather watch *you* dress."

With a low curse, she strode over to where his clothes were piled and began tossing them at him. "Well, you can't. I'd be mortified if some servant found us in here alone together." She started to throw his coat to him, then halted when something fell out of it. A folded sheet of vellum.

She stared down at it, her heart sinking into her stomach. In a daze, she bent to pick it up. Though she unfolded it, there was no reason. She knew what it was. It shouldn't even surprise her, yet it did. She'd almost begun to think he might care for her.

A deep sadness stole over her. She should have known better. To him, she was simply one more acquisition—the adoring wife who happened to also be a wanton. But certainly no one whose feelings would require him changing his plans.

Woodenly, she tucked the paper back into the coat pocket and walked to him. As she handed him his coat, tears welled in her eyes. He must have seen them, for he caught her by the hand before she could escape. "Rosalind—"

"I see that your haste to run after me didn't prevent you from grabbing the certificate first. God forbid you should leave that behind." Only then had he followed her to make his insincere declarations. "At least I know where I stand with you."

She tried to tug free of his hand, but he wouldn't let her. "This has nothing to do with you or how I feel about you. It's business, that's all." When she refused to look at him, he softened his tone. "If I don't attend to business, darling, we won't eat, will we?"

It was Papa's I-am-the-man-so-I-know-best tone of voice, the one that always infuriated her. To have

Griff use it only proved her worst fears about him. "Don't speak to me as if I'm some witless female. You've never done so before, so don't you dare start now. We both know this isn't about business, and it certainly has no effect on whether anyone eats."

Muttering an oath, he dropped her hand and began pulling on his drawers with jerky movements. "Then what do you think it's about? I assure you, if I wanted vengeance against your father, I'd choose something more devastating than the mere loss of his title. I could have bedded you and refused to marry you, you realize. I could have ruined him financially fifteen times over. For God's sake, I could have had him poisoned! But that would have been pointless, foolish, and yes, morally wrong. Despite what you think of me, I do have morals. I should think you'd know me well enough to realize I wouldn't do this for something as petty as vengeance."

"No, you'd do it for something as petty as ambition."

Leaping to his feet, he began to pace in front of the settee. "Ambition is not petty. Without it, there'd be no Knighton Trading. I see no reason why I should ruin my firm's chances to garner a large share of the Chinese trade simply because you don't want a few people speaking badly of your sisters."

She tossed back her head. "You know me, Griff— I'm not as 'practical' as you. I happen to care more about people than property or your bloody company's success."

"You care about your family perhaps, but not me. You'd rather save your sisters from gossip than see me succeed. I *am* practical, thank God. I don't listen to nonsense like gossip when making decisions that benefit my company and its many employees."

Oh, he made it sound so noble. He made it sound as if she were the one selfishly pursuing her own interests. But she wasn't fooled. She'd heard the emotion in his voice earlier when he'd confronted her father, when he'd spoken of the pain of being a bastard. This ran deeper than any "practical" reason.

The truth came to her in a flash of insight, a simple truth that tore her heart. "Keep telling yourself this is all for the benefit of your employees, but you know better. The truth is, you do care about nonsense like gossip. You care too much."

Her throat felt raw with anguish, for him as well as for her. "You hate being denied your legitimacy. You resent all those who call you bastard, all those in society who dismiss you for consorting with criminals, all the lords who still won't let you into their little circle because you're illegitimate. You want that title, and you want it publicly, so you can grind their noses in it and make them see that you were unfairly wronged by all of them, that you're better than what they always thought."

His stricken expression proved that she'd hit it exactly.

She went on. "You've tried to prove yourself with your success, yet it hasn't satisfied you, so you intend to find a bigger, more impressive way to do it. That's the real reason you're willing to sacrifice anything and anybody to gain your title, isn't it?"

"Like hell it is!" he hissed, but his face said otherwise. His lifelong hurt and humiliation and anger drove him.

He needed to prove himself to his naysayers, yet he'd never succeed. He'd never be satisfied, no matter what pinnacle he reached, because someone would always hold him in contempt. Besides, what he really wanted was to fill the empty space where his heart should be, and those ridiculous men in the House of Lords couldn't do that for him.

"I'm so very sorry that my father did this to you,

Griff. If I could change what happened, I'd do it in an instant. I'd remove your pain if I could. But I can't. You must do it yourself. And you're going about it all wrong."

"You're entitled to your opinion," he ground out, "but it changes nothing."

"Yes, I know." That's why she couldn't marry him, why she must leave tonight. Because her opinion would never change anything for him as long as his past entangled him so inexorably.

She hurried to the door, but he got there first and braced his hand against it. "It changes nothing," he repeated. "We'll be married, no matter how our opinions differ on this. You admitted you cared for me despite my supposed faults, and I won't let you take it back, damn it!"

She gazed up at his dear face, her stomach knotting painfully. She'd probably not see it again for some time. In a burst of tenderness, she laid her hand across his rigid cheek. Her poor fierce, tormented griffin. She now knew why he hoarded treasure and tore apart his enemies. Someone had stolen his treasure long ago, and now he only felt safe when amassing ever greater quantities of it.

Unfortunately, there was no place for love in the midst of all that amassing of treasure, was there? There was no place for her, whether he admitted it or not.

"I do care for you," she whispered. "I love you, and that is my curse. But you don't know how to love—and that is yours."

When she finally dropped her hand and slipped from the room, she didn't look back.

Chapter 21

Faith, Sir, we are here today, and gone tomorrow.

Aphra Behn, English playwright, The Lucky Chance

I *love you, and that is my curse. But you don't know how to love—and that is yours.*

Long after she left, Griff sat on the settee in his drawers, fingering his parents' marriage certificate and staring blindly at the Swanlea coat of arms on the wall across from him.

Rosalind loved him. His Amazon said she loved him, and he knew she meant it. She might have used a deceptive ploy or two in her attempt to save her family, but he knew her character. When it came to matters of the heart, she didn't lie.

He tossed the certificate aside and buried his face in his hands. Goddamn it, she loved him? What was he to make of that? He'd never believed in romantic love. Familial love, yes. But romantic love was a fanciful term women used for physical desire, nothing more. Or so he'd always told himself.

319

Now he wasn't so sure. Unlike most women, Rosalind seemed to feel no need to call her physical desires by another name. She accepted them, even reveled in them. For God's sake, how many gently bred women would engage in a frank discussion of the euphemisms for one's privates? Rosalind might rail against her desires for conflicting with her morality, and she might rail against him for rousing her desires, but she didn't pretend they were something else—like love.

No, if she said she loved him, then she did. The thought terrified him.

Affection he could handle. He felt a great deal of affection for her, too. But Rosalind in love . . . By God, the woman never did anything by halves. If she'd given him her love, she'd given her whole heart into his keeping.

Now what was he supposed to do with it? How could he ever satisfy her, please her if she wanted love from him in return? She was right—he didn't know how to love. He hadn't the faintest idea.

Feeling as if someone had punched him hard in the chest, he rose and mechanically began to dress. What of her other accusation about his reasons for wanting the certificate?

He scowled. She was wrong about that, completely wrong. Rosalind was merely being her usual suspicious self and seeing deep meaning where there was none. He did *not* want to "grind their noses in it," as she had put it. That wasn't it at all.

Was it?

Swearing loudly, he snatched up the certificate and stuffed it into his pocket. No, it wasn't, and she'd realize it once the matter was settled. He'd make sure he achieved the title so discreetly she'd hardly be bothered by the ensuing scandal. Once she recognized how much success it brought to Knighton Trading and how much wealth . . .

He groaned. Rosalind didn't care a fig for wealth. The bloody woman would probably spend all his money in support of theaters and God knows what else. He'd have to keep a sharp eye on her expenditures, for they were sure to be wild and impractical.

He rolled his eyes. As if he could ever begrudge her anything she wanted. Thanks to his "willful St. Peter," she could ask him for the Thames, and he'd bottle it for her.

But in one matter, he'd remain firm. She wouldn't keep him from regaining his title in time to be part of that delegation. No, indeed.

You're going about it all wrong.

Damn her! Must her absurd opinions torment him even when she was absent?

Trying not to heed them, he strode about the study, making sure he'd left nothing for the servants to find, then headed up to bed. The house was unnaturally quiet, as if holding its breath. Perhaps it was—waiting for the old earl to die, for the daughters to marry, for him to inherit. No, he reminded himself sternly, that would come before the earl died.

Once in bed, however, he had trouble falling asleep. Rosalind's words plagued him, no matter how much he tried to squelch them.

All right, so perhaps he did wish to prove himself. What was wrong with that? Most men sought to prove themselves. Why should he be any different?

You're going about it all wrong.

With a groan, he turned his cheek to the pillow and tried to shove her voice from his head. After a while he did fall into slumber, but only a fitful one. He tossed half the night, never comfortable, never able to drive her words away. Then shortly before morning, he began dreaming.

He stood in the House of Lords, waving his parents' wedding certificate as a loud, sonorous voice pronounced him the rightful Earl of Swanlea. Secure in his success, he glanced around, but to his shock, the lords in their robes had all become children. When he looked down at himself, he was a child as well. He was twelve again, fatherless, friendless, and the boys jeered at him. He tried to explain that he was legitimate now, but their clamor drowned out his voice.

Then he saw her. Rosalind stood above him in the visiting chamber, watching the proceedings. He called to her, but couldn't make her hear him either. With a sad glance, she turned away and left. Panic struck him. He tried to get to her, but the boys surrounded him, blocking his path, preventing him from following. *Rosalind!* he cried. *Rosalind!*

He woke up thrashing about in his bed, still calling out her name. It took him several moments to realize where he was, and to get his racing pulse under control. When he did, he rolled onto his side and pounded the pillow, cursing and moaning.

Oh, God, she was right. The woman had seen clear into his soul, damn her, when even he had refused to see it. His quest wasn't merely healthy ambition, was it?

He shifted onto his back and stared up at the ceiling. No, if he examined his motives thoroughly, he knew it wasn't about that at all. He had no guarantee that gaining his title this year would put him on that delegation. And not being on the delegation wouldn't necessarily prevent him from gaining a foothold in the China trade. He hadn't had a title when he'd carved out his place in the India trade, after all.

Something else was at work, and Rosalind had

seen it. He closed his eyes with a groan. Indeed, she'd been kinder to him than he deserved. For what he wanted was even smaller, pettier than she'd said. The realization made his stomach lurch.

He didn't want to prove himself to his peers. No, he wanted to go back in time, to prove himself to all his Eton classmates, to reclaim his tainted boyhood. That was the meaning of his dream.

And that was ludicrous—as Rosalind had realized. Trying to rewrite the past was a child's game, a pointless, ridiculous child's game no one ever won.

All the titles in the world couldn't make him forget that tortured little boy's humiliation. Even if all who'd ever held him in contempt changed their opinions overnight, it wouldn't erase his past. That would stay with him all his life, no matter what he did.

I'd take away your pain if I could. But I can't. You must do it yourself. And you're going about it all wrong.

His eyes shot open. Yes, he'd been going about it all wrong. But not anymore. He'd been acting like a child demanding his way; it was time to grow up. What did it matter if he gained his spot on the delegation but lost Rosalind's heart in the process? He couldn't lose her heart. It meant too much to him. Perhaps she was right, and he didn't know how to love, but he could learn. For her, he *would* learn.

He sat up, praying he wasn't too late. Despite his skepticism about portents, the last part of his dream worried him. It left a bad aftertaste, a foreboding that disturbed him even after he'd left his bed and gotten dressed.

Nor did it help when he came down to breakfast to find Rosalind absent. Everyone else was there, if less friendly than the morning before. Lady Juliet had reverted to her initial shyness. Lady Helena was colder than usual. Even Daniel wouldn't look at him, but merely ate his breakfast in a sullen silence.

"Where's Rosalind this morning?" Griff asked as he took his seat.

Lady Helena regarded him with undisguised dislike, but said in much too mild a tone, "She told me she wanted to sleep a while longer. Apparently, someone kept her up quite late last night."

He raised an eyebrow. It hadn't been all that late. Then again, yesterday had been a tempestuous day. She might need her rest.

When she didn't appear at any time during the morning, he repeated that explanation to himself. He tried not to worry while he packed his trunks and made arrangements for the trip. But when she didn't come down for the luncheon that Lady Helena had inexplicably delayed until nearly 2 P.M., he grew alarmed.

At Lady Helena's assertion that Rosalind was still "resting," he left the dining room and headed up to her bedchamber. He needed to talk to her and tell her what he'd discovered about himself, what she'd taught him. He needed to reassure himself that she was still his.

Lady Helena followed him up the stairs, protesting that he ought to have some "notions of decency."

That tore it. He halted on the stairs to glower at her. "Where Rosalind is concerned, I've no notions of decency, madam. I'm sure she'll confirm that if you ask her."

When Lady Helena blushed violently, he wondered if Rosalind hadn't already told her sister a great deal. He wasn't sure whether to be pleased or ashamed as he continued up the stairs.

He reached Rosalind's bedchamber moments later and rapped loudly on the door. No answer.

"I told you, she's sleeping," Lady Helena said stoutly. "Rosalind sleeps very soundly."

He tried the door. It was locked. "Open it," he ordered.

"I will not!"

"Very well, then I'll break it down." He moved back a pace, fully prepared to do just that.

"Wait!" Jerking out a ring of keys, she muttered, "All right, I'll open it."

She took her damned time about it, however, so when the door at last swung open, he wasn't entirely surprised to find the room empty.

Swearing under his breath, he whirled on Lady Helena. "Where is she?"

Lady Helena shrugged. "I have no idea. You know Rosalind. She could be anywhere—consulting with the housekeeper or riding or—"

"Don't play games with me, damn it!" he snapped. "Where is she?"

"Mr. Knighton, I do not respond to men who curse at me," the woman said with her usual air of dignity.

Daniel came up behind Lady Helena, looking concerned. Griff barely spared him a glance. "Tell me this then—when will she return?"

When mutinous silence was her only answer, he strode past her into the hall. "Perhaps Lady Juliet can tell me."

That seemed to ruffle Lady Helena's composure. "Now see here, you scoundrel, you will not browbeat my little sister! She doesn't know a thing about Rosalind's plans!"

He stopped short and faced her. "Then you'll tell me, Lady Helena, or I *will* browbeat Juliet, and afterward your father and every goddamned servant in the house until somebody tells me the truth!"

"Rosalind was right—you *are* a monster!"

The word echoed hollowly in his brain. "Did she . . . actually call me that?"

Lady Helena searched his face, then sighed. "Not exactly. She called you a griffin. But that is a monster, you know."

Yes, it was. He well remembered her telling him in the deer park how appropriate his supposed nickname was. The griffin, who stood guard over treasure and tore his enemies asunder. She thought of him that way? Still?

It didn't matter, he told himself, ignoring the sudden rawness in his throat. She would change her mind once he told her about the marriage certificate. What mattered now was finding out where she'd gone.

"Lady Helena," he said softly, "I need to know where she is. I must know, and you must tell me. She's my fiancée—don't I deserve at least that consideration?"

Lady Helena's contemptuous glance reminded him of one his mother had used on those who'd dared to insult him as a boy. It made him markedly uncomfortable.

"She's not your fiancée anymore, I assure you, if she ever was. It's precisely because she won't marry you that she's gone to London."

At first, he thought he'd misheard her. "Gone where?"

"To London. To go on the stage. It's what she always wanted to do and—"

"To go on the stage?" he shouted. "For the love of God, has she lost her mind?"

Lady Helena drew herself up to her full height. "Not in the least. You could hardly expect her to marry you when you plan to drag her entire family through a scandal."

The words closed around his conscience like a fist, adding more bruises to the ones already there. "She told you about the certificate."

"Of course she told me. I'm her sister."

And clearly detested him for it. Not that he blamed her—to echo Daniel, he'd been a "bloody arse." Or worse. "You're saying Rosalind has run off to London to go on the stage instead of marrying me."

"Yes. Since we're shortly to be without a home," she paused for effect, "she went to London to find a means of income for herself and lodgings for the rest of us. She's always wanted to be an actress, so that's the means of income she's attempting."

For a moment, his pain wiped out even his ability to breathe. Rosalind had left rather than marry him. After everything they'd shared, after she'd claimed to love him, after their goddamned sweet lovemaking last night, she'd left him. How could she?

But he knew the answer to that. He hadn't given her much of a reason to believe in their future last night. He'd run roughshod over her, seduced her, told her that her wishes didn't matter. He'd driven her to run away as surely as if he'd held that damned sword of hers to her throat. What else did a battle goddess do when cornered? She retreated, gathering her strength for the next battle.

But she'd retreated to London, for God's sake. She couldn't have much ready money, she was alone, and there were villains roaming the highways and lurking in the inns. Not to mention the villains roaming London . . .

His blood chilled. The woman had never been to London in her life. She had no idea of the blackguards who preyed on females arriving in town alone. Even his Amazon might be hard-pressed to defend herself against some of them. He glanced at

Daniel, whose dire expression showed that his thoughts ran in much the same direction.

"When did she leave?" Griff asked hoarsely.

"Shortly after midnight."

"After midnight?" Daniel said before Griff could even retort. "Christ, the woman is mad to be on the roads at night alone!"

Lady Helena's glare included them both. "She'll be fine. She rides well and—"

"She went on horseback?" Griff's heart sank into his stomach. "She's on horseback alone?"

"Yes." Griff's fear must have penetrated the woman's armor, for she eyed him a bit anxiously. "She'll be safe, won't she? I mean, she took Papa's pistol."

"Has she ever even shot a pistol?" Griff's fear was rapidly exploding into terror.

"Well, no, but you know Rosalind. She can take care of herself."

Griff swore vilely. Goddamn it, had no one ever cautioned these three about the dangers to a woman traveling alone?

"Take care of herself?" Daniel put in. "Against highwaymen and criminals? Don't you see what could happen to her if she met up with men like that?"

The disdain on Lady Helena's face would have cowed even the king. "They can't be much worse than the two deceitful wretches standing before me now."

Daniel loomed up over her, thick brows furling. "Now see here, m'lady, I'm bloody sick of your condescension and your—"

"Enough, both of you! I only care about Rosalind." Besides, Lady Helena was right about him, at least. His treatment of Rosalind was no better than any villain's. He forced himself to meet Lady Helena's gaze. "Where did Rosalind go in London?"

She tilted her chin up stubbornly, the very picture of her sister.

Temper flaring, Griff pinned her with a hard stare. "You told me you'd been to London once, so you should remember what it's like. Not the balls and the parties, but the streets you passed through, the pickpockets lurking in alleys, the keen-eyed rooks and panderers your father probably hustled you past. London is no place for an unprotected woman, especially one with no connections."

"But she does have connections," Lady Helena protested. "An actress friend of Mama's is helping her find a position and somewhere to live."

An actress friend? That didn't exactly reassure him. "Is this 'friend' expecting her? Does Rosalind know for certain she's in town and not away with a troupe or visiting friends or even on the Continent?"

Looking shaken, Lady Helena glanced away. Obviously such a thing hadn't occurred to her.

"Tell me this friend's address in London," Griff said.

"I . . . I don't know it."

He bit back an oath. "Then tell me the woman's name."

"I don't know that, either."

"Like hell you don't! You know it—you simply won't give it to me."

"Why should I tell you?" she cried. "So you can go break her heart again?"

That inflamed his already raging guilty conscience. "I didn't set out to break her heart."

"Perhaps not, but you did all the same."

"I realize that. But I won't anymore, I swear it. If she still doesn't want to marry me when I find her, I'll leave her be." He swallowed down the fear rising in his gullet. "I just have to see her safe, don't you understand?"

Lady Helena eyed him uncertainly. "She'll soon be appearing on the stage in London. That should give you ample proof that she's safe."

Panic built in his chest. "And what if she doesn't find a position at one of the London theaters? Most actresses begin in traveling troupes. They're poorly paid, mistreated by their managers, and taken advantage of by every drunken lout who fancies them. It's no life for her, don't you see? She's too good for that." Damnation, what if she did join one of the troupes? What if he couldn't find her? Or something happened to her before he could?

"You truly are worried about her," she said in a bewildered tone.

"Of course I'm worried about her! What did you think, you blasted—" He broke off, struggling to contain his wild anger. And his paralyzing fear. "Please, Lady Helena, I beg you. Tell me how to find her."

She swallowed. "What reason could you possibly give me to justify my breaking her confidence?"

The words were out before he even thought about them. "I love her. I love your sister. And I have to know she's safe."

It was true, he realized in shock. If loving her meant needing her more than breath, caring more about whether she was safe than about winning her, then God knows he loved her with an intensity that terrified yet exhilarated him. She'd seen clear into his soul and uncovered his petty hatreds. For that alone, he must find her—to thank her, to tell her that her words hadn't been in vain.

And if she could still find it in her heart to love him, then by God, he would hold on to her for the rest of his life. If she could not . . .

He choked back an agony that stole his breath. He would face that possibility later. First, he must make sure she was all right. But judging from the

skeptical look in Lady Helena's eyes, that might
prove difficult.

"You love her?" she snapped. "You have a peculiar way of showing it."

"I'm perfectly aware of that. I intend, however, to
improve upon my courtship skills. But I need your
help. You must tell me where she's gone in London."

For a moment, he thought she might be wavering. Her lower lip trembled, and she wrung her
hands. Then she said in a small voice, "I-I can't. I
promised her." Her earnest gaze swung back to
him. "Besides, you've told so many lies over the
past few days, I don't know how to determine when
you're speaking the truth."

His heart sank. He hadn't thought all his decep-
tions would return to haunt him in quite this way.
Something shattered inside him at the thought of
Rosalind traveling alone, staying in inns with no
protection. And what about once she reached London? She'd be wandering the streets of London in
search of a position, possibly penniless and friendless. All because of his childish posturing last night
and his arrogant belief that he could somehow gain
her compliance in his foolish plans for her family.

"Very well," he said to Lady Helena. "You do
what you must, and I'll do what I must." Full of
impotent rage and frustration—most of it directed
at himself—he added, "I'll find her, however, if I
have to scour every goddamned theater in the
country. And I swear, if she's been harmed in the
least, I'll lay the responsibility for it on *your* head."

He started to walk off, but her voice halted him.

"I make the same promise to you, Mr. Knighton.
You've already broken my sister's heart. So help me,
if you now rip it out, I'll rip yours out in return and
feed it to those London 'sharks' who worry you so."

He didn't respond, didn't even look back at her.

But as he strode away, he heard Daniel snap, "At least the poor man's got a heart, m'lady. That's more than I can say for you." Then Daniel hurried after him.

Tears welling in her eyes, Helena watched both men stride down the stairs. How dare Daniel Brennan call her heartless? If anybody lacked a heart, it was that great oaf of a highwayman's son who'd taken money to help his employer deceive and destroy them all. How dared he criticize *her* after all his lies?

She struggled to regain her calm. It didn't matter what the wretched rogue said—she refused to let it bother her. With any luck, she'd never have to lay eyes on him again—him and his sly charm and rough courtesies and subtle ways of making a woman feel as if she actually were desirable and whole—

She groaned. *A pox on you, Daniel Brennan! You and your wicked employer both!*

Still, she wondered if she'd done the right thing. She hadn't once considered the dangers to Rosalind in going off to London alone. Rosalind had always been perfectly capable of taking care of herself. And after what Rosalind had told her about Mr. Knighton's plans, Helena had been so irate she'd been eager to see Rosalind thwart him.

But what if he did love Rosalind? What if he meant it?

Well, she wouldn't stand in the way of it, even if Mr. Knighton *was* a toad and his man of affairs a snake. She'd write Rosalind to warn her of his coming and to tell her what he'd said. Then Rosalind could decide on her own about seeing him.

Yes, that's what she'd do. And then Daniel Brennan could at least acquit her of being heartless.

Chapter 22

*Players, Sir! I look upon them as no better than
creatures set upon tables and joint-stools to make
faces and produce laughter, like dancing dogs.*

Samuel Johnson, patron and critic of the theater,
as quoted in James Boswell's Life of Samuel Johnson

Three days after arriving in London, Rosalind
leaned against a pillar at the entrance to the
Covent Garden Theatre, munching an apple and
watching as an assortment of equipages streamed
down Bow Street—brilliantly painted barouches,
sedan chairs, and phaetons driven by reckless
young bucks. London had everything Stratford did
not—theaters and shops and coffeehouses.

And people. All sorts of people. Only last night,
Mrs. Inchbald had brought her to a gathering of the-
ater folk that included Richard Sheridan himself.
She'd even spoken with him, and that was *without*
Griff's help.

She cursed under her breath. Blast Griff. *He* was

the reason she couldn't enjoy London as she should.
The bloody man plagued her thoughts every waking hour.

She'd tried to put him out of her mind. She'd
tried to forget him—but apparently forgetting Griff
wasn't as easy as it seemed. Every time she ate
plums or read Shakespeare or saw men playing billiards, she thought of him. Every time she disrobed
she remembered their lovemaking. She hadn't met
any men in London who compared to him, and she
was always comparing them to him. One man was
not as quick-witted as Griff. Another lacked his
intensity. Yet another roused a strange repugnance
because his hair wasn't black and his eyes not
blue—

Damn him! She hated him for doing this to her,
poisoning her for any other man. For not loving her
as she loved him. She wiped away the tears that had
filled her eyes without her even noticing. She
wouldn't cry over that wretch. She would not! He
didn't deserve it.

He'd probably washed his hands of her already,
anyway. He had his bloody certificate, after all.
What would he need with her?

Eventually, however, he was sure to cross her
path in London. She only prayed it would be many
weeks away. By then, she'd be ready for him, ready
to appear cool and unaffected.

As if she could ever hide her feelings around Griff
Knighton. She swore and stuffed the half-eaten
apple in her apron pocket.

"Your mother would turn over in her grave to
hear you use such language," a voice commented at
her side.

She turned to find Mrs. Inchbald smiling at her.

"Yes, I suppose she would." Rosalind prayed her
reddened eyes wouldn't reveal all her misery.

"Mama's strictures about foul language had no effect on me, I'm afraid, although Helena took them quite to heart."

At sixty-two, Mrs. Inchbald was still a pretty woman, as slender and graceful as she'd been in her youth when she'd played in Convent Garden herself. With a mobcap covering her curls, she seemed as modest and reserved as any older widow, but she was actually quite lively and possessed a fine command of dramatic literature. She was also more generous than Rosalind had expected, for she'd invited Rosalind to live with her until Rosalind got on her feet.

"Speaking of your sister," the woman said now, "I came by the theater to bring you a letter from her that just arrived. I thought it might be important."

Rosalind took the letter with an aching heart. Helena would probably have news about the family's reaction to her mad flight. And Griff's reaction, too. She tucked it away in her other apron pocket, not wanting even Mrs. Inchbald to watch her read it.

Mrs. Inchbald merely raised an eyebrow. "You know, I was only nineteen when I ran away to the theater, but I remember it well. I expected it to be thrilling but instead found it hard and tedious. Mostly, I was terribly homesick. That's why I moved in with my actor brother after only a week of being 'independent.'"

"I'm not homesick in the least, I assure you." Well, perhaps a little. She did miss having Helena to talk to. And walks in the orchard. She missed Swan Park's huge open spaces, perfect for reciting lines without worrying who might hear.

That was all she missed at Swan Park, however. Truly, it was. And Cook's apple tarts, of course.

"You've made a promising beginning," Mrs. Inchbald said. "I wasn't so lucky. I had to start in a

traveling troupe. I hope you appreciate how difficult it is to win a role at Convent Garden on your
first try—even a small one like Iras in *Anthony and
Cleopatra*."

"I do appreciate it, especially since I know I have
you to thank for it. Your influence is the only thing
that garnered me the role. To be truthful, I'm mortified that I never knew you wrote plays and were
friendly with all the managers." Indeed Rosalind
had realized very quickly that the manager of
Covent Garden—John Kemble—and Mrs. Inchbald
were . . . well . . . quite good friends. "You didn't
speak of your new profession in your letters. If I'd
realized how highly you were regarded, that your
plays were published and acted, I should never
have dreamed of imposing—"

"It's no imposition in the least." Mrs. Inchbald
chucked her under the chin. "I'm delighted to help
the daughter of my dearest friend. Besides, it wasn't
only my influence that got you the role. Your
knowledge of Shakespeare had something to do
with it." Mrs. Inchbald cast her a smile. "Not to
mention that the actress who was supposed to play
the role eloped with an army captain, leaving John
in dire straits. He'd despaired of finding anyone in
time for tomorrow night who could learn the lines."

"I'm grateful he considered me."

"This part will show your talents nicely and
should lead to other things." She paused, searched
Rosalind's face, then added, "If that's what you
really want."

Rosalind bit her lower lip and averted her gaze.
"Of course it's what I really want. And I'll join a
traveling troupe if I must."

"No need for that, I should think." Twirling her
walking stick on the floor of the stone portico, Mrs.
Inchbald said in too casual a tone, "John tells me

your speeches are prettily spoken. He did say, however, that you were a bit . . . opinionated."

Rosalind sighed. "It's true, I know, but I can't help it. They want me to cut out some of the best parts. They're having me play the role all wrong—making Iras into a milksop. She may only be Cleopatra's attendant, but Shakespeare clearly meant her to be vivacious and clever. I mean, look at that scene with the fortune-tellers—"

Mrs. Inchbald laughed. "You do have an enthusiasm for Shakespeare, don't you? I'd forgotten that the bard was your father's favorite. I fear you'll soon learn that actresses in small parts have little say over what lines are cut or how the role is to be performed."

"What about actresses in larger parts?"

"That depends on the theater manager."

"I see I'll have to become a theater manager," Rosalind mumbled under her breath.

Mrs. Inchbald's eyes twinkled. "Why? Don't you like performing?"

Rosalind thought of this afternoon's rehearsal, and being told always where to stand and how to speak and what to wear when she knew perfectly well how it should be. "I haven't decided. I like having the attention, I think, but I should like it better if it were done right."

Her friend looked as if she were trying not to laugh. "Do you think your fellow performers aren't playing their parts adequately?"

"They miss some of their lines, you know." She sighed. "But I suppose they're tolerable. Well, except for that nasty Mr. Tate, who pats my bottom every time he passes behind me."

"You'll get used to the men's attentions. A sharp word will usually gain you some breathing room, though it's best to be careful how you refuse some

of their overtures. Some actors are more powerful
than others—you wouldn't want to offend them."

That comment gave Rosalind pause. "A...
um... friend of mine said that some men consider
actresses little better than whores. He—that is, my
friend—said that being an actress is degrading.
That's not true, is it?"

Mrs. Inchbald shot her a curious glance. "It
depends on the actress. You're talented and pretty
enough, so you'll be able to do as you please without anyone thinking ill of you once you're established. Those who lack talent or looks, however,
have to... cultivate the right people. I don't mean
resign their virtue, of course. But in such cases, marrying a man who can forward one in the profession
isn't a bad idea. I found it very useful to marry an
experienced actor like Joseph Inchbald."

Rosalind eyed her with shock. "You didn't marry
for love?"

Mrs. Inchbald chuckled. "Love of the theater—
that's what I married for. Why? Is that what you
want? To marry for love?"

"Certainly." She straightened her spine. "If I can't
find a man to love, I shan't marry at all. I'm quite
determined on that point."

"I see." She gave her stick another twirl. "Speaking of marrying... while I was talking to John this
morning, a man came in looking for you."

Rosalind caught her breath. "Oh?"

"Oddly enough, it was the same man you wrote
to ask me about some time ago. That Mr. Knighton,
the one who's illegitimate."

"Griff's not illegitimate!" she cried, then bit her
tongue when Mrs. Inchbald raised an eyebrow. "I
mean... well, some of the gossip about him is false,
that's all."

"Well, whatever his legitimacy, it seems he's been

quite generous to Covent Garden over the years, judging from how John fell all over himself offering his aid. Mr. Knighton claimed he was looking for his fiancée—you."

A blush rose in Rosalind's cheeks before she could stop it. Griff here? Looking for her? She hadn't thought he would go so far. "You didn't tell him anything, did you?"

"Of course not. I figured if you were desperate enough to run away from home and take a new name on the stage, you had your reasons for avoiding the man." She shifted her walking stick from hand to hand. "He did seem rather anxious to find you, however, and if we hadn't fed John that tale about you being my country cousin, he would undoubtedly have told the man who you were at once. But John didn't mention you except to say he'd hired my cousin."

Rosalind released a pent-up breath. Griff was looking for her. Why? Because his foolish pride was hurt over losing her? She tilted up her chin. Well, if that was the reason, he'd get over it soon enough, the arrogant scoundrel.

"Thank you," she told her friend. "I appreciate your discretion. Papa arranged a marriage between me and Mr. Knighton, but I found that we didn't suit."

"Then why do you blush at the very mention of his name, my dear?"

She swallowed. "Because at one time I thought we might suit. Unfortunately, I expect a great deal from the man I marry, and I discovered it was far more than Mr. Knighton was willing to offer." She pasted a false bright smile to her lips. "In any case, thank you for telling me of his visit. Now if you don't mind, I should like to read my letter since they'll be calling me back to rehearsal any minute."

"Certainly. I'll see you later. Tomorrow is the big day, so we'll eat at home tonight to give you a chance to prepare."

Impulsively, Rosalind kissed the woman's perfumed cheek. "You've been so kind to me. I can never thank you enough."

"Nonsense. I'm not entirely sure that introducing you to the theater is a kindness. But we shall see." She smiled secretively. "Yes, we shall see."

As soon as Mrs. Inchbald strode off down the street to her lodgings, Rosalind broke the seal on her letter, desperate now to hear what Helena had to say. She quickly scanned Helena's account of all the ways she'd tried to delay the men's departure. The next paragraph, however, arrested her attention at once:

> They are on their way to London, and Mr. Knighton seems determined to find you. He was furious when he heard of your flight to London, though that soon gave way to worry. You know the man better than I, so you will know if his concern for your well-being is feigned or genuine. He spoke most anxiously of your safety on the roads and in London. He asked for your direction, and I refused to give it.
>
> But one thing you should know. He said he wanted so desperately to find you because he loved you. You may make of that what you will. He seemed in earnest, but I am not a good judge of either his or his friend's honesty, for both have repeatedly played us false. He might have said it only to get what he wanted from me.
>
> Indeed, his friend, that scurrilous scoundrel . . .

Rosalind paid no attention to her sister's ranting about Daniel. Helena distrusted men in general, so

she was sure to feel most unfavorably toward
Daniel now that he'd proven to be a highwayman's
son and erstwhile smuggler.

Instead she reread the paragraph about Griff saying he loved her. She clutched the letter to her chest
and stared blindly off into the street. Could it be
true? Surely even Griff wouldn't speak so cruel a lie
only to gain an advantage.

Then again . . . She reread the letter from beginning to end, her heart sinking as she realized that
Helena made no mention of the certificate. Even if
Griff thought that he meant what he said, it was
only words. As long as he proceeded with his dark
intentions, she couldn't ever believe he loved her.

Or was she being unfair? He'd spent all his childhood under a cloud, and now that he wanted to dis-
pel it she wouldn't let him. Was that small-minded?
Was she asking too much of him?

Dear God, she wished she knew. Because the
truth was, she'd not had a moment's peace from the
time she'd left him until now. Despite all the wonders of London and the intriguing aspects of the
theater, she missed him sorely. The thought of being
an actress paled in comparison to the thought of
loving Griff.

She wasn't, after all, like Mrs. Inchbald—willing
to do whatever it took to gain success in the theater.
Some things were more important than that to her,
she was rapidly discovering. And she very much
feared that all the success at acting in the world
wouldn't make her happy if she couldn't have Griff.

Griff paced his office impatiently while Daniel
gave his report.

"No one at the Pantheon or the Lyceum has heard
of her," Daniel said, "and there's been no new
actresses at all to hire on. I spoke with all the agents

for the troupes, but no one they'd hired sounded like her either."

"Perhaps she's in disguise. There's no telling what Rosalind will do."

"I doubt she'd go so far as to work in disguise, Griff," Daniel said, a hint of exasperation in his voice. "If you wish, I'll try to get a look at each woman, but that will take weeks as they've been sent off to join their troupes already."

Feeling the same helpless terror that had tormented him for the past few days, Griff halted at the window to stare out at the teeming streets that might or might not hide Rosalind. "I tried Drury Lane yesterday, but their two new actresses are both blond and short. You know Sheridan's tastes. Kemble in Covent Garden said he hadn't hired anyone new other than the cousin of that playwright Mrs. Inchbald. I don't think Rosalind would consider the burletta or pantomime houses, but we'll try the Adelphi and the Olympic this afternoon."

"And when you find her?"

"What do you mean?"

"Well, if she ran off to avoid marrying you before, what makes you think she'll marry you now?"

He gripped the windowsill. "I don't know that she will. Some things have changed since she and I last talked, but it may be too late to make a difference. All I want is to be sure she's safe. I must know that, at least."

Days of worrying about her, of contemplating the dire things that might have happened to her, had nearly driven him mad.

"What has changed since you talked?" Daniel asked. "Didn't she give you the certificate? She won't be any more likely now to stand idly by while you use it than she was before."

Griff flinched at Daniel's cold tone. It was hard to

remember what he'd been like only days ago, before he'd realized the true depths of his selfishness, which had driven Rosalind to flee from him. "I've decided not to act on the certificate until the earl dies. After that, we can all claim that the certificate was found among some old forgotten papers. It's better for the women that I inherit the property, since otherwise it would go to someone else or even to the Crown if no heir is found. But I'll do my best to preserve his good reputation and make it seem as if the court case were all simply a tragic oversight."

"Had a change of heart, have you?" Daniel said quietly.

"Yes." He left it at that, his thoughts full of worry about Rosalind.

Of course, that didn't put Daniel off in the least. "So you're not concerned about your delegation to China anymore?"

"No, damn it! You were right—I was wrong. Now can we stop discussing it? I have more important things to consider." He drummed his fingers on the sill. "Who have we left out? Perhaps we should go over that list of theaters again."

Daniel drew out the list, but said, "The lass has certainly got you by the ballocks, hasn't she?"

"That's not the only thing she's got me by," Griff said quietly. Daniel could torment him endlessly about Rosalind, but he wouldn't rise to the bait. If anything happened to her, he'd never forgive himself.

"She'll be all right, you know." Daniel's voice held pity. "She's a hardy thing, your Rosalind. We'll find her, don't worry."

"How can I not worry?" Griff threaded his fingers through his hair distractedly. "It's as if she vanished without a trace, as if she—"

He broke off at the sound of a loud commotion

outside his office, followed by the dramatic entrance of the one woman Griff did not want to see just then. His mother.

His clerk rushed in after her, red-faced and worried. "Begging your pardon, Mr. Knighton, I tried to explain you were in a meeting, but—"

"In a meeting, hah!" his mother snapped at the clerk. "Can't you see he's merely talking to Daniel?"

Griff waved his agitated clerk off. "It's all right. Go on back to work."

As soon as the door closed, his mother strode up to him, her slender shoulders shaking with anger. "Where the devil have you been? You disappear, and nobody will tell me where you went or when you'll return. Though they did tell me you'd taken Daniel." She paused in her tirade to shoot Daniel a chastening look.

"Good afternoon, Mrs. Knighton," Daniel said cheerily. "Nice to see you again. You're looking quite lovely today."

"Don't try your flatteries on me, Danny. I know your ways, and I don't fall for them like all your tarts. I should have known you'd have a hand in this. You ought to be ashamed of yourself." She turned her glare on Griff. "*Both* of you. I thought you said you'd put all that unsavory business behind you. That you and Daniel weren't going off on any more secret trips to God knows where—"

"I was in Warwickshire, Mother."

She blinked. "Warwickshire? Whatever for?"

"To visit our mutual friend, the Earl of Swanlea. I was invited."

She paled to an unnaturally sickly color. "*He* invited you? But . . . but why?"

Griff shot Daniel a glance, and the man beat a hasty retreat. Daniel might have a certain affection for the only woman he ever allowed to call him

"Danny," but he knew better than to stay around when the generally mild-mannered woman was upset.

Once Daniel was gone, Griff leaned back against the windowsill and folded his arms over his chest. He'd hoped to delay this until he'd settled things with Rosalind, but now that his mother was here . . .

Briefly, he related the story of the letter he'd received and how he'd gone off to Warwickshire with the intention of retrieving the marriage certificate without having to marry one of the spinsters. It was more difficult to explain why he'd wanted it, for now that he'd seen the error of his ways, his motives shamed him. He knew his mother wouldn't approve, yet he had to tell her all of it, partly because she deserved to know the truth. And partly because he wanted the truth from her.

It took her a moment to digest his tale, but when she did, she sank into a nearby chair. Silver curls bobbed beneath the brim of her bonnet as she shook her head. "I can't believe it. Did you . . . did you manage to find the marriage certificate?"

"I did." Reaching into his coat pocket, he pulled it out and handed it to her.

Her fine-boned fingers stroked the paper wonderingly. "So he really had it all this time. He really . . . stole it. I was never sure."

"Yes, he admitted it."

Her gaze shot to his in alarm. "You talked to him about it?"

He nodded, then dragged in a weighty breath. "Indeed, he told me . . ." He paused, wondering how one asked one's mother such a question. "He said . . . that is, he claimed you were in love with him before you married Father. He even claimed you told him you were still in love with him on your wedding day. That was his reason for stealing the certificate—partly to punish you for not marrying him and partly to gain what he saw as a fairer division of the Swanlea properties."

His mother's silence, coupled with her haunted expression, made something twist in his chest, yet a quest for truth drove him on. Shoving away from the window, he strode to his desk. "Of course, I called him a liar to his face." He paused, half-fearing to ask the question, half-fearing not to hear the answer. "He *was* lying, wasn't he?"

When she didn't answer, he turned to see his mother crying silently, fat tears rolling down her thin cheeks. He struggled for air. "It was a lie. Tell me it was all lies."

She lifted an anguished gaze to him. "I was so young, Griff, and lonely for attention. My father was too busy managing the theater in Stratford to pay me much heed, but Percival . . . he shared my love for plays and protected me when boys insulted me and made advances. He was living at Swan Park as the previous earl's ward. That was long before I met your father, who was off at school. Percival and I . . . became close. He wasn't like other men I knew. He was a gentleman, and he always flattered me. When you're seventeen, you like to be flattered."

Griff gripped his hands together behind his back. "But did you *love* him, Mother?"

A look of deep sorrow settled over her still pretty features. "Yes, I did love him. Very much. But I knew he had no future. He was something of a wastrel, whereas your father—"

"Was the heir presumptive to the fourth Earl of Swanlea," Griff snapped, wondering how he could have so misunderstood everything from his childhood, how he could have let it blindly shape so much of his life.

His mother set her shoulders stubbornly the way

she always did when she was cornered. "Yes. Your father had a future, a very bright one. When he came to stay at Swan Park and both he and Percival would visit me, I found I liked him. I didn't love him as I did Percival, but I liked him. I knew if I married Percival, we'd be ... poor and always looking for income. And I'd grown up poor. I despised it. I wanted something better."

Though he certainly understood that, he couldn't help comparing his mother's response to Rosalind's. Rosalind would never have married to avoid being poor—not his Athena. "Well, if it was poverty you were avoiding, Fate certainly paid a cruel trick on you, didn't it?" he said, somewhat unkindly.

She regarded him with a melting sadness. "No. Fate meted out a suitable punishment. That's how I consider it. I married your father for his prospects rather than following my heart, and I paid for it later." A wan smile touched her lips. "I did grow to feel a deep affection for Leonard, you know. He was quite the rakish character. When you were born, I was so happy I thought I'd die of it. My husband was to be a wealthy earl, and I'd borne him his heir to the title. I was beside myself with joy."

The smile faded abruptly, and she glanced away. "But such happiness isn't meant for mere mortals, especially when gained at the expense of someone else. I treated Percival very badly. I didn't even have the decency to ... lie to him on my wedding day, to tell him I didn't care for him. He looked so lost, so forlorn, and I foolishly thought it would help him to know I still cared." A shudder wracked her delicate frame. "It only hurt him further when he realized I simply didn't love him enough."

"And he nursed that hurt for months," Griff finished coldly. "So when you and Father flaunted your 'happiness' in front of him by inviting him to see me as a baby, he lashed out. That's when he stole the certificate and had me proclaimed a bastard."

Her gaze swung to his, full of remorse. "I wish to God I could have kept you from that suffering, my son. I deserved to suffer, but you certainly didn't. I'd hoped that your father and I could shield you, could prevent it from mattering too much." She shook her head. "Once he died of smallpox so young, however . . ."

Griff's throat felt swollen and raw. "That's why whenever I railed at Swanlea, you told me not to. Why you never railed against him yourself. Why you never blamed him or sought revenge."

"How could I blame him? I drove him to it." She paused, then asked shakily, "Is that what you're doing now with the certificate, seeking your revenge against him?"

Two weeks ago, such a question would have infuriated him, probably because despite all his denials, it had been somewhat true. "No. Not anymore. That might once have been part of my intention, but now . . ." He scrubbed his hands wearily over his face. "I suppose I should thank you for not marrying him. If you had, I would never have been born. And neither would Rosalind."

"Rosalind?"

An urgent need to tell her about the one he loved possessed him. "Swanlea's daughter, the middle one. I'd hoped to marry her. But she . . ." He swallowed down the bitter lump in his throat and sat down wearily behind his desk. "She took exception to my plans for the certificate and ran off before I could tell her I'd decided not to use it. I haven't yet found her. I think . . . I hope she's somewhere in London." He stared blindly past his mother. "I pray she's at one of the theaters and not on the road being—" He broke off, unable to voice his terror.

"Do you love her?"

He nodded.

"Does she love you?"

"She said she did."

His mother rose and came to his side, placing her hand on his shoulder. "Then do what you must to find her and win her back, my son. Because no one knows more than I how important it is to follow your heart."

Beset by a complex mix of emotions—envy, hurt, and perhaps a little betrayal—he lifted his head to gaze into her tearful blue eyes. "Is that why you never remarried? Because you were still in love with Rosalind's father?"

She sighed. "I never remarried because I learned the hard way that some people only love once. And there's simply no point to marrying where you do not love."

He shook his head, trying to take it all in. There'd been so much in his world that he hadn't seen, too wrapped up in his own concerns to pay it any notice. "I never dreamed you felt all this. That certificate belongs to you more than to me, yet I never once considered that. I never even considered telling you about it or my plans or—"

"You're telling me about it now," she said, smiling. "That's all that matters."

She squeezed his shoulder, and he clasped her hand tightly, feeling a connection to his mother that he hadn't felt in years. He hadn't realized until now how much he'd shoved her out of his life, as he'd shoved away everything and everyone who hadn't been material to Knighton Trading.

The door suddenly burst open and Daniel hurried in. "Griff, an invitation of sorts has arrived for you. I think you'll want to look at it. It's from Mrs. Inchbald."

Griff sat up straighter and released his mother's hand. "The playwright. She was in Kemble's office at Covent Garden when I asked about Rosalind."

"She used to be an actress there, and I believe she was on the stage around the time Rosalind's mother would have been." Daniel strode to the desk and tossed down a paper with a note attached. "She's sent you this playbill. It's for *Antony and Cleopatra* at Covent Garden."

Shakespeare. Damnation, of course! Where else would Rosalind go but to the theater that not only contained a marble statue of Shakespeare, but had scenes from the plays painted in the lobby?

What a dunce he was. Rosalind must be Mrs. Inchbald's "cousin." His heart pounding, Griff read the note first. All it said was "You may find this performer interesting." He glanced at the top of the playbill. It was for tonight's performance, the first. He scanned the bill, hoping against hope until he noticed a circled item that listed the actress for the part of Iras as "Miss Rose Laplace." Nothing else.

"The woman who married Percival was named Solange Laplace," Griff's mother said, reading the playbill over his shoulder. "Does that help?"

Griff nodded as relief coursed through him. "It's her, thank God. It has to be. And if Mrs. Inchbald was the 'friend' Lady Helena spoke of, then Rosalind is at least safe, for the woman is well respected and responsible. Though I do wonder why Mrs. Inchbald decided to send this to me today when she said nothing about Rosalind yesterday." He stared down at the playbill. "It doesn't matter. I'll be at that performance tonight, you can be sure."

Then what? He had to see Rosalind, if only to make sure she was happy and well. He wanted so much more, but he feared he didn't deserve it, and she'd surely feel the same. She might even truly want to remain on the stage. Well, she could perform on horseback at Astley's amphitheater every day for all he cared, as long as she agreed to marry him.

But what if she wouldn't even see him? Or worse yet, suppose she saw him and refused his offer of marriage again? He didn't think he'd survive that. Yet how the devil was a man to convince a woman he loved her when she'd lost her faith in him, when she thought he cared for nothing but himself and his company?

You will do anything for Knighton Trading—whether consorting with smugglers or defaming innocents—so what place could a mere woman like me have in your life? Well, I can't marry a man who cares so little for me.

It suddenly came to him what he must do. Rosalind wouldn't believe mere words anymore, and he couldn't blame her. But he could offer her something she would believe.

He glanced at the time for the play, then at the clock on the wall. He only had five hours to manage everything. It would have to be enough—because he couldn't wait another day. Not for this.

"Mother," he said as he rose from his chair, "I'm afraid I must leave you. I have some urgent matters to attend to before the play."

She arched one silver-streaked eyebrow. "I hope you plan to bring me to this performance tonight. I should like to meet my future daughter-in-law."

"I warn you, it's by no means certain she'll agree to marry me. I'll ask her, but I won't try to change her mind if she refuses. I did that before, and the result was disaster."

"She'll marry you. I know she will." His mother

eyed him fondly. "How could anyone refuse my son?"

"For my sake, I hope you're right and not just speaking from motherly affection." He forced a smile. "I suppose this would be the right time to ask for your blessing."

"As if you'd pay me any heed if I didn't give it," she teased. "You don't care in the least if you have my blessing. You never have, you rascal."

He stared at her, realizing for the first time how much his ambition must have cost her, how often he'd thoughtlessly left her alone to worry while he pursued his own dreams. Why had he never seen it before?

Because he hadn't had Rosalind to show him all his faults before.

Impulsively, he caught her hand and kissed it. "I confess that if Rosalind will have me, I plan to marry her even if you do protest. But I don't think you will. I may have disappointed you in the past, Mother, but this is one time I think you'll be pleased. And yes, it does matter to me that I have your blessing."

Her eyes again filled with tears as she gazed into his face. "Of course you have my blessing, dear boy. And you could never, ever disappoint me."

Scowling at her tears even as a lump caught in his throat, he dragged out his handkerchief and handed it to her. "Then stop that crying, will you?" he said gruffly. "I swear, you and Rosalind with your tears—you'll drive a man mad."

As she sniffed and made good use of his handkerchief, he turned to Daniel. "All right, man, let's go. You and I have business to take care of at my solicitor's."

"Business?"

"Yes. I'm going to do what most decent men do

when they plan to marry: I'm getting rid of my mistress. The woman I love won't have me unless I do."

And without bothering to explain his enigmatic statement, he strode from the room.

Chapter 23

*For my part, I confess I seldom listen to the play-
ers: one has so much to do, in looking about and
finding out one's acquaintance, that, really, one
has no time to mind the stage ... One merely
comes to meet one's friends, and shew that one's
alive.*

Fanny Burney, English novelist, diarist,
and sometime playwright, Evelina

Rosalind paced backstage, surprised she
wasn't more nervous. She'd seen the packed
theater—it ought to terrify her, yet it didn't. She
wasn't sure why. It might be different if her family
were here or . . .

She squelched that thought at once.

Mrs. Inchbald approached to survey Rosalind's
costume with obvious approval. "I'm delighted to
see they made it fit. Your first appearance shouldn't
be marred by a shabby costume."

"Once again, I'm in your debt. If I'd realized I'd

be better off providing my own costumes, I'd have brought clothes from home to remake."

She glanced down at the flowing gown Mrs. Inchbald had loaned her. Its gold threads and filmy fabric made it look more Egyptian than anything in the properties room, though it consequently displayed a scandalous amount of flesh. Then again, a dressmaker could only accomplish so much when the original wearer of a costume was as slender as Mrs. Inchbald and the new one as full-bodied as Rosalind.

Tugging the deep bodice higher, she smiled sheepishly. "Perhaps I shouldn't have started as an Egyptian handmaiden after all."

"Nonsense. You look lovely." Mrs. Inchbald pulled aside the curtain and scanned the audience, then smiled. "It's a good thing, too, since your Mr. Knighton is here."

Rosalind's curst heart fluttered uncontrollably. "He can't be!" She hurried to look out at the woman's side.

Mrs. Inchbald gestured to a box near the stage. "There. That's him, isn't it?"

Rosalind immediately spotted the dark-haired man standing in the first-tier box with his profile to the stage. Dear God, oh, dear God. "Yes, that's him."

"He's a handsome one, isn't he?"

She nodded as she examined every inch of him. He was, more's the pity. She should have guessed he'd look delicious in evening clothes. The perfectly fitted tailcoat and breeches suited him. But he was wealthy, after all. He probably spent more on a tailor in one month than she spent on gowns in a year.

He was accompanied by Daniel and a silvery-haired woman Rosalind could only assume was his mother. Rosalind eyed "Georgina" with painful curiosity. So that was the woman Papa had once loved so much that he'd destroyed her son for it? Rosalind could see why. Georgina was still pretty, and her smile held a brightness that would captivate any man.

The woman sat down, and Rosalind returned her attention to Griff. She thought he looked pale under the light from thousands of candles. He wasn't smiling, though Daniel seemed to be doing enough of that for both of them. Seeing him so close and yet so inaccessible made her heart twist in her chest.

The orchestra started playing, and Rosalind jerked back from the curtain. She was in the second scene. She didn't have time to stand here gawking at Griff.

When Mrs. Inchbald also drew back and smiled, a sudden suspicion leapt into Rosalind's mind. "How did Griff know I was here?"

Her friend shrugged. "Perhaps he likes Shakespeare."

Rosalind groaned. "Of course." How stupid of her to take a role in a Shakespeare play, especially the only one currently being performed in London. Well, perhaps he wouldn't realize it was she. How would he make a connection between Rose Laplace and her? He couldn't know her mother's stage name, and besides, she was in costume.

She rolled her eyes. Oh, yes, a costume that hid nothing. She wasn't even wearing a wig, for pity's sake, since they'd deemed her hair dark enough for the role. And that box he was in practically sat on the stage.

The play started.

Now she was nervous.

The first scene passed before she was ready, and all too soon she was entering the stage with the other eight performers. Thankfully, her first line came well into the scene. By then, she was caught up in the story enough to put Griff from her mind. Or as much as she could ever put him from her mind.

Iras, along with the character of Charmian, was Cleopatra's attendant, destined to die with her. In their scene, Iras and Charmian were having their fortunes told by a crafty soothsayer whose every word had a double, more dire meaning. For most of the scene, Rosalind easily fell into her part.

There was one frantic moment, however, when she lost her role. The soothsayer had just told Charmian that she had the same fortune as Iras, and Iras had asked if she wasn't at least an inch of fortune better.

Charmian's next line was, "Well, if you were but an inch of fortune better than I, where would you choose it?"

The meaning behind Iras's rejoinder, "Not in my husband's nose," struck Rosalind suddenly. She blushed and nearly tripped over the line, but thankfully recovered in time to give it the comedic delivery it deserved.

Throughout the rest of the scene, however, she was only too painfully aware of Griff, though she didn't dare look at him. All she could think about was their discussions of Shakespeare's bawdy humor. Dear God, how would she ever perform Shakespeare without thinking of it? Of Griff? Would the man intrude even here, in this part of her life?

She half feared, half hoped he'd seek her out during the interludes between the acts, but when the third act came and went with no sign of him, she decided perhaps he hadn't recognized her after all. She told herself she ought to be relieved.

Instead she was annoyed. Here she was, making

her great debut on the stage, and he didn't even know it. It was enough to make her flounce out there and tell him. Of course, that would be foolish in the extreme.

Then again, he might have recognized her and not care. She scowled at the thought, then cursed herself for scowling. Why did it matter what he did, how he felt?

Because it did. It just did.

By the last scene, the one in which she was to die with Cleopatra, she finally worked up the courage to look at him during the first part, when she had no lines and nothing to do but stand by on stage.

She regretted it instantly. He'd certainly recognized her. His gaze was locked on her—earnest and grave, mirroring her own desperate need. Daniel and his mother conversed in low whispers beside him, but he ignored them. Cleopatra spoke, and he ignored *her*. He only had eyes for Rosalind.

And she only had eyes for him. She drank him in greedily, wishing she could see him better past the candles at the foot of the stage.

In that instant—when all her attention was off the play and focused on Griff—she realized that nothing mattered to her except him. The acclaim of the audience meant nothing next to his; the demands of the play were as dust next to his. If he attended all her plays and looked at her like that, they might as well take her out and shoot her, for all the good she'd be as an actress. Because right now, for her, the only person in the entire huge Covent Garden Theatre was him.

She played the rest of the last act in a daze, hardly caring how she gave her lines. All she wanted was to see him, and now she felt sure she would. The fact that he hadn't tried to interrupt her performance by accosting her between the acts touched her, but surely he wouldn't delay once the play was done.

She was right. When she exited after the final curtain call, he was waiting in the wings. Actors and actresses milled around, chatting about the performance, evaluating the crowd, but she saw no one else. She walked toward him, a sudden apprehension piercing her. What if he didn't want her back? What if he was here merely to be polite?

But Griff never did anything to be polite. He watched her expectantly, and he held a satchel tucked under his arm. She felt a twinge of guilt to see lines of weariness etched into his brow and black circles under his eyes. He looked as if he'd been eating and sleeping as little as she. Surely that showed he loved her, didn't it? Perhaps not the way she loved him, but—

"You were wonderful," he said as she reached him, his voice barely lifting above the din backstage. A faint smile touched his lips. "But I knew you would be."

"Thank you." *I love you.*

They stood apart, awkward, so much to be said and both uncertain how to begin.

He cleared his throat. "I see you decided to start on those bawdy passages of Shakespeare without me."

She had no chance to answer before a young man pushed between them to thrust a half-wilted bouquet of flowers at her. "Miss Laplace, you outshone them all!"

Not sure what else to do, she took the flowers and murmured another "Thank you," though this one was distinctly wooden.

The young man leered down at her breasts. "A

few of us are having a late dinner at the Crown and Anchor, and we'd love it if you joined us."

"No, I—"

"We're not taking no for an answer, are we, Darnley?" another young man interjected as he joined his friend. He winked at her. "Two of the other girls are coming with us. You've got to come. It'll be jolly good fun."

She glanced at Griff, but he just stood there silently, with an uncharacteristic reserve. Though she didn't know what to make of it, she certainly had no desire to go off with these two coxcombs. She leveled a cold gaze on them. "I'm afraid I have a prior engagement."

She started to push through them to get to Griff, but the one named Darnley slid his arm about her waist. "At least give us a chance to talk you into it, won't you?"

"I believe the lady told you she wasn't interested, Darnley," Griff bit out as he stepped forward to clasp her arm. "And her prior engagement is with me, so why don't you and Jenkins find another actress to play with?"

Darnley blinked at Griff. "Knighton! I beg your pardon. We didn't see you there, old chap."

Griff just glared at him until Darnley dropped his arm and pulled his friend away, grumbling.

"Could we talk privately?" he then asked her in a low voice. "Kemble has offered me the use of his office. That is, if you're willing to come with me."

"Of course I'll come with you."

This sudden odd restraint of his worried her. She let him draw her through the throng and down the backstage stairs, but his silence preyed upon her imagination until she could stand it no longer. "Thank you for stepping in with those two."

"You know who they are, don't you?" he said tightly.

"I haven't the foggiest idea."

"Darnley is the Marquess of Darnley. And his companion Captain Jenkins is his cousin and Prinny's current favorite. They both attended Eton with me." He shot her a bleak look. "Perhaps now you regret rebuffing them."

"Don't be absurd." Deliberately, she tossed the bouquet aside. "I wouldn't even have let it go as far as it did if they hadn't taken me by surprise."

"Taken you by surprise?" he grumbled. His eyes scoured her costume, narrowing as they focused on her low-hung bodice. "I don't see why. That gown is designed to have half the male audience slavering over you."

Cheered by his jealousy, she ventured a smile. "Mama's friend, Mrs. Inchbald, gave it to me."

"I see I must have a chat with the woman if you plan to keep using her costumes."

Her heart sank. That didn't sound like a renewal of his proposal. But then, why was he here, asking to speak to her privately?

As soon as they reached Mr. Kemble's office and went inside, he released her arm, further heightening her distress. He strode away from her to Mr. Kemble's desk and set down his satchel. For a moment, he stood there with his back to her, making her more uneasy the longer he remained silent.

The room was cold, though there was a fire lit. Nervously, she rubbed her bare forearms and tried to read Griff's mood. She'd expected recriminations, accusations, and certainly more of his attempts to seduce her. Not this unnatural quiet. Not from Griff. Then he faced her, and the stark pain in his expression made her breath catch in her throat.

"I want you to know," he said, "that I've spent the last few days becoming intimately acquainted with my black soul. I'd never examined it before, but after your father held a mirror up to it, then you, and finally my mother, I could hardly ignore the image. I confess it was an ugly one. Resentments lurked there that I'd never recognized; vanities were exposed to the light so vexing I couldn't bear the sight of them."

"Oh, Griff—" she began.

He forestalled her with a quick wave of his hand. "Let me say it all first before you say anything. Please?"

She nodded, though what she really wanted wasn't to speak but to enfold him in her arms and kiss away his hurts.

He shifted his gaze to the curtained window at her right, as if looking at her was more than he could stand. "One thing that became horribly clear to me was that you were right. About everything— my ambition, my selfishness, everything. You were certainly right about my reasons for wanting Knight-on Trading to succeed. I realized it the morning after you left me when I dreamed—"

Breaking off, he rubbed the back of his neck and grimaced. "Let's just say I had a dream that made me finally understand myself. You said I wanted to lash out at those who'd called me bastard to 'grind their noses' in it. That was true, but it was even smaller than that. I wanted to strike back at my boy-hood tormentors, a lot of children who'd long ago ceased to matter. Everything I wanted came down to that—a need to beat a lot of stupid Eton dandies like Darnley and Jenkins, a need to show them I was better. To do it, I was even prepared to act like a child myself—spoiled and selfish and caring only about what I wanted."

She hadn't thought her words had affected him so. He'd seemed so angry over them that night.

A muscle jerked as he clenched his jaw. "I finally realized that all my hopes for China came down to that. In truth, Knighton Trading was fine without my having a spot on that delegation, and I knew it. I wouldn't admit it, but I knew it." His gaze swung back to her. "As its owner—as a grown man rather than a child—I should have seen how contemptible my plans were. You saw it. Daniel saw it. Even your damned father saw it. The part of me that still had a sliver of conscience saw it, too, or I would never have attempted to gain your hand in marriage without telling you of the certificate. Still, I ignored my conscience until you left me."

She held her breath, moved beyond words by his obvious remorse. Dear God, how she loved him!

"I came to tell you that I do see it now, that I see it and regret it, that I'm sorry for all that my plans may have cost you. And I came to give you something." Turning to the desk, he removed some papers from the satchel. When he faced her, he held them out.

Not sure what to expect, she took the papers warily.

"The document on top you will recognize," he said hoarsely. "It's the certificate. I have my mother's permission to give it to you." When she glanced up at him, perplexed, he added with a wry smile, "You see, one thing you taught me was that I ought to consult all the parties concerned, instead of pursuing my plans as if only I was involved. Since the certificate was my mother's before your father stole it, I thought she should have a say in how it's used. She agreed I could give it to you."

Her throat felt clogged with happy tears as she stared down at the piece of paper that had brought so much grief to so many.

"You will need it after your father dies," he went on, "in order to execute that second document in your hand."

Seized by curiosity, she flipped to the next document and stared at it. It was a contract of some kind, written in typically impenetrable legal language.

"That document assigns ownership of Swan Park to you and your sisters when your father dies and I inherit." When her gaze flew to his, he added with a hint of remorse, "That was the only legal way to accomplish it, I'm afraid. As his daughters, you can't inherit it, and only after I'm proven the legitimate heir can I even give it to you. But if you use the first to prove I can inherit, then you can exercise the second that allows the three of you to receive it from me as a gift."

Pure shock kept her silent. Could this be the same man who'd manufactured an elaborate masquerade so he could regain the title withheld from him? Could he actually be giving away not only the title, but the property and everything in it?

As if sensing her disbelief, he said, "It's all legal, I assure you." He flashed her a wan smile. "I had to stand over my solicitor and his clerks to get it finished in time for tonight, but it's legal. If you don't believe me, take it to an attorney or—"

"I believe you." Fear suddenly seized her chest, making her heart thump madly. "But does this . . . does this mean you don't want to marry me anymore?"

"We're getting to that." A desolate pain scored his brow. "I want to marry you more than ever. But I want you to choose me because you want me, too. You can't choose freely if you're encumbered by responsibilities to your sisters. If you own Swan Park, then you have a choice. If you don't marry me, this will enable you to—" His voice cracked a little. "Make your way on the stage if you like or manage the estate. Either way, you and your sisters will be provided for. It's a small enough thing to offer in repayment for my . . . base behavior."

She could hardly bear his self-recrimination anymore. "Please, Griff—"

"Let me finish, my sweet." He closed his eyes briefly, as if marshaling his strength. When he continued, his tone was wrought with guilt. "Among the hard truths I've had to acknowledge in the past few days, one was that I treated you and your family badly. Perhaps your father deserved it—I don't know—but none of the rest of you did. I manipulated you, lied to you, and seduced you, yet you forgave me. Until I held firm about my stupid title—a title I'd never really needed, that I only thought I needed."

He leaned back against the desk, gripping the edges until his knuckles gleamed white. "You probably won't be surprised to learn that I really hadn't thought I'd done anything wrong, not until after you left Swan Park. Then I realized that any woman so hurt by my actions that she would risk danger and uncertainty to be free of me must be desperate indeed. And I'd driven you to that desperation. I'd driven you away."

Staring off past her, he went on in a choked voice. "That's when I knew the truth. You said I didn't know how to love. Well, about that one thing, you were wrong. Perhaps I didn't know how before, but I do now." His gaze met hers, fierce, intent. "I love you. I'll always love you. After you left, I realized that my greatest fear was losing you. It mattered more to me than the certificate or the China delegation. It mattered more to me than Knighton Trading."

Her heart felt full to bursting with her own love

for him, yet it was clear he wasn't finished, and now she desperately wanted to hear it all.

He shoved away from the desk, approaching her with solemn determination. "You once accused me of having a mistress with whom you could never compete. Well, my love, I'm relinquishing my mistress. To you." Gesturing to the papers in her hand, he added, "That last document assigns to you the ownership of Knighton Trading."

"What?" she exclaimed, half-certain he was joking.

"I'm giving you the only thing I own of any worth. It's yours now. You may keep me on as manager or clerk or whatever you wish. Or dismiss me. It's your choice."

"Oh, my love—"

"If you choose to marry me, of course, Knighton Trading will once more belong to me as your husband, but as far as I'm concerned, it matters not—you'll still have a say in the running of it. Therefore you needn't worry that it means more to me than you. And if you choose not to marry me—" He glanced away as if that possibility were too painful to contemplate. "Then none of it matters anyway. Because I've discovered in the past few days that without you, my life is nothing. At least this way I'd have the satisfaction of knowing I'd given you the wealth to ensure you a happy life."

"A happy life?" She looked at the tormented man she loved, who'd faced his own darkness for her. It was her turn now. Walking to the fireplace, she threw the documents for Swan Park onto the low-burning fire. "I told you before that running Swan Park would not make me happy."

As they burst into flame, her heart lightened, floated. She tossed the documents for Knighton Trading on top, her happiness soaring as high as the smoke rising from the fiery consumption of all her fears. "And I'm bloody certain that running a trading concern—even as your partner—could not make me happy."

The certificate, she folded carefully and tucked in the band of her skirt. "This, however, I shall keep." With her heart brimming over, she returned to where he stood watching her uncertainly. "We'll need it for our son someday, won't we?"

As hope softened Griff's features, she cupped his face tenderly between her hands. "There's just one thing I require for a happy life, and it isn't your wealth. But only you can give it to me. Indeed, it's the only thing I want from you."

"What is that?" he choked out, his wonderful blue eyes riveted on her face.

"You. Your heart. Your love. Your—"

Hauling her into his arms, he kissed her sweetly, achingly, a kiss that promised more love than she'd expected from any man, but certainly from him. When he drew back, that same love shone in his dear face. "You have it, all of it," he said earnestly. "My wealth, my heart, my love. Marry me, and you may do as you wish—strut the stage, run Swan Park, or lie about all day while I feed you apple tarts. But never leave me again, darling, for I can't bear the thought of living without you."

"Nor can I." Feverishly, she pressed kisses to his cheeks, his chin, his broad temple. Joy danced through her, sweeping away all her uncertainties. He loved her so much he'd wanted to sacrifice everything for her happiness. How could a woman resist a man like that?

She drew back to beam at him. "You didn't need to do all this, you know. The minute I saw you in the theater, I realized I could never leave you again. I knew I never wanted to let you go."

That earned her another kiss, only this time he lingered forever over her mouth, worshiping it, plundering it . . . loving it. And as always, when he finished he left her weak-kneed and trembling.

"I hope you realize what marriage to me will mean, darling," he warned. "Since I'm determined to keep your father's secret, in public I must pretend to be what I was before. So you'll be marrying a man widely proclaimed to be both illegitimate and heartless. Certainly someone unworthy of an earl's daughter in the eyes of the world."

"Do you care what the world thinks?"

He stared down at her sincerely. "All I care about is having you as my wife."

She searched his face but saw only worry for her, and that warmed her to her toes. "Then I'm perfectly content." She smiled. "Besides, we're both good at playacting, so we can manage any role. As long as you're my husband in private, I don't care what else you pretend to be in public. We both know the truth."

Laying her hand on his chest, she added, "As for being heartless, I'll challenge anyone who calls you such. For I finally know that Daniel was right. Until now you ignored your heart—but you have one. Oh, yes, my love, you had one all along."

"And it's yours," he told her as he clasped her hand tightly in his. "It will always be yours."

Epilogue

The iron tongue of midnight hath told twelve.
Lovers, to bed; 'tis almost fairy time.
I fear we shall outsleep the coming morn.
As much as we this night have overwatch'd.
This palpable-gross play hath well beguil'd
The heavy gait of night. Sweet friends, to bed.

   William Shakespeare, A Midsummer Night's Dream

Griff stood sipping champagne at the end of Swan Park's terrace as he watched his wife of one hour regale their guests with tales of her career on the stage. Her three-week-long career in a small part. Rosalind still knew how to captivate an audience, even though she'd chosen to give up the stage.

Apparently even she could see that her talents lay elsewhere. During the play's short run, she'd often complained to Griff of her irritation at being ordered about, and more than once she'd argued with Kemble over the staging.

Griff smiled. No one would ever call his wife

docile, to be sure. Or lazy. She was already making grand plans for her newly chosen role as lady patroness of the theater. Kemble might be dancing with glee at the thought of all the Knighton money Lady Rosalind intended to bestow upon Covent Garden Theatre, but he'd soon learn that the money came at a price—endurance of milady's willful tongue.

Daniel strolled up, followed the direction of Griff's gaze, then laughed. "Already thinking of the wedding night, are you? That lass has *still* got you pining after her."

Not even Daniel could dampen Griff's good mood today. "Enjoy yourself at my expense while you can, my friend, because someday I intend to see you pining after a woman yourself. I only pray that the woman, whoever the poor wench proves to be, puts you through hell before she accepts you. That will give me the chance to repay you for all your barbs."

"You might be waiting an eternity then."

Griff eyed him askance. "Didn't you tell me when we battled in the study that you intend to marry one day?"

"I should like to. A man needs a woman looking after him once he tires of whoring. But the right woman won't be so easy to find, and my poor breeding is likely to put her off even if I do find her."

"What about Rosalind's two sisters? As I recall, you said they were 'fine women.' And they both like you."

Daniel snorted. "Lady Juliet only likes me if I don't have amorous intentions. Poor lass, my size terrifies her. As for Lady Helena . . ."

Daniel glanced across the room to where Helena stood remote from the others, serenely talking to

Griff's mother. For a moment, something dark and intense burned in his gaze.

Then a look of resignation crossed the burly man's face. "That woman thought little enough of me when I pretended to be you, but now she knows I'm little better than my highwayman da, so she'd not be fool enough to consider any suit of mine." He laughed harshly, then tossed back his champagne. "Besides, what man in his right mind would want a stiff-rumped woman like that for a wife?"

Griff's eyes narrowed in speculation. He glanced from Daniel to Helena just in time to see Helena shoot Daniel a furtive look, then blush and avert her gaze when Daniel met it shamelessly, as if daring her to look her fill. A slow smile spread over Griff's face. So that was the way the wind blew. Perhaps he would have his chance to gloat sooner than Daniel thought.

Griff handed his empty champagne glass to a passing footman. "At least Helena and my mother seem friendly with each other. That bodes well for Mother's visit here. Swanlea invited her to stay with the family while Rosalind and I are on our honeymoon on the Continent. After all, it's been years since Mother was here, and she does have family in Stratford."

"It doesn't bother you to see her here? With *him*?" Daniel asked, nodding toward where the earl sat in the chair he'd been carried down in.

Griff looked at the man, but felt little of the ire that had burned so fiercely in his chest before. "Not really. In any case, it's time to put the past behind us. All of us." With a smile, he shifted his gaze to his wife, who looked particularly fetching in the vibrant blue gown she'd chosen for their wedding. "The future interests me far more these days."

The crowd around Rosalind had dispersed,

drawn by the lure of the feast being laid out beneath tents on the lawn. As if sensing his gaze on her, she looked over, and her face brightened with love. Quickly, she strode toward him like Athena following her arrow to his heart.

When she reached him, she tucked her hand in the crook of his elbow, then gazed up at him, eyes alight with mischief. "I hope the two of you aren't over here plotting new strategies for Knighton Trading. I realize Daniel is taking your place during the weeks we'll be gone, but I draw the line at having my husband discuss business on our wedding day."

"I wouldn't dare," Griff retorted with a chuckle. "Knowing you, that pesky sword of yours is lying in wait for me behind some bush." He lowered his voice, but not so much that Daniel couldn't hear. "As mine is lying in wait for you in its scabbard."

She blushed.

Daniel rolled his eyes. "I can see when I'm not wanted." He gazed over to the heavily laden tables. "There's a leg of lamb crying out to be eaten, and I don't want to keep it waiting."

As the giant man strolled off toward the tents, Rosalind squeezed Griff's arm hard. "I swear, you're shameless—and in front of Daniel, too! You embarrassed the poor man dreadfully!"

"Embarrassed *him*? Don't be absurd." He skimmed his gaze down her sumptuous, seductive form. "Besides, I thought you'd become rather fond of my roguish ways. You wouldn't want me to reform simply because I've married you, would you?"

"Certainly not!"

When he laughed heartily she blushed again, but drew a little closer. He laid his hand over hers and began stroking the underside of her gloved wrist with his thumb. Although he smiled and nodded at their guests, all his awareness was reserved for his lovely wife: the woman he adored, the one he'd keep always in his heart.

And the one he desired madly. Between her stint treading the boards and all the preparations for the wedding, they hadn't made love in weeks, so he was as eager for his wedding night as any groom.

He shot her a sidelong glance. "You needn't worry about my reforming, darling. I'm still rogue enough to be looking forward to tonight." He teased in an undertone, "And to trying that variation on lovemaking you were so curious about in your father's study a few weeks ago."

She glanced furtively about them, but no one was close enough to hear. "Oh, you are, are you?" she said saucily.

"Most assuredly. That and several other variations. 'Lady, shall I lie in your lap?' "

"Why, Griff Knighton," she reproached him in a low, mocking voice, "you ought to be ashamed of yourself, quoting the naughty parts of Shakespeare! Have you no decency?"

"None whatsoever with you, my love." He squeezed her hand. "As I told you before, we bastards are a naughty lot. And when it comes to you, I fear I'll always be one in the bedchamber."

She laughed. "Then thank God for bastards."

Author's Note

The year after my book was set a delegation to China took place that opened up the China trade for England. I'd like to think that Griff would have been on it.

Mrs. Inchbald was a real actress and playwright from this period. I took no liberties with her life history that I know of. Her relationship with John Kemble was very close until her death, a relationship that began even before her husband, Joseph Inchbald—who was a bit of a philanderer—died. She's a fascinating character who's only now being rediscovered by historians.

As for the wedding of Griff's parents at Gretna Green, there were indeed court cases disputing marriages made at that illustrious spot. Most such disputes concerned the willingness of the woman involved—a family might accuse the fortune-hunting groom of kidnapping so they could obtain their daughter's release from a disadvantageous marriage.

The legality of the wedding of Kitty Barnes to Lord Cochrane, heir to the Earl of Dundonald, however, was disputed by their children, who argued over who was the legitimate heir to the family fortune and title once their father died. The marriage was upheld because of Kitty's testimony. But I wanted to write about what could happen when such a marriage was *not* upheld by the court system.